PRAISE FOR *THE WITCHES AT THE END OF THE WORLD*

Tor.com's Best New Fantasy Books of October
Gizmodo's Best New Sci-Fi & Fantasy Books of October

"A perfect fall read, full of dark, foreboding curses and a Norwegian winter. This tale of two sisters and the bond of magic between them is recommended for all fiction collections."

—*Booklist*

"Chelsea Iversen's magical debut, *The Witches at the End of the World*, is a story for the ages. Minna and Kaija are two young witches living in the wood. They are also sisters, separated by grief, who must find their way back to one another before it's too late. The powerful themes of revenge, redemption, and healing are beautifully rendered in a story where love is the most potent magic of all."

—Adriana Trigiani, author of *The Good Left Undone*

PRAISE FOR *THE WHISPER*

"I didn't know I needed *Practical Magic* and *The Craft* to have a baby, but *The Whisper* gave me that and so much more. Chelsea Iversen deftly navigates the power of female friendships and the secrets that bind us in a harrowing reminder of why the woods are so scary. A girl's girl's thriller through and through, *The Whisper* kept me turning pages late into the night. Obsessed."

—Chelsea Conradt, *USA Today* bestselling author of *The Farmhouse*

"Atmospheric, magical, and deliciously twisty, *The Whisper* is a haunting, witchy thriller about the bonds of friendship and the dangers of returning to the past. Equal parts enchanting and chilling, I couldn't turn the pages fast enough!"

—Nichelle Giraldes, author of *The Forest of Missing Girls*

PRAISE FOR *THE PECULIAR GARDEN OF HARRIET HUNT*

"Iversen's latest takes the closed world of a sheltered young woman in 1860s London and, with magic, crisis, persistence, and power, cracks it wide open. Fans of Rowenna Miller and Rena Rossner will particularly enjoy this coming-of-age tale in which the magic that surrounds Harriet Hunt provides both her greatest vulnerability and her greatest strength."

—Greer Macallister, author of *The Magician's Lie* and *The Thirteenth Husband*

"An endearing tale with a heartfelt heroine trapped in a cruel world of men and a sentient garden where magic, vengeance, and second chances bloom. *The Peculiar Garden of Harriet Hunt* will shock and delight readers at every page."

—Ava Morgyn, author of *The Witches of Bone Hill*

"Iversen's novel will appeal to fans of character-driven historical fantasy with feminist themes and just a touch of magic."

—*Library Journal*

"Iversen writes compelling historical fiction that is both a fantastical story and also one that realistically conveys the horrors of domestic violence. Readers will cheer for Harriet as she discovers her own agency and seeks freedom to make her own choices. Comparisons to authors like Alice Hoffman or Sarah Addison Allen are apt, and Harriet would fit right in with those authors' magical women. Highly recommended for all fiction collections."

—*Booklist*, Starred Review

"A haunting gothic tale of madness and aspiration set in a Victorian London suburb… Iversen leisurely unfurls a sweeping tale of a woman on the edge… The slow accumulation of spooky atmospherics makes it work…plenty to enjoy."

—*Publishers Weekly*

ALSO BY CHELSEA IVERSEN

The Witches at the End of the World

The Peculiar Garden of Harriet Hunt

THE WHISPER

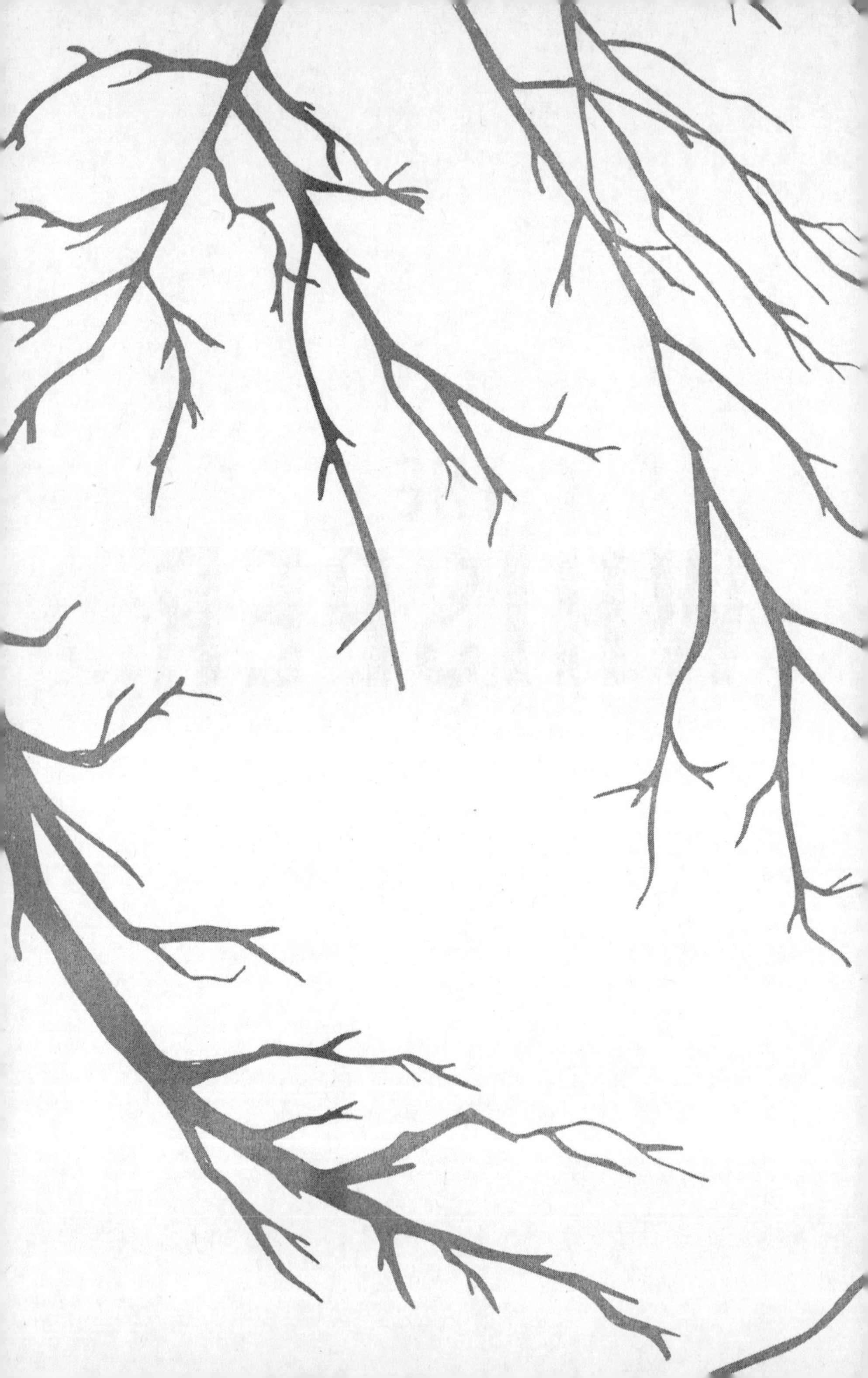

THE WHISPER

CHELSEA IVERSEN

sourcebooks landmark

Cover design by Sarah Brody/Sourcebooks
Cover images © Valentin Valkov/Shutterstock, Nosyrevy/Getty Images
Internal design by Laura Boren/Sourcebooks
Internal images © Insh1na/iStock

Published by Sourcebooks Landmark, an imprint of Sourcebooks
1935 Brookdale RD, Naperville, IL 60563-2773
(630) 961-3900
sourcebooks.com

Cataloging-in-Publication Data is on file with the Library of Congress.

Printed and bound in the United States of America.
LB 10 9 8 7 6 5 4 3 2 1

For Ryan

"When the trees whisper, listen."

—Rule #1, *The Book of Aspens*

The room is bright behind her eyelids, her first sign that she's not dead.

She can hear someone moving nearby. That's another sign. You can't hear sounds if you're dead. But there is also a hint of a memory. Something transpired before this that started the splitting pain in her head, the blood racing to mend some wound. She was hit with something. She feels a steady wave of pain move through her, then recede, then pulse through her more urgently. The pattern, in and out, is the same as her consciousness.

A sharp sting in her lower leg surprises her. A figure slides into her vision. The person above her is indistinct, and she can't seem to keep her eyes open. The images before her move too fast for her to hold on to. And she can't move her head. She is cold too, she realizes, and growing colder. She thinks maybe, given another few minutes, she will be fully awake. She can feel herself coming around. Just a few more minutes.

She wonders what the person above her is doing. And then she sees the flash of what looks like a needle, and she thinks, *Yes, good. I must be in a hospital.* She doesn't remember going to a hospital, but she doesn't remember anything, not really.

She hears a voice very close to her. "Stop…" Then she hears a name she recognizes. "Quinn…" Her childhood friend Quinn? But soon, sounds become muffled by a ringing inside her head. The cold is consuming her. Her hands, her legs. Can someone bring her a blanket? She wants to sit up, to call the nurse, because she's in a hospital, isn't she? But she can't. Instead of gaining strength, she seems to be losing it.

Darkness begins to creep in; it shows up as little spiders on the outside of her vision, which is already too spotty to see anything useful, like clues about where she is or why she's here. The spiders grow, taking everything over, and there's suddenly pain everywhere. Where there was cold a moment ago, now there are sharp contractions all throughout her body, as if her organs are seizing, one by one. She registers a loud noise somewhere nearby, a crash maybe, but it doesn't feel real. It doesn't feel important.

It's an odd sensation, but she knows what is going on now. Somehow, she knows, beyond a doubt, what is happening. The distant pain. Her fading awareness. The black mold of nothingness closing in.

She is fading. She is—

And it's in that moment, just before she can name it, that it comes.

FIVE DAYS EARLIER

1

JOEY

Joey hears the trees whisper just as she starts mile seven.

She isn't dressed well for the cold, but she curls her fingers into fists and lets her speed do the rest. She flies past slender tree trunks, one after another. A climb up a steep hill makes her heart thunder; a hop over a downed tree sends blood pumping through her legs. A runner's high is one thing, but there is an extra pleasurable pain in the elevation changes of a wooded trail.

Since the moment she started running, before the sun rose and the trees were simply shadows blinking in and out of her headlamp, she's heard nothing more than her shivering breath and the beat of her footsteps.

She is here to clear her head. To recalibrate. To forget about last night.

She picks up speed now as she nears the bend in the path. If she makes a left and veers off-trail, she'll end up in the aspen grove. She can imagine the spell circle there, but she doesn't look that way; she just keeps her eyes trained ahead as the light from her lamp bounces up and down. The aspen leaves quake around her, and she feels a shimmer of magic. It's strong, even at this distance. She thinks she can feel it tickling her bones, but she shakes her head. It's been so long. She's not even sure if it is the magic she's sensing or just her subconscious remembering the feeling. In a fit of recklessness, she flicks off her lamp and bounds down the trail—away from the aspen grove—at a full sprint, speeding up even more as the slope pitches down.

She tries to pretend she doesn't know why she chose this trail today. She tries to pretend it was just a coincidence. She wants to shoulder away the thoughts that pulse in time with her quickening steps. *Fifteen years. Fifteen years. Fifteen years.*

The ground is dark and soft beneath her, but the faint light of morning is purpling the sky, and the trees blur gray around her. Even her wide stride and expansive breaths—breaths that billow like smoke in front of her—can't get her out of her own head. Now that she's here, the thoughts won't leave her. She's come this way because, deep down, she's a masochist. She has done it before, and she wonders, not for the first time, if she has some kind of psychological condition. Being near here feels like pressing a bruise, a dull reminder of pain. But she likes to press on that bruise. She needs to, if only to know that she can still feel.

Fifteen years.

Joey saw her first. Quinn's lifeless eyes stared up at the empty sky. It was strange to see her there, so near where they often came together, except sprawled at the bottom of the rocky crag instead of above it.

The coroner's conclusion was that she had died around five o'clock on Wednesday evening. She left her mom's that afternoon and wasn't found until ten the next morning. There was no moment of psychic *knowing* for Joey, no tug of an internal string that told her Quinn was gone. And Joey would never forgive herself for that. She'd never forgive herself for not paying closer attention.

In the end, they ruled it an accident. A snapped clavicle, broken shoulder and arm, and fatal trauma to the skull. One misstep, an unlucky fall, and a single jagged rock in the wrong place at the wrong time. The evidence was unmistakable. A careless slip while hiking alone, an accidental tumble down the ravine, and that was the end.

But Joey knew Quinn would never come hiking out here alone. Not here, where the woods were thick with magic only they could feel, where it buzzed, hive-like, beneath their feet. They weren't ever supposed to come alone. They were supposed to stay together. It was one of the rules.

So no, Joey has never believed it was an accident.

After that day, the world stopped turning. They couldn't do magic, even if they wanted to. Four best friends broken and scattered. Quinn was buried. Elena left within days. Sophie left within a few months. It all happened so quickly. Joey stayed but did not grow roots. She was blindsided at first, ice-cold with grief. But over time, her heart started to thaw, and all she could do was let time pass. There were times she'd thought about starting fresh somewhere else, but she never did. Someone had to stay here. Someone had to remember.

She did eventually find a sliver of relief, but that's something she tries not to think too much about. The shame of it makes her feel sick. And after last night, it's clear things have gone beyond her control.

A surge of wind kicks leaves up into Joey's face, and she's temporarily distracted. As she bats the leaves away, she feels a sharp change in momentum. She jolts as her toe snags on a rock. Her body hurls forward, launching through the air. Her palms, her chest, and her thighs smack against the ground. She bumps and skids over the earth. A rock slices into her knee.

She curses and wipes dirt off herself, examining the tear in her pants and trying to catch her breath. She's in the thick of the aspens here. The grove—their grove—is just behind her. She closes her eyes and wishes she'd chosen a different trail this morning. The memories and the pain are still unbearable, and yet, she cannot seem to let them go.

Then, without warning, the wind spirals. Leaves blind her, violently flipping and twisting, devouring everything beyond a one-foot radius.

The sound comes next. At first, she thinks it's the wind, but soon her thoughts are drowned out. It's a shushing, like white noise, but so earsplittingly loud, it could be a jet engine. She scrambles to her feet. Something else is there, intermingled with the wind—barely there, like it's coming up from the ground, from the tangle of roots that reaches down into the earth and stretches beyond this trail, deep into the mountains. Is it a voice?

Then, in the way an orchestra finishes tuning before the performance, silence descends over the aspens around her. It's a blanket, soothing and still. For a few moments, all she can hear is the in and out of her breath.

Her heart slams against her rib cage.

A voice—she is sure that's what it is this time—comes from every direction. Softened by the whispering trees, it is raspy and wild. And so familiar, her knees almost buckle.

Quinn, Joey thinks. She looks around desperately, as if she'll see Quinn standing behind her, as if that were possible. But it's only the aspen trees standing guard, with their leaves that look blood-black against the morning sky.

She leans her back against the nearest tree to steady herself. The cold of the trunk seeps through her shirt, like ice against her skin.

Quinn's voice is all around her now, above and below her, repeating and echoing from every direction. It sounds edged with fear, with a sharp inflection Quinn only used when she was cornered.

Two words. Joey hears them over and over again, a dozen times, maybe more. And she looks around, over her shoulder, and then between the trees because she wants more than anything to see the real Quinn, to hear her real voice, but it's not her. Just a couple of words, whispered through the trees, again and again and again.

Before long, the whisper of shivering leaves grows louder than the words, and Quinn's voice is hurried away with the wind.

Everything goes silent. Joey holds her breath. It's in this space, this supernatural quiet, that she understands the significance of the two words she's just heard.

She waits another minute, then sprints back down the trail.

Holy shit.

2

SOPHIE

Sophie's phone is in her hand when it vibrates with a text. She taps the screen absently, but Leah yells from the kitchen before she can see who the text is from.

"Mo' eggs!"

Sophie stuffs the phone into her pocket and hurries down the stairs, pulling a shirt over her head as she rounds the corner.

"More eggs, *please*," she says to Leah, and then scoops some scrambled eggs onto her little plastic plate. She looks delighted that food has appeared, just as she requested, and Sophie's stress melts a little. She loves this phase. Leah is learning so much so quickly—how to run and jump and new words every day. To her, the world is one big place to explore. She has no clue about the difficulties that come with being alive year after year.

"All good, Soph?" Talia asks, coming up behind her. She looks fantastic in a white flowing shirt, ironed and buttoned neatly up the middle, and her slim black pants that flare at the bottom. Sophie pushes down a wave of jealousy. She's not even a year and a half out from giving birth; of course she doesn't look as good as Talia. And Talia always did have an athlete's body, while Sophie has always had a full figure. *Voluptuous*, they call it, but only when you are taller than, say, five-foot-six, which Sophie, decidedly, is not. The thing she's most jealous of, though, is the fact that Talia has had time for a shower.

"I love you guys so much," says Talia as she sneaks up behind Leah and plants a kiss on her curly hair. The move is practiced and goes off without incident, but it would never work for Sophie. If she tried it, Leah would inevitably swing around, hands flailing, desperate to be picked up, and Sophie would get greasy egg all down her front. It's exactly why Sophie can never wear white.

Then Talia leans in to give Sophie a warm, comfortable kiss. They always kiss before leaving the house and before falling asleep. What if something were to happen while they were apart? Sophie fears abrupt endings. The kind you don't see coming.

Talia brushes a hair away from Sophie's ear. Sophie is surprised at this extra bit of affection. She even feels her heart rate begin to pick up, just a little. Then Talia whispers, "Your shirt's on backward."

She gives Sophie a playful bite on the earlobe and a smile that's part I-love-you, part sorry-for-leaving-you-with-all-this.

The cat swishes past Sophie's legs just as Talia's out the door. Sophie remembers something and calls out, "Did you feed Trixie?" but the door closes before she can finish, and her words echo in the house.

"Twixie," says Leah. She chucks a handful of egg at Sophie's back.

It's forty-five minutes round trip from her house to the day care center on foot, which includes time for kissing away Leah's tears and prying little hands off her shirt. It's new, this full-time day care schedule, and Sophie lets herself cry after she says goodbye. But she doesn't have time to dwell because another mother stops her on her way out and complains about the construction on Colfax, and Sophie agrees that it is inconvenient, but yes, the road will hopefully be in better shape once it's done. Once she finally wrangles free, she realizes she completely forgot to review the presentation for her Zoom meeting at nine. She pulls out her phone to open the Slides app. She'll look over what she can on her walk home. But then her eyes catch on the date. Today is the eighth. Her breath seizes in her chest, and she closes her eyes as the wave of grief hits her. It's viscous as it moves through her body, thick from fifteen years of distance. How could she have forgotten it was the eighth?

A truck honks loudly. She's in the middle of the street, hasn't looked left or right, and there is no stop sign. The truck is barreling toward her. She's forced to leap out of its way or be flattened. The driver gives her a crude hand gesture, and she hops onto the sidewalk, mouthing, "Sorry!"

The phone vibrates in her hand as she catches her breath.

"Hey, Dad."

"Hey, Pumpkin." He sounds distracted, probably doing a puzzle while watching the news after his Monday pickleball game. Even in retirement, he has his routines. Sophie can hear him chewing. "How's the day going?"

"Not bad. Just dropped off Leah at day care."

"Aw, give her a kiss from Grandpa. Listen, I meant to tell you, they're filming that movie in town. You should come. Leah would love to see all the cameras and the lights and what have you." There's such hope in his voice, like maybe today is the day he will finally convince her to visit.

She is so busy acknowledging the rising guilt that it takes her a minute to register what he just said. They're filming a movie in Whisper Ridge? But then she remembers him mentioning this a few weeks back. The first movie ever to be shot there. She guesses she can see the appeal. The town is charming in an undiscovered sort of way.

But when Sophie thinks of Whisper Ridge, she doesn't think of the historical buildings, the mountainous backdrop, or the miles of rocky forest. She doesn't even think of her dad. She thinks of Quinn. And she thinks of the magic. The picture that comes to mind right now is so vivid, and maybe it's because of what day it is, but it's like she's there with her. Sophie can imagine Quinn sitting in the aspen grove, long legs crossed in front of her, the ends of her hair a soft lavender, like she'd dipped them into a bucket of wine, smiling as the magic races through their veins.

"Maybe, Dad," Sophie says, and she feels bad, but the thought of going back makes her chest tighten. She hasn't made the trip in fifteen years. She thinks of the date again, and she suddenly can't keep the memories from coming. "Hey, can I call you later?" she asks.

In twenty minutes, she is through the door and sitting at her kitchen table, which also seconds as her work-from-home desk. She is thankful for the hot cup of tea and the workday in front of her that will keep her from dwelling.

Only then does she remember she got a text earlier and hasn't checked it. The meeting starts in five minutes. She won't have time to finish her review, but it is what it is. She loves the life she has built, but in some ways, everything seems to be happening around her. She is so busy. There's never a thought for what she might like to do or what she might want or even a long enough moment to stop and take a breath, let alone savor what she has. But when it's good, it's so good. There are toothy giggles and soft cheeks and story-time snuggles, and she wouldn't trade any of it. It's these thoughts, of little Leah, that finally steady her. Everything is okay now. The past is in the past.

She taps through and the message appears.

Sophie's tea wobbles in her hand, nearly spilling all over her lap. She hasn't heard from Joey in at least a year, and even then, it was just a two-word message to wish her a happy birthday. It's strange to see her name on her phone now. Sophie looks at the time. She has two minutes. She considers, takes a steadying breath, and reads.

Everything around her slows. She places the phone down and stares, bringing a fingernail to her teeth as she reads the message again.

I know what happened to Quinn.

3

ELENA

The text comes as she spots her car across the street. Elena knows it's probably her agent, asking her how it went. She doesn't look right away. She wants to savor the moment. The director said she had "*the perfect inflection*" when she delivered the line about asking your doctor about Protenly. Not too happy, not depressed. And she'd felt pretty in that kelly green shirt they'd put her in. A good morning and a relatively easy six hundred dollars—more if they decide to run it. Her last three gigs were not so lucky, but hopefully this one will be.

The sun is shining. Of course, this is LA, and a woman with the tiniest dog she's ever seen stops right in front of her on the sidewalk. Elena's bright mood wavers slightly as she tries to step over the leash, but her foot gets caught on it, and she stumbles. The dog lets out a little whimper, and the owner, a blond woman in matching mint green yoga pants and bra, gives Elena a dirty look.

She swallows the comment that pops into her head.

Just as she spots the familiar dent on her car's left bumper and the deep scratch near the driver's side door handle, she sees something else. A slim piece of paper is tucked under her wiper blade. She glances at the sign down the street, the one she should have looked at before parking. "No parking for street cleaning, 2nd and 4th Mondays of the month." *But it's Tuesday,* she thinks. And then she remembers. *No, it's Monday.* She squeezes the parking ticket in her hand.

Monday, June eighth.

For a moment, she's back in the woods, sitting next to Quinn in their circle and reading from the book. She can smell summer forcing spring away. There is a warm breeze toying with the hair at the nape of her neck, making her itch. The magic is rising around them. "*It feels like a bathtub filling up,*" Quinn said once, and that was exactly it. It streamed into them, through them, before spilling over, and then the spells were released into the world. And every time—every single time—they shook their heads with amazement. *They could do magic.* And now she can almost hear Quinn correcting her. They didn't *do* magic. It was the *place* that was magical. The aspen grove was a mile north of Whisper Ridge, and you could feel the crackle of something powerful in your bones when you were there. The aspens held the magic. The four of them were merely the stewards. Yes, Quinn's tree-hugger vibes were sometimes grating. But, god, that feeling was something special.

A sour taste fills her mouth, and the memory disintegrates. What was the point of all that magic if they couldn't save her? Sometimes Elena's not even sure the magic was real or just something her mind invented to escape the shitstorm that was her life. And then Quinn died, and it all got even harder.

Once she climbs into her car, she crumples the ticket into a ball and throws it on the floor of the passenger side. But then she thinks better of it and flattens it out, sticking it in her bag. She huffs and leans back into her seat, the upholstery making her feel hot. She pulls out her phone, her bright mood officially dimmed.

Maybe it's because she was just thinking about the four of them, but she's not surprised to see Joey's name on her phone. They haven't talked in forever, and Elena's embarrassed that she plugged Joey's and Sophie's numbers in from memory when she got a new phone years ago. She sent a group text that simply said, It's Elena, and then instantly regretted it. They both responded, but she ignored them. They haven't spoken since. She doesn't know if she wants to look at what Joey has to say, today of all days, and so she hesitates. Does she really want to dredge all this up again? She's put the past behind her—spent years doing it. Opening this revived text thread feels like opening an underground crypt.

The inside of her car is starting to feel as hot as an armpit, and she won't run the AC just to get another ticket for idling. Best to just read the message and get it over with. Whatever it says, she plans to just reply with a heart emoji—a yellow one so it's not depressing—and then get home. She has to clock in for lunch service at eleven.

She taps the message and reads Joey's words. Immediately, she flushes with anger. *Joey knows what happened to Quinn? What the hell is she talking about?* They all know what happened to Quinn. It was an accident. Case closed. Elena can feel irritation making her jittery. This is the kind of thing she did not want to feel today. Joey was never one for melodramatics, but this message has the stickiness of desperation, the kind that can drag you down if you're not careful. It's been fifteen years, and she hasn't even written a preamble. No, *"Hey, I know this is out of left field, but…"* Nope, straight to the point. That is pure Joey. Elena's head suddenly feels heavy, and she doesn't like it.

She starts the car. The phone vibrates in her palm just as she's starting up the podcast, *The Second Act*, episode thirteen. She closed Joey's text, planning to pretend she didn't see it at all, but now another message comes through, this one from Sophie.

She opens Sophie's text, sent only to her. It's a long one. She almost doesn't have the stomach to read it, but she exhales and gets on with it. She laughs after the first sentence. Sophie wants her to go to Whisper Ridge. That is something Elena will absolutely not be doing. There are several reasons for this—one of which she decided years ago. Too much baggage for one small town. Too many memories. Okay, yes, some memories were good. But it doesn't matter, does it? Bad memories are like spots of mold. They eventually shrivel the whole fruit.

The other reasons she can't go back have to do with her life here. Gael, for one. Plus, her agent has said she should be available as much as possible. "*Try not to go out of town unless you have to,*" she said. "*In case your big break comes knocking in the form of an insurance commercial,*" is no doubt what she meant. But Elena hasn't had any place she's *wanted* to go. Her mom lives down in San Diego, where they moved after her life in Whisper Ridge blew up. But it didn't take too long—just a few months, really—for Elena to get the hell out of there. Her mom would probably call it a misunderstanding. Elena would call it an escape. Either way, she doesn't speak to her anymore, let alone drive three hours for a hug and a catch-up.

Even though Elena is fully expecting to send that yellow heart emoji, her eyes catch on something Sophie has written, between one run-on sentence and several nonsensical autocorrected words. Elena reads the words through once, then again. They are filming a movie in Whisper Ridge.

She thinks for a minute, then starts the car and presses Play on her podcast. When she gets home, she calls off work. Then, after a quick Google search, she calls her agent.

She's going to be "out of pocket" for the next few days.

"Four will be initiated from each generation."

—Rule #2, *The Book of Aspens*

4

QUINN

OCTOBER 2007
FOUR YEARS BEFORE THE FALL

We're all thirteen, but I'm the oldest. Sophie is the youngest, and Joey and Elena are in the middle. That's the order we're walking in now. The trees are watchful around us; their trunks lean and are bone white with small black knots like eyes. My mom leads our group, followed by Joey's mom. The six of us are silent except for the crunch of the leaves beneath our shoes, but inside I am on fire.

The moms kept us up until midnight last night, telling us everything about the magic. We sat around the kitchen table with mugs of hot chocolate, switching between quiet shock and fits of giggles. It didn't seem real. It couldn't be. They told us there was magic in the trees. And that it was going to be ours.

"You four have been chosen because we have decided you'd make the best stewards of the magic," said my mom. She wore a headscarf printed with red roses and dangly earrings that swayed as she spoke. Joey asked what *stewards* meant, and we all listened carefully. "You will wield the magic," my mom explained. "We will show you the spells. But you will also protect it. This is crucial. You will be the protectors of the magic. It's a huge responsibility. Are you prepared for it?"

We all said we were, of course. Then Elena made a joke about our periods giving us *blood power*, and Joey's mom laughed. "It is amazing," she said. "You girls will love it. Just don't get carried away."

My mom looked at her, then at us. "Look, I know it sounds fun, and it is. But it is extremely serious too. A long time ago, someone died trying to keep the magic from falling into the wrong hands." That silenced us. "It's why we have a formal initiation process. It's why, back then, they established the five rules—to help keep the magic safe." She stood to pour us more hot chocolate. "Above all, you *must* follow the rules. They're for your protection."

They told us stories about the group of girls they were initiated with back in the eighties. There was my mom and Joey's mom, of course, and Elena's mom, who stopped practicing magic to become *born again*, which I didn't really understand, because how can you be born twice? And then there was a woman named Tammy, but she moved away years ago. I couldn't believe it. Why would someone *choose* to stop doing magic?

When they were done explaining, we were allowed to ask questions. And we had about a thousand. It took until our hot chocolate was cold and our heads drooped toward the table, but they answered every single one.

The ritual has to be done at dawn, they said, so we only got five hours of sleep last night. But I am wide-awake. I can tell the other girls are too. Elena jokes loudly as we walk, trying to make Sophie snort-laugh, and Joey looks like she's going to puke from nerves. I'm lightheaded with excitement. Finally, we come to a stop at the end of the trail. It's still pretty dark, so it's kind of hard to see, but I can just make out a circle of stones sitting at the center of a ring of aspen trees. My heart races, and Joey wipes her palms on her pants. I catch her eye and see that she seems to be thinking exactly what I am. *This can't be real, can it?*

They jostle us by our shoulders into place, the four of us pressed together, back-to-back inside the spell circle. Joey's mom places *The Book of Aspens* on the ground in the middle of us before taking her place inside the spell circle with her arms above her head. My mom does the same, and she tells us to hold hands. Surrounding us as best they can, they both close their eyes, and so do we.

Within seconds, I feel something tickling me, like fingernails sliding over my skin, only it's on the inside of my body. My mom drops to the ground suddenly. At first, I think she's fallen, but when I look down, I see her leaning between my feet and Sophie's. She begins to read. Her words are musical. I don't understand what she's saying, but I know she is casting a spell because she told us this is how it would happen. The tickle inside me grows. It becomes a fizz that bubbles through me like Pop Rocks—*pop, pop, popping* beneath my skin. Up to my hair and back down to my heels. Out to each fingertip, passing directly through my heart. I hear one of the other girls gasp and another one release a breath of a laugh. It makes me feel so strong, so excited that my friends are here with me, knowing that they are feeling this too.

And then, just like that, the spell is finished. The words stop, and the Pop Rocks fade. They don't leave completely, though. I can still feel the faint crackle of them in my blood, and I secretly hope the feeling will last forever. We unclasp our hands and spin around to look at each other.

"Was that it?" asks Elena. Sophie starts to laugh. Soon, the rest of us join in, and the spell circle is filled with our sudden, uncontrollable giddiness.

When we have recovered, the four of us circle up again, and Joey's mom guides us through some practice spells. We take turns giving it a go. Sophie reads too quietly, and Elena too fast. Joey is frustrated with her pronunciation and starts over. It takes all morning for us to get the hang of it. Until I finally do a perfect illusion spell, turning a golden aspen leaf green. It's such a small spell, but it is the best feeling I've ever had. We all stare at the leaf like it's the start of our new life. Because it is.

5

JOEY

The coffee shop is the busiest it's been in weeks.

The temperature is expected to touch seventy today. If Joey was in a clearer headspace, she would have put a sandwich board outside advertising their cold brew. And she would start selling cold brew.

She's on edge and hasn't eaten at all today; it's already almost one.

Her mind is still back in those woods, the whispers all around her.

The bell jingles as the door swings wide. A child runs in, followed by her grandmother. She gives Joey a friendly wave. Beyond them is Front Street, which is busier than usual. Small clusters of people she doesn't know stand nearby, not ogling the mountains but the movie set, which Joey can't see from here, thankfully. Other than the gawkers and what she assumes are film crew, the town looks just as it always has from her vantage point. The square lines of old brick buildings look small against the shadow of the mountain behind them. Beyond that, though she cannot see, she knows there are two more peaks, making up the famous Three Elks that surround the town. The tallest is capped white with snow.

The credit card machine beeps, making her jump. She gives Zach an apologetic look as she passes him yet another order for a lavender latte.

"We need more lavender syrup from the back," says Zach, wagging an empty bottle in her direction. There's a small stain of sweat on his chest just below his beard. He does not look happy.

"I'll go," she says quickly. She should give her employee the break and not take it for herself, but she doesn't. She can tell Zach notices this lack of good management, but she is desperate for a minute of quiet. She just needs to think.

She ducks into the storeroom, where the din is a little more tolerable. A fleeting thought about how she wishes she ran the kind of coffee shop that served freshly infused syrups to her customers. She'd serve it as a latte with a sprig of lavender on top of thick foam, and the air would smell of wildflowers and steamed milk. While she was at it, she would get rid of all the old tables and replace them with something natural but colorful—a hygge-meets-mountain-town vibe. Quinn would have loved that.

But as it is, Joey barely cares if anything is nice. What right does she have to dream about rattan light fixtures when Quinn is in the ground? Joey's mom too. That happened five years after Quinn, almost to the day, which made the dulling pain sharp again. And Joey has been bouncing between sharp and dull ever since, never quite free of the caked-on grief that, at some point, had stuck to her bones.

But this morning, when the trees whispered to her, something changed.

Everything changed.

She climbs on a sturdy box and reaches up to the top shelf. She heaves herself to her tiptoes, pulling down the bulk syrups she ordered online, bottle by bottle. This is the kind of thing she has done since she took over the place six years ago. She pretends she doesn't know about the rumors that the coffee shop has gone downhill and that she doesn't maintain the same level of quality as Barbara did. Barbara used to wake up at four in the morning to bake lemon blueberry scones and spent her evenings slicing vanilla beans to make her own syrup while on the phone debating the high school athletics budget with the school board. After what happened to Quinn, Barbara didn't want the coffee shop anymore, and, honestly, neither did Joey, but it was the least she could do. A thin cloud of guilt, one she has gotten used to by now, moves into and out of her thoughts.

"The director is Phillip Granger," someone at the table closest to the storeroom is saying. "Cal Pierce is in it and, what's her name, Nicola Bianco." The speaker's companion doesn't seem to know any of these people, so there ensues a long explanation of previous movie titles and accolades that sounds like it's read straight from IMDb. Joey rolls her eyes as she arranges the bottles on the tray she'll bring out to the front. Though the weather is nearly perfect, and the promise of a seasonal change is so close you can smell it in the air, that's not why the coffee shop is busy today. It's this stupid movie. The whole town is in heat over it.

She stops for a second and thinks about what she heard in the woods this morning. Fifteen years is a long time to go without knowing the truth. But today, a slow trickle of terror and exhilaration has been filling her veins, making her feel out of control, like she's hooked up to an IV drip with the wrong medication. She's been searching for answers for so long. Now that she thinks she has something, what is she supposed to do with it?

She lugs her tray of fresh syrup bottles out to the front. In her absence, the noise has grown to middle school cafeteria levels.

Zach runs the steamer, and there's an extra ringing that stays in Joey's ears for a minute afterward. He says something to her, asking her a question, but she can barely hear him. Someone stands at the door looking straight at her, someone who makes the rest of the world disappear. Joey goes completely numb and knocks a bottle onto the floor. It shatters, but she doesn't even flinch.

Sophie.

6

SOPHIE

Being back inside the coffee shop makes Sophie yearn for the family karaoke nights of years past, when the four of them belted Leona Lewis into one microphone. She steps inside, catching a glimpse of Joey, who looks almost the same as she did fifteen years ago, but then she turns away, and Sophie is forced to order from an unhappy-looking barista and wait, heart pounding. Joey keeps her head down for a half hour, pouring drink after drink. When she finally has a moment to come over, she just says, "You came," in a tense voice that makes Sophie's heart squeeze. That crisp alto—she hasn't heard it in a million years.

They don't linger. Instead, Joey peels off her apron, and Sophie follows her to her house, watching her, amazed at how long it's actually been. They stick to small talk—"What have you been *up to*?" "It's been *forever*."—even though Sophie is aching to ask Joey one thing in particular. What exactly did her text mean? What does she know about Quinn's death?

The Three Elks rise up behind them in the distance as they walk, three familiar peaks stretching into the brilliant blue sky and overlooking the town. She's struck by the snuggled-in beauty of Whisper Ridge. They pass the bar, the brewery, and the old inn. The warm brick buildings blend with the steep exposed rock face of the mountain behind them. There are a few new shops, but it's otherwise the same quaint Front Street of her youth. Two bored teenage girls sit on a curb in front of the inn. One girl must say something funny because the other goes wild with laughter in the way that only teenage girls do. Sophie feels the tug of nostalgia, and at the same time, she's unexpectedly jealous. She had all those years to change her mind and come back to this town. Why didn't she?

Joey's house is a few blocks away. A small faded blue bungalow. Weeds sprout along the front path, and the front porch step has a bow to it, warped from time or cold winters, or both. She jiggles her key into a stubborn lock and shoves open the door. Sophie doesn't know what she was expecting before she steps inside—tidy bookshelves, maybe, or a cozy single girl's setup, with scented candles and throw blankets. She sees none of that. In fact, the place looks stark. It's neat, which is very much Joey's style. But that's only because there's hardly anything in here. A few boxes sit in the corner, and the couch and coffee table are plain, sparse, and definitely IKEA. There's a TV and a dining table—if you can call it that. It's a small pine square with four legs and four neat chairs tucked underneath.

Sophie hesitates. "Did you just move in?"

Joey shakes her head. "I've been here four years."

"Four years?" Sophie tries to keep the shock from her voice. She really has no idea how someone could live like this. Sadness grips her.

"The boxes," says Joey. "That's stuff I keep meaning to get rid of, but I just haven't yet."

Sophie thinks of her own home, with its round-the-clock messes and tufted rugs and plush pillows she sinks into after long days. She thinks of the tiny hands that cup her cheeks before planting big unsolicited kisses and the burning smell from her oven that tells her the homemade pizza is ready.

"Do you want something to drink?" Joey is still being formal. An awkwardness hangs between them. "Bubbly water?"

Sophie says yes and thanks her. When Joey disappears into the kitchen, she pokes around. She's looking for a sign of something, anything, that will tell her what Joey has been doing all these years and who she has become. Maybe it's just Sophie's way of assuaging her own guilt, but she would love to see photos of Joey with a significant other or a dog or a friend, or maybe proof of a cheerful hobby like baking or cross-stitch. But there's nothing. In Joey's room, there's a closet full of shelves, most of them empty, a few stacked with black running gear. Three pairs of identical trail running sneakers are lined up underneath, and a copy of *Outside* magazine sits next to her bed. The bed itself is flat with a thin black-and-white striped duvet on top and a phone charger snaked between the headboard and mattress. No pictures anywhere. Sophie's guilt crystallizes into concern.

She rounds out of the bedroom and into the hall. There's another room next to the bathroom that's cracked open slightly. A guest room, most likely. She nudges the door open with her foot.

"Wait," calls Joey from down the hall. She's speeding toward Sophie with a clinking cup in her hand. But she's too late.

Here are all of Joey's pictures. And then some. They're taped to the wall. All over the wall, in fact, and they are all faces Sophie recognizes. There are little notes and strings—actual strings—between them. Sophie steps inside the room and spins around, holding her arms out wide, realizing what she's seeing. "Joey, are you still…?" Her voice breaks, and she doesn't finish the thought. She can't finish the thought.

Joey sighs, steps into the room, and forces the drink into Sophie's hand. "I've just been keeping up with it."

"Are you *investigating*? Oh my god, is this like a true crime thing?" Sophie can't keep the incredulity out of her voice.

"Of course not. It's just where I keep the information I've learned. Everything I know in one place."

Sophie turns, takes a sip, and sets her cup down on the desk with control. This is not what she was expecting. Joey seems to be completely consumed by Quinn, even after all this time. Has she even lived at all? Her text suddenly has context, and Sophie feels so utterly sad that she hasn't been here to help her move on. She tries for measured when she says, "These pictures are from back then. How did you even get them?"

Joey runs her hands over her face and exhales into them, like she's gearing up for a long story. "I printed them from Facebook years ago."

Everyone from the town, or just about everyone, is here. Even Sophie's own face stares back at her from a photo. *Disturbing* is the word that comes to mind.

"I don't actively look at this stuff anymore," Joey says. "I'm not investigating, and I'm not doing any true crime anything. I just can't bring myself to take it down."

Based on the message this morning, Sophie doesn't know if she believes that. Maybe Joey wishes it were true. Maybe seeing someone else here has made her self-conscious, but this is too much. She is absolutely still actively involved in…whatever this is. There's an uncapped pen on the desk next to a splayed legal pad. Sophie catches sight of Quinn's name and turns away. She examines the photos on the wall. They're arranged in unlabeled columns. One note says, *Where is The Book of Aspens?* Now that she looks, there are several pictures of Quinn—smiling, scowling, jumping, head turned, purple hair flashing. Sophie has to take a deep breath. All of this seems to rule out any chance of Joey having a significant other.

She's about to ask about the notes but sees embarrassment on Joey's cheeks that bleeds through her stolid exterior. Sophie falters for a minute. Then, she's overcome. Instinct plunges her forward without thinking, and she pulls Joey into a hug. Joey's not skin and bones, but she feels fragile, and Sophie's afraid to squeeze too hard. She waits several seconds, holding her like this, feeling warmth grow between them.

And then Joey softens, just a little, into her embrace. Her wiry arm muscles slacken and wrap around Sophie's shoulders. There's an unsteady breath and then an exhale.

"I'm so sorry," says Sophie. "I don't know why it took me so long to get back here. I don't know why I didn't come. I—"

"It's fine," says Joey.

Sophie nods because her face is suddenly wet with tears, and she doesn't want to speak in case her voice wobbles. The moment is taut between them, a stay that could hold or snap, depending on the wind. Sophie waits, breathless. She wants to say so many things, to tell Joey about her family, about her life. She wants, most of all, to try to explain why she's built this formidable wall that's kept her away from Whisper Ridge. It's seizing her now, the guilt. If only she'd reached out. If only she'd come back. She should just say what she needs to say. But she doesn't trust her voice not to shake if she speaks again, so she stays silent and waits for Joey's response.

"It's fine," Joey repeats.

Sophie sniffles, pulls away, and wipes at her face. "What is wrong with me? I should be comforting you."

Joey shakes her head.

"Yes," says Sophie. "I'm the one who left. I can't explain it other than to say that I hate myself for it. I missed you so much. I missed Elena. I missed—" She stops short of saying Quinn's name.

"It's okay," says Joey, with the air of someone who wants to stop blubbering and change the subject. "I didn't text you this morning because I wanted you to feel guilty. I texted you because"—she blows out air between tight lips—"I want your help." Joey looks away and stares blankly at the wall of suspects, theories, and questions. Though she hasn't changed much, her eyes have a hardness to them now.

"We should go," she says, changing the subject, presumably before Sophie can ask more questions. She turns and strides out the door. Sophie is left in the guest room alone and suddenly feels the memories swell above her head and crest down again. All these faces, this place, these people she's tried so hard to escape—they surround her like underwater creatures pulling her to the depths.

She wonders how Joey stays afloat.

7
ELENA

Planes are disgusting places. Cesspools. The man behind Elena coughed the entire flight. She wouldn't be surprised if she and Gael both got the bubonic plague.

But after a shitty flight she could barely afford and a four-hour drive in a potent rental car, she's here. They're here. And wow, this place hasn't changed one bit. It's still the gritty town it always was. The old square buildings stare down blankly. A few people eye her curiously as they walk by. She forgot this feeling, like she's constantly being watched. Judged.

At the house, she showered beneath a tap that didn't stay warm while Gael set up the laptop. She dried her hair and reapplied concealer. She's aging well, but still. Things have happened. Life has happened. Fifteen years is a long time.

Front Street is busy. Two boxy trailers sit on either side of the road, taking up several parking spaces each. A video village tent with cameras and equipment is set up near the old bank building. On the other side of that, the road has been covered in dirt to make it look old-timey. There are other set design props too, and livestock. The Three Elks peaks rise behind it all, jagged and ominous in the dusky light. Hollywood has come to Whisper Ridge.

Elena's agent secured her a job as a background actor in the film. Being so last-minute, it was lucky the casting company was still booking even though filming had already started, probably because they were shooting in the middle of nowhere. Elena's two-pronged plan: Secure a day of work, and use this as the networking opportunity of a lifetime. Then, after filming is wrapped in a few days, get the hell out of here. Being here isn't the most practical thing she's ever done, since she'll miss a few shifts at the restaurant. But she's finally in a place in her life where she can dip her toes into risk. Rubbing shoulders with Phillip Granger seems like a good place to start.

She slings her cross-body bag over her head and makes her way down the street. Gael wanted to stay in, but when Elena told him they would probably be filming right now, he jumped up and grabbed his camera. Elena did not want him to come to Whisper Ridge at all. Too much history here. She reminded him of his other commitments and said she just needed a few days to herself. But he did not take no for an answer and all but threatened her if she didn't let him come. Now he's playing with the settings on the camera as they walk, not even watching where he's going. He asks absently if she believes in the tommy-knockers, the terrifying little creatures they said would knock on the walls just before a mine collapsed. Locals here love these kinds of stories, but she's surprised Gael even knows about them.

He shrugs. "I looked it up."

He tells her he's going to go check out the horses, and she watches him wander away. It's surreal seeing him here, on this street where she used to spend her weekends. As for her, she's ready to get the hellos over with, deciding to say something generic like, "*Wow, you look great.*" That will set the tone, keeping things as peripheral as she needs them to be. She's thought about this moment before. Of course she has. She's only human. But she always imagined their reunion to be on some Southern California rooftop with lowball cocktails, where she could gloss over the details of her life.

Today, she chose a pair of white pleated pants and an earthen brown tank top—both thrifted—and paired them with a plain black baseball hat just for this occasion. She hopes it says, *"I'm back but I'm not really back."*

She uses the group chat to message them now to tell them she's here instead of dragging it out to the point of awkwardness. When she hits Send, she doesn't have to wait long at all. Within minutes, they appear from the opposite end of the block. Despite the low evening light, Joey is unmistakable with her black jeans and tee and ramrod-straight ponytail. Next to her, Sophie is short and chaotic. She wears a messy blond haircut and a flowy purple shirt.

"Here we go," Elena says to herself through clenched teeth before gluing on a smile.

"Elena!" Sophie is speed-walking toward her. "You came." She doesn't hesitate when she reaches her; she just grabs her for a long, warm hug.

Joey is at her heels, a cautious cat, betraying almost no emotion except maybe a trace of surprise and something obdurate, like she's not sure she wants Elena to be here.

Elena shrugs, then points vaguely in Sophie's direction. "Wow, you look great."

"So good to see you," says Sophie, emphasizing the word *see* like sight is somehow not a given. "Joey and I thought we could go for a little walk." Sophie looks to Joey, as if for permission. The way she says it, in a loud whisper, makes Elena understand immediately that she doesn't mean *walk* at all. They're going into the woods. On cue, almost on instinct, it seems, all three of them look around toward First Street, where there's a small, completely hidden trailhead.

The thought of that trail disturbs something inside Elena. She changes the subject, hoping to buy herself a pass without explanation. "They started filming, I guess?" She nods to the tent at the end of the road.

"Last week," says Joey, turning to look. "They're all obsessed with it."

A small crowd has formed a semicircle around video village. Gael is there, standing near one of the horses, oblivious to this moment, his neck still hunched over his camera's screen. Elena watches as a woman in ripped jeans and a headset walks over to him. They talk for a minute, and then he puts the cap back on his camera and slings the strap over his head.

Sophie places a hand above her eyes to block out the setting sun. "Anyone know what the movie is about?"

"According to my agent, it's a historical gold rush thriller," says Elena. "A schoolteacher is brutally attacked by wolves or something, but the sheriff thinks someone else is behind her murder. It's a Phillip Granger film."

Sophie quickly turns to Elena. "That's right. You're an actress now. You have an *agent*."

Elena's surprised Sophie knows this about her.

Sophie waves her hands as if to erase any misunderstanding. "I'm not stalking you. Just found you on social." She gives a rueful grimace.

"Huh," says Elena, preferring not to comment either way. It's not that she tries to be private. She has to be online if she has any chance of making it as an actor. Now that she thinks of it, she does remember seeing Sophie's face pop up during a flurry of follows after one of her reels went semiviral. It's an odd feeling knowing that Sophie has kept tabs on her. It makes her wonder if anyone else has too. Anyone that she might not want to.

"Oh, come on," Sophie says, playfully. "You're lying if you say you haven't looked us up."

"Nope," Elena says.

Joey crosses her arms. "You two moved away. I assumed you didn't want to be looked up."

She's right. But Elena doesn't do guilt trips. "Well, we had to escape this sinkhole," she says, hoping to drive her stake into the ground where it's visible. She does not really want to be here, or at least wants to make sure that's the impression she's giving.

In response, Joey scrunches her lower eyelids in a movement so small it's nearly imperceptible. Elena's hit a nerve; that much is obvious. Maybe she was trying to hit one. Joey was going on the offensive. Elena's response was just self-preservation.

"We're here now," says Sophie, and she gives Joey a knowing look that tells Elena they've already had some time to catch up. Elena has questions, but this doesn't feel like the time or the place. Her curiosity almost wins over her indignation, but in the end, she stays quiet.

"Let's walk," Sophie says, sounding flustered, maybe hoping to quell some tension. "Stretch our legs before it gets too dark."

Before Elena can respond, the woman in the ripped jeans who was just talking to Gael jogs toward them, pushing the headset away from her face. "We're clearing this block," she says, tapping on a smartwatch.

"Got it. We were just leaving," Elena says to the woman, who seems relieved she didn't get pushback. She strides away, toward a trailer, presumably to tell others to move off the block in question too. In the distance, Gael begins to saunter over. Elena watches his familiar movements. In thirty seconds, she will have to introduce him.

"It's so weird seeing all these people here," says Joey, breaking the silence. "It's like we've been discovered. Tourists will be next."

"I don't know. I think it's exciting," says Sophie, standing on her toes to see more of the film equipment.

"Tourists already," says Elena, pointing an elbow toward Sophie. Elena sees Joey's lips twitch. It's not a smile, but it feels like a temporary truce. Something inside Elena unwinds gently, and she lets her eyes close. She's been Spandex-tight, fretting all day over whether coming back was the right thing. She shoved Whisper Ridge so far back into the cobwebbed recesses of her brain, she thought she'd forgotten it altogether. But this place sticks to you like gum on your shoe. When she booked the last-minute flight, she tried to convince herself she wouldn't feel anything when she arrived. That she was just traveling to a set. But, deep down, she knew better. And she can feel this place pulling at her already.

"That woman said we have to leave this block," Gael's voice rings out nearby. Elena opens her eyes instinctually at the sound. He stands a few feet away, and she takes in all of him: his thin face, a wave of black hair with that enviable shine, and his enormous feet and beanpole legs.

Sophie and Joey both turn toward this new voice, and Elena can see Joey preparing her retort. *"We said we were going."* But once they see who has spoken, they're silent, stunned maybe. They were clearly not expecting a child.

Gael's eyes bounce between the three of them. He seems just as confused as they are, and for one manic moment, Elena feels like laughing out loud.

He doesn't say anything, just walks around Sophie to stand next to Elena to wait, not shy or bothered, just curious. For a second, none of them speak. Gael's presence has made them incapable of continuing their conversation. Then Elena says, "Gael, this is Joey and Sophie. We grew up together."

Sophie is the first to recover from her surprise. "Nice to meet you, Gael," she says with the warmth of a woman who is good with kids.

"Hi," he says, coolly. He's unconcerned in his typical, fourteen-year-old way.

Joey offers him a small wave, then slips her thumbs behind the straps of her backpack. Gael must deem this a sufficient introduction because he turns to Elena and says, "Food?"

"We literally just ate," she says, referring to the two burgers he wolfed down in the car less than an hour ago. He shrugs with one shoulder as if to say, *"What does that matter?"*

Joey pulls her bag to her front and rummages through it, eventually producing a small wrapped energy bar. She holds it out to him, her eyes still wide with shock. "Peanut butter?" she asks.

"Hell yeah," he says, taking it from her. "Thank you."

They observe him tear at it with his teeth for a silent minute, like they're watching a creature in the wild. "I guess no walk?" Sophie asks eventually, her eyes moving between Elena and Joey. Joey looks at Gael, who's already finished the energy bar and is crumpling the plastic wrapper in one hand. Then she looks back at Elena like she isn't sure exactly what to do.

"No walk," says Elena, relieved that at least this part is over. "Let's get a drink."

8

JOEY

The Strike is divey.

It has that natural mountain charm that makes locals proud—warm century-old buffed wood and a stone wall lined with rail ties and fairy lights. It also offers a shot of tequila and a can of PBR for three dollars, which doesn't hurt either.

It's cool and quiet inside, almost like they've escaped down a hole into the earth. The film hubbub is audible outside the closed door, but only faintly. There's a haze in the air, and it swirls around in the dim light from the small stained-glass windows at the front. The smell is of beer and pine cleaner.

It's a Monday, which means there are only a few locals here besides Ken behind the bar. Joey's nerves are jangling. She is bursting with anxiety about telling Sophie and Elena what she heard in the woods, not least because she knows how insane it will sound.

Elena's kid is as tall as Joey's chin and is surprisingly confident as he steps up to the bar. "Can I get a Coke, please?" he asks. Without hesitation, Ken fills a pint glass with ice and dips the soda hose inside. He shoots Joey a look that says, *"Anyone above age having a drink?"*

Joey thinks about getting a water, but she orders an IPA instead. Sophie gets a margarita. Elena, a whiskey, neat.

They settle into a table in a dark corner of the bar, cradling their drinks in silence and watching the fake candle pretend to flicker. Sophie places her phone face up on the table, and Joey can see a little girl on the home screen. Ringlet curls and a beaming smile. She has Sophie's eyes. It occurs to her that they should be spending the afternoon catching up on the years they've missed. Sophie has a baby, Elena has a teenager, *and* she's on TV. And Joey has—

What does Joey have?

Elena pulls a five-dollar bill from her wallet and hands it to Gael, then motions to the Mortal Kombat arcade game in the corner. "Nice," he says, and heads back up to the bar, where Ken takes his money and gives him a handful of quarters in return. Gael seems like he's in his early teens, and it occurs to Joey that Elena must have had him not long after leaving Whisper Ridge. She wonders if Elena ever thought to tell her old friends about this enormous life change. But that was just how Elena was. Once she was gone, she was gone completely.

"Okay," Joey says, finally, taking a sip of beer. It's bitter but satisfying. She leans in and lowers her voice, deciding, finally, that there are things more pressing than small talk. "Thanks for coming."

Sophie and Elena exchange a look, and it's not lost on Joey. Her leg is bouncing uncontrollably beneath the table.

"You said you know what happened to Quinn," says Sophie carefully, folding her hands in front of her.

Elena studies her fingernails, says nothing.

Joey tries to still her bouncing leg, hoping to calm down, but it doesn't work. Finally, she just comes out with it. "I was in the woods yesterday, near the aspen grove," she says. "And I heard whispers."

"You heard whispers?"

Joey takes another sip, then a deep breath. "It was the trees. They were...whispering."

At this, Sophie's face shifts to a look of bald concern. Elena looks up, with an expression like she's being punked. A viscous silence spreads between them as sounds of kicking and punching ring out from the arcade machine.

"What do you mean they were whispering?" It's Elena who speaks eventually. Her voice is low and mumbled, almost as if she doesn't want to know, but something has compelled her to ask.

"It was the trees, but the whispers sounded like...Quinn's voice."

Sophie chews on a nail.

"I'm confused," says Elena. "Was it Quinn's voice or the trees?"

"Both, maybe. I don't know," says Joey. "I think it was a memory of her, of something she said at the end. She sounded scared."

Elena shifts in her chair. Her face tells Joey that she thinks this is a sick joke and she's trying to anticipate the punchline. Joey's throat is scratched and dry. She takes another prolonged sip of her beer, which is warming quickly. She places herself back on the trail, dirt on her knees and a recklessness she couldn't explain at the time. Now, she wonders if the magic somehow called to her, and that was why she chose that trail, so close to the place where Quinn was found.

"All she—the voice—said were two words, over and over." She can feel herself pressing on that bruise again. It hurts, but she wants them to know. "She was saying, *'Dad? No!'* It was a whisper, but it was also kind of a scream. Like she just realized something. She sounded terrified."

An intake of breath from Sophie makes Joey's heart start to pound faster. Part of her is still back in those woods, listening.

"Huh," says Elena, not bothering to hide her skepticism.

Sophie takes her fingernail from her mouth. It's bleeding a little at the corner. "You mean, like she just realized her dad was about to—"

Joey shrugs.

"Okay. More drinks, I think," says Elena. She pushes herself back from the table. After a few minutes, during which Joey and Sophie stay silent, Elena returns, dropping three fresh drinks on the table, even though none of them are done with their first.

Joey taps the rim of the new beer with her thumb.

"It was definitely Quinn's voice?" Sophie asks.

"I'm positive," Joey says forcefully. And she is positive. It was the most heartbreaking sound she's ever heard. That's not the kind of thing someone just imagines, is it? The beer is making her head fuzzy. "I've been thinking about it. I think for some reason they were out there together…Quinn and her dad…right before she… It was like the aspens were remembering the moments before she died and wanted me to know. Otherwise, why did I hear those words? Why that one moment? Out of all the times we spent out there. There must be a reason."

"Joey, today is the anniversary of her death," Sophie says carefully. Doubt drips from her words.

"Thanks for letting me know."

"Do you think you could have imagined it?" Sophie looks to Elena as if for moral support. Elena pulls back her lips in a cringe. "Do you think it's possible you *wanted* to hear something while you were out there on a day when you were probably feeling pretty vulnerable?"

"I know what I heard." Heat blossoms beneath Joey's cheeks. She's drinking too fast.

"Okay. I'm just asking if you think it's possible. I read about something called *delusional daydreaming*. It can happen to people with a history of trauma."

"Thank you, TikTok, for your official diagnosis," says Elena with a wry smile. "But seriously, Joey, I don't know about this. It could have been anything. A rustling of leaves. The wind."

Joey can't help it. She snaps. "*Wow.* I didn't think I'd have to convince you I was telling the truth. You know there's magic in those trees. You've lived it. And you know the rules too. Rule one is to listen when the trees whisper."

"Fair enough." Elena mashes her lips together. "The rules do mention whispering trees, but I always thought that was a metaphor or something."

Sophie nods in quick agreement.

Joey cannot believe what's happening right now. "I thought you'd get it. It didn't even occur to me that you wouldn't." She pauses, waiting for someone to say something, anything, to contradict her. "It seems I miscalculated." She is expecting her words to rile them or at least shake the doubt from their faces, but it only seems to deepen their concern. Even Elena is wearing a look of pity. "Fine, whatever. I know what I heard."

"Joey..." Sophie says, but Joey can't handle this.

She whisper-yells across the table, "Do you not understand what this means? It means we know at least part of the truth about what happened. It wasn't an accident."

She thinks she can see a glimmer of regret in their expressions—at least in Sophie's—but it's fleeting because they're interrupted by a sound from the door. A chill floods the room, and a second later, bodies stream through, voices raised. Laughter rings out, echoing in every corner. Suddenly, it's as lively as a nightclub, and Stevie Nicks sings from the jukebox.

Sophie reaches over the table and grabs her hand. Joey thinks she's about to relent and tell her she believes her. But instead, she lets out a nervous laugh. "Oh my god. That's Cal Pierce. *The* Cal Pierce. And is that Nicola Bianco? She's so gorgeous in real life. I thought this was a little indie film. I didn't realize there would be actual celebrities here." She spins around to glare at Elena, as if she has some explaining to do. Joey's hope deflates.

Elena doesn't look at them when she replies. Instead, her eyes are locked on someone. At first Joey thinks it's Gael, but he's on the opposite side of the bar.

"I didn't know who the actors were," Elena says, distracted. "I just knew the director." Then she stands. "Hey, I'll catch up with you guys later." Without waiting for a response, she walks over to Gael and tells him something. He nods without looking away from his game, and Elena turns to the crowd of people, drink in hand, where she transforms into someone completely new. She's suddenly magnetic, flashing a warm smile and pushing her long black hair over one shoulder as she introduces herself. The people she's speaking to laugh pleasantly as if she's just said something clever.

Irritated, she turns to Sophie, who seems to have clocked her change in temperature. Sophie gets that pitying look on her face again. "You okay?"

This gives her an extra jolt of frustration. Even empathetic Sophie doesn't believe her. She offers a conciliatory nod, even though she is not okay. Sophie's phone begins to vibrate.

Joey watches as, without hesitation, Sophie grabs the phone, holds it up in front of her and swipes at the screen. Over the din of the music and voices in the bar, Joey can hear a crackle of a voice come through. "Hi! How's home?" Then, before Sophie can answer, an adorable shout follows it. "Mama!"

Joey has never seen anyone's face do what Sophie's does now. She beams with genuine, unfiltered joy and is somehow also close to tears. "Hi, baby."

Joey is suddenly self-conscious witnessing this private family moment. She stands up. "I'll see you tomorrow," she mouths and gives Sophie a quick wave, but Sophie barely looks away from the screen as she raises a hand back toward her. On her way out, Joey walks by Gael, who is expertly roundhouse kicking his opponent, completely consumed by the old-school graphics. Elena sits on a barstool across from him, leaning into a small circle of people and gesturing emphatically. Joey doesn't say goodbye.

It's only when she reaches the door that she realizes what Sophie's wife asked her. She didn't ask, *"How's Whisper Ridge?"* She asked, *"How's home?"*

Strange that even after all this time, Sophie would still call this place home. But this isn't her home anymore. It's not Elena's home either. They've outgrown this place; they've outgrown her. Joey is alone.

Finding the truth about what happened to Quinn may not be a living, breathing thing, but it is all she has.

9

QUINN

FEBRUARY 2011
FOUR MONTHS BEFORE THE FALL

I need new hiking boots.

My left heel has lost its traction, and my foot slips every few steps. There's some snow on the ground, and if it wasn't *our* trail, it would be closed this time of year.

Joey's up ahead. She cuts through the winter air with her breath billowing and her sleek dark hair pulled back into a ponytail. I watch the sharp outline of her calves, visible under her long, tight running pants, as she takes on the trail with her usual vigor. She's quiet, but I know her mind is going a million miles a minute. I'll have to ask her about the hiking boots. She'll know which pair I should get. She's the gear girl.

Elena strides just in front of me, head bent toward a flip phone. "Oh my god," she says, cackling. "Tanner sent another one." Elena, the queen of the universe. She's not heartless, despite what everyone says. She's just herself all the time and doesn't care what people think. Never has.

Elena holds out the phone behind her, and I cover my face with my hands. I know what it is without looking—a dick pic—and it's one image I do not need to see. Behind me, Sophie adjusts her beanie and turns away. She stops to watch a rabbit hop over the snow and dart between the trees, and I know she's deliberately making space between herself and the image on the phone. Tanner McGrath has made her cry enough times that I don't imagine a picture of his penis is on her list of things to see this morning. Unlike Elena, Sophie does care what people think—and say and feel. She is the kind of friend who will listen as you divulge your deepest fears and share her Red Bull with you between classes. She is all heart.

"We have the book, right?" Joey asks.

I reach behind me and give my pack a squeeze. "Of course." I pinch the familiar edges of the book and am, as always, exhilarated to be the keeper of secrets. To be the one who knows that things aren't always what they seem.

After our initiation, the four of us became as inseparable as vines. We'd been friends before, but after that day, we were always sneaking out to do magic, obsessed with our new power. We used illusion spells to change the color of my hair every few months. When Joey sprained her ankle in volleyball, we healed it. When Elena couldn't remember where she put her cigarettes, we summoned them.

Above us now, clouds wrestle overhead, threatening to douse the world in snow.

"I can't believe I got a C," says Sophie, who walks alongside me again.

Elena laughs. "You know a C is average, right?"

"Not when you want to get into AP world history."

Around us, bare aspen branches shudder in the wind. Along the snow-spotted trail, rocks crown through the mud like icebergs. I am reminded that now this is a path only we can see. Our illusion spell keeps it hidden.

Joey turns to walk backward so she's facing us. "We all agree it should be an illusion spell, right? Change the grade on the test, and change it in his grade book?"

"Even though the grade book is online, you still think it will work?" Sophie asks.

Joey shrugs. "We changed that Facebook post, remember?" As she finishes the thought, her heel catches on a rock. She reaches for Elena, who then reaches for me. Sophie yips and grabs my elbow, but instead of breaking my fall, she slips. Together, we tumble down, an avalanche of limbs, into the snow and earth. After one second of silence, we burst into laughter, unable to stop ourselves. We're muddy and bruised, but we help each other to our feet.

A thirty-minute hike is all it takes to get out here, and the anticipation is like sugar on our tongues. Soon, the woods open around us, and we're surrounded by knobby white aspen trunks, looking on like stacked-together bones. There's a sharpness in the air that bites the inside of my nostrils—the smell of the trees. Alongside the smell is a vibration, a constant hum, like there's a grid of electricity beneath our feet. This is the magic. I savor it for a moment, excited for the spell work to come.

Then, beneath the feeling of the magic, an unexpected, unwelcome prickly feeling sweeps over me. Goose bumps rise in warning on my arms, itching me through my sweatshirt. Something doesn't feel right. I look out at the enormous snow-covered crag at the far end of the clearing. It's an abscess bulging from the earth. Beneath it is a thirty-foot drop. If you stand at the edge and look out, there is an insane view. But none of us would dare to go close to the edge, not in winter, not in any kind of weather.

Then, I realize what the prickly sensation is. It feels like someone's watching us.

This, of course, is not possible. We are hidden behind our illusion spell. A spell we have mastered and tested time after time. Despite knowing this, fear compels me to glance around. I see the aspen trees around us and the dark, lurking conifers beyond them. There's the crag and the expanse beyond that. Nothing seems to be out of the ordinary, even though my body is telling me otherwise.

We stand in our usual places. Elena to my left, Sophie to my right, and Joey directly across from me. I'm still wary as I hand Sophie the book, but I tell myself to calm down. It's nothing. It's just me being in my head too much.

In my hands, the spell book looks old, its black edges frayed. My favorite black and gold ring—a gift from my grandma—catches an arc of sunshine and reflects a dagger of light. Sophie takes the book. Without opening it, she sets it on a lump of snow in the center of the circle and lays a hand on it, reverently. The rest of us take a seat on the cold ground. I try, but I can't shake the weird, creepy feeling.

"Wait," I say.

They look at me with surprise.

"What if we tried a time-turning spell? If it works, Sophie can just retake the test now that she knows all the answers." Something suddenly lathers and foams inside me, an urge to try something new, as if it might somehow scratch an itch.

"Really?" says Joey, skeptically. "It's never worked before." She's right. We've tried it. My mom even tried it back when she was our age. It hasn't worked for generations.

"I just... I have a good feeling," I say, and I think it's true. Maybe this strange sensation is just me being hyperaware. I can't exactly say why, but I just don't think I'll be satisfied with a simple, benign spell today.

There's a long silence, during which no one disagrees. Their eyes connect with one another's.

"We can try it," Sophie says. I can tell she doesn't want to, but she wouldn't say no to a fly.

Elena shrugs, and Joey gives a resigned, "Whatever."

Excitement spreads through me, warm and thick. I say nothing, though, just nod to Sophie and close my eyes. This is her cue to begin.

In another second, I know she is raising her hands above her head. She is channeling. It's almost religious, the way the magic comes to us. It's second nature now. We've done spells more than a hundred times. The trees wait in quiet contemplation. Inside Sophie's head, I know she's cleared all her thoughts except one. She has to start channeling with a specific vision, a focal point. If we were doing an illusion spell, that vision would be of the object or objects she wants to draw an illusion over and what she wants to replace them with. In the case of a time-turning spell, I think it would be a specific point in time.

The silence drags on too long, and I open one eye. Sophie is still standing with her arms raised, but she's staring down at the book with a frown.

"It's not working," she whispers. Joey and Elena open their eyes too.

"Did you clear your thoughts?" My tone is sharper than I mean it to be.

"Yes," she says, defensive.

The book is still closed in the center of the circle, and it's obvious nothing has happened. It should be opening to a blank page—any page, all of them are blank—and words should be appearing there.

"Dammit," I say.

"Told you," says Joey. She's frowning, clearly annoyed that we even entertained the idea.

Elena claps her hands together. "Well then, we have confirmed that we still can't turn time. Let's just do the illusion spell for Sophie's test. It's fucking freezing out here."

Sophie nods her assent. But I'm disappointed. Strangely, I think of my dad. I think of his bumper crunching into the telephone pole at Second and Front Street at four in the afternoon yesterday, and the way he stumbled out, splashing vomit onto the sidewalk. I wasn't embarrassed, although who knows how many people saw. What bothers me is that I couldn't help him, even though I can do magic. He's changing into a man I don't recognize, and no simple illusion or summoning or wound-healing spell can change that. It's made me wonder, for the first time ever, what the point of the magic is.

They're all looking at me. How could I possibly explain all this? In the end, I just say, "Fine. Illusion spell."

"You okay?" Sophie asks and gently places a mud-splattered hand on my shoulder.

I change tack, shove the confused thoughts away. "I'm good." My voice squeaks with the lie.

Joey's frown deepens, and Sophie looks at me quizzically.

But Elena squawks. "Clearly." She gives me an ironic thumbs-up, but she doesn't ask what's wrong. None of them do. They think I will tell them what's wrong when I'm ready to. They trust me enough to do that.

But, for the first time, I'm not sure they should.

We resume our positions, and I try to forget about my dad, about how I'm feeling. I smile as genuinely as I can, and they seem relieved. We refocus.

Sophie starts the illusion spell, and I surrender to the magic as it fills me. This time it seems to be working. It feels familiar, like liquid sunlight tumbling through my veins. It's hot and bright and fast. And then I'm a tiny cup under a gushing tap. The magic spills over, making me open my eyes. We all do. Sophie drops to her knees, and we lean in. This is the part when we can see the spell in action, and, despite it all, it's still amazing.

The book opens on its own, and a page that was blank before suddenly fills and fills with words. This is how the magic always works. Our presence in this aspen grove turns on the tap, then we concentrate on the spell, and the pages of the blank book begin to fill. We read from the page to set the spell in motion. Once it's done, the words disappear again.

Before us, crimson letters creep across the page, as if written by a pen dipped in blood by some invisible hand. We're mesmerized.

Somewhere close by, there is a sudden revving sound that makes us all jump. It sounds like a dirt bike.

I whip my face around, jaw clenched in fear. The bike sounds far too close. Joey and Elena and Sophie have heard it too. For a second, it seems like it's coming toward us, but then the sound stops abruptly. We wait for it to come back, but nothing happens. The aspen trees are silent, slim, and watchful. Tender young saplings crowd the space at their feet. All is quiet.

Sophie takes a deep breath, realigning our attention back to the book. "Right," she says. "Here we go," and she starts to read.

10

SOPHIE

Sophie didn't tell her dad she was coming.

It's not that she was afraid to say anything; it was more that she wasn't sure what she could say. *"I'm coming home because a friend needs me, even though I haven't been to see you in fifteen years. Oh, and I'm not bringing your granddaughter."*

Just because Sophie hasn't been to Whisper Ridge doesn't mean her dad hasn't been to see his grandbaby as often as possible. Otto Stringer has been to Denver plenty. He's made the four-hour drive five times in the last year alone, including once during a pretty treacherous snowstorm. It warms Sophie's heart to know that he loves her family so much he's willing to overlook her lack of effort. She hasn't stepped foot in this town since she was a teenager, and he's never once made her feel bad about it. Not on purpose anyway.

But here she is, stepping foot. She wonders how this is going to go, being inside her childhood home. She puts her bag down and knocks.

While she waits for him to answer, she rocks back and forth between her sneakered feet, and her thoughts stray to Joey again. She's worried about her. Really worried. That murder wall, with all the pictures and the strings. And her claim about the whispering trees…

Joey texted the group chat a few minutes after she left the bar, letting both Sophie and Elena know she was planning to go to Barbara's tomorrow morning to talk to her about Tom. Sophie replied as soon as she was off the phone with her family. Regardless of what she believes is true, she doesn't think Joey should be alone. It's loneliness, she realizes, that probably dragged Joey into this delusional pseudo-investigation in the first place.

And then, before she has another thought, she sees her dad, on the other side of the open door, standing in his socks and sweatpants. He blinks when he sees her.

"Hi," she says and gives him a wave.

He pretends to stagger backward, steadying himself on the hall table. Then he says, deadpan, "No thanks, we don't want any," and closes the door.

Sophie shakes her head and waits. In less than three seconds, he flings open the door again with the biggest grin she's ever seen. Reflexive tears spring to her eyes. "You're here," he says, but she can't reply because he pulls her in for a lung-crushing hug.

"Frozen pizza or grilled cheese?" he calls from the kitchen.

Sophie's in her childhood bedroom. It's exactly the same. Not exactly the same, actually, because it's clean, which was never the case when she lived here. But her bed is still covered in the lavender floral bedspread she remembers. The walls are still the same buttery yellow, but they look fresh. She wonders if he repainted it recently.

Three different collages—all tacked with pictures of Sophie, Quinn, Joey, and Elena—line the far wall next to the window. One for each year of high school. There isn't one for senior year, of course. After what happened to Quinn, Sophie did what she had to do to graduate early. She was gone, working at a museum in Denver to pay her rent, by New Year's Eve. Standing here, she knows what drove her away, but what kept her away—that isn't possible to capture in a collage.

"Never mind," her dad calls out again. "Grilled cheese it is. This pizza expired in 2007."

Sophie drops her bag to the floor and takes out her phone. When Sophie told Talia she was going to Whisper Ridge, she asked if it was because of her dad, and Sophie, for some reason, didn't say no. Seeing Quinn's name in Joey's message unnerved her. She hadn't seen or heard it in so long, and somehow, she could sense that this was Joey's version of a cry for help. She could have told Talia this, of course, because Talia was her wife. She knew about Quinn's tragic death. But Sophie had never told her about the magic. She let Talia think it was an issue with her dad so she didn't have to explain, surprised at how excited she was just at the thought of speaking about it again with Joey and Elena.

She sends a quick check-in text. It's the dinner-bath-bedtime hour, so Sophie's not expecting a response, but she stares at the phone anyway, hoping to see Leah in her little cat jammies. She realizes she forgot to tell Talia about the chicken defrosting in the fridge and the carrots she bought yesterday that she meant to make for dinner today, and a moment of panic seizes her. She hopes Talia remembers to help Leah brush her teeth *after* her last glass of milk, and—*oh my god*—she left Teddy in the dryer this morning.

"Hey," says her dad, poking his head into her room. "Dinner in ten." He must see the tears that she hasn't had time to hide because he comes in and puts a hand on her face. "We doing okay?"

She nods, afraid to speak. "I just miss Leah," she manages.

He dips his head down so his eyes are level with hers. "I know you'll tell me eventually why you're here, so I won't ask." He hesitates. "This stage is tough. Believe me, I know. All couples struggle when the baby is young. Just—don't give up on them." He raises his hands. "That's all I'm going to say."

Sophie looks at him. "Oh, Dad, no." She realizes why he thinks she's here. "I'm not leaving Talia and Leah. Never. Never, ever."

She softens as she sees his face. Relief that Sophie hasn't turned out like her mother.

"I'm here," she says, finally mustering the courage to explain, "because Joey says she needs my help. Honestly, I think she just needs a friend."

What Sophie doesn't say—and neither does her dad, to his credit—is that Joey needed a friend fifteen years ago when all her then-friends abandoned her and needed one again ten years ago when her mother died.

He looks her dead in the eye. "You'd tell me if something was wrong, right?"

"Of course," she says, squeezing his hand. She's not sure if it's true, but she likes to think it could be.

"Shoot," he says, suddenly, sniffing the air. "The grilled cheese."

When he leaves, Sophie dumps her bag onto the bed. She doesn't even know what she's brought. She shoved a bunch of things in here without taking time to see if anything matched or fit. At least she remembered her toothbrush. She puts her toiletries in the bathroom, which still also looks the same as it used to. Same pink tiles on the walls, same matte white bathtub, same polka dot shower curtain. But again, clean. No more pimple cream or body scrub from her youth, but also no toothpaste splatters on the mirror, not a single tissue in the trash. Her dad has never been a particularly tidy man, and he wasn't expecting her, so she's wondering why his house looks this neat on a random Monday.

Back in her room, she tries to flatten a shirt on the bed, but it's like the wrinkles are permanent. At this point, she wouldn't be surprised if they were. The closet, with its bi-fold slatted doors, calls to her, and she scoops her clothes up into her arms.

Inside the closet, there's a little lightbulb with a drawstring that she pulls, and the light flickers on. The drawstring swings, and she's distracted by this little movement. She spent mornings staring at this same drawstring, hating her clothes, annoyed that when she pulled a shirt over her head—one that looked so cute on the hanger—it would cinch in all the wrong places, giving her a lumpy look. She's been working on her body positivity, but she still has a way to go, especially since Leah was born. There are no more of her drapey sweaters in here anymore. Her dad brought boxes to her in Denver over the years, filled with clothes and books and things from her life before. However, there are a few items she doesn't recognize neatly stacked on the white iron shelves. A pair of jeans and some slippers. What looks like a nightgown, and hanging next to it is a blue floral sundress. It's cute, though not something Sophie would wear.

"Dad?" she calls out, hoping to ask him who these items belong to, but before she can, something else catches her eye.

A journal sits in the back corner of the closet. She drops the pile of clothes from her arms and bends down to see it more closely. It's a rosy pink, and the words *live for the journey* are embossed in small gold letters across the front. The cover looks worn, smudged by fingers and pen marks. She has never kept a diary, never liked the idea of analyzing her days this way. She'd rather sit with someone and talk it out face-to-face. This journal is not hers. And yet, here it is, sitting in her closet next to this strange dress.

"Soph," her dad calls to her from the kitchen. "Food's up, love."

She picks up the journal. It's a hardcover, and the pages are edged with gold. "Coming," she calls over her shoulder, but she doesn't move.

It's obvious that this journal has been held by anxious hands. She can tell by the broken spine and the way the pages want to splay out instead of pressing together. But when she opens to the middle of the journal, she stares at a blank page. There are no words there.

She flips through pages and pages, but still there is nothing in this journal. It's strange because it feels like she should see ink, but there isn't any. Eventually, she gets to the end, and still, nothing at all. Then she cracks it open to the very first page, just to check something.

She pinches her eyebrows together. On the inside of the front cover, it says, "THIS JOURNAL BELONGS TO:" and then on the line following, someone has written their name in faded blue pen.

Quinn Winter.

11

JOEY

Sophie comes skittering up the gravel road just as Joey's about to knock.

She's thrown back to days in the past when they would all show up at Quinn's together, pillows bunched under their arms, ready for a sleepover or for hours jumping on the trampoline in the backyard. Quinn's house—or, just Barbara's house now—is quiet. Dew-damp flower beds line the front path, and a bird feeder hums furiously as tiny wings vie for space.

"Morning," says Sophie. She's wearing a very rumpled pale blue peasant top and a bright, sleep-creased smile. Something about the smile feels put-on. Joey is sure that Sophie is still turning over what she said about the whisper in the woods. She seems to be deciding how to be with her without immediately referring her to psychiatric care.

Barbara Winter greets them at the front door with a look of unfettered delight. "Oh my days," she says, after she hugs Joey and sees Sophie standing behind her. "Look how beautiful... Come in, come in."

Joey's been here a few times over the years. She and Barbara discussed business around the same kitchen table where she used to serve them blackberry pancakes on Sunday mornings. Before, Barbara was so full of energy, so bubbly, always making the girls laugh. She was always everything to everyone. A city councilwoman, present at every PTA meeting, volunteering for events at the school, and running the town's annual lights parade in December, plus she owned Aspect Coffee, which, in its heyday, doubled as a kind of community center. A sparkle of a woman. But after Quinn died, especially by the time Barbara was ready to get rid of the coffee shop, her eyes had sunk into tired skin, her hair had thinned. She quit almost everything, and now it's just the baking. All the time. Today, she wears her hair in a bob, her natural curls completely gray. Despite it all, Barbara still has a bit of her old spirit. Maybe it's the long gold earrings hanging from her ears in the shape of snakes with tiny black stones for eyes.

The house smells of cinnamon and bread. The kitchen walls are a ruby wallpaper decorated with sketched pomegranate halves. A brass kettle billows steam. A crystal suncatcher dangling in the window refracts light around the room.

Joey is surprised to see Gael here. He is busy setting out small plates and napkins, seeming right at home. "Buns are almost ready, madam," he tells them with a napkin draped over his forearm, as if he is a butler. Behind him, Barbara grins, proud. Sophie laughs, and Joey wonders why Gael is here but not Elena. He offers them a choice of tea or coffee.

Joey takes a coffee.

"Thank you very much, sir," Sophie says, opting for tea. To Barbara, she says, "It's so cozy in here. I've missed this." The kitchen is warm, and the counter is speckled with flour. A window is cracked so they can hear the birds, who seem thrilled that the sun is shining. Barbara slides a tray of homemade lemon curd and freshly whipped butter onto the table.

"Barbara is teaching me to bake," says Gael. He looks like he's never seen a spread like this in his life, and she is struck with how much he looks like Elena. The same thick black hair, the same deep brown eyes. And yet he has an easygoing, jovial personality she doesn't recognize.

Joey notices too, his use of Barbara's first name. They've all called her that ever since Joey made the mistake of calling her Mrs. Winter one morning when they were kids. *"Oh, use my first name, honey,"* she said. *"It was a gift from my mother."* She was not one of those first-name moms who tried to get in on the gossip or put in her two cents about who she thought was *cute* at school. That was more Joey's mom. Barbara was a mother hen, a collector of friends and the busiest woman alive. Someone who would wrap you in a hug and listen, no questions asked, but who would also then spearhead antibullying training at school on your behalf.

Joey feels her molars grinding. Of course she would compare her own mother to Barbara, even though she has no delusions that hers was so maternal. Joey's mom seemed so young, sometimes more like a sister than a mother, all the way up to the end. But god, Joey loved her.

From somewhere in the house, Elena emerges. Her hair is styled in beach waves that look effortless but likely required at least twenty minutes in front of the mirror. Joey notices the wet smell of shampoo wafting down from upstairs, the two extra pairs of shoes by the front door, and the white cross-body bag hanging on a hook, and she feels an instant twinge of irritation. "I didn't realize you were staying here," she says. The words are out before she can check them.

"Oh, awkward. Sorry." Elena makes a little oopsie face to show that Joey's comment has made her mildly uncomfortable. "Now you know, I guess." She grabs a coffee mug from a rack beneath the cabinets.

"I was more than happy to open my home up to Elena and Gael," Barbara says over Joey's shoulder, "just as I would be more than happy to do it for either of you." She wipes her hands and pats Joey on the arm as if to say, "*and that is that.*"

"Of course, we know that," says Sophie.

But Joey feels bruised. She knows Elena probably stayed in touch with Barbara on Barbara's insistence and that she has no right to be jealous. Maybe she wishes things had been different between them, that they could have banded together after Quinn died, not scattered. Joey lets herself picture Quinn here now, sitting across from her, telling her not to let Elena get under her skin, laughing as she dips a finger into the curd and then licks it clean.

"Good," Barbara chirps. "Chelsea buns will be ready in five minutes."

"Bless you." Sophie gives Barbara a look of such gratitude, it looks like she might be considering staying forever. Elena pours herself some coffee. The smell fills the room, and the moment seems to pass. Imaginary Quinn disappears.

"So Gael says he's been taking pictures around town," Barbara says, patting him on the shoulder.

"He's pretty good," Elena says, and Joey detects a small glint of pride in her eye. "But he is completely obsessed."

"I am," he says as he swallows down some orange juice. Then he grabs a camera from the counter and holds it up to his face, pointing it directly at them. A few speedy clicks, before they even have time to smile, and then he examines his work.

They settle into the silence. Morning sunlight floats around the oven-warmed room. Maybe it's the way they all seem so at ease right now, in this familiar kitchen, or maybe it's the soft jazz playing on the speaker or the smell of something baking. It's at odds with the restlessness inside Joey, with the reminder that the trees wanted her to know something about Quinn.

"Barbara, can I ask you something?" Joey's interruption is louder than she intends it to be. Everyone looks at her.

Barbara is alerted by the change in energy. She flips a kitchen towel over her shoulder and tilts her head to the side in concern. "Everything okay?"

Back in the day, when Joey asked the questions no one wanted to hear, she was not taken seriously. And rightly so. She was a nervous kid whose ideas about corroboration and timelines and alibis came from watching *NCIS*. But despite being the subject of town gossip, just asking the questions gave her a strange buzz, like one piece of an interrogation might lead somewhere. It never did, of course. But right now, she feels an ounce of that old buzz again.

"How much do you believe Tom's alibi?" The words spill out of her.

There's a palpable silence after the word *alibi*. And with it, the kitchen's cottagey warmth chills slightly. Barbara frowns. Gael looks up from his camera. Sophie and Elena both take longer than normal sips.

Fifteen years ago, Joey spoke to Tom Winter while he sat at the bar in the Strike. Her obstinate glare dared the bartender—still Ken, even back then—to kick her out. He didn't, even though he knew she was underage. She didn't order anything, and she didn't make small talk. She just watched Quinn's dad tap his ring against his glass over and over again while she asked him where he had been the night of her death. He didn't make a single sound except for the clinking of metal on glass, and her only thought at the time was, *You're divorced. Why are you still wearing your wedding ring?*

Barbara slides into a seat and looks Joey in the eye. "If you're asking whether I believe he was at poker the night Quinn died, then, yes, I do. He is a lot of things, but a good liar is not one of them."

"Joey, his friends vouched for him," Sophie adds quietly.

Barbara squints. "Why do I think that's not the answer you were looking for?"

Joey shrugs, deciding how to respond. It's not the answer she wanted, but what does she want? She can't go into detail about Quinn's words in the woods. Not with Barbara. But she can't pretend everything's fine either.

"You weren't living with him at the time, so how can you be sure?"

Sophie examines her drink like it's going to somehow save them all from this awkwardness. Elena and Gael, on the other hand, can't seem to look away. Barbara puts up two palms in her defense. "Yes," she says. "That's fair. You're right about that. I *don't* know for sure. But listen, I'd like to say one thing. You called it an alibi. Honey, even though I appreciate you still caring about what happened to our girl—I do, so much—it was an accident. There is no such thing as an alibi for an accident. I'm sorry. It does no good to keep these vengeful thoughts in your head. Quinn wouldn't want you to worry so much about it. Miss her, yes. Love her, yes. But don't suffer for some answer that's not going to come." She stretches a hand across the table. It doesn't quite reach Joey's, but the sentiment is there.

"You know, I used to think—" Barbara cuts herself off and brushes crumbs from her chest. "It's really nothing, and it's probably just hindsight, but I think Quinn worried about her father too much. I should have made her see there was nothing she could do about his alcoholism. A child shouldn't have to help their parents. That's not how it's supposed to work. But she had this insatiable need to save the world and everyone in it." She twirls her finger around in a circle.

Collectively, they breathe, and it feels as if Quinn is really sitting here with them, so spot-on is Barbara's characterization of her. Melancholy mixes with their anxiety and floats around them like dust motes. They've stirred latent bereavement debris, and it's irritating their noses and eyes. Gael reaches out a hand and puts it on top of Barbara's. Gael, the only child in the room and the only one who never knew Quinn. It's a gesture so unexpected, it makes Joey's throat constrict.

"Tom has a good heart," she continues. "Though it may be deep, deep down. Please don't go digging there again. You'll only unravel a man who is threadbare already."

The oven timer beeps. Barbara releases a giant exhale and jumps up.

The mountainside directly behind the house towers over the tiny backyard. Dark green conifers darken the fifty yards between the property line and the rocky upslope, which is peppered with even more trees. The trampoline is still there, in the far corner, nestled between shadows of huge Douglas fir branches and pine cones that litter the ground around them. Joey, Sophie, and Elena sit on the low deck with their legs dangling over the edge. Joey is still antsy. Frustrated.

"Oh my god, remember our camping nights?" Sophie says, swinging her feet.

"Yes," Joey snorts, despite herself. "And the night you swore you heard howling, and I had to go check every hour that we weren't surrounded by wolves."

Sophie looks mock outraged. "Everyone was scared."

Elena shakes her head vigorously. "That was all you."

Camping nights were typical in the height of summer. The four of them squashed their sleeping bags together, yelping when their flashlights finally died, and cracking up when their shrieks woke Sophie, who was always the first asleep.

"How many times do you think we played Uno, like in total?" Elena says. "Ten thousand? A million?"

Sophie lets out a breathy laugh. "Oh my god, Uno." Then, suddenly, she perks up. "Guys, our carvings. Do you think they're still there?"

Joey doesn't move. The day is steaming by. All she wants is to go through the night Quinn died, find some detail she missed, but she knows Sophie and Elena don't believe her about the trees whispering, and she doesn't feel like dealing with that again.

"I didn't come here to reminisce," Joey says, and it comes out cold.

Elena laughs out loud. "Neither did I." She's already on her feet, hopping off the deck and rounding the corner.

Maybe it's her perpetual belief in the good of people, but Sophie doesn't seem offended by Joey's lack of enthusiasm either. "You're not even a little curious?" she asks gently.

Joey shakes her head. "Nope."

Elena peers at her through the bars of the deck. "How could you not want to see our pubescent angst carved eternally into this decking?"

Without giving Joey a chance to respond, Sophie reaches her hand down. "Come on, let's kill five minutes. I desperately want another Chelsea bun, but I feel like I have to wait a socially appropriate amount of time."

Joey doesn't take Sophie's hand; she just watches as her look morphs into one of profound disappointment. She hops off the deck too.

"Some gnarly spiderwebs down here," Elena calls up. "What are the signs of a black widow bite? Also, thank god I'm wearing brown pants." Her voice is muffled, and Joey knows she's crawling under the deck. It's only about three feet off the ground.

"I just want to go," Joey says to Sophie, who she hopes will allow her to escape, even if it's out of pity. But Sophie drops to her knees and crawls under the deck, ignoring her. Joey turns, catching a glimpse of Barbara through the sliding glass door. She's cleaning a mixing bowl. The domesticity is incongruous with Joey's churning insides. But then Barbara stops scrubbing to lean both hands on the counter and hangs her head. Her shoulders shudder lightly.

"Oh my god, we were ridiculous," calls Elena. "Look at this one. *PB&J milkshake*. Like, what?"

"I think this one says, *sugar babies*?" says Sophie. "Honestly, I don't remember half of these inside jokes."

Wanting to move out of Barbara's sightline, Joey hauls herself up and makes her way down to the grass. She sees Sophie's feet sticking out from under the deck like the house has landed on her, and she sighs before lowering herself down and squeezing in next to them.

"Oh, hey, sugar baby," Sophie says, shining her phone's flashlight right in Joey's eyes.

"Stop." Joey can't help but let a small smile break her stony mood. For an instant, she feels warm. A sliver of what it used to feel like. She accidentally bumps Elena's elbow. Apologizes, but doesn't inch away.

Sophie points the light at the wood above their heads. This space used to feel so much bigger when their bodies were small and flexible. Years of words are scratched here. It's strange to see them again, as if her childhood has been condensed to just the CliffsNotes. The four of them came out here whenever they were bored, which was unsurprisingly often. Whisper Ridge is a tiny town. Joey's eyes catch on a few words randomly. It's impossible to know who wrote what. *Witches, bitches. I hate Tanner. School sucks. Get high like planes.* She's suddenly young, and tiny rocks are digging into her knees, and she's knocking into Quinn and Sophie, and they're all laughing because Elena is scratching the word *vagina* into the wood with a box nail.

"Look," says Sophie, stopping the roving flashlight on one spot. "See the 'Q + R' with the little heart?"

Joey looks, and there it is, bigger, more pronounced than the other carvings.

"Who's *R*?" asks Elena.

Joey swallows. "I don't remember that one." And she doesn't remember. But she can guess. Her shirt suddenly feels too tight around her arms.

"Oh, duh," says Elena.

Joey bites her lip, praying she doesn't say it out loud.

"*R* is *River*," Elena says, answering her own question. "Quinn and River. This must be from junior year."

Joey feels sick. Should she say something to them now? Rip off the Band-Aid? But she can't; the words won't leave her mouth.

"There's something written right next to it," Sophie says. "This one's weird."

Elena scoots closer. Joey is beyond relieved that they seem to have moved on, though she hasn't. How can she?

"What is it?"

"Not sure," says Sophie, keeping the light still until they all can read it clearly. "It just says... *bloodspell.*"

12

QUINN

APRIL 2011
TWO MONTHS BEFORE THE FALL

"We don't have to talk about it if you don't want to."

Joey sits at the corner of the bed hugging a pillow. Her long legs make neat triangles beneath her. My window is open, and a breeze snakes inside. The last tendrils of winter. I know Joey can tell I'm distracted. She's right.

Joey's not looking at me and instead seems focused on the closet door in the corner of the room. I turn to see if there's a spider or something there, but there's nothing.

"It was…good," I say.

She laughs. "Well, River's crazy about you, so of course it was."

It's freshly dark outside, just after eight. Last night, I dreamed that I was on a hill and Joey was on the other side, reaching her hand out and calling my name. Sophie and Elena too. Between us was this tumultuous, uncrossable whitewater. Waking up to that made the day seem bleak before it had even begun, and that mood has stuck with me all day. I have the sadistic urge to pass on my bad mood to someone else.

I lean on the side of the bed, and it squashes down beneath my forearms. My rings press into the flesh on my fingers. "Do you ever wonder if there's more we should know about the magic?"

Joey's lying on her side with her foot tucked behind her as she stretches her quad. There's a shift in her demeanor now that I've changed the subject. "What do you mean?"

The wind picks up. I can hear it whistling through the trees behind my house, traveling down the slope of the mountain toward us. I watch Joey with her running shorts and bare toes. "Aren't you freezing?"

She rubs at her knees in response, which seems insufficient to me because the cold is so present, it's like a third person in the room. I close the window.

When we were all fourteen, less than a year after our initiation, we found a small alpine lake. I was the first to lower my body into it and swim out to the center. Minutes later, Joey came paddling behind me, dragging an inflatable inner tube. She didn't say anything, just treaded water until I finally hooked an arm over the top. She didn't make a big deal of it, just quietly rescued me. And the thing is, I was starting to ache from the cold. My breathing was speeding up, and my lungs were constricting; I was shivering uncontrollably. But part of me *wanted* to feel cold and alone out there. I didn't want her to rescue me. And I don't want to be rescued now. I want to know what it feels like to swim on my own, body numb and goose bumps like needles, all the way to the other shore.

"Do you ever think there's more to it?" I ask. "Like, don't you think it's weird that the book we use for spells is completely blank?"

"I've never really thought about it."

"Well, think about it now." I'm needling her, gauging her reaction. I'm not sure of my aim—maybe I want her to guess what's going on so I don't have to lie.

She folds her arms. "I don't understand."

"Like, what if there is magic we don't know about? Hidden in those pages. What if we're purposefully being shielded from its true potential? Our true potential."

"Quinn, what are you talking about?"

Suddenly, my question feels urgent. I know I'm not explaining it correctly because Joey is smart. Born to work out puzzles.

"Okay, so we are the stewards of the magic, right?" I point, generally, to the woods beyond my backyard.

She nods slowly, as if to say, *"I am aware, yes."*

"What if we are actually capping its potential by only using it for benign shit, like little summoning spells and illusion spells and healing our zits? What if we could do more with it? Like, more *good*." I emphasize the last word to make my point.

She's nodding quicker now, clearly thinking, and I'm starting to feel warm, loose. Possibility is taking root. If Joey understands, if she gets it, then my conflicting feelings might dissipate.

"But we can only do the spells that the trees write for us in the book," she says, ever practical. "And there are only a few of those. That's how it works." She leans over to stretch the other leg.

"Okay, but hypothetically." My hope is starting to ebb away.

"I don't know what you want me to say."

"I've just been thinking about it. Like, don't you think we have a responsibility to do more? We have access to *magic*, Joey." I know I sound imploring now, maybe even desperate.

She looks like I just told her I wanted to take a trip to the moon. "I think we have a responsibility to follow the rules," she says. "To keep the magic safe."

We fall silent then, the rapids widening between us, almost uncrossable already.

A noise comes from the front of the house. Voices. They're hushed. Distantly, the front door opens and closes. Joey and I hold each other in a suspended look.

And then, Elena and Sophie burst into the room. "Hey, hey," says Elena. "I brought a movie and a bottle of Smirnoff."

Joey and I break our eye contact, and the moment snaps.

"Shh," I say as I hurry behind Elena to close the door. "My mom is home."

"We know," says Sophie, who holds out a plate of homemade whoopie pies. "She gave us these."

Elena plops a DVD on the bed. *Shutter Island*. "Love me some Leo."

"Isn't that one supposed to be scary?" asks Sophie. She places the cookies in the middle of the bed.

"You're a witch, Soph. And you're afraid of a movie?" Elena takes a cookie and licks the marshmallow fluff from the center, then puts the cookie bits back on the plate. Her smile is devilish.

"*The Witches of Whisper Ridge*. I'd watch that," says Joey, clearly unfazed by our earlier conversation. She pops an entire whoopie pie into her mouth.

"We could watch *Planet Earth*?" I say.

I can see on Sophie's face that she likes this suggestion.

"Boo," says Elena.

"It's fine," concedes Sophie. "I'll probably just fall asleep anyway."

"I knew you'd come around," Elena says. "You always do."

Sophie gives her a look like "*ha-ha*," but I'm not sure she finds the jab entirely funny.

Satisfied, Elena pulls out the vodka. The top is off in a second, and she takes a swig. She passes it to Joey, who sips once. Sophie pours too much into her mouth, which makes her cough and pull a face. I'm last. The smell reminds me of my dad. I put it to my lips and pretend to take a sip, just for appearances. I can tell Joey notices, but she doesn't say anything. She just grabs the blue Gatorade from the side table and pours vodka into it, passing it around like we've done a hundred times before. When it gets to me, I skip that too.

Whenever we watch movies, Sophie is always the first one asleep. When I look up from my spot on the floor, she's on her side, facing away from the TV, fully committed. Joey and Elena share a single pillow, their eyes closed too. I look past the credits flickering black and white on the screen, toward the open window. The clouds must have moved away from the moon because the trees beyond my yard look skeletal in the moonlight.

Silently, I pull on my socks and a sweatshirt. Then, I tiptoe to the nightstand. The cookie plate is speckled with black crumbs. The empty Gatorade bottle sits discarded on top of it. I close the cap to stifle the stench of alcohol. Then, I quietly tug at the drawer underneath. It slides out easily. Even with just the flickering TV light, I can see the rough edges of the book clearly. I take it in my hand. There's something about the feel of it that's different tonight. It's warm to the touch. I know it's just my imagination, though, because I want there to be some sign, some physical proof that what I am wondering about could exist.

On my bed, Joey, Elena, and Sophie are cuddled into each other like cats. I hesitate at the door.

But the pull is too strong, and within a minute I'm tugging on my hiking boots, shrugging on my coat, and slipping silently into the night.

13

JOEY

River is at her door.

He stands with his hands in his pockets and offers a nervous smile. Joey knew it would be him as soon as she heard the gentle knock. He looks hopeful, but still, she doesn't want to talk. She's about to say so, but then she sees that next to him, in a perfectly happy, obedient sit, is Walter. His tongue flips out of his mouth, and he pants enthusiastically.

"Hello, sir," Joey says, bending down to greet the dog. His marbled Aussie fur is soft and fluffy, and he has black markings over one crystal blue eye. He offers her a playful paw, even though he's almost sixteen and has arthritis in his old joints.

"I didn't think you'd talk to me if I came alone, so I brought reinforcements." River peers at her cautiously beneath waves of hair the color of oak. His beard is short and thick, while his build is tall and strong.

Joey waits a beat before inviting them inside. She was hoping to avoid this conversation, or at least put it off as long as possible. After the morning at Barbara's, she had to put in time at the coffee shop, working, cleaning, apologizing to Zach, her one disgruntled employee. All the while, she wished she knew what to do about Tom Winter.

"Wow, smells great," he says, stepping through the door and slipping his shoes off.

She disappears into the kitchen, saying, "Chicken parm," over her shoulder. She can practically hear him salivating, and she suddenly wishes she'd chosen something else.

Soon, Walter is curled up at her feet, and River's bringing salad to the table. They start to eat in silence. To break it, he tells her about the trail he helped clear this morning. He's worked for Parks & Wildlife since high school. "We cleared, I don't know, four huge downed trees. It was kind of grueling, but it felt good to use the saw again."

When that line of discussion dries up, she stares studiously down at her plate. He asks her if she went for a run this morning, clearly just trying to fill the awkward gaps. She says no and doesn't elaborate.

Then he takes a sip of water. "I heard Sophie is back in town."

She looks up.

He spears a lettuce leaf with his fork. "Otto cornered me at the store, going on and on about her surprise visit. I take it you've seen her?"

Joey lets her gaze linger on his face. When he finds her eyes, she coughs and studies her plate. "Elena is back too."

He whistles, one dipping trill. "Really? What's going on? Is hell freezing over?"

"I don't know." She instantly knows her tone is too cutting.

He bites his bottom lip. "Sorry. It's probably bringing up a lot for you." River is the kind of man who is the first to apologize and always means it. It's infuriating. There's a pause, and she sees something familiar in his face. His candor is about to bubble over. He's going to ask her about the other night. She can sense it. At her feet, Walter's ears perk up, like he can feel it too.

Joey stands suddenly, startling the dog and River—even herself a little bit.

Without saying a word, she walks around the table. His face is a question. Gently, she grabs his hands. They're warm and dry and strong. Without saying anything, she places them on either side of her hips and moves in closer to him until she can smell his smoky shampoo. Her mind is going fuzzy. She tries to stay in control, takes his hands again. He swallows as she moves them to the front of her body, sliding them up and, finally, placing them on her neck. He keeps them gripped there until their eyes meet, his thumbs resting gently on her throat. Then he stands, slowly exhaling. The fingers of one hand snake behind her head and weave into the roots of her hair while the other hand slips her hair tie loose and lets it fall to the floor.

Afterward, they're in her bed. Sunset is on its way, and a sideways glare of light exposes his broad, bare shoulders.

They've lain here like this, after sex, so many times Joey has lost count. She knows the contours of his chest, the way his skin feels surprisingly smooth against hers. She knows that he's minutes away from kissing her on the forehead and padding out barefoot to go feed the dog. He doesn't keep a dog bowl here, but he knows exactly where the silver baking bowls are that she never uses. They have, somehow, at some point in time Joey can't quite nail down, braided their little habits together.

It's this thought that makes her roll over. She pulls on a bra and running shorts. Hearing the rustle of the blankets behind her, she hurries out of the room. With every step, she can hear the echo of Sophie's voice in her mind. *"Bloodspell."* A word that seems like it should mean something, but it doesn't. Not to Joey, anyway.

The guest room is dark, and her fingers find the light switch on the wall. It illuminates the pictures the way a CT scan illuminates the brain. They're all here. Tom, Barbara, a handful of teachers, her old volleyball coach, River's dad, Sophie's dad. And then of course, there are pictures of Joey, Quinn, Sophie, Elena, River, and a few peripheral friends like Marissa Berg and Tanner McGrath.

A couple of strings tie pictures together and a few more tie pictures to notes. She leans toward one image she took of the crag months after Quinn's death. It looks like a tourist photo, perfectly capturing the view of the valley below and a snow-capped peak behind it.

The truth is that Joey's sleuthing turned up nothing in the years following Quinn's death. The number of people who said they were simply at home when Quinn died meant that it was impossible to get a clear picture of anything. To them, Joey was a source of gossip, a play detective, a lost cause. They all thought she was chasing something that wasn't there. Because it was an accident. Everyone knew it.

Greg Hunstad listened impatiently while she had tried to explain. *"She wouldn't come out here alone,"* Joey swore. *"Not here."* She couldn't mention the magic, of course, but she had made it clear that they had agreed to only go there together. And yet, by the time Mr. Hunstad and the other officer bushwhacked their way to the crag above Quinn's body, it felt like they'd already decided. No one was going to take Joey seriously. She even tried to appeal to Barbara, who knew Quinn wouldn't go out there alone because she knew the rules better than anyone, but Barbara only said something about there being no evidence of anything other than an accident and that they needed to accept it, as hard as it was.

Joey pulls the picture of Tom Winter off the wall. Aside from one conversation, she stayed away from Quinn's dad when she was first investigating. God, *investigating*—that sounds far more official than it ever was. Every resident of the town was accounted for that day, at least by their own testimony. There was a group of tourists staying at the inn who had dinner in town. Front desk staff had them heading up to bed around nine thirty at night and not coming out of their rooms until morning. They spent the next day on a fly-fishing excursion. These were facts Joey learned later, after doing her own digging.

Tom Winter's two-dimensional face looks up at her now. A thick string of greasy hair hangs limply over one eye and a scraggly beard streaked with gray. The man himself is permanently hunched over, and his eyes are watery. As far back as Joey can remember, Tom always seemed to have a beer in his hand. Despite that, he functioned relatively well until his divorce from Barbara. Then, cracks began to form. The drinking got worse, he forgot Quinn's birthday, and he drove drunk into town and crashed into a telephone pole. Quinn tried to mend things with him all the way up to the end. But after she died, he nose-dived. From what Joey gathered, he stopped going to his weekly poker nights and became a complete picture of self-neglect. These days, he only surfaces once a week or so to go to the market or the liquor store. She stares into his flat eyes now and wonders if it's guilt that's driven him deep into reclusiveness these last fifteen years.

Knuckles tap on the other side of the door. Joey jumps.

"Knock, knock."

She lays the picture on the desk and flicks out the light before swinging the door open. The hall is dark too. River is there in silhouette, head bowed.

"You don't have to say, 'Knock, knock,' if you actually knock," she says, and she means it to come out light, but she's not sure it has because he releases a heavy sigh and leans against the doorframe. Outside, the sun must have set because the hall behind him is a deep, thick blue.

"What are you doing, Joey?"

Joey goes hot. She shrugs.

He reaches by her and flips on the light. "I thought you were done with all this."

"All this?"

He looks disappointed or resigned. She can't tell which. "What happened to Quinn was…"

"You don't know what happened to Quinn," she bites back.

"I do, though," he says, ignoring the sharpness in her tone. "Everyone does. She fell."

Joey looks away, feeling herself seethe but not wanting to get into it right now.

"Look, I'm worried about you," he says. "Fifteen years is a long time to hold on to so many questions."

"I'm not just going to let it go," Joey says. *I can't*, she thinks but doesn't say. She takes the opportunity to turn the light out.

River runs a hand over his beard and exhales. "Anyway, the thing I said the other night…I'm not going to bring it up again, so you don't have to worry about that. You don't have to hide from me."

Joey's body begins to warn her of some small impending danger. A flutter in her chest, a hitch in her breathing.

"I know you don't want to talk about it, and that's fine. I'm okay with it. I just want to—" He inhales and moves his hands up and over his hair. Joey feels a spasm of alarm when she sees that motion, as if he's reaching the end of his tether. As if he's ebbing away from her. She's not sure she wants that. She's not sure what she wants.

"I just want to be with you," he says finally.

Joey has to swallow. Her throat is dry. When did she last have a drink of water? She feels rooted to the spot, feet nailed to the floor. In the end, she says nothing. What is there to say? The pause is excruciating. She knows what he wants her to say. But she can't say it. To reply would be a kind of betrayal.

Joey is a thief. She has no right to be happy. Quinn is dead, and Joey won't steal the life she could have had. Fresh waves of grief and guilt move through her, and she resists them yet again by closing the door behind her and stepping past River to turn on the hall light. It's shocking, the sudden brightness.

River squints at her, and she says the only thing she can think of. "You should go."

Another sag of the head, and she knows she's let him down. She pinches her bottom lip, harder than she means to, as she watches him go down the hall. She doesn't move but hears him shake Walter awake. The front door clicks gently, and she is alone.

14

QUINN

MAY 2011
ONE MONTH BEFORE THE FALL

It takes ages to get out there.

We take it slow. Joey is scowling, cradling her hand to her chest. We walk in silence, but there is something stirring inside me, and it's not the magic. Secrets have a kind of energy all to themselves.

Neon green aspen leaves blink and twist as the wind picks up. I zip up my soft pink hoodie, wishing I had another layer. As I look at the red rims around Joey's eyes, I feel a stab of guilt, just as I did when I first saw her an hour ago.

All is quiet except for the uneven beat of eight shoes on dirt.

"Mark was looking hot yesterday," says Elena, breaking the silence.

"Oh my god, call him Mr. Collingswood," says Sophie.

"Whatever you want to call him, he's the reason I started masturbating."

"That's wrong on so many levels," says Sophie.

Joey fakes a smile, but I see her wince from the pain in her hand. I want to tell her that I'm sorry I've been absent. I've just been…busy. And I have. But I can't tell her with what. I want to tell her I know the feeling—that I recognize the helpless frustration of watching a parent disappear and not being able to do anything. It sucks.

"Also, you know he'd never look at any of us that way."

Elena presses her boobs together and makes a pouty face as she looks Sophie up and down. "You're right. He doesn't like nice girls."

I see the clearing between the trees and hurry my steps. A ring of rocks at the center marks the spell circle. I feel a pull toward it, though I'm not sure if it's the magic itself or my desire to be near it. Stepping into the clearing feels like entering a private room walled in by glinting, shuddering aspens, whose leaves always seem to be in motion. I read recently that, after a fire, at certain elevations, aspen trees like to root in the charred earth where other trees recently burned. They thrive in the aftermath.

"He's our teacher," Sophie is saying.

"Well, our *teacher* told me he wants to put his tongue on my—"

"Okay," I say. The usual banter, the back-and-forth that is typical when we're all together—it's grating my nerves. "Let's just put Joey here, and I'll grab the book."

"Joey can put herself here," Joey says, and she finds her way to her spot at the other side of the circle. I watch her, assessing her mood. She's not looking at me, and her hair is uncharacteristically messy, covering her face on one side. The T-shirt she has wrapped around her hand is soaked in blood, and she holds it above her head. She sits clumsily on the ground, looking pale. Any other friends would have forced her to go to the hospital. She almost certainly should get stitches. Possibly surgery. It's a deep gash right through the center of her palm. She says she can't feel anything around it, which actually sounds worse, and the bleeding has slowed but not stopped.

"I don't think we should wait much longer," I say, taking charge as I tend to do, and I can see the mix of emotions on Joey's face.

Last night she and I smoked a joint together because her mom wasn't home, and then we ate pizza, and it felt so normal. Until she asked me why I haven't been around lately. I told her I've been spending tons of time with River, and she seemed satisfied with that, or at least she didn't ask any follow-up questions. That wasn't the whole story, not even close, but I just wanted things to be okay between us. And they were. We ate too much and listened to Lady Gaga and sprawled out on her living room floor.

When, around nine o'clock, we heard voices outside, Joey became immediately serious. I turned down the music as the voices grew louder and more alarming until, without warning, Joey's mom burst through the front door. There was no time for me to understand what was going on. Joey just ushered me out through the back door as quickly as she could and said I should go and she'd call me later. She was stoic, practiced almost. She locked the door behind me. And I was—this sounds horrible, I know—but I was relieved. Confused too, but also relieved. I did what she asked and left without a word, deep down, happy to have the rest of my evening freed up for something else. Someone else. As I left, I watched her mom's boyfriend hop into his black pickup and slam his palms against the steering wheel.

It was 6:16 a.m. when my house phone rang. My mom answered quickly. There was a beat of silence and then she said, "Joey?" I could hear the urgency in her voice, even through my bedroom door, and I stumbled out of bed. My mom wrapped herself in a coat and stepped into her sneakers. Then, she was gone. Guilt at letting Joey push me out last night because I wanted to be somewhere else anyway—it chewed at me. My heart thundered for the whole chilly walk to her house. When I got there, the first thing I noticed was that the boyfriend's pickup was gone. And I knew what it was. Another breakup.

The front door was cracked open, and my mom was in the bathroom at the back of the house. I could hear her speaking slowly, asking questions about which pills she took and saying something about sleeping it off. All the while she opened and closed drawers and made sounds like she was cleaning up. I walked into the kitchen, and there was Joey, standing in front of the stainless-steel sink with one hand wrapped in a bulky gray shirt. With the other hand, she was rinsing a knife under the tap. I said her name, tried to get her attention, but she didn't even look up. It was like she couldn't hear me. She just kept rinsing and rinsing. I pieced it together eventually. The boyfriend left, and Joey's mom had an episode. Joey had to wrestle a knife from her mom before she could harm herself—and got a huge gash in the process.

Now, in the woods, Joey does the honors. I hand her the book, and she places it on the ground where she runs a gentle finger across the cover and then the spine, sits back on her haunches, and hugs her injured hand close to her chest. She nods and closes her eyes.

As if it's a call and response, I nod and close my eyes too. We all do.

The magic starts as a trickle, but it builds. It's flowing quickly now, a slipstream inside me, and I know it's going to burst free soon. I can't hear anything, just a ringing in my ears growing louder with every passing second. We've talked about it before. We all experience the same sounds, the same heat moving through us. The magic is like liquid power flooding our inner thoughts, the essence of us, the very blood in our veins and then spitting out as ink on the page. When we read aloud, that's when it becomes real. The person leading the spell focuses their thoughts on what they want the magic to do, with as much specificity as they can manage. It's that focus that calls the spell to appear on the otherwise blank pages of the book.

And then it's time. The magic spills over. The book flips open, and words appear on the page splayed in front of us. Joey reads quickly to try to catch them all.

Sometimes the words are plain English, the spell complex but readable. Sometimes they are in an old near-English that takes some effort to pronounce. And sometimes they're not words, not really. They're more like sounds strung together. This spell is one of those. The spell before us now is in an ancient language, we were told when we were initiated, from old Germanic paganism. Unintelligible.

"*Sose benrenki, sose bluotrenki, sose lidirenki—*" Joey reads, unfaltering, even though I know she's in pain. The words continue to spill onto the page, and she reads and reads. Until there are no more words, and the ink dries up and the page is empty once again.

We sit in the wake of the spell, just as we've done so many times before, stealing looks at one another, still in awe that this is how we get to spend our Saturday morning. Joey unwraps the T-shirt. She pulls a water bottle out of her bag and douses her hand, shaking pink drops into the dirt. We all wait with our breaths held. When the blood is washed away, her hand is there, clean, dripping, and completely healed. She wipes her palm on her pants and wiggles her fingers, one by one.

"Good," she says.

"Joey." Something like bravery takes control of my voice.

She looks at me and blinks, as if she forgot I was here.

I inhale, and then I ask the question that has been worming around inside my head since I found her this morning. "What if we did a healing spell for your mom?" I see a flicker of confusion, and I take advantage of the pause. "If the magic can heal a physical wound, maybe it can heal…a mental one."

"It won't work," she says abruptly.

"But what if it could?"

She leans forward and studies me, as if she's never seen me before. "We've tried before. There is no mind-healing spell. What's going on with you?"

I look away, feeling like she's trying to read something in my eyes. But then she just takes the book in her hand and flips to the inside of the front cover. There is a thin piece of paper there, taped onto the book.

There are scratches and tears and remnants of old tape, reinforcement from over the years.

Sophie and Elena and I exchange looks. We hardly ever open to this front page, the only page that's not blank in the entire book. It's one that we memorized the contents of long ago. But Joey places the book back on the ground and presses her fingers into the crease.

"I just thought we should review," she says.

Her look, directly into my eyes, tells me she knows my secret. Or thinks she does anyway because there's no way she can know.

"Who wants to go first?" She looks around the circle, and I bite my lip.

"We don't need to read them. We know them by heart," says Elena. She and Sophie are sitting away from us, as if to offer space, perhaps sensing a confrontation brewing.

"Who wants to go first?" repeats Joey.

"We're bossy today," says Elena. Then, after a beat, she says, "Fine." And she scoots closer to the book. "Rule number one," she reads. "When the trees whisper, listen." On instinct, I look around. The aspens stand papery and attentive, as always.

Elena pauses, giving someone else the chance to read. When no one does, she continues. "Okay. Rule number two. Four will be initiated from each generation."

Joey nods along, as if Elena's a child learning to read.

"I'll go," says Sophie, turning the book in her direction. "Rule number three. Never channel without another present."

She leans back reverently and turns the book to Joey, who traces a finger on the page. "Rule number four," Joey says. "Our magic is benign. Benevolent when necessary. Never malevolent."

I know the book is coming to me next, and I am starting to feel lightheaded. But I don't let on. Instead, I lick my lips and start to read.

"Rule number five," I say, staring down at the words. "Tell no one."

I'm positive they can all see the trickle of sweat that's formed at my hairline and is now making its way down toward my ear. I cannot look anywhere else but at the words. I can't look at my friends. I don't know if Joey knows, but she's acting like she does. As if, by reading the rules, she can smoke me out.

Because, of these sacred rules, I've already broken one.

And I'm well on my way to breaking another.

15
ELENA

Elena is back at the Strike. Just as she'd hoped, the film crew is here. There are no other drinking options in town, so it didn't take her long to guess where they might go.

The bar is as cliché as it is grimy. It stinks of beer, and the little twinkle lights are supposed to be charming, but a few of them are dead, giving the whole strand the look of a hockey player's mouth. The patrons, new to this kind of town, look out of place in their bright, short-sleeve button-downs and nineties-style hairstyles. Pure LA, and yet, they seem wide-eyed with awe as they hover over a real working jukebox. Maybe they can't believe that a place so remote, so *small*, could still exist in the world. And sure, anyone would be enamored for a few days. Give it a month, though, and you'll be bored out of your mind. Better yet, give it seventeen years.

Elena catches Ken's eyes from behind the bar. He looks surprised to see her there. She's reminded again of the feeling of constant surveillance in a town where people have little else to do but watch each other. She smacks on a smile and orders a double Buffalo Trace, neat. He doesn't say anything but keeps his eye on her as he pours. Elena pays and turns away, bumping into a twentysomething woman as she does. The woman apologizes, though she has done nothing wrong, and Elena jumps at the chance to start a conversation. She is a production assistant, apparently, and is as chatty as she is young. As they talk, Elena doesn't reveal that she's a background actor. Instead, she chooses to play up her localness. *Yes, I grew up here, in the mountains. Yes, it was such a unique childhood. Hiking trails right out my back door!* This faux-rosy depiction of her adolescence throws her inadvertently into real memories. The four of them—Quinn, Joey, Sophie, and Elena—were freezing their asses off as they lowered their bottom halves into an ice-blue alpine lake. Summer days spent sitting on the curb and drinking Dr Pepper, tossing Reese's Pieces into each other's mouths. Summoning cigarettes to the spell circle and, later, lying to her mom about the smell. Afternoons in junior year English class, holding eye contact for just a bit too long.

She is lost in these dregs of the past—the reminder of which she blames on the carvings under Quinn's deck—when someone speaks quietly, almost intimately, into her ear.

"You're not one of mine."

When she turns, she nearly chokes on her drink. It's Phillip Granger. The director. He wears a black ball cap on top of a pile of Wonder Bread–white hair and ears that stick out sideways. Not handsome but distinctive. She turns toward him, slowly enough to catch the production assistant darting away, lizard-like, behind her. Standing next to Phillip Granger are two other people she recognizes. Nicola Bianco and Cal Pierce. Nicola is petite and sprinkled with gold jewelry, owl eyes glancing about. She looks mildly curious, like a child at the zoo for the first time. Cal, on the other hand, is looking straight at Elena and beaming with boyish white teeth. Veneers? She can't tell and doesn't want to stare too long. They are a trio of fame and untouchability.

"Not yours *yet*," she replies. She extends her hand into the space between her chest and Phillip Granger's. "Elena Alvarez." He responds to her flirtation with smiling eyes. They shake. Elena raises her glass to all three celebrities and says, "Welcome to Whisper Ridge. The last place in America where you can still smoke inside. Not because it's legal, but because no one gives a shit."

For the next forty-five minutes, she keeps Phillip Granger's attention by asking as many questions about him and his career as she can think of. He is responsive, even attentive. Elena knows she is attractive and delightfully charismatic when she needs to be. Her charms seem to be working especially well tonight. At one point, he even says to her, *"Call me Phil,"* and she almost high-fives herself under the bar. She is on her game more than she thought she would be. The bourbon is helping a bit. Just as more drinks are ordered, Elena tells them all she's actually a background actor in the film. She's working up to telling *Phil* that she has a demo reel she can email him, in case he needs fresh-face talent for future projects. But before she can, Ken yells, "Last call!" far too loudly, like this is a real bar in a real city. A groan of disappointment moves through the crowd. It's only ten o'clock.

Slightly drunk, Phillip Granger steps onto the rung of his barstool. "Bedtime, kids," he yells over the din. "We have an early start tomorrow."

It's patronizing. A few people laugh, but it's halfhearted, as if they are only humoring him. Elena gets the sense that they're all used to this kind of thing from him. Then he turns to her. He is flushed with alcohol, his words slurred together and his movements unpredictable. A hand lands on her bare arm, squeezes.

"What are you doing tonight?" he asks, like it's a secret.

She catches a small gesture to her left. Nicola Bianco taps a fingertip on Cal's forearm, and they share a look that tells her this isn't their first time witnessing Phillip Granger attempting to pick up a stranger at a bar.

"Phil, buddy," Cal cuts in. "We should get some sleep." Elena is grateful she doesn't have to respond.

Phil seems to digest this. Then he snaps his fingers. "Cast party on Wednesday," he says to her. "My place." A smile showcases the brilliance of this idea.

"Oh, yeah?" Elena is, of course, aware that he is just looking to get laid, but she also senses an opportunity.

"Extras—I mean *background actors*—are part of the cast." He glances at Cal, a challenge in his eyes. "Extras are part of the cast, aren't they, Cal?"

"Where exactly is *your place*?" Elena asks. If she goes to this cast party, she can continue her charm offensive, then do a little bait and switch.

"The hideous glass house up the side of that mountain." He flails a hand in the direction of the door.

Elena finishes her drink. "I know the one."

Cal Pierce claps a hand on Phillip Granger's back. "You're a true man of the people, Phil," he says coolly. Then, "Okay, let's hit it. I'm beat."

Once the Hollywoods are gone, Elena sits alone at the bar. Ken raises his eyebrows at her as he wipes the taps down. She glares at him until he looks away.

Fifteen minutes later, Elena is scrubbing the makeup off her face in Barbara's low-lit guest bathroom. Gael and Barbara are both long asleep. Being back here has been more full-on than she'd expected. Getting Phillip Granger to consider her for future projects is going to take some creativity, but she can manage a man like him. It's more everything else. Last night, Sophie insisted they humor Joey because she seems fragile, but Elena refuses to live in the past, always has. She always assumed

Quinn's death was an accident, just like everyone else. Only, now, she keeps picturing Tom Winter pushing Quinn off the crag. It's fucked up, but it is playing on repeat. Just the mention of Quinn's death has had dark thoughts battling for space in her head. And then there was that creepy word carved into the deck. *Bloodspell.* It sounds like a word they should know—its allusion to magic is obvious—but none of them do.

From the counter, her phone chirps at her. Low battery. She searches her purse and suitcase before remembering she used her charger on the drive from the airport. She curses and tiptoes past Gael asleep on the upstairs couch, stopping to cover him with a throw blanket. Down the stairs, then through the front door. She feels the cold of the front walk on her bare feet. Wind hisses between trees, but otherwise, the night is silent. And that smell. She'd forgotten it, but it hits her now, piney and cool and filled with memories. She wrinkles her nose and tries to recall smoggy LA, but somehow she can't. Whisper Ridge's high-altitude crispness, the distinct odor of dry wood and cold stone, overwhelms everything.

When she opens the car door, the click echoes, and the yellow overhead light flickers on. She yanks her phone charger free from the port and crawls out backward, closing the door and snuffing out the light. It's then that she feels it. A creeping feeling, like someone has just said something to her. She spins around, clutching the small white cord to her chest. But she is alone in the driveway. Nothing but darkness swimming around her. In the distance, a lonely streetlight illuminates a neighbor's house and—she takes a small step closer, heart skittering—the outline of a figure. It's no more than a dark shadow, but it's in the shape of a person. Her chest goes tight, and her breath momentarily leaves her. She glances back at Barbara's house and the darkened windows, wondering if she is being watched.

But when she looks toward the streetlight again, just a few seconds later, no one is there at all. She scrubs at her face.

She waits five minutes, listening to nothing but the chirp of a frog somewhere in the dark. Then she runs back into the house and double-locks the door.

"Never channel without another present."

–Rule #3, *The Book of Aspens*

16

QUINN

MAY 2011
THREE WEEKS BEFORE THE FALL

Sunshine pours in through the tiny bathroom window as I wash my hands. The four of us stand in a row before the mirror, pink-painted stalls like gates at our back.

"Sleepover at my house tonight?" Sophie says. She examines her reflection and adjusts her shirt, tugging it down as far as it will go. Elena leans in and applies a sticky gloss. The room begins to smell of cotton candy.

"I can't," I say, and I catch Joey's eye in the mirror. She's glaring at me with her arms firmly crossed at her chest. She steals a look at Sophie and then Elena, and in a second, they're all standing around me. I take a step toward the sink. I'm not sure what's going on, but it seems like they've planned this. They followed me in here with the intention of cornering me.

"It's been, like, weeks since you've hung out with us." Elena puts her lip gloss away and zips up her bag without taking her eyes off me. She flicks an eyebrow up in question.

"Sorry," I say. I don't want to tell them why, so I just say, "Maybe next weekend?"

Joey examines her feet. "If it's River, just tell us. We won't care."

"It's not River," I say. "It's…my dad. He needs me. I'm working up to an intervention."

"Oh, wow," says Sophie, softening. "Do you need us there for support?"

I shake my head. "Not yet."

Sophie rubs my arm. "I think you're absolutely doing the right thing. He needs professional help. But make sure you have your mom and maybe a friend or two of his there. And call us. You shouldn't do it on your own."

"So we'll hang out next weekend then," says Joey. "You won't back out at the last second?" Her words cut, as I assume they're meant to. I can hear the shouts and laughter from students lining up at their lockers.

"You know," I say. "You don't need me to be friends with each other."

Elena smacks her lips together, unbothered. "Yeah, but Quinn, you're like the glue. On our own, we're terrible. Joey is a robot. Sophie is emo, and I'm a bitch. You're the balanced, down-to-earth friend."

"Hey." Sophie looks genuinely hurt. "I'm not emo, am I?"

Elena tosses her a look that says, *"Do you really not know this about yourself?"*

I'm flustered. I know Elena's words are intended to be funny, but for some reason, they make me feel boxed in, like I only have one role. "I'm not your mom," I say. "So maybe you should just figure it out." I turn to leave.

"Wait, don't go." Joey suddenly has a firm grip on my arm and a desperate look in her eye. Her touch surprises me. "Just tell me we'd still be friends if it weren't for the magic," she says.

I feel their eyes on me. It feels like tiny burns.

"Of course we would," says Sophie in an almost whisper. I'm glad she answers so I don't have to. "It will be summer soon. We'll have plenty of time to be together."

At that moment, the bell rings, echoing throughout the mauve-tiled room, and I pull my backpack over my shoulder. They watch me without making any moves themselves, and I push down the feeling of guilt that threatens to make me turn and confess everything.

Instead, I say, "Just because I can't go to a sleepover doesn't mean we're not still friends." Then, without turning back, I shove open the door with my foot and disappear down the hall.

A few minutes later, I'm hurrying away from the school, making sure none of them are watching me as I turn the corner away from my house.

He finds me before I see him. I hear my name from somewhere behind a tree. The way he says it, low and intimate, chases away the guilt I felt lying to my friends.

I stride over to him and look up into those icy eyes. I see hunger there. The same hunger I feel. A sharp wind throws my hair into my face, and he brushes it away. Then he tugs at the loopholes in my jeans until my hips are flush against him. He leans in, and I disappear completely into the kiss, into the softness of his lips, and my guilt dissolves without a trace.

Why have I chosen to spend tonight with him instead of my friends? It's simple. He understands me. They don't.

17

SOPHIE

Sophie watches the sunshine pour through the front windows of Aspect Coffee. The tables are worn and from another decade, and the decor is still the same, only somehow grayer. She remembers the small faded painting of the general store that still hangs above the napkins from way back when Barbara owned the coffee shop. The walls are streaked white, a slapdash paint job barely hiding the homey peach color they used to be. It's all just a little depressing, and Sophie's reminded again that Joey does not seem to be at her best.

Sophie's plan today is to supply Joey with resources. She spent the morning trying to forget about Quinn's haunting blank journal by compiling a list of links and medical articles about PTSD. She even reached out to a grief counselor on Joey's behalf. It feels important to help, but she must play it carefully so Joey doesn't react badly.

The bell above the door clatters as Elena comes in. Her white pants and Panama hat make her look put together, but the bruised half-moons under her eyes show an obvious lack of sleep.

Joey texted this morning saying she had something to run by them. Immediately, Sophie texted Elena separately to make sure she was planning on coming. It's important to be here so she can, gently, tell Joey that what she heard in the woods may have been unprocessed grief and to have Elena here as extra support.

"The place looks great," Sophie says to Joey as they approach the counter. She isn't sure why she lies, but probably because she hopes to cheer her up a bit.

Elena is dubious. "Can you do an Americano?"

Joey glares at her, and Sophie goes full-on cheerful to try to combat the tension, ordering a chai latte with a sprinkle of cinnamon.

"Anything to eat?"

They survey the baked goods counter. A couple of flat things that look like they could be croissants. A pale tart with what could be cream cheese in the center. A muffin wrapped in plastic. Next to her, Elena says she's good. Sophie is also unimpressed, but she masks it beneath a pert, "Whatever you recommend."

They wait at a table by the window. Sophie sips her chai and watches Elena. "So..." she says. "Gael."

Elena tips her own cup up to her lips, peering into the depths of her espresso as she does, then sets it down again. She looks like she's about to say something but then checks herself.

Sophie puts her mug down carefully. "You seem to be doing a great job. He's a sweet kid. Truly."

"We manage," Elena says at last, pressing out a smile.

"He's, how old, fourteen?"

Elena nods without making eye contact.

"Hm," says Sophie. "Did you have help? I mean, is his dad still in the picture or..."

Elena buries her face in her drink again. "His dad was no one special. And no, not in the picture."

"But you must have been so young when you had him. How did you make it work? Did your mom help?" Sophie remembers Elena's mom.

Her dad died when she was six years old, and after that, eventually, her mother transformed into a closed-minded, sometimes violent religious zealot. But bless her, Elena still snuck out, smoked, drank, and fooled around with half the school. And when she got caught, she took the punishment and then was back at it again the next night.

"Are you kidding?" Elena laughs. "That bitch did nothing. I relied on neighbors and friends. I even dragged him along to work with me a bunch in the early days. And somehow, he turned out okay. No idea how that happened. But what about you? You're a mom now. How's that going?"

"Great," says Sophie, and warmth fills her when she thinks of her family. "Leah is eighteen months. To be honest, the postpartum really knocked me out for a while. Talia was worried, but I upped my therapy sessions to twice weekly, and it helped a little. You know, during that time of my life, I used to imagine seeing you or Joey…or even Quinn sometimes, when I was out running errands. It used to make me so sad. I was not well. I thought being back here would be triggering, but it's honestly not that bad." She wants to say something about the journal she found in the closet, but the thought of speaking about it out loud it makes her nervous. Elena looks winded by Sophie's complete mental health history anyway, so she decides to bring it up at a better moment.

The bell above the door jingles.

A woman Sophie recognizes appears in the doorway with her hands on her lower back. Marissa Berg wears a navy blue uniform and a gun at her hip and—unexpectedly—a pregnant belly that protrudes over her pants. It's jarring to see Marissa again. She was always trying to include herself when they were young. Of course they couldn't include her in the magic, since she wasn't initiated, but Sophie sometimes said yes when Marissa invited herself to hang out with them after school. Elena, Joey, and Quinn didn't get it. They said she was a hanger-on. Elena called her a self-important bitch. But Sophie felt bad that the four of them were, by default, exclusive. She didn't like the idea of someone clawing at the outside trying to get in. More importantly, though, she was highly allergic to the word *no*. Still is.

"Marissa, hi. How are you?" Sophie says as Marissa spots them. Her eyelids peel open in shock as she strides over.

"Sophie Stringer and Elena Alvarez, both of you? My gosh, what on earth are you doing here?" Marissa's greeting comes across as a bit saccharine. She leans into Sophie for a one-armed hug.

"Marissa, wow. You look great," Elena says, completely monotone.

Marissa beams and runs her hands over her baby bump. "Six months next Tuesday," she says.

"Do you still live here?" asks Sophie, eyeing the uniform.

Marissa laughs. "Are you kidding? I could never leave. We're down at Sixth and Pine. But what on earth are *you* doing here?" Marissa looks between them, waiting.

"We're just visiting," Sophie says.

At this, she clocks a prolonged look from Marissa that she can't quite read. "I thought maybe it was because of Quinn. Maybe Joey finally got a break in her case." She says this with a not-so-subtle mocking tone, as if Joey is going around town calling herself Carmen Sandiego.

Sophie bristles inwardly.

Elena says, "Nope," with emphasis. Sophie's surprised to hear her speaking up for Joey.

"It's the fifteen-year anniversary of her death, isn't it?" Marissa picks an invisible fuzz off her shirt.

"Monday was."

Marissa nods. "Right… So is that why you're in town?"

Sophie makes a noncommittal noise. She wonders why Marissa's presence makes her so uncomfortable.

Joey walks over then, looking tired and bunching up a filthy black apron. "Done for the day," she says. "Zach's not happy, but I promised him overtime pay I can't afford." She looks around with the air of clearing her mind. "You guys ready?"

She's speaking to Elena and Sophie; that's perfectly obvious, but Marissa doesn't seem to read the room. She checks her watch. "I have to be back in...half an hour," she says. "That's enough time for a quick cup of something."

Joey squints at her and gives her the approximation of a smile. There's a moment of quiet, and Sophie feels things start to tip. She has an old familiar feeling that, in just a moment, when it becomes unbearable, she won't be able to let the silence grow any longer. She will have to jump in and invite Marissa to hang out. She can almost hear herself saying it. *"Sure, let's all get a fresh coffee and catch up."*

Before she can, thankfully, Joey jumps in. "Wish we could, but we are on our way out for a hike."

Marissa is skeptical. "Are you?"

"Are we?" asks Sophie. Elena looks up in surprise.

"We are." Joey says it with certainty as she faces down Marissa. "Next time?"

"Shoot," says Marissa, running her hand over her belly again, as if the act might somehow change Joey's mind. When she gets no response, she says, "Well, I do want to catch up with you all at some point. Call me if you end up doing brunch or something. Joey, you have my number." And she leaves them to approach the counter and order a to-go skinny latte—*"Make it a decaf!"*

She's all smiles, and yet as she makes her way to the door, she turns toward Sophie. Her eyes linger for a few seconds, her expression unreadable, until Sophie feels a flush of embarrassment rise in her. And then the moment is gone, and so is Marissa, and Sophie is left with the bizarre feeling that she's been caught out for something, though she has no idea for what.

Minutes later, they are outside, hiking the familiar old trail that leads to the spell circle. Sophie follows Joey and Elena over the lattice of downed logs. When her shoes sink into the soft dirt on the other side, it's at once familiar and satisfying. A text hums from the depths of her bag. She rifles through receipts and pacifiers and tissue packets to pluck it free.

A message from Talia. Leah has a fever.

Sophie worries at the drawstring of her hoodie. Talia's never done sick-kid parenting on her own. Sophie is the one who administers Tylenol and who takes temperatures, even in the middle of the night. Sophie is the one who lies awake, fearing that the sleep sack is too hot, that the room is too cold, or that she will miss some hidden danger should her eyes close.

Now, an image starts to come through. It takes a second to load, and Sophie is tense with anticipation. It's Leah. Her cheeks are red, her eyes wet-rimmed, and she clutches her favorite elephant blankie. Another message from Talia. My mom is here to help. Just call us later. Love you.

Sophie's about to type out a reply when she sees that she has no service. She considers going back, but then she sees the slender foot-trodden path, lined with shimmering green aspen leaves. It rolls out before her like a bridge to the past. Slowly and with real effort, because she's not sure she's making the right decision, she slips the phone back into her pocket. *They'll be fine without me,* she says to herself, and she almost believes it.

Summer is almost here, and the aspens always signal it first. It occurs to her that this trail isn't hidden anymore. The illusion spell that used to hide it has long since worn off—it would have been ten years ago now. Illusion spells need to be updated, since they only last for five years, but she and Elena have been gone fifteen. This fact reminds her how invincible they once felt. And how wrong they were to feel that way.

"So now that we're a mile out of earshot of the pregnant cop, can you tell us why we're out here?" Elena avoids an elbow-shaped root that juts above the ground. Her incongruous black boots look like a cross between army-issued and Spice Girl.

Joey plods on. "Let's just get there first," she says over her shoulder.

They walk for several minutes in silence, and soon, Sophie settles into the rhythm of their footfalls as they sidestep puddles. It smells of fresh spring mud. Busy birds converse above their heads. Spots of sun fleck the ground like splatters of paint.

Soon, though, they are at the spell circle, and memories press into her chest. Why is it always the happy ones that hurt the most?

Joey breaks the moment by turning to face them. "So," she says, "I was hoping that maybe, if the trees oblige, you could hear it for yourself."

Sophie tosses a glance at Elena, who returns it.

"Maybe it sounds stupid," says Joey. "But I think if you could just hear them for yourselves..."

"How exactly are we supposed to do that?" Elena seems annoyed.

"I thought we could try to channel the magic."

"No book," Elena reminds her.

Sophie has ached for the magic over the years—not in the same way she ached for their friendship or for Quinn—but she remembers how powerful the magic used to make her feel. And then the book disappeared around the same time as Quinn's death, and she knew they would never get that feeling back. As years passed, Sophie learned to silence her inner voice. It repeatedly warned her that by leaving Whisper Ridge and not finding the book, she was not protecting the magic. And yet, as much as she tried to silence that voice, another, devastated voice grew louder. They may have been responsible for protecting the magic, yes, but was the magic not at all responsible for protecting them? It did not help them when they needed it most. She feels it now—the strange combination of love and resentment. Like two daggers in her side.

Joey is undeterred. "I didn't have the book when the trees whispered to me on Monday. And somehow it still worked."

Silence drips from the branches all around them. It creeps along the earth and fills every space inside the clearing.

Then Elena clears her throat. "Let's get this over with."

Sophie isn't sure if she wants to encourage Joey, but she wonders if maybe, when this doesn't happen how she wants it to, Joey will realize that the trees never whispered at all.

Joey closes her eyes and so does Elena, after a questioning glance at Sophie. Sophie shrugs and decides she might as well follow through. She tries to focus her mind like she used to. *Trees, whisper to me*, she thinks, and she feels ridiculous. There is no book in front of them to catch any spells. This is entirely pointless, but she goes through the motions anyway. A minute passes. Two minutes. Three. Elena sniffles.

Eventually, they open their eyes. "Fuck." Joey stomps out of the spell circle and toward the crag.

Sophie's heart cracks, and she hurries after her. The top of the rock is crusted with lichen. Careful steps bring her up to the edge. She spreads her toes inside her shoes for balance. It's a rush, looking down. Inches from the tip of her shoe, the rock face ends sharply where some ancient ice shelf or landslide or crack of lightning lopped it off. She'd guess it's about thirty feet down. A sheer drop. Below them, a cluster of sharp peaks wait like hungry piranhas, one among them the peak that ultimately ended Quinn's life. One wrong step, a slip on a rainy afternoon. Life is so unfair.

She coughs quietly. "Joey, listen. Would it be okay if I gave you my therapist's number? She's incredible. The real love of my life."

Joey says nothing, just stares down at the space below them, as if searching for an answer there. Sophie continues carefully. "She does virtual appointments. I really think you might benefit from talking to someone. If you want." She stops to give Joey a chance to think it through.

Elena, who lingered in the spell circle for a while, steps up alongside them.

"It's not just Quinn," says Joey. "We were supposed to protect the magic too. We haven't seen the book for fifteen years."

"We were busy grieving. I think that's reasonable," says Sophie, lacing her fingers through Joey's, grateful that she lets her.

Elena clears her throat. "I, for one, didn't feel like summoning a few bottles of Mike's Hard Lemonade would help at all, not when our best friend was dead."

Before them, a tiny bird dips and soars in the open sky. Sophie can't decide whether the move is a show of grace or power. It's somehow both at once.

Joey scuffs her shoe against the rock. "I have a theory...about what happened that night."

Sophie and Elena let her speak.

"Quinn died at about five o'clock. That's what the coroner's report said. After the last day of school, she went to her mom's, but then she must have gone to visit her dad, and they must have gotten into an argument—maybe she was threatening him with rehab, or maybe he was just drunk and angry. I don't know. Then, she ran to the woods, and he followed her, and they ended up right here, still fighting, and he..." She makes a shoving motion with her hands.

Sophie gives it a moment and keeps her tone controlled so she doesn't upset Joey. "Interesting. I wonder, though, if Tom would get mad over his daughter suggesting rehab, no matter how drunk he was."

"And he'd have to be pretty fucking mad to, you know..." Elena mimics Joey's shoving motion. "Plus, the illusion spell would have hidden her if she ran this way."

Joey is nodding, like she is agreeing with them. *Maybe*, Sophie thinks. Maybe she will come around on this all on her own. Maybe she'll let it go without having to be convinced.

"You're right on both counts," says Joey. "But something happened with Tom that day. I know it did."

Sophie hasn't forgotten the words the trees supposedly whispered to Joey.

"Dad? No!"

She thinks back to that day. She remembers it all more vividly than she'd like. Finding Quinn's body, legs twisted unnaturally, creek water soaking her sneakers. The police, the businesslike way they took care of her body, as if they saw this kind of thing all the time. She recalls the time-turning spell they attempted hours after they found Quinn's body. They had never managed to turn time before, but they desperately wanted to go back a day to save her, and for some reason they thought their desperation would be enough to make it work. They sat in the spell circle and tried through their tears. The problem was that, just like today, they didn't have the book. They couldn't find it. Sophie remembers the moment she realized time-turning would be impossible. She remembers the sudden crushing blow right to the center of her. Quinn was gone. The magic was gone. Nothing could help them.

Something about this memory bothers her. "Was the book already missing before Quinn died?"

Elena bobs her head. "She said she lost it. It was the day before, and I wanted to do magic for something, but Quinn told me she couldn't find it. I guess I should have asked her more about it then, but I thought she was lying. Like, how could you just lose the book? We were at school at the time so I couldn't do much, but I planned to confront her about it later. Never got the chance."

"We went looking for it the day we found her, remember?" says Joey.

"We checked everywhere. Her room, the spell circle. We thought about asking Barbara, but we didn't want to worry her."

They're quiet for a long time. Sophie watches the small bird swoop above them with startling speed. It beelines for a giant hawk that is circling a treetop. The sudden change of direction must take the hawk by surprise because it rears up. But the little bird does not relent. Fearlessly, it goes straight for the eyes. The hawk swoops away just in time.

They're getting carried away with all this. Quinn went out for a hike and slipped. She fell. No one followed her. No one pushed her. It has nothing to do with the book. Sophie does not believe Joey heard Quinn whispering her killer's name fifteen years after the fact. They grew up with impossible things happening, but that is beyond the scope of even her imagination. Joey wanted some kind of sign that Quinn was killed, and so her subconscious invented one. Although Sophie has to admit that the book disappearing right around the time Quinn died is really odd. She remembers thinking about that coincidence back then, but Elena left town the very next day, and Sophie herself decided to push through summer classes so she could graduate early. Neither she nor Joey had any desire to even step foot in the spell circle after Quinn and Elena were gone.

In front of them, the hawk is back, reassessing its approach, thinking it has a clear shot. But the small bird comes out of nowhere and speeds toward it with exacting precision, clawing at its face again. The hawk flaps and changes direction, but the bird doesn't relent. It goes for the eyes again. At long last, the hawk gives up, its broad dark wings carrying it slowly away. Having diminished the predator's power through desperation and grit alone, the tiny bird, understandably exhausted, returns to the tree, disappearing into the cover of needled branches. The little nest it was protecting isn't visible, but Sophie knows it's there.

"I want to go talk to Tom," says Joey. She tightens her ponytail in one self-assured tug.

"Terrible idea," says Elena. "What could you possibly have to say?"

"For one, I could get a sense of what he and Quinn might have fought about. And two, maybe he knows where the book is. Maybe he even has it."

"I agree about the book," says Sophie. "It's been missing a really long time, and I think we should find it. But Joey, Barbara warned us not to bug Tom. He's not well. I don't know if we should push him over the edge."

Joey folds her arms over her chest and glares at her.

"You know what I mean," Sophie says.

"Sounds like a huge waste of time," Elena says with a sigh.

"But what if we did find the book?" says Joey. "We could do a summoning spell. Maybe there are clues out there that could tell us exactly what happened that night."

"I'm sorry, Joey." Sophie tries to be as gentle as she can. "It's just… what proof could there be that they didn't uncover back then?"

"Could be anything," says Joey, obviously undeterred. "A fiber, a hair, a fingerprint."

There was a formal investigation, of course. Sophie recalls the burly frame of Mr. Berg, Marissa's dad, in his police uniform. He was the one who moved them away from Quinn, ushering them into their new bleak existence. He and Jim Hunstad, River's dad, strung up yellow police tape, the kind she thought was only in movies. At the time, they still had the illusion spell cast over the spell circle, and thank god for that because it served as a sort of secret hiding place. They stood mere feet from the two police officers, whose heads were bent against the drizzle, holding notebooks and rubber gloves inside windbreakers, poised for evidence collection. But ultimately, they found nothing, no trace that anyone else had been with Quinn. There are dozens of hiking-related deaths every year in Colorado, and this is a slippery rock with a treacherous drop. It was cut-and-dried.

"I think instead of going to talk to Tom, we just take a breath," says Sophie. "Two days ago, it was the anniversary of Quinn's death. There are bound to be emotions wound up in that. Let's work through it instead of obsessing over clues."

As she says the word *clues*, the pale pink journal sitting in her closet with Quinn's name in it slithers into her thoughts. She feels a flutter of nerves.

"How about this," Joey says. "You guys come with me to Tom's. We'll just see what he has to say about that night and ask about the book. Maybe he'll let us check through any of Quinn's old stuff he might have. If it's a dead end, I'll drop it."

Elena looks up at the sky. "Still a terrible idea."

Sophie takes Joey's hand. It's warm. She wishes it would bring back good memories from back then, and it does, but they are fleeting. "We'll come." She stares at Elena, and Elena glares back until, finally, she sighs dramatically. A concession. "But please," Sophie says, turning back to Joey, "after this, promise me you'll seriously consider talking to someone."

"Deal," says Joey.

Sophie sees the hawk again, this time diving into the trees with a ferocity and speed it didn't have before. Something about this decision doesn't feel quite right, but she can't go back on it now.

18

JOEY

Tom's house is tucked into the woods.

It's deathly silent here, his old white truck nowhere in sight. The surrounding trees seem to be sick with trunk rot, their branches shrouded in caterpillar webbing. The front step is home to a sunken lawn chair and a littering of cigarette butts.

Joey unclicks her seat belt and lifts herself out of the car. Sophie follows, closing the door carefully behind her. Elena clomps out of the back seat in her combat boots.

Joey knocks on the front door. The sound is like three gunshots in the silent woods. On the third knock, the door slowly peels open. She and Sophie look at each other suddenly; then Joey leans in. The latch where the door should close is broken.

Joey is about to push it farther, but Sophie snaps a warning arm across her middle. She calls out, "Mr. Winter?" Her voice is too high, like they're kids, and she's asking if Quinn can come out to play. Joey's hands have begun to sweat.

There is no answer from within, though they wait a minute in silence to make sure. Joey reaches out for the door again, and she jumps as Sophie's hand lands on top of hers. "Don't," she says in a whisper.

"He's obviously not here," calls Elena from behind them, sounding impatient. Her shoes crunch on the uneven earth as she disappears around the corner of the house. There is no sign of him, but Joey knows that, if he's out, it means he's probably just stocking up on booze or frozen dinners and could be back any minute. They should hurry.

Joey ignores them both and uses her fingertips to push the door. It's featherlight—probably made of plywood—and gives way easily.

"Joey!"

The shout comes from around the house, sending Joey's heart into her mouth. It takes her a second to register that it's Elena.

"Soph!" Elena shouts again, louder this time. Joey thunders down the two front steps and around the corner, imagining Tom is back there. Imagining Elena at knifepoint.

Soon she sees Elena forty yards away, at the edge of a down slope. She's turned away from them, staring out at the woods. Tom is nowhere in sight.

"What is it?" Joey calls out as she runs toward her, feeling an itch at the back of her neck.

Sophie runs up alongside them, panting, and they follow Elena's gaze out toward the woods. It's getting dark, and there's not much to see. But something catches Joey's eye. It's the glass house at the top of the hill in the distance. A long-abandoned ultra-eighties eyesore they dared each other to break into when they were young but never actually did. She didn't realize it was visible from here.

"Did you know?" asks Elena, and Joey is confused. *Know what?* And then she turns to see that Elena is not pointing up the hill, but down.

Two hundred yards in the distance, the way the trees clear out in a wide opening—the woods take on a familiar shape.

The itch on the back of Joey's neck suddenly feels like an insect burrowing under her skin.

Sophie gasps. "Look." She doesn't have to say anything else because Joey sees it now. It's suddenly there, as if trees had been cleared just for this view.

Straight through the woods, hauntingly close, is a circle of rocks surrounded by a ring of aspen trees. Tom Winter has a clear view of the spell circle.

Minutes later, Elena shoves a shoulder into the back door, and it gives with a snapping sound that can't be good. She tosses Joey a toothy grimace as if to say, "*Oops.*"

The smell of stale smoke hits Joey first. Then, it's the faint dampness of mildew. Sawdust and dried mud crackle under her shoes as she steps into the kitchen. A skylight casts a murky glow from above, illuminating the scratched-up table in the center. On the table is an empty vodka bottle next to a shot glass, smudged from recent use. The tabletop is peppered with black crumbs, old ringed coffee cups, upturned fly carcasses. A sharp professional-grade kitchen knife gleams from the corner, the only clean dish Joey can see.

Back by the door, Joey spots the dustiest minifridge she has ever seen. She crouches down, careful not to touch the floor with her hands or knees. Just breathing the air in here makes her feel like she needs a shower.

It takes an effort to open the minifridge door with the sleeve of her shirt. Once she tugs it open, she sees a flimsy shoebox that contains small white tubes that look, at first, like Styrofoam. She leans closer. No, not foam. They seem to be...bones. Tiny animal bones. There are dozens of them. What the hell are they? Birds? Rats?

"Guys." The urgent whisper comes from a distant room. Joey jumps. She kicks the fridge closed and hurries from the kitchen.

She passes through the living room. An old floral couch is faded and torn. Yellow stuffing herniates out the middle.

"Oh, good," says Sophie as Joey and Elena come down the hall. "Just wanted to make sure you didn't leave me here."

There is no door on the hinges of what appears to be Tom's room. Inside, there's a mattress in the corner with a blanket on top of it and a ratty pillow. Next to the makeshift bed is a half-empty bottle of whiskey and a small collection of empty beer bottles.

Sophie picks up something that looks like an old DVD. She finds a remote and clicks on the small TV. It reminds Joey of the TV that used to sit in the corner of Quinn's room, on top of her bookshelf.

Joey can't help but wonder what Tom would do if he came home now. If he saw them in his room. Looking through his things.

Behind her, Sophie yelps. "Oh my god, how do I turn it off?"

Joey turns. It's hard to tell what is happening, but the screen is showing lots of skin and black leather, and then a loud moan reverberates around the room.

"Turn it off," shouts Elena, over the din.

"I'm trying." Sophie fumbles with the buttons and drops the remote. When she takes a step toward it, she accidentally kicks it, and it goes sliding across the room.

Elena puts her head in her hands, and Joey goes after the remote. She has to crawl under the TV stand. She reaches, wondering when the last time this floor was cleaned. Finally, her fingers find it. She stands and jabs at the power button. The TV snaps off in a staticky click, and they're left in the silent aftermath.

Sophie rushes out of the room.

"So he's into bondage porn," Elena says, following. "That's a choice."

Joey rubs her arms. She takes a few steps out of the room and stops at the end of the hallway, before a closed door. Fearing the worst, she turns the handle and nudges it open. An involuntary sharp breath fills her lungs. The floor is so clean, it shines. The hardwood, preserved in this way, looks like it belongs in another house altogether. She uses her hip to push her way in, and that's when she sees it.

A photo resting in a gold-plated frame. A photo of Quinn.

Her hair is tinged green at the tips and in streaks around her face, and she's smiling a broad smile that makes Joey's chest flood with sudden, unexpected sadness. Of all the pictures she has ever seen of Quinn, she has never seen this one. It seems to perfectly capture her essence. A few steps inside the room reveal more photographs, all framed, resting on a polished oak table. Every image is of Quinn. Quinn running. Quinn eating ice cream. Quinn as a little girl, grumpily hugging a stuffed bunny. Scattered around are candles melted down to various heights, there's a rosary, and what she recognizes as tiny animal bones, arranged like offerings. Then, she sees a piece of dirty string. Only, on closer inspection, it's not a string. It's a shoelace. Mud-stained and stiff, as if it hasn't been touched for years. Next to it is a floppy stuffed bunny with fur that might have once been soft but is now matted and rough. It's the bunny from the photo of Quinn as a girl, only it's missing an eye, and stuffing protrudes grotesquely out of its ear.

There is nothing else in this room. No chair. No bed. Importantly, no book. Only the table and two black curtains, parted down the middle, allowing a slice of dying daylight into the room.

"I was not anticipating a shrine," Sophie says quietly from behind her. She brushes past and lifts a photograph of Quinn. The frame is delicate, covered in curled gray aspen bark. Gently, she replaces the photograph and spots the bones. "Are those—" But she doesn't finish the thought. Instead, she rubs her hands over her eyes. "This is heartbreaking."

"Heartbreaking?" Elena stands next to them now. She pokes a finger into the bunny's missing eye and makes a disgusted sound. "This is some serious serial killer shit. What's with the candles and the rosary? Is he religious?"

Sophie picks up a small laminated card and shows it to them. On the front is a picture of a horned satanic beast.

"Not discerning about his worship then," Elena says.

As Sophie replaces the card, Joey notices a lumpy bit of clothing, faded pink, just behind the stuffed bunny. It's soft between her fingers as she picks it up. Thin. It's not immediately recognizable, but when she unfolds it, her pulse pounds. Quinn's pink hoodie. Her favorite pink hoodie—the one she was wearing beneath the raincoat the day they found her body. Opening it up, she sees that the front side is completely discolored. A deep brown, nearly black, stain covers almost the entire thing. She lays it on the floor, and as she does, Sophie and Elena peer over her shoulder. Joey kneels, frantically scanning the entire thing. Her focus snags on a little rip in the fabric, just to the right of the zipper. She uses two fingers to gently peel the rip open. It's two to three inches across, like someone stabbed a blade through it.

"Oh my god," says Sophie breathlessly.

Joey notices more of the little rips all over the front of the sweatshirt. There are six, no, seven of them. Her fingers are pulsing with her heartbeat. She can barely hear anything.

Elena kneels next to Joey. "I'm going to take a risk and say that's not coffee spilled on the front?"

"Right," says Sophie. "I think I'm ready to leave now."

"We should take it with us," says Joey. "Find out if it's Quinn's blood."

"Absolutely not." Elena extends her arm, blocking Joey from grabbing it.

"Why not?" *We should take the evidence*, Joey thinks, *prove that it's a match with Quinn*. She knows it will be.

Elena doesn't relent. "If Tom comes back, which he's likely to do any minute, and sees this sweatshirt missing, don't you think he'll be wondering where it is? No offense, but your little sleuthing hobby seems to have earned you a reputation around town. You're the first person he'd suspect. And I'm not risking your life or mine for some child-killing psycho."

"I think what Elena is trying to say," says Sophie with a gentleness that only she could muster at a time like this, "is that this is insanely suspicious. I can't believe I'm saying this, but I think you, or the whispering trees, were right about Tom." She gestures in the direction of the table as if to prove her point.

Elena says, "Whether the trees really whispered to Joey is irrelevant. It does seem, though, that our friend Tom is trying to hide evidence in plain sight. And look at these holes. They're so exact. Is it just me, or does this sweatshirt look less like she fell and more like..." She takes a breath. "Like someone stabbed her six times."

"Seven," says Joey. "There are seven holes."

They all flinch, even Elena.

Sophie says, "If the sweatshirt looked like this when she died, imagine what her body looked like underneath. Oh god. I can't imagine the pain." She buries her face in her hands. When she looks up again, her eyes are red. She sniffles. "Is it at all possible that, when she fell, she actually did land on her front? That these slashes are from rocks?"

"No." Joey is quick to reply. "I *know* she was on her back when we found her. If she died on impact like they said, she couldn't have just rolled over."

"You're right," says Elena. "Look where they are. They're clean. Intentional." She points to the left side of the sweatshirt, right where Quinn's heart would have been.

Joey closes her eyes. She's tried to imagine what happened to Quinn so many times over the years, but for some reason seeing her actual clothes, this real piece of her, is so much harder.

"She was wearing a raincoat too," says Sophie. "Remember? It could be the reason we didn't see the blood then. It must have been covering it."

"But the police would have seen it," says Joey. "Why didn't they say anything? How did we not know about this?"

Sophie shrugs. "Maybe Tom took it off her before they got there?"

"We should take this to the police," Joey says, "test the blood—"

Elena grabs her arm. Her eyes are clear and determined as she slowly shakes her head. "We were never here." Then she stands to take out her phone. She snaps several pictures. A series of vibrations from Joey's pocket signals that she's just sent the images to the group text. She snatches up the sweatshirt, bunches it up, and shoves it back behind the stuffed bunny.

"We have to go now."

Sophie is nodding so much that stray hairs fall loose from her hair clip and swing over her face. "We've already been here too long."

Joey takes a fraction of a second to decide, and then she nods too.

They run.

19

QUINN

MAY 2011
TWO WEEKS BEFORE THE FALL

I agree to go to the party but tell Joey I have to go to my dad's right after.

We turn the corner from my house, on our way to Tanner's. The weather is changing. I think there's rain coming. For now, night settles in, resting on our shoulders. The trees are the first to go black. She makes a sound like *hmm*, and we walk on.

It's a lie, of course. I don't have to go to my dad's. I wonder, momentarily, if she knows, if she is reading me. I twist my gold ring with its hefty black stone and raised droplet of gold around my middle finger. But she just says, "We have to go to the spell circle tomorrow. Will you be around?"

"Possibly." I say. "What's up?"

"We need to update the illusion spell to keep the trail hidden." She sounds impatient. It's my fault we've started to grow distant. This party is the first time we'll all be together outside of school in I don't even know how long. Weeks, I think. "It's important," she says. And she's right. I nod.

Her hair is pulled tidily into a hair tie, not loose like mine, which picks up every tiny wisp of wind. I feel so weird lately, like a snake folding out of my old skin and growing a new one underneath. With Joey and Sophie and Elena, it's been a little awkward. That's why I wanted to come tonight. To put in some face time and maybe see if things could be normal. I've been busy with *him*, but truthfully, I've missed us a little.

I look over again and see that Joey is watching me carefully. She pulls her ponytail to the front of her shoulder. "What's going on?"

I scuff my shoe against the dusty pavement. "What?"

"You can tell me."

I open my mouth, and I can feel myself reaching for another lie. When did lying become so automatic? "Nothing," I say. "Just stuff with my dad. I don't know."

We see Sophie waving at us from the corner of First Street, and Joey drops it. The night adds greasy layers of darkness around us, and the peaks of the Three Elks are somehow darkest of all, three hulking shadows in the night sky. The streetlights flick on with a hum, illuminating all the closed-up shops. Voices from a couple of restaurant-goers trickle down the wide street, but no cars pass. It's a ghost of a night.

Elena crosses the street, lighting a cigarette without breaking stride. Slivers of thigh are visible through slashes in her tight jeans. "Quinn," she says, approaching, her mouth full of smoke. "Glad you could make it." I don't respond, even though I can feel all their eyes on me. She exhales and pulls a bottle of schnapps from her coat pocket, trading a drag for a sip. Everyone takes a drink when she offers it around, even me. I feel like if I don't, I'll just get more questions, so I push through the smell and swallow it down.

"Party time," says Elena.

Tanner's parents are out of town for a wedding, and so we descend on his house like moths, eating up all available space. He stands in the middle of the room, with a stocky frame and the same buzz cut he's had forever, looking out over his domain.

More people are filing in now, a maximum of twelve or thirteen, which is a lot for this tiny town. We gather around Tanner's kitchen island as he doles out shots and encourages people to set up beer pong. Sophie takes two shots right in a row, and I want to tell her to slow down, but she's laughing with Joey, and they both look like they're having fun.

The hairs on my arm prickle, and I glance at the sliding glass door. I think I see a flash of something out there, but it's so dark outside and so bright in here that I'm sure it's just my own reflection, my tie-dye maxiskirt and lavender hair. A patched denim jacket I have yet to take off. I feel strange. If someone was out there watching me, they would be able to see me clearly. It should scare me, this thought, but instead it gives me a little thrill. I slowly run my hand under my denim jacket and push it down to expose my shoulder, watching my pale flesh in the reflection.

"Hey."

The rumbling voice comes from behind me. I close my eyes as I feel River's body heat next to me, and I slide my jacket back up onto my shoulder. He wraps his arms around my top half and gives me a tight squeeze. His head rests on top of mine, and I wonder if he can tell what I've been thinking, if he can see my desire circling like a vulture. "All good?" he asks. I look at our reflection again, watch his hair fall into one eye.

I grab his hand, and he looks surprised. I pull him away from the kitchen and into the front hall, toward the stairs. At the edge of my line of sight, Elena slips out the front door into the night, and I wonder where she is going. I don't stop to check, though, because suddenly I need to do this now. My fingers entwined with his, I pull River upstairs to a quiet room where we can be alone.

The door slides closed behind me, and I realize we're in Tanner's parents' room. The bed is made, the window cracked so a little of the night seeps inside. The music from downstairs thumps distantly.

"I want to break up." I blurt the words out quickly.

He stares at me, blinking. "What?"

I don't respond.

He perches on the edge of the bed, elbows resting on his long bent legs. After a few seconds, he lies back, sliding his hands beneath his head, elbows out wide. "Honestly, I'm surprised, but also not. You've been…distant lately. I was actually shocked you came tonight."

I can't tell if his words are meant to be sharp or resigned. I look down at my shoes. "Sorry, I didn't know the best way to tell you."

"It's fine." He turns his head so his eyes are focused on me. There's something there, anger maybe, and it makes me retract. But then, his eyes are closed and he's inhaling deeply.

"Do you want to talk?" I ask because I'm not sure what else I should do.

He offers nothing but a small "Hmm," but he doesn't move. I interpret that as a dismissal.

As I reach for the door, I hear him sit up. "Is there someone else?"

I pinch at the bottom of my jacket. "No. I just want to be by myself for a little while."

He eyes me. Another dark look makes me step closer to the door. I grip the handle. His gaze drops to my hand, and after a second, his expression softens a few degrees. "Friends?" he asks.

I nod.

When I close the door quietly behind me, I know I should feel bad. I should feel horrible for hurting him. But I just feel free. It was a lie, of course. There *is* someone else. And now, I let myself think of him. He's there, in my mind, looking at me, looking into me, eyes like glaciers. Suddenly, with a passion so fierce it stings my throat, I want nothing more than to tangle myself up with him and watch the stars. With him, I can be myself.

As I descend the steps, I hear a muffled noise from one of the other bedrooms. It's Tanner and Marissa Berg in there, I'm guessing. Dating on and off for a tumultuous ten months. The kind of thing you are forced to care about in a town where your whole school can fit into one picture in front of the school's front steps. Everyone's business becomes your business.

Downstairs, I poke my head out the front door, expecting to see Elena having a smoke. But the night is thick with silence, and it smells of pine. No Elena. I could just make my escape now. It's tempting, but I don't want to have to explain anything tomorrow, so I duck back inside.

Inside, the living room opens seamlessly to the kitchen. Calvin Harris thumps from the speakers. Someone has spilled a drink on the Persian rug and made a vague attempt to clean it up by throwing a striped kitchen towel over top, which is now soaked through with a cherry-red stain. The smell of beer and Kool-Aid is strong. A cheer goes up from the small crowd that sticks to the kitchen island like a swarm of flies. They all tip their cups up to their faces at once.

I don't see Sophie or Elena, but Joey sits on the couch by the window, nursing a drink. She shoots me a smile, then looks past me. I follow her gaze. It's River. He makes his way into the room, squeezing my shoulder as he passes. His grip is tight, and I think for a second he's going to squeeze harder, and my breath catches, but then he just lets go.

Joey is watching me from her corner of the room. The disconnect I feel is hard to explain. At parties past, I would have plopped down next to her on that couch and started up a game of Guess Who's Going to Puke Tonight. Elena and Sophie would have eventually pulled us up off the couch, and we would have danced and changed the playlist to only our favorite songs, as if the party were just for us. Now, I glance at Joey and then away, feeling torn because I miss the way things used to be, but I also feel alive in a way that I haven't since we first learned about the magic. Something is changing within me.

I accidentally connect eyes with Marissa Berg, who stands leaning against the refrigerator. She wears two long braids like some kind of horror movie doll. A bejeweled silver cross gleams at her neck. I half smile with no teeth, wondering, briefly, who is upstairs in Tanner's room if Marissa is down here. She shuffles over.

"What's going on there?" I can smell her cloying, trying-too-hard perfume. In middle school, Marissa used to follow us around, constantly trying to push her way into our conversations at recess, always running to catch up as we walked home from school. But once we were initiated, we spent every waking hour just the four of us. She was muscled out of the group.

"What?" I ask.

"Isn't she flirting with him?" I watch River grab Joey's cup and cross the room to fill it with beer. Joey's gaze stays glued to him. When it's obvious I'm not going to respond, Marissa says, discreetly, "Does it make you wonder what they're up to?" She pauses, looking down into the drink in her hand. As she swirls it, red liquid splashes up the side of the cup and slides down in slow streaks.

"Not really," I say.

"Oh," she says. Then, without moving her eyes from her cup, "I think Tanner cheated on me." She fiddles with the chain of her necklace. "I think it was Sophie."

Indignation draws a laugh out of me. "That's insane. Sophie would never."

Marissa whispers urgently when she says, "They send messages to each other. Did you know that? Like *graphic* messages."

I do know about the messages. They exist, but they only go one way, from Tanner to Sophie, and they're entirely unwelcome. I think of the dick pic that Tanner sent and the way Sophie hid from it, shamefaced, like it was somehow her fault.

A laugh that's short but loud pulls my attention to the corner of the couch. River stands above Joey, who uncrosses and then recrosses her legs and tries to smother a smile. She looks up quickly as if she knows

I'm watching her, then away again, this new awkwardness between us like another person in the room.

"Just saying," Marissa says. "Be careful who you trust."

I study her eyes, which she has now locked with mine. They are laced with hope and seem to be asking a silent question. I know exactly what it is. She wants to know if I will turn on my friend and join her little broken-hearts club. She has tried a hundred times to winnow into our group, and I've always felt bad for her. Suddenly, I feel an incredible surge of unexpected power. I have access to magic, and she doesn't. There are people who would give anything for that.

"Sorry, hun," I say, handing her my cup. "Sophie's not hooking up with Tanner." I stride to the front door without looking back and swing it open.

Outside, the air is fresh, and I feel energized. I start to walk up the hill. But I don't take five steps before distant voices float toward me from behind the trees at the end of the block. I advance toward the tree line as the voices grow louder. An argument intensifying.

"It's over," a man is saying. The voice is familiar but out of context. I can't place it. Silence fills the cool night air.

"It's not," says a woman. No. Not a woman. Elena.

I freeze, hardly breathing. I'm close enough to hear, but it's very dark, and they are obscured by the trees. Then, there's a rustle of something and a deep, masculine moan.

"Stop."

"Stop what?" I have to strain to hear her voice because it's soft and sultry, and then there's another moan.

"I said stop." His voice is sharp, as sudden and cutting as a slap.

"I could tell everyone about us," Elena says with forced bravado. "I have pictures. I could make it very bad for you."

There is a long pause, and I can't hear what's happening. My pulse quickens.

"Get the fuck off me," says Elena. Urgently, I scan the dark ground, searching for a way into the trees. I find the beginning of a trail between the trees and take two steps toward it. Before I can go any farther, I hear running in my direction. In another second, a body collides with mine. I fall backward, and Elena is there, groaning, grabbing her nose. The collision has thrown her hair into her face, and she looks at me the way a deer looks at an oncoming car. She glances back to the woods where another set of footsteps grows louder. Her eyes fall back onto mine. "What are you doing here?" she asks. It's the first time I've ever seen shame on her face, and it jars me. I want to say something, anything, but she doesn't give me the chance. She just turns and scrambles away.

I barely have time to stand before a figure steps out of the shadow of the trees. Mark Collingswood. English-teaching, chinos-wearing, friendly-with-students Mark Collingswood. His needle eyes find mine, and he holds my gaze, maybe assessing how much I saw, how much I heard. I give nothing back, just blink at him in the dark, doing my best to hide my surprise. I know Elena is wild and impulsive and unbound by social expectations, and I know she talked about him like that, but I never thought it was true. I just assumed it was her brand of raunchy, over-the-top humor, meant to shock. Mr. Collingswood is our *teacher*. And at least twenty years older than her.

"Miss Winter," he says, interrupting my thoughts. It's a mundane, monotone greeting. He doesn't seem nervous or caught out. Instead, he's strangely confident. I dip my head in a nod, not sure what I'm acknowledging exactly. He thrusts a hand out, gripping the top of my arm with a suddenness that stops me. The cold denim of my jacket presses against my skin. He tries to make eye contact with me. I can feel it, but I avoid his face. I can hear his ragged breath. Eventually, without saying anything else, he lets go and brushes past.

I don't move. Instead, I stare into the gap in the trees, my heart skittering. I'm trying to make sense of it.

Mark *Collingswood.*

Mr. Collingswood.

And then, unexpectedly, the shock slowly morphs into something else. The darkness of the woods in front of me like a mirror, reminds me—for the second time tonight—of my power. I inhale deeply and recognize a sudden insatiable desire to do something about this. To fix it for Elena.

But what?

20

ELENA

Elena is inside the glass house. She sits on a black leather couch that is not comfortable at all. She takes another sip of whiskey and rests her cup on the cold slate coffee table, resisting the urge to prop her feet up there too.

She recalls how she just saw this house not two hours ago from Tom Winter's backyard. The shrine with bones of dead animals was one thing, but Quinn's sweatshirt covered in her blood, the holes that looked like stab wounds? Was it like that when they found Quinn fifteen years ago, or did Tom put those holes in it during some weird, sick ritual? Regardless, there's no way those cuts were from rocks. She didn't believe it before, but now she is certain someone took Quinn's life.

Earlier, Elena had tried to tamp down the violent surge of anger that the visit to Tom's stirred in her as Gael helped bring a roast to Barbara's dining room table. Browned potatoes, homemade rolls, freshly churned butter with chives, and a salad with radishes and blanched asparagus. His eyes had never been so wide, the impossibility of such a feast canceling out every drive-through chicken nugget he's ever had. Elena had watched her son polish off two entire plates and marveled at the fact that he is only two years younger than Quinn was when she died. Anger fired through her again, and her appetite waned. After eating, Barbara put a firm hand on Elena's shoulder and told her she shouldn't feel one ounce of guilt, that she should, *of course*, go to the cast party, and that she should lean on her while they were here. Besides, she wanted to get to know Gael, and this would give her that chance to get a sense of *"what's in his soul."*

It took almost an hour to walk from Barbara's to the glass house on the hill, since she went the long way as opposed to through the woods. Still, she checked over her shoulder every ten steps. Once, she thought she heard footsteps behind her, but when she turned, she was the only one on the darkening street. Was there a chance Tom had seen them leaving his house or saw something out of place when he got home? He could have sensed something off with the sweatshirt. If he did, she didn't want to think about what that meant for them.

Sitting inside here now, she feels ten thousand miles from Tom Winter's hovel and strangely safe in this house that's almost entirely decked out in glass. The walls are floor-to-ceiling windows, cleaned to perfection. There are glass vases and mirrors on every wall that's not a window. Whoever decorated seems to have taken the glass-house theme to the extreme and then scrubbed it clean of any life whatsoever. It sparkles with neurotic germophobia.

This house is a local legend. The original homeowners moved out in the eighties, and the place was abandoned for decades. All Elena knows about the woman who lived here then was that she was a *godless heathen*—that was according to Winona Alvarez, Elena's mother, who actually said those words, like she was some seventeenth-century witch hunter. Elena isn't a fan of the decor, but it does look like it's been renovated from when they pressed their faces to the window in the early aughts. Leave it to a film production crew to resurrect an abandoned mansion halfway up a mountain.

She observes the sterile room around her, taking in a sculpture that is maybe the one beautiful thing in here. Small enough to fit in her hand if she were to try, it's a dense mountainscape of heavy-looking glass with three jagged peaks jutting up at different heights.

"I was like, '*yes*,' when the location scouts told me about Whisper Ridge," Phillip Granger is saying. He touches her arm, yanking her away from her observations. "It just seemed like a place with a dark soul, squeezed between these huge mountains. Choked by industry, disconnected from the pace of modern life." His knee presses against hers. She keeps herself rooted to the couch, waiting for the opportunity to talk about her career goals and the classes she's taken. She has talent—this, she's been told more than once. But she's not naive. She knows it wasn't her talent Phillip Granger was interested in when he invited her here. Still, she thinks she can thread this needle just right to get on his professional radar.

Phillip leans forward to top up her glass with a whiskey she is sure is more expensive than her monthly utility bills. He wants details, he says, because details are what make the audience feel like they're *really there*. He tells her he's glad she's an extra, that her local presence will add authenticity to the film. She searches his face for signs that this is a joke, but there are none.

The young production assistant she met at the bar yesterday sweeps in front of them, offering to bring fresh cocktails like a nervous housewife. Then she hurries away toward the kitchen where Nicola Bianco pinches the delicate stem of a cocktail glass and touches Cal Pierce's arm at regular intervals. Elena takes in Cal's square jaw and distant eyes. There's something about seeing him—a bona fide movie star—here, in Whisper Ridge. It's jarring. He's actually good-looking in real life in a way that most of them are not. He catches her watching him and smiles his practiced, benign smile with those radioactive veneers. Nicola, who looks tan and tiny in her blush V-neck sweater dress, says something that pulls his attention back to her. Last night, Nicola mentioned that she has been staying down at the inn instead of up here at the big house with the boys. Elena is curious why, especially when it's rumored that Nicola is secretly dating Cal Pierce. But then, maybe she gets it. Secrets require discretion.

The party is strangely intimate. Cal and Nicola have their corner of the open-plan room, and Elena and Phil have theirs. Everyone else dips in and out of conversations, and as they do, Elena begins to feel territorial. She has another sip, assessing her odds of getting him to look at her demo reel tonight. She's just a lowly background actor with too-big dreams, and she needs his help. That is how she'll spin it, anyway. He's a man with an ego. He'll bite.

Ridged potato chips spill out of the art deco glass bowl as Phil digs a hand in. "Any good Whisper Ridge stories to, you know, add color to this place?" he asks. He seems at home here, despite the sharp, clinical surroundings. He leans back, chewing, and slings an arm behind her. Never mind that it's not the kind of couch for lounging. On cue, the stiff leather squeaks beneath him.

"What kind of color?" she asks.

"Sordid insider knowledge, that kind of thing. Local lore."

As if he's just spoken a trigger word, Elena feels the room hush around them. In the space of a breath, she glances up to see Cal and Nicola staring at her over their drinks.

"Let me think," she says to buy time.

She rifles through her mind, unsure which sordid tale would fit the bill, but she keeps hitting a brick wall. They're all too personal.

"Well." She shifts and looks up to the ceiling to show she's thinking hard about the question. "It was magical growing up here. The way the sun hides behind the mountain after four o'clock every afternoon, casting the town in shadow. The way the winter closes the town off from the rest of the world, like you're living in a palace of snow and ice." It makes her slightly nauseous to describe Whisper Ridge like this, since it was always the exact opposite for her, but she says it because she thinks this is what he's fishing for.

Nicola and Cal round the couch then, taking up position in the chairs opposite. The rest of the cast and crew seem to follow their lead. The party, at Phillip Granger's apparent command, is now listening to Elena.

Phillip, though, looks disappointed. "But what about grit? Lawlessness, anarchy, the Wild West? Because I think that's what you have here. Desolation." This last word he slows down for emphasis.

"Oh, that goes without saying." She pivots without missing a beat, realizing she missed the mark and trying a different tack instead. "You know, there are legends here of miners who came back from the dead. And it's believed that gold and silver deposits created a dark and mysterious magic in the woods." At this, he shifts toward her. She has his attention now. She doesn't look at the others but can feel their alert silence. "There are tales, too, of stranded prospectors who ate each other to survive and of ghostly tommy-knockers haunting the old mines. And the Ute people had their own legends, long before they were forced to leave. There is plenty of local lore to make your skin crawl." She watches his face broaden with interest and is happy she's struck the right chord.

"And now?" Phillip asks.

"Now?"

"What is it like now? Give me something I wouldn't know unless I was from here."

"Rumor has it, they're filming a high-profile Phillip Granger film as we speak."

Breathy chuckles fill the space, but then a hush. They are waiting for her real answer. She considers what to say since she may never have another chance to captivate quite like this. Any one of these powerful industry players could take her seriously if her story is memorable enough. She's suddenly buzzing with the thought. The game is in her control now. Ironic that being from Whisper Ridge has turned out to be a winning card. *Play it right*, she tells herself.

"About fifteen years ago, a girl fell off a cliff in the woods nearby," she hears herself say. "Her name was Quinn Winter." Phillip raises his eyebrows expressively. She pauses and uncrosses her legs, feeling a tingling as blood rushes into her foot. "Police said it was a hiking accident, but there are some locals who don't believe it. They say she was pushed."

At once, she can see the resonance of what she's said splashed across their faces. It's raw, delicious excitement, like she tossed them a New York strip when they were expecting kibble.

Phillip cradles his chin with a thoughtful hand.

"Fascinating," says Nicola, whose eyes glitter with delight.

Spirited conversations blossom around her, but Elena isn't listening. She looks out the window, wishing she could see anything beyond the glass of this monstrous house. Still, there's nothing but her own reflection. It's not as if they couldn't have found out about Quinn online if they looked, she tells herself. It's not like she revealed a secret. But she feels an intestine-twist of guilt anyway.

She has just crossed a line.

21

JOEY

Joey really doesn't want to be wiping coffee splatters off the wall.

She wants to be cornering Tom Winter, shoving him into a chair, and yelling into his face. *Why did you kill her?* This detective drama fantasy isn't new. She's imagined herself doing it to the right person over the years. The problem is, she never found the right person. Now, they have him dead to rights, but there are still questions. Why would he keep evidence in his spare bedroom for anyone to find? And why did the police, the coroner, or anyone who examined Quinn's body after her death not mention the stab wounds? Something isn't adding up. She resists the urge to pull up the photo of the sweatshirt on her phone. When she gets home, she'll check the notes she's examined a hundred times, in case there's something she's missing.

She wipes the wall, then dips her rag back into the bucket and wipes again. When she finishes with that, she goes after the floor, where something sticky has formed a solid puddle. She may need a mop for this one.

Zach doesn't do a great job closing up. There were cups in the sink when she came in a couple of hours ago, and she's almost certain he hasn't bothered to clean the espresso machine grates. He's fantastically reliable at showing up for work, and that's about it. But he's all she's got, and she feels like she owes him for taking off early today and yesterday. The influx of customers over the past few days has strained day-to-day operations, and she wants to blame the film, but she can't. This is on her.

A faint sound makes her look up. The door is closed and locked. She can't see anything out there, though she has the sudden sensation that there's someone there, just beyond the sidewalk where the light reaches. Her pulse vibrates in her throat.

But after a few seconds of silence, she sees no one and doesn't hear the sound again. She does her best to shake it off and gets back to wiping the floor. Being in Tom's house felt like crawling barefoot through a dumpster, and it sparked in her a sudden, irrepressible need to clean something. Besides, no one but her is going to make sure this place is ready for the morning rush. So even though she feels uneasy being here alone tonight, here she is.

A knock on the glass.

Joey jumps, sending water tumbling out of her bucket and bleeding across the hardwood. She rights the bucket.

A vaguely familiar woman bundled in a furry pink coat salutes her hand over her eyes and peers through the glass. In a moment, she spots Joey and throws a palm to her heart in an *oh, thank god* gesture. And then she smiles and mimes opening the door.

It's Nicola Bianco. The actress. Joey has no idea what she's doing here, but she guesses she's about to find out. She stands, peels off her rubber gloves, and cautiously walks to the door. When Joey cracks open the door, Nicola makes a face like she's just been saved from oncoming traffic. "I am dying for a coffee," she says with a barely detectable European accent that Joey assumes is Italian.

"It's ten o'clock at night," says Joey, glancing at the *Closed* sign that hangs from the door.

"Oh, it's fine. I'm a night owl." Nicola looks at Joey expectantly.

Joey presses her lips together, hoping to convey that she doesn't negotiate with entitled movie stars, but in the end, she doesn't have the energy to put up a fight. She opens the door wider and gestures for her to come in. Nicola, with no self-awareness whatsoever, saunters inside, shivering and pulling her coat tighter around her. *It's fifty-five degrees out*, Joey thinks, *and at least seventy in here*, but she says nothing. Resigned, she ducks behind the counter and fires up the old espresso machine. Zach has left beans in the grinder, she notices, and just as she suspected, the grate beneath sloshes with murky brown liquid. She places a mug down, sees that it's chipped, and replaces it with two unchipped mugs. If she's going to the trouble, she might as well have one too. Then she gets out the mop and quickly cleans up the spilled water.

"You work here?" Nicola scrapes a chair across the floor and watches while Joey finishes mopping and begins to make the drinks.

"I own it."

She looks around appraisingly. Joey guesses what she's thinking. It's the same thing she'd think if she was in Nicola's shoes. Suddenly, she feels defensive. "We're updating the decor soon," she says.

"Ah," says Nicola politely.

They fall silent as the machine whirs.

"How is the inn?" asks Joey. She doesn't really care, but she figures making conversation is better than sitting in silence. She's trying to get a read on Nicola, and she can't. She appears girly and petite, and the request for coffee after dark from a closed café fits the entitled cliché. But she also seems candid. Almost likable.

"It's great," Nicola says, surprising her. "To be honest, I thought I would hate it here. But everyone is so nice. And no paparazzi."

Joey finds herself laughing. "Don't be fooled. We have our own version of the paparazzi. They're named Ingrid and Jasper Hardy, and they live on Third Avenue. They run the local online paper. I'm sure you've already been featured in Tuesday's 'Around Town' column."

"Oh," says Nicola, reluctantly smiling. "I guess I don't mind a little paparazzi now and then. It means I'm still relevant."

Joey can feel herself softening to the low-stakes conversation. In the hours since Tom's house, she's felt trapped by her own thoughts. For years, she has known that Quinn didn't just fall off that crag. She's known it like she's known her own name. And yet, after finding the sweatshirt she was wearing when she died, stained with her blood and slashed seven times over, she can hardly bear to think about it. For the moment, Joey appreciates the levity of sitting with another soul who has no idea about Quinn or Tom or any of it. She almost doesn't mind that she's making coffee this late at night for someone who, she just has a feeling, has no intention of paying.

"How's the filming coming along?" Joey asks as she brings the drinks over. She hands one to Nicola, who takes a desperate sip.

"It's awful. A toxic working environment. The director is..." She trails off. "He is a bully. I have never worked with him before this film but have heard rumors. Well, the rumors are not as bad as the real thing. Two crew members have quit because of his little tantrums."

"That's... Yikes," says Joey. She tries to recall the name of the director. She knows Elena mentioned it, but she can't fish it from her mind.

Nicola rubs a thumb along the side of her mug. "Men like him are everywhere. Especially in this business. But I suppose they're not all like that. There are some good apples."

Nicola has curtain bangs that are cut perfectly to frame her face, and Joey marvels at how put together she looks for this time of night, like she's just come from a party. Maybe she has. Her expression is dreamy, as if she's thinking of someone in particular—one of the good apples, no doubt. Joey's about to agree. *There are bad men everywhere. There are bad men here.* But she doesn't. Because her heart stops.

As Nicola tips her cup to her mouth, Joey stares.

There. On her middle finger. A gold band with a witchy-looking black stone. In the center of the stone is an overlaid gold charm shaped like a droplet of water. Or blood. Instant recognition sends Joey to her feet, and Nicola looks startled.

"Where did you get that?" Joey sets her cup down and points at the ring with a shaking hand. She's breathing fast, like a feral animal, both terrified and indignant. It's impossible that Nicola Bianco has Quinn's ring, but it's right there.

Nicola looks caught out for a second and brings the coffee mug to her lap. "I found it," she says finally. She looks at Joey from behind her curtain bangs.

Joey's heart is hammering. She narrows her eyes. "Found it where?" Her teeth are clenched, and she thinks she might jump on top of this woman and pluck the ring off her finger herself.

There's a long pause, and Nicola's face eventually softens into a nostalgic smile. "At a vintage shop I love just off South Beverly. They have some really unique jewelry. This one is Victorian. Eighteen ninety-one, I think she said. It's gorgeous, no?"

"Oh," says Joey, feeling thrown. She's studying Nicola's face, but there's nothing. No flinch, no sign of a lie.

"Are you alright?" asks Nicola. She's peering at Joey inquisitively, and Joey realizes she probably looks unwell, the way she's staring with heat and fear behind her eyes. She thought for a minute—

But it really does look like Quinn's. It's almost exactly the same.

Nicola tugs at her finger and twists the ring free. She holds it out. "Try it on if you like it that much. I will send you Marilyn's website. Maybe she has something similar."

Joey takes it in her hand and turns it around. She slips it onto her finger. As much as she wants to feel something, as much as she is hoping for a sign from the ring that it is, indeed, Quinn's, there's nothing.

She's even less sure now that she's seeing it up close. She can't tell. Was Quinn's this shape? Was it this heavy?

Nicola takes the ring back and stands quickly, looking uncomfortable. She sets her empty cup on the counter and waves a delicate, manicured hand. "Good night."

Joey gives her as much of a smile as she can manage.

As she goes back to the storage closet to get more towels for the wet floor, she's not thinking about the extra cleanup or the fact that Nicola did not, just as predicted, offer to pay. Instead, she thinks about the ring. Not Nicola's, but Quinn's. She strains to picture it on Quinn's finger when she brushed her hair back or sipped on a Coke, but just like staring too hard at a faint star, the images go dark and blurry. Joey is certain Quinn wore a bulky black and gold ring on her middle finger. Then, her memory swerves from practical to morbid, and she squeezes her eyes tight. She wishes desperately that she could be the kind of person who finds the positive in things, the kind of person who could celebrate her friend's short, beautiful life. But Joey is emotionally impotent. Optimism, if she ever had it, has been wrung out of her. Now, all she can see—all she ever sees—are the things that go wrong.

Sophie's right. She needs therapy.

She thinks she hears a noise at the front of the store, and she thinks Nicola might be back. But when she rounds the corner, she realizes it's just her growing unease. The store is empty. Feeling the churning of espresso on an empty stomach, Joey cleans up quickly and flicks off the light before heading out and locking the door. The street is dark, and she can hear an owl in the distance. She thinks about turning left to her house but changes her mind and turns right instead.

She doesn't want to be alone.

22

QUINN

MAY 2011
TWO WEEKS BEFORE THE FALL

I am walking back from another amazing night with *him*, though I'm lost in swirling thoughts about Elena. It's been less than twelve hours, but my anger has already doubled, like a bowl of dough sweating on the windowsill. Collingswood is taking advantage of my friend. I know Elena acts grown up, but she's not. He could ruin her life.

I almost miss Otto Stringer watering the lupines by his mailbox as I walk by Sophie's house on the way to mine. When I see him, I think about doubling back and taking a path through the woods instead, but he catches my eye and rights his watering can.

"If it isn't Quinn Winter," he says brightly. "So good to see your face."

"Hi, Mr. Stringer."

"Haven't seen you around in a while. Everything okay between you and Soph?"

Warm fingers of embarrassment wrap around my neck and cheeks.

He looks back at the house, then at me again. "Hey, can I bother you for a few minutes? She's upset about something, but I can't get her to talk to me. Will you…? I know it's a lot to ask…"

My senses perk up instinctively. "What's wrong?"

He just shakes his head, and I realize then that the crease between his eyebrows is deep with worry. He watches me walk all the way to the front door before splashing more water into the dirt.

Inside, Sophie is curled in the fetal position on her bed, facing her closet. The blinds are closed, and the darkness is a contrast to the expansive morning sunlight, closing out the promise of summer.

"You want to tell me what's going on?" My voice startles her, I can tell. But she doesn't turn around, just tightens her hug around a yellow throw pillow with tasseled edges. I hear a sniffle.

"I'm going to open the blinds now," I say.

"No." She turns toward me. "Don't. It's... I don't want it."

I take a few steps toward her and climb up onto the bed. I rest my chin on her upper arm. Her eyes are puffy, and her face is splotched red. She's been crying for a while. "Let's see," I say. "Is it because the Nuggets are out of the playoffs?"

She wipes her face with the back of her hand. "You know I'm a Lakers fan."

"I guess they do have Kobe."

She shakes her head. "It's their colors. Purple and yellow." She turns to me, and even though she doesn't smile, she swallows and prepares to tell me something. "Last night," she says, then pauses.

"Last night," I echo, waiting for more.

"I don't remember all of it...just snippets, like flashes. I must have been really drunk. I don't know."

Her hand curls around mine, and she squeezes, like she needs the reinforcement of human contact.

"He took pictures... He undressed me, and he took pictures of me. Or I don't know, he told me to undress. It's... I don't remember everything, but he—oh god, this is mortifying." She buries her face in the pillow.

My heart begins to hammer in my chest. "Are you saying someone forced you to pose for naked pictures?"

She nods, barely.

"Did he…?" I start, and then I wait, my jaw starting to hurt because I can't finish the thought.

She shakes her head. "He is going to send them to everyone. He said…he said he was going to send them to my dad." Fresh tears flood her eyes now, and she shudders in what looks like a herculean effort to keep from sobbing.

"What the fuck is wrong with him?"

"I don't know what I did to him. I honestly don't."

I'd ask who it was, but I know. I've always known he would do something like this. "He's been after you since we were kids, Soph. It's not your fault."

"I know. But I'm humiliated. What if he sends those pictures around? I know he's going to if he hasn't already. I can't go to school on Monday. What if my dad sees them?"

"We won't let that happen." It's all I can think of to say because I am flush with the injustice of it. Tanner and his infuriating assholeness crashing head-on into wonderful, tender, loving Sophie, who's never hurt anyone in her life. Was this happening to Sophie last night while I was in the next room with River? It must have been. I realize now that I hadn't seen Sophie for hours. At the time, I'd just assumed she was somewhere, playing a game or adding songs to the playlist like she usually did. But I was so anxious to leave, I didn't even check to see if she was okay. I think of what Sophie's dad said to me outside. *"Haven't seen you around in a while."* I know I've been distant, but now I'm wondering if my absence has actually shifted things for my friends. Joey's mom attempted suicide—which Joey had to thwart all on her own—Elena is sleeping with a man in his late thirties, and now Sophie has been sexually assaulted. I can't help but feel a little responsible for all of it. We're supposed to be here for each other. I've lost sight of that.

She searches my face, then sits up and sweeps her fingertips back and forth beneath her eyes. I hurry to the kitchen and fill a glass to the top with ice and pink lemonade from a plastic pitcher in the fridge. It's something my mom has kept in her fridge for years, and I wonder, fleetingly, if she's been swapping notes with Otto. When I come back in the room, Sophie's slowly opening the blinds.

"I feel like it's been so long since you've been here," she says quietly. She wipes at her nose with the back of her hand. "I think we should go to the spell circle. We could do a summoning spell to try to get those pictures off his phone. There's still a chance he hasn't shared them yet, so it's worth a try."

I nod absently, but I can't seem to speak. A thrill slams into me, as if it has just run, panicked, out of the dark closet. The magic. It can reach inside the brain of someone like Tanner and rewire it. I know it can. And Collingswood for that matter. And Joey's mom. The magic can do more for Sophie than just a simple summoning spell. It can fix bad people—and save the good ones. Before, I thought maybe it was possible, but now I can *feel* it, as if it's a solid, powerful truth. I know it's possible. But I still don't know how. I've never heard of any spells that can do it, but I am suddenly struck by the certainty that the answer is hidden in the blank pages of the book.

My hand almost slips from the condensation as I hurry over to her and hold out the glass. "No," I say as she takes a long steadying drink. "You stay here. Eat something, watch some reality TV. Take your mind off it. You shouldn't have to see those pictures, Soph. I don't want it to trigger you. I'll take care of it."

"But are you going to use magic? You can't go by yourself," she says.

"No, no magic," I lie. "Just good old-fashioned convincing. Or maybe I'll just distract him and steal his phone. That could work too."

Sophie looks skeptical.

"If it doesn't work, I'll come back and we can go to the spell circle together. With everyone. Okay?" I am quickly formulating a different plan. I try not to let my face betray me.

Sophie looks at me and then at the door. She's torn. I can see it. She seems to be weighing it up, trusting that I will protect her but also believing this situation is irreparable without magic.

Eventually, she breaks the silence. "Okay."

I kiss her forehead, and before she can take another sip, I'm out the door.

23
SOPHIE

Sophie pauses *Survivor* and stands up.

"I'm going to bed." Her dad stirs in his recliner, like he's going to stand.

"Don't get up," she says, handing him the remote. Yawning, she dips into the kitchen for some water. On the counter, she sees a plate of homemade chocolate chip cookies that look delicious and out of place. Otto has never been a baker. He must be so lonely here on his own that he's picking up new hobbies to pass the time. She places one on a napkin and brings it out to him.

"Don't mind if I do," he says with a greedy smile when he sees the cookie.

"Love you, Dad." She kisses him on the head. His hair is thin and soft.

"Love you too, kiddo."

In her room, she sits at the foot of her childhood bed, knees tucked up to her chest. She can hear faint sounds of the TV from the other room. She calls Talia. With every ring, Sophie thinks of Leah's hot little hands and feels the worry deep inside her.

Just as she thinks she's going to be sent to voicemail, she hears a groggy voice on the other end. "Hey."

"How is she?" Sophie can't keep the anxiety from her words, though she tries. She's imagining Leah curled up in Talia's lap, sweating and struggling to breathe.

"Sleeping." Her tone is warm, comforting, but there's a hint of something else too.

"What's wrong?" Sophie asks.

There's a slight hesitation until Talia says, "Don't freak out. Her fever went up slightly after her last dose of Tylenol wore off, but the doctor said only to worry if it's above one hundred and two."

"Is it above one hundred and two?"

Another pause, this time, it's laced with annoyance. "No, of course not. I have an alarm set for every two hours so I can keep tabs on her temp all night."

Tears are starting to build up in Sophie's eyes. "I'm sorry I'm not there. How did she seem at bedtime?"

"Snuggly, a little whiny," says Talia, and Sophie can hear her softening. "She will not let go of Bear. And she asked for you a few times."

Sophie closes her eyes. "What did you say?"

"I said '*Mama is coming home soon*,' and that seemed to work."

"How are you doing?" Sophie asks after a pause.

"Oh, let's see," says Talia with a sigh. "I miss you."

"Me too," whispers Sophie.

Talia's response comes quickly. "But listen to me. It's still a low fever. We are going to be fine. I want you to stay there. I want you to enjoy this time with your dad. I promise I will call you if her fever goes up."

A clatter outside her window makes Sophie's breath catch. She's about to whisper, "*What was that?*" before she realizes that Talia's not actually in the room with her. She stands slowly and walks to the window, then peels open the blinds so she can see out. She sees nothing but the dark street.

"Soph?" she hears through the phone. The sound makes her jump.

"I'm here," Sophie says eventually, turning from the window and racing to the bed to tuck herself under the blankets. "What about work tomorrow?"

"I already called off." Talia hesitates. Then she says, "I can do this, Soph."

Sophie's therapist is in her head. *"Do you trust Talia to take care of Leah?"* Sophie's answer to that would be *"Of course I do, but..."* But what? Is Sophie really so controlling, so overbearing, that she can't let her wife handle their daughter for a few days?

She nods, deciding to heed her own internal advice. "I love you. Call me the minute her fever goes up. I don't care if it's the middle of the night. I want to be the first person you talk to after the doctor, and I'm coming home if it gets any worse."

Sophie can almost see Talia at the kitchen table, dressed in sweatpants and a Buffs T-shirt and those adorable black-rimmed glasses, glaring into a blue-lit laptop, Tylenol bottle at her elbow. Sophie lets herself lean into this image, lets herself feel the safeness of it, especially as the image of Quinn's bloody sweatshirt crashes through her thoughts. She feels slightly uncomfortable as they hang up, like she's forgotten something, but she tells herself it's the same feeling she always has when she's forced to rely on someone else, and so she tries to ignore it.

On her phone, she turns on some music to drown out any sounds that might make the anxiety worse. Her feet are suddenly freezing, she realizes, and she walks to the closet, peeling open the doors. She sees the pair of purple slippers sitting there on the shelf and shoves her feet into them. Maybe her dad bought them for her? But he couldn't have because he didn't know she was coming. If they're not for her, then whose are they?

She's about to close the closet door when she lets her gaze fall on Quinn's journal. Half-hidden beneath a crimson cable-knit sweater, just where she left it. She doesn't want to think about the journal right now, and she goes to pull the chain to turn off the light.

But something catches her eye.

A flash of pink between the sweater and the journal. She doesn't remember seeing that before.

She squats down, carefully peeling the sweater away with two fingers, like a layer of old, dead skin. Then she sees the sticky note. Neon pink and stuck to the cover of the journal, right in the center. Two words written in jet black marker across it.

Read me.

She spins around, as if an explanation will reveal itself somewhere else in the room. A stack of Post-its on her dresser, perhaps. Or maybe she stuck one on the journal yesterday and didn't remember? But the thought is ridiculous. Of course she didn't.

She is certain that when she last saw the journal, it did not have a bright pink sticky note on the front of it. She searched the thing from front to back. The pages were empty—empty except for Quinn's name scribbled inside the cover. But this note. This note was not here.

She reaches out to open the journal without lifting it from the floor. She turns the first page, and then when she sees nothing else written in it, flips through the rest. It's still blank. She isn't sure what she expected to see. She sits back on her heels, thinking.

"Dad?" A minute later, she's out in the living room again, trying to suppress the insect of fear creeping through her veins. She leans on the back of the sofa.

"I thought you were going to bed," he says over his shoulder without pulling his eyes from the TV. Two soaking wet participants high-five on the screen.

"Dad." She is schoolteacher stern now, and it gets his attention this time.

He fumbles for the remote and pushes the recliner upright with his feet. "What's wrong?" he says, searching her face. She takes a deep breath, but the weird feeling is still there.

"Has anyone been in the house?"

He looks at her in confusion. There's a cookie crumb stuck in his mustache. "What do you mean? Besides you and me?"

She nods.

He looks away for a flash, his own thoughts occupying him. Sophie doesn't know what to make of this hesitation, and her mind tries to interpret it.

"Dad?"

"No," he says quickly. "No, just us."

"So, no one has been in my room?"

He looks furtively down the hall, then shakes his head.

"You're sure?"

"Of course I'm sure."

Something occurs to Sophie. "At night, and when you go out, you lock up, yes?"

"Yes," he says with a note of incredulity.

"What about the back door?"

He looks toward the kitchen, where the door in question stares back at them. Sophie senses he's about to say that he locks that too, all the time, but they can both see clearly from here that the deadbolt is turned to the right. Unlocked.

She looks back at him, and he glances up at the ceiling, letting out a chuckle of self-admonishment. "The lock is finicky. I've been meaning to get it fixed for a few months."

Sophie hurries into the kitchen, where she picks up a chair and shoves it under the knob of the back door. Just in case.

When she comes out, her dad walks over and leans down so he can look her in the eye. "I promise you, we're safe."

She studies his face, and she can feel her heart rate slowing just from the weight of his hands on her shoulders. She collects herself and says, "Whose things are in my closet?"

There's a moment when Sophie can see him thinking. He gives her an extra hard squeeze that feels unintentional, a kind of instinctual reaction to ground himself at her words. "They're yours, aren't they?"

"No."

"Huh," he says.

"What about the journal?" she asks. "How did that get there?"

"Journal? I don't remember a journal." He rubs at his neck, searching her face. Then he digs his fingers into his eyes, looking suddenly exhausted. The creases on his forehead that were once the cornerstone of his whole expressive personality have deepened over time into permanent folds. Two pockets of skin rest on top of his cheeks.

"Are you okay, Dad? I mean here, on your own?" She asks it gently.

With no hesitation, he pulls her toward him in a robust embrace. His barrel chest and strong arms grip her so she can't move.

"I'm the dad. Let me do the worrying."

She allows herself to relax into him.

Later, though, when she's lying in bed, something occurs to her. The way he rubbed at his neck. It's what he does when he's hiding something.

24

ELENA

Early-morning light heaves through the naked window.

Phillip Granger lies next to Elena on his back, blond furry legs tangled in silvery sheets, dehydration crusting the corners of his lips. She slips out of bed, praying he doesn't wake.

Last night, after she spoke of Quinn to a room full of strangers, Elena felt herself check out. She tried to refocus, keeping Phil interested in her with her questions about his favorite topic. Himself. She even mentioned the word *genius* and nearly gagged. By then, she still hadn't mentioned her demo reel. More whiskey was poured. *Fuck it*, she thought. If there was ever a night to get drunk and see what happened, this was it. She texted Gael to make sure he was okay and Barbara to apologize. Stay, Barbara wrote back. Enjoy. Gael and I are fine.

She checks her phone now, grateful she doesn't see any where are you texts from her son. Joey and Sophie messaged the group thread, though, both saying they have something they want to talk about and agreeing to meet at the coffee shop. Elena punches out a reply. She needs to see Gael and shower before she goes anywhere. It takes her a minute to find her underwear, which is tucked beneath a pillow. The rest of her clothes are in a pile by the door. She tugs them on quickly, wincing at the sudden throbbing in her head. Way too much whiskey. She fishes through her purse and plucks out two Advil. Extra strength. She gags but gets them down eventually. She would kill for some water right now.

She pads out of the room and closes the door silently behind her. Daylight crashes through the floor-to-ceiling windows.

In the kitchen, she fills a glass from the tap all the way to the top and drinks it in one go. Her stomach sloshes, but after a minute, she feels an ounce better. She fills it up again, taking her time with this one, confident Phillip Granger will not be waking up, offering to make her breakfast. She remembers snippets from the night. His woolly hands on her waist, his wet lips, the way he pulled her hair a little too hard. He was clumsy and overconfident, the worst combination. Nausea moves through her, and she takes a steadying breath.

Glass in hand, she wanders over to the bookshelf near the leather couch. Her finger traces the spines of old books. Some look like first editions. She's not very literary, so she doesn't recognize any titles, but these old books are out of place in a room that could otherwise be a contemporary art museum. She finds the glass sculpture she saw last night and admires it again. Three peaks. It really is beautiful, she decides, the cloudy pastel colors like mountains cast in the glow of sunrise. That's when she realizes it's not made of glass but crystals. Quartz, topaz, maybe aquamarine too.

"Good morning."

Elena turns. Cal Pierce stands behind her, leaning on a barstool. His cool blond highlights and pale blue T-shirt give him a good-boy look that she would normally roll her eyes at, but right now, he's an angel because he's not Phillip Granger. She smiles weakly and brings her glass to the sink.

"Let me get that," he says, taking it from her and sticking it in the dishwasher. It's a bit unexpected, this act of domestic gallantry, and she wonders briefly why she set her aim at an egotistical director when she could have focused on someone who might actually be willing to help her. She tells herself she will make her move as soon as she sees Phillip Granger on set. Right now, though, she is suddenly ravished with hunger, feeling an urgent need for Barbara's blackberry pancakes. She hopes she can still get back before Gael wakes up.

"See you," she says, pulling her purse over her shoulder.

"Can I give you a ride?" He gestures to her footwear.

"It's fine," she says. "They're hiking grade." She doesn't even know if that's a term. The Advil is working its magic, and her headache has dulled enough for her to think straight.

He clears his throat as she is about to turn toward the front door. "Hey, I wanted to say…I'm really sorry about your friend. Who died."

Elena stares at his hands resting on the kitchen island. Her heart thrums. She was hoping they had all forgotten. "How did you know she was my friend?"

His smile looks like an apology. "I lost someone too. Just recognized something in the way you said it." He examines her face as he begins to turn pink. "But now I can clearly see that I shouldn't have said anything. I'm sorry, I—"

"No, it's fine." Elena swallows, longing for a shower to clean the lingering shame off her.

"It's just…" He flicks his eyes toward the staircase. "Well, it's probably not my place, but there are some people I wouldn't trust with things that are personal to you. I would hate for your pain to become someone else's next big film, if you know what I mean. Just saying, it's happened before."

Elena's insides curdle as she follows his gaze upstairs. Another reason she shouldn't have said anything. What kind of a person exploits their friend's death mere hours after seeing evidence that she was actually murdered? Elena has no idea where her loyalties lie.

"Thanks for the heads-up." She swallows down a spasm of nausea.

"Anytime," he says. A self-conscious laugh escapes.

There's a sound from upstairs, a door opening. The last thing she wants is any awkward morning-after conversation with Phillip Granger. She checks her phone. Joey is on her way to the coffee shop. Sophie has asked if Elena is good to meet there in an hour. "I have to go," she says. "It was nice meeting you."

"You're taking an Uber though, right?"

She shakes her head. "Walking."

He juts his chin out in shock. "I'm more than happy to give you a ride."

She glances again toward the stairs, considering his offer. But no, she just needs to get out of here. "Truthfully, I would rather walk."

He puts up two palms in resignation. "See you on set then." Elena hesitates, a little surprised that he remembered she's a background actor in the film. She thinks about asking him if he has any idea which day they'll need her on set, but she says nothing. Hunger, and a desire to see Gael, drive her out the door and down the hill.

One foot then the other, over a branch, avoiding a rock to the right, to the left, taking care not to twist an ankle in these shoes. She estimates it will take her forty-five minutes to get home, though she really doesn't know. That will be just enough time to punish herself properly. Amazing how one night can make you feel so fucking low.

25

JOEY

Joey is half-dressed, leaning her elbows on the foot of the bed, hovering over her phone.

River comes in with two mugs of coffee. His hair is still wet, and he smells like shampoo. Joey clicks off her screen and turns, taking one of the mugs from him.

They're both up with the sun, Joey to get to Aspect before the rush and River to get out to the trails to before the first hikers. They move around the room, pulling socks out of drawers, sliding past each other with hands on each other's hips.

"How are the girls?" River asks. She's too distracted to reply. Her mind tries to pick one thing to focus on, but she thinks about all of it—the ring that looked like Quinn's, the bloody sweatshirt, and Tom Winter's creepy shrine.

"You okay?" River asks as he slips on his shoes.

"They're good. We're meeting up this morning."

"Tell them I say hi," he says, taking a sip of his coffee. "If they're staying for the weekend, maybe we can grab a drink or something. It would be great to see them." He watches her check her phone again and then slip it into her back pocket.

"Maybe," she says absentmindedly. "I'm not sure how long they're staying."

He waits a beat before leaving, even though it's past seven and he doesn't like to be late—they're a good fit in that way, she has to admit, but punctuality does not a relationship make. He says he's okay not talking about their discussion the other night, but it's still there, lingering between them. Joey wishes it wasn't, but she can't give him an answer right now. She turns away a few degrees. Instead of taking the hint, he slips her mug from her hand and puts it on top of the dresser, then he rests his forearms on her shoulders and digs his fingers into her scalp, massaging. She resists slightly, even though she can feel the scratch of his sweater and the shape of his chest underneath. He's warm. She wants to sink into him because he knows she turns to butter when he does that to her head, but she doesn't let herself. He must sense her reticence because he lets her go and pecks the top of her head. With a distinct air of disappointment, he leaves. Soon she hears the faint jingle of Walter's leash and the click of the back door.

She closes her eyes, wondering, not for the first time, what the hell she's doing.

Then, she pulls her phone from her back pocket and opens her text messages. She taps one of the pictures Elena sent from yesterday. It's overexposed and slightly out of focus. Quinn's pink sweatshirt lies flat and lifeless on the floor, creasing unnaturally at the elbows. Why would a father want to keep the clothes his daughter died in, especially if they're covered in her blood? It's morbid. In the blurred background is the shrine. Picture frames, Quinn's disembodied face, a dangling rosary, one dirty shoelace.

A massive coffee-black stain and seven similarly sized slashes paint the front of Quinn's sweatshirt. The best theory Joey has come up with so far is that Tom followed her out there, they argued, and he pushed her. But these seven knife-blade-sized holes, the bloodstain—they point to another cause of death altogether. Seven stab wounds on her abdomen. Joey does not remember seeing these the day she found her. The raincoat, she guesses, is the only explanation.

She pads to the spare room in her socks and pulls a pile of pillowcases off the closet shelf. Underneath is a file folder. This is something she's not supposed to have. She only has it because River's dad worked the case, and River somehow managed to swipe it for Joey long before they started sleeping together, before his parents moved away. It's something she knows River still feels guilty about, even though he accepts that her obsession with Quinn's death is just a part of her, and even though his dad is long retired and has likely forgotten this case file even exists. No one at the police force has come looking for it, in any case.

She has no idea how it has been so easy for everyone to just move on when it feels like she never will. She tucks the file into her backpack, pulls on some clothes, and heads out the door.

26
ELENA

They wait as Joey puts in a couple of hours at the coffee shop.

Gael is quizzing them with a 1998 edition of Trivial Pursuit, and Sophie is being polite, though neither of them pays much attention. A couple of low-level crafties run in and out with drink orders for the movie cast and crew. Locals pile in like fruit flies, hoping—she can tell by their craning necks—to catch sight of one of the actors. She wonders what state Phillip Granger is in today. She scratches the pad of her thumb with the sharp corner of a trivia card as she debates the intelligence of sleeping with him.

Gael stands and announces that he's going to go explore, even though she tells him flat out that there's not much to explore.

"Cool camera," Sophie says as he pulls the second strap over his head.

"Thanks. My art teacher gave it to me. It's an SLR. Super old, like from 2015, but it still works great. Want to see?" He shows Sophie while Elena slips a few dollars in his pocket for lunch. In another minute, he makes the two of them smoosh together at the table and snaps a photo. Elena's head pounds with the sudden movement. Then, he's out the door. Elena tries to imagine what this town looks like through his young unjaded eyes, but she can't.

Sophie is agitated and keeps hugging her bag to her chest. It's an annoying tick. Elena wants to tell her that no one wants to steal her diaper bag that she's disguising as a purse, but she holds back the urge to open her mouth about it. It's this hangover. It's making her snippy.

There's a sound behind her. Elena turns to find Joey hovering.

"All done?" Elena asks. Joey nods and glances back at the counter. There are only two other people in the whole place, but Joey's aproned peon sloshes milk into a pitcher, looking like he'd rather put a dagger into Joey's back than watch her socialize.

"He seems nice," Elena says.

Joey is distracted. "No," she says. "I mean, yes, he is. But no, I... Sorry, it's the weirdest thing. Remember that little painting that was hanging on the wall over there? I'm not sure where it is." They all turn to look as if to assess for themselves, and Elena does remember a very amateur bit of artistry from back in the day, a modest, book-sized painting of the old general store. They spent so many afternoons here. Elena is surprised that she remembers, but the wall there does look strange without it, like it's been stripped and exposed against its will. She untwists the lid on a Perrier and sips. The carbonation is gone, and it tastes all wrong.

"Ask your guy over there." She nods to the grump behind the espresso machine. "He is probably just doing some redecorating."

Joey waves a hand through the air as if dismissing the missing painting and, with it, the fact that she should probably still be working. She takes a seat and rummages through her backpack.

"Joey, I've been thinking," says Sophie quietly. "I know we said it was dangerous, but I think we should go to the police and tell them about the sweatshirt."

Joey doesn't answer. She just tosses a file enclosing a stack of papers onto the table. It lands with a slap, and both Elena and Sophie jump. Elena almost knocks over her Perrier but rights it before it can spill.

"What is this?" says Sophie, lifting the front flap of the folder.

Joey puts a finger to her lips to hush them. "At first, I thought we needed the police too," she whispers. "But now I don't think it's such a good idea." Then she nods at the file, indicating that they should open it and find out what she means.

Sophie sifts through it with the care of a rare book archivist. Elena looks over her arm, and when she sees what it is, she feels an immediate, visceral jolt of danger. "How did you get this?"

Sophie has caught on now, and she is flipping back and forth between two of the pages. "Are you supposed to have this?" she whispers.

Joey doesn't seem nervous at all. Maybe it's because she owns this place, and it's given her false confidence. Or maybe she is just done giving a shit about what anyone in this town thinks. That, at least, Elena can relate to.

"Look," says Joey, all business. "There are no pictures of Quinn's body or clothes in the file." *Thank god*, Elena thinks. "But there are notes from the coroner." Joey finds the right page and points her finger at some hand-scrawled notes.

Elena reads. There is a reference to a "sharp force injury to the right posterior skull—likely fatal" and a mention of a broken humerus and clavicle. A few "contusions on the upper back," but that's it. It's only one paragraph. Quinn had a broken collarbone and shattered shoulder. The impact from her fall was on her right side and back. And, of course, her head.

"No mention of the wounds on her front abdomen," Elena says, realization dawning. "Seven stab wounds on a victim and no one even writes about it in the police report?" Her hand is shaking, she realizes. She isn't sure if it's the hangover or the image that's implanted in her brain, resurfacing. Quinn lying there. Dead and alone. She squeezes her drink and feels the plastic flex beneath her grip.

Sophie pushes the Trivial Pursuit box to the side as if that will help her get a better look. "Maybe they didn't know what they were looking at?"

Elena has never admired Sophie's relentless optimism or her insistence on believing the best in people. From Elena's experience, most people are shit. She shoves the pages back inside the folder and presses it closed. "Who were the police officers that worked on this case?" she asks Joey.

"Jim Hunstad and Bill Berg. River's dad and Marissa's dad."

Sophie's fingers pick mindlessly at the damp top of a Saran-wrapped muffin. It's making Elena feel sick. "This is sort of unrelated," Sophie says. "But you said Jim Hunstad, and it made me think of something."

Elena notices Joey fidgeting. The lean muscles in her arms tighten as she reaches behind her and works at her apron string.

"River and Quinn were dating back then," continues Sophie. "Is it too far-fetched to think she gave River the book? To hide it for her?"

"I don't know," says Joey. "It doesn't make sense that she would hide the book from us."

"It's a good theory," says Elena. "What are the chances River still lives in town? We could check."

Joey finally unties her apron and then wraps the strings around her hands until they go white. "He does, but Quinn wouldn't give it to him. He didn't even know about the magic."

Elena is fed up with Joey shooting down their ideas. "It's not like whoever has it can use the magic anyway. Only the four of us—three of us—can. Quinn would have known that. To anyone else it looks like a bunch of empty pages inside an old book. But we should still look. A summoning spell might help bring us something substantial, like you said, Joey, remember? Worth a try anyway because you're right..."

She motions to the file on the table in front of them. "We cannot go to the police."

Before anyone can respond, there is a squeal of tires on pavement. A rusty white truck bumps onto the curb right in front of the coffee shop. It grazes the side door of a car that's parked right next to it, but the impact doesn't stop the truck's momentum. It keeps going. In fact, it looks like it's going to smash right into the window right in front of where they're sitting.

They all jump to their feet at the same time just as the truck finally jerks to a stop. Joey scoops up the paperwork and clutches it to her chest. A man tumbles out of the truck. Straw hair covers one eye. The other is shot straight through with red veins.

Tom Winter. Elena didn't realize how familiar his face would be. It's been more than fifteen years since she's seen him in person. He spots the three of them inside the window, and his eyes meet hers. She takes an involuntary step back. She's seen that look before. When she was fifteen, Elena's mother shoved her into a closet and rage-screamed fifty-three Hail Marys through the slatted door. When Elena was seventeen, her mother bound her to a chair with a shoelace before pelting her in the face, hard, with the Bible. *"You don't earn God's love by being a slut!"*

It comes from the soul, that kind of fury, and she would recognize it anywhere.

Tom flings open the door, nearly taking it off its hinges, and marches toward Elena. He leans in until his red-spidered nose is touching hers. "Whatdidyoufuckingdo." His words blend together, consonants slurred. His breath is rank. Elena grits her teeth, her hand tight on the chair. She does not lean back. She doesn't give an inch, even as his sweaty forehead touches hers. Adrenaline lights up the muscles in her limbs, and she shoves him away with a forearm. He grabs her, his watery gaze unsettlingly direct.

In another second, he's being pulled back. The grumpy guy from behind the counter is there, grabbing Tom's arm, pushing his body between them. Tom growls, keeping his eyes locked onto Elena's. He spits as he talks. "A woman came to my house. From the movie. Somehow, she heard about Quinn. Asking all these questions, wanted to use Quinn as inspir—" he fumbles over the word—"inspiration for her character in the *goddamn movie.* I asked her how she found out about Quinn, and get this, she told me it was *you* who told her, Elena." He breaks off as a new emotion ripples through his anger. "Said you told her what happened to Quinn wasn't an accident. Said you thought it was murder. Now why would you say that?" He tries to wriggle free, gasping. "Tell me why, goddammit! Why would you drag my little girl into this?"

Elena's thoughts are yanked back to the warning Cal Pierce gave her this morning. He was right. She shouldn't have trusted any of them. And as for Nicola Bianco, who she has no doubt is the "actress" Tom's referring to, that was lightning quick. What did she do, wake up this morning, fresh-faced, and think, *Gee, I'll go track down the dad of the deceased teenager Elena told me about twelve hours ago*? It's true that Elena shouldn't have polished up Quinn's death like it was in-person clickbait, but what a weird thing for Nicola to do. Like, what the actual fuck?

There are a few patrons in the coffee shop now, and each of them—every single one—is glaring at her. She can feel their gazes like shards of glass in her back.

"Leave her alone." It's Joey who says it, and Elena wants to tell her it's fine, she can handle it, because she doesn't need Joey to stand up for her, not after she did this to herself. She can blame Nicola all she wants, but this was her. *What is wrong with you, Elena?* she thinks.

But Tom Winter is not done. He turns to Joey now, inches from her face, spitting rage. "And you. I saw your car leaving my house. Yeah, that's right. I saw you. The knife you left on the counter... What was that, a warning? And her sweatshirt. Her beautiful sweatshirt. What the hell did you do to it?" It's a statement, not a question. "I told that lady cop. I told her you broke in, that you messed with my baby's stuff. You'll go to prison for breaking into my house. You'll go to hell. What is wrong with you? You were supposed to be her friends. It's not right. It's not right what you did." With each word, his passion deflates slowly, giving way to sorrow. Finally, exhaustion seems to strong-arm his anger altogether, and he begins to shake. "Why, goddammit? Why did you touch her stuff?"

Elena sees him crumble, noticing how slender he is, how his bones look like they would crack under the slightest pressure, and how he stands with a stoop, as if in constant pain. She watches him as he loses control of himself and slides to the floor. She is horrified that she has caused this, that she wrecked a man still consumed by grief. He is angry, but this does not seem like a man who killed his own daughter.

She becomes aware that everyone in the coffee shop is still staring at her—at Joey and Sophie too—but mostly her. And she knows why. She has been home for two days and already she's kicked a hornet's nest. At her feet, Tom Winter brings skeletal fingers up to his face and sobs.

27
SOPHIE

They sit, now, in the storage closet at the back of the coffee shop. It's cramped in here, and it smells like coffee beans, a smell Sophie would normally like, but it's too potent. Half-open boxes of paper cups and napkins line the walls. She takes a seat on one of the boxes, and a mop clatters onto her knees.

Joey rounds on Elena and whispers aggressively. "What was that? Did you tell Nicola Bianco that Quinn was murdered?"

Elena doesn't back away. She only stands taller. "Yes," she says, not betraying any emotion.

It feels like a punch. "Why would you do that?" Sophie asks.

A moment of something passes over Elena's face, but she prepares her defenses fast. "I don't know. It just came out. I guess it was on my mind."

"*You guess it was on your mind?* Elena, you can stop pretending. We know why you're here. You think you're hiding it well, but it's so obvious that you're not here because you care about Quinn. You're here for the movie, for your career."

Elena laughs abruptly and tosses two hands into the air. "You caught me. I am background in the film. And yes, maybe I want to network with some people in the industry while they are, frankly, sitting ducks in this little fucking town. And maybe that led me to say something out of turn. But honestly, who gives a shit? I'm here now, and I saw the same sweatshirt yesterday that you did, and I can't get it out of my head. Whether I came because of Quinn is irrelevant. I'm pretty sure, at this point, it's the staying that matters."

"Enough," Sophie says. She needs to cool them both down before this goes too far. "All that matters now is finding out who did that to our friend."

They both breathe heavily, still facing off. Joey hasn't dropped her pissed-off face, but she has slackened her grip on the door handle.

Sophie says, "Listen, Tom said he told *the lady cop* that you broke into his house. Is the lady cop Marissa? What do you think he told her?"

Elena shrugs. Joey makes a "hmm" sound.

"I've been thinking," Sophie goes on. "Tom did drink a lot, and yes, the state of his house yesterday was…ick. But he was never a mean man—current behavior aside. Plus, Barbara said Quinn was spending a lot of time with him in those last few weeks. They were close, or as close as they could be. Maybe it's just me, but it just doesn't feel right. I know he was pissed off at Elena, but he was also sobbing. I don't know. I just don't get murderer vibes from him."

"It could be an act," says Joey.

"Or guilt," adds Elena.

They drop into a thoughtful silence, and Sophie is at least glad the tension is at a simmer. "Okay, listen," she says, finally ready to change the subject entirely. "I need to show you both something."

They turn toward her, and she realizes she's sweating. She reaches into her bag and plucks out the journal. She sets it on her lap. The watermelon-pink sticky note sits dead center on the cover. *Read me.*

"What is this?" Joey asks. She leans in closer. Elena leans in too.

Sophie exhales. "I found it in my closet at my dad's house." She opens the journal's cover. The spine crackles, and there is Quinn's name, written in her inky scrawl, the *i* with a little circle instead of a dot.

"Whoa," says Elena.

Joey runs a finger over Quinn's name, reverently.

Sophie gives her a second, then rifles quickly through the blank pages from back to front. The flutter disturbs the wisps of hair at her forehead. "The weird thing, though, is that there's nothing written in it. It's completely—"

But that's when she sees it. Something she didn't notice before.

On the edge of a page in the center of the journal. A faint but dark-colored thumbprint.

"What the hell is that?" Joey spins the journal toward her and hovers her own thumb over top. Almost the same size and shape. It even has print markings on it.

"Is it blood?" Elena is leaning down now, trying her finger over the print.

"I don't know," says Sophie. "The journal was blank before. I swear. This is the first time I'm seeing this." The fingerprint looks like it's similar in color to the old bloodstain on the sweatshirt, but it's impossible to know for sure. She opens the journal wider so they can see the entire page, hoping to find a clue as to what this exactly is. What they see steals their collective breath.

The words on the page are in blue ink, with loopy letters and circles over the *i*'s—the same as Quinn's name on the inside front cover. Only these words are new. They were not here the last time Sophie looked through this journal. There were no words on any pages besides Quinn's name. And she definitely, *definitely* didn't see any bloody fingerprints.

The words stare up at them in all caps, big and bold and underlined with deep pen marks that almost slice clear through the paper.

IT DIDN'T WORK.

Sophie's senses dull at the edges. She traces the letters' deep indents with her finger with a thudding in her ears. She flips to the previous page.

And she's not prepared for it.

One entire page, covered from top to bottom in one single repeated word.

Bloodspell.

Bloodspell, bloodspell, bloodspell, bloodspell, bloodspell…

She drops the journal as if burned.

Elena bends to pick up the journal and flips it open again.

"Guys, I know—*I know*—the last time I looked through this journal there were no words on any pages other than Quinn's name," Sophie manages. "How could I have missed this? There's no way." She's met with silence as her friends again examine the page.

Joey shakes her head. "Well, it's Quinn's, isn't it? So what if it has some kind of magic in it?" She closes the journal gently and holds it out to Sophie.

"Maybe, but what kind of magic?"

Elena says, "Could be similar to the book if the words truly did just appear. Maybe we should take it to the spell circle." She pauses to hold Sophie's eye for a long second. "And if there's no magic in that journal… Not to freak you out, but I think it means someone has been writing in it. Like, in real time."

Sophie goes icy. She's had it with her since the moment she found it. Except…she left it in the closet while she was sleeping. And she slept hard, didn't she? A landslide of exhaustion pulled her under—worrying about Quinn, about Leah, and about her dad. She didn't even dream. Could someone have snuck into her room and written in it while she was asleep? Someone who knows something about Quinn? The idea makes the blood rush from her head to her feet.

"Bloodspell," says Joey. "That was the same word carved into the deck at Quinn's. What do you think it means?"

Elena plays with a strand of her hair. "The way it's written on this page a hundred times, over and over and over again, it's like someone possessed wrote it."

Joey has her hand on the doorknob again, all business. "I think we should split up for a bit. I'm going to go to River's house and make sure the book's not there. Elena, you can go to Barbara's and check Quinn's room for the book. Maybe it's hidden there somewhere. Sophie, see if you can figure out what the deal is with the journal."

"Sir, yes sir," says Elena with a salute.

Sophie's mind is a vacuum, sucking up any logical thought. *I need to talk to my dad*, is all she can manage to think before they're all out the door and heading in different directions.

28

JOEY

Joey stands outside River's door, hesitating. It's just past midday, which means he's most likely out on backcountry patrol or clearing more local trails for summer hiking.

Either way, he's not here.

Doubt roots her to the front step. Does she really want to do this? *Yes*, she concludes. She's just checking a box. She knows the book is not here. She's been here enough times to know that. She would have seen it. But she needs to bring back this conclusive information to Elena and Sophie. And for some inexplicable reason, she needs to check. Just to know for certain.

To the right of the front door is a woodpile. She wiggles a small paving stone next to it and is rewarded with a glinting spare key. She hesitates again but snatches it up before she overthinks it. She jams the key into the lock harder than she intends to. It gives with a click, and she's inside. Walter immediately bounds toward her, his tail sweeping the floor in excitement. She bends down to greet him and makes her way to the kitchen.

She holds out a piece of jerky, and he takes it with careful teeth.

"Don't tell on me," she says before he trots to the other room. She stands and examines the empty kitchen. There's an old coffee cup on the counter with black sludge at the bottom, but otherwise, it's tidy. Mountainscape hand towels hang neatly on the oven, and a few pictures hang by magnets on the fridge door. School photos of his niece and nephew, who live in Montana. Walter leaping off a rickety dock into a lake. Then she sees her own face looking back at her. She's smiling in the picture, her hands pulling at the straps on her hiking pack, Rocky Mountain juniper trees behind her.

There's only one more picture on the fridge, and she's in that one too. It's a group shot from when they were in high school. Quinn is there and so are Elena, Sophie, Marissa, Tanner, and a handful of others. They're at a party at Tanner's house and look caught in the act. River wears a wry smile. Joey stands next to him, looking so young. He told her once that she's the reason he loves this one, but she doesn't like looking at it. It was right before everything fell apart.

When she makes her way to the living room, she's surprised she's never noticed that his smell is everywhere. She checks all the nooks around the fireplace where other books live. She checks the hall closet, rummages through the junk drawer, and briefly glances in the dining room where a Scandinavian-style wooden table sits bare beneath an industrial light fixture. Eventually, she makes her way upstairs.

In his room, the bed is made, and there is a bookmarked Muhammad Ali biography on the bedside table. There are other little touches too—an Edison-bulb industrial lamp, a stack of national parks coffee table books, vintage whiskey bottles lined up by year. Hiking boots. The comforter has his smell. Shampoo. Campfire. She searches his closet, his underwear drawer, and under the bed.

She only saw the inside of his childhood bedroom once as a teenager, and she has done everything she can to keep that memory under lock and key. Now, she lets it in just for a second—the all-black walls, the snowboarding posters, his vinyl collection, the window overlooking the backyard, and the trees beyond. The records are still here, but that seems to be all that remains of his youth. The room is home to a Peloton and some weights. No books. She flips the house key over and over in her hand.

In the office, there is a metal desk with a dark wood top and a leather swivel chair in the center. The desk is backed by bookshelves, which are mostly empty, except for a few trinkets. A fancy pen still in the box, Pokémon cards for his nephew, a pocket-sized multitool, and loose change. She's starting to relax, grateful that she hasn't found the book here. She doesn't want River to have it. She doesn't want Quinn to have given it to him.

She's about to leave the room when she sees something to her right. A small door next to the bookcase stands two feet tall. A storage space or something. She's never registered it before. The tiny door sticks as she tries to open it, like it's been covered in a fresh coat of paint. Inside is a hollow, dark crawl space. She scans the inside with her phone's flashlight. Dust, dog hair, a spider web. No book.

But there is something. She holds the light still.

In the back corner is a full-grown buck antler. Sixteen, seventeen inches maybe, with five curved tines. It looks like a hand with bony webbed fingers cupping the air and glows ghostly white in the beam of her flashlight. She's not an expert, but there seems to be dark, dried blood on it. Her eye is drawn to a flash of neon toward the base of the antler.

A pink sticky note.

She leans in to read it and drops the phone in shock. With unsteady hands, she pulls it into the daylight, letting it rest on her lap.

The words on the note are written in bold black marker.

Ask Joey about bloodspell.

Her head is pounding. She can't track her thoughts, even as she recognizes the word, *bloodspell*. It was carved into the wood under Quinn's deck two days ago.

"Joey?"

She whips around at the sound, a fork of tines jabbing her in the middle.

River stands at the door to the office with one hand frozen on the brim of his hat.

"I didn't hear you come in," she says. She sounds cool, but she's boiling inside.

He sets his hat on the desk and walks toward her, peering down at her from the other side of the desk. "Decorating?"

She lets a nervous laugh escape and then realizes she's clutching the antler like a weapon. Her knuckles are growing white. He reaches out a hand, and she doesn't know if he's reaching to help her up or take it away from her. "What is that?" he asks.

"Not sure," she says, standing on her own.

He examines it. "Is it real? Looks real."

She shrugs. She has no idea why this has been stuffed into his crawl space with her name stuck to it or why there seems to be old blood on it.

He examines it without revealing any signs of recognition. What is she hoping to see? Nothing tells her he knows what this is or what it means. She pulls the note free, sticks it to her palm, and holds it out.

It takes him a second to process what he's seeing. "Ask Joey about bloodspell," he reads. Then he frowns. "What am I looking at?"

She closes her fist around the note, then shoves it into her pocket. "I found it in there." She points to the gaping crawl space door.

"Huh," he says, running a hand over his beard. Joey can hear the rough bristles scratch his fingers. "I haven't been in there since the renovation."

"Why is my name on this?"

"I honestly have no idea. What did it say again? Ask you about what?"

Joey hesitates, then pulls the pink sticky note out of her pocket again. The wrinkles run like forked lightning through the words, giving them even more power than before.

He looks at it and then at her. His eyelashes are long, which has always given her the impression that kindness has been baked into him, genetically speaking. But she doesn't see that kindness now. A darkness moves across his face, subtly, but enough to set her on edge. "You found this in the crawl space?" he asks.

"What is bloodspell?"

"It says to ask you."

"Did you hunt this deer?" She points to the dried bloodstain smeared over half of it.

He laughs, then stares as it seems to dawn on him that it wasn't a joke. "No. You know I don't hunt."

"Why is there blood on it?"

Walter prances in with a stuffed duck between his teeth, thrashing it around and pushing it against River's thigh. Distracted, River runs a hand over the dog's head. "Joey, I have no idea. I've never seen this before in my life."

Walter spots the antler and drops the duck. He sniffs it and sits at Joey's feet. She can't tell if he thinks it's a treat for him or if he recognizes the smell.

"What are you doing home?" she asks. "Shouldn't you be working?"

"Early start today, so I finished at three." He rests one hand on the desk and rubs at his eyes with the other hand. "Why are you here if you thought I would still be working?"

She only pauses for a second before reaching for the lie. "I thought I left my bra here. The red one with the..." She points to the middle of her chest where a tiny bow would be.

"Okay, and did you find it?"

"No." She eyes the door behind him.

"Maybe it's my dad's from the last time he was here?" he says, gesturing to the antler. "He doesn't hunt either, but I don't know, maybe he's storing it for someone. I have no clue." He holds her gaze now.

Joey takes a step to the other side of the desk. He reaches out a hand to stop her. Slowly, he wraps the other around a point of the antler. She holds her breath for a few seconds, aware that he's standing between her and the door. He seems taller than normal somehow, and there's something in his eyes that she's never seen before.

"I have to go," she says.

There's a beat of silence, and his eyes flick down to the antler, then back up again. He's still blocking her path to the door. "Don't," he says.

Joey quickly calculates how she can sidestep him and get to the door as quickly as possible. "I'm meeting Elena and Sophie."

River's eyes seem to darken, and his expression suddenly pulses with something strange, an emotion Joey can't read.

He leans in slowly then, so close to her ear that she can feel his breath. "Stay," he says, with a voice that's low and hard and floods Joey's insides with frigid water.

She closes her eyes, fear unexpectedly moving through her. Everything has slowed around her now, everything except her heartbeat. "River," she manages, and it comes out as a whisper.

There's a pause, a moment that she thinks he's not going to let her pass.

But then he stands up straight and nods. Joey releases her grip on the antler. Wordlessly, he slides it away from her and steps to the side.

She feels his eyes on her as she hurries down the stairs and fumbles with her shoes. Then, to Walter's obvious disappointment, she backs out of the front door, slamming it a little too hard.

29
ELENA

Elena opens the email from the casting agency as she walks back to Barbara's. Her call time is tomorrow at seven. A small leap of excitement breaks through her grim thoughts about Quinn. This is it. She may be just background, but she intends to speak to Phillip Granger, or track down a casting director, and send along her demo reel. She'll do what it takes to make sure she's on *someone's* radar for future projects.

"Elena?" The deep voice comes from closely behind her. She jumps and spins around. A tall man stands less than a foot away, up on the curb. She wonders how long he's been there. She didn't hear him at all. "I thought that was you," he says.

It takes her a minute to place the shape of his face, the color of his eyes. He has a beard now. "Oh my god," she says, recognition dawning. "River Hunstad."

He shoves his hands into his pockets. "Heard you were in town."

"You still live here?"

"Still in my parents' house actually. Bought it from them when they moved to Montana to be with my sister and the baby." He hesitates. "That's a lie," he says, forking a hand through his hair. "They gave it to me. Technically, I paid out their taxes for the year, but they had no more mortgage to pay down, so zero dollars on the actual house." He lets an awkward laugh escape. She feels it too, and this is exactly why Elena hates reunions. "But hey, if you're not busy, you should come by for a drink," he says. "You can meet Walter."

"Who's Walter?"

"My grandfather," says River. "It's been a few years since he passed, but I've been able to preserve the body pretty well."

Elena's heart skips.

River's face breaks, and he lets out a small laugh. "Sorry, that was my terrible attempt at humor. Walter is my dog. Very much alive. So, yes? Time for a drink? I have wine. I have soda. I think I have some tortilla chips."

"Oh, now? I can't. I have to go back and then I'm meeting Sophie and Joey."

River digs his hands into his pockets, though it's not cold. "Ah, she did say you guys were getting together." He hesitates. It looks like he wants to say something else but seems to change his mind.

"Nice to see you," she says, waving and stepping away, realizing now how close she actually was to him. She could smell his shampoo.

"Let's get together while you're in town and catch up," he says and lifts a hand. He's walking backward, but his eyes are pinned on her. He watches her longer than seems necessary, something indecipherable on his face. A centipede of unease crawls over her skin, but she shakes it off and turns the corner toward Barbara's.

Quinn's room is almost exactly how Elena remembers it.

She didn't let herself come in here before, partly because she wasn't sure Barbara would want her to, but mostly because *she* didn't want to. The same black and blue tie-dye comforter covers a full-sized bed. Her dresser stands to the left of the door, decorated with a few pictures. One depicts Quinn as a young kid leaning into both her parents. Another is of the four of them, faces pressed together so close that it looks like they're sharing one long continuous smile. Elena turns away. She opens the closet where Quinn used to shove bags, coats, dresses, and anything else that didn't fit in her drawers. It's no longer bursting but is instead a neat approximation of what it used to be. A denim jacket, a long flowy skirt, a couple of hippie shirts, and not much else. She sniffs, imagining she'll get a whiff of something that will set her memory alight, but instead she only gets traces of cinnamon and vanilla, and it makes her sad because she knows these are the scents of Barbara's house. The smell of Quinn, whatever Quinn *did* smell like—because, truthfully, she can't remember—is long gone.

There is no sign of the book, so when she's done looking, she closes the door gently and heads into the guest room across the hall.

"Hey," says Gael without looking up. He lies on his stomach across the bed with knees bent and feet crossed in the air. His face is inches from the laptop screen, examining some small detail.

"Remind me," she says, setting her bag down on the floor. "Why did you want to come here so badly? Don't you wish you were at home with your friends getting into trouble? It's summer vacation."

He looks up and blinks at her like he's not sure she knows him at all. "No way," he says. "It's cool here."

"It's not," she says, offhandedly searching for her phone in her bag.

There's a long pause, and she can feel his eyes on her. She looks up to see him staring at her, serious. "Can you come look at this? I found something weird."

He waves her over, and she flops down next to him on the bed. "What are we looking at?"

On the screen, it's a picture of Elena, Joey, and Sophie, at a distance, on Front Street. They're standing close together and talking. Elena has her hands on her hips, Joey's arms are crossed, and Sophie is reaching out toward them both, possibly for a hug. They're cocooned by old brick and peeling-paint buildings on either side and standing in the long imposing shadow of one of the Three Elks peaks.

"It's a great shot," she says. He has captured the discomfort of their first meeting in fifteen years so perfectly that she feels herself cringe inwardly at the scene.

"Look," he says, and he brings a finger to the screen. He points at a person even farther in the distance, standing half-hidden by a parked pickup. It looks like a man, but that's about all she can tell. Most of his face and body are obscured by the truck. She can't even see what color hair he has.

"Okay, what's weird about that? It's just a person on the street."

He clicks out of the photo and then scrolls for a second before clicking another thumbnail. An enlarged image bursts onto the screen. The first thing that strikes Elena about it is the colors. It's bleak and dim—the sickly yellow and black of a night shot. It's taken from a second-floor vantage point, from this very room, she realizes with a start. Gael is partially reflected in the window, perhaps on purpose, his camera raised to his face. Beneath his reflection, the window is open a few inches, and there's a view of the light at the end of the street. The streetlight illuminates the road…and something else. Elena leans in closer, her stomach flipping. It's a man. Standing beneath the streetlight, facing the house. Again, it's impossible to see his face—he's just a dark shadow—but there is clearly someone there.

"I think it's the same guy," Gael says, bringing up the two images side-by-side and zooming in until the pixelation obscures anything worth identifying.

"When did you take this one?"

"The other night. You were out, and I thought the reflection was cool. I didn't see a person there until I looked at this picture today. I swear."

She remembers the chill that followed her that night. She'd felt the tingle of someone's eyes on her when she went out to the car looking for her phone charger, and when she turned toward the streetlight, she saw a figure. Or, at least she thought she had, but she wasn't entirely sure. Now, the certainty is like two strangling hands.

Her instincts were right. Someone is watching her.

30
SOPHIE

Otto is waiting for Sophie as she walks in the door, eager, like she's just getting back from her first day at school.

"What's up, Dad?" She slips off her shoes and hangs her bag on the rack, careful not to look too closely but certain the journal is burning a hole straight through the faux leather.

"Oh, nothing. How was your day?" He has a can of beans in his hand that he's shaking back and forth mindlessly. She can't maneuver past without bumping into him.

"Good," she lies, taking the can from him. She guesses he hasn't heard about Tom Winter's outburst. He will soon, she knows. "Pinto beans?"

"Chili," he says brightly. He looks at her with expectation. "You hungry?" She nods, and he strides away, mindlessly taking the beans back and turning the can over and over.

But she's not hungry. She's thinks of the slimy blueberry muffin she ate at Aspect, which is still churning in her stomach. She slides the journal out of her bag and clutches it to her chest.

In the kitchen, her dad stands with his back to her. His jeans are a little loose around the waist, though he has tucked in his shirt in an attempt at tidiness. He's fussing with a big pot and spices and cans of tomatoes, moving quickly and clumsily, which seems just slightly counter to his usual routine confidence. It's been so long since he's cooked chili for her in his kitchen. He reaches for the can opener and knocks it off the counter. When he bends down, she notices that his hairline is clumped and damp.

"Dad?" She lowers herself into a chair, setting the journal beside her.

He doesn't respond, just cuts open a package of bacon, his secret ingredient, and nicks his finger in the process.

Sophie jumps up. Droplets of blood drip onto the floor beneath where he holds his finger out to her. He looks helpless.

"Band-Aids?" she says.

"Ah, sorry," he says. "Look at me. Band-Aids, yes. In the cabinet under the sink in your bathroom. Behind the shaving cream."

She finds one inside a first aid kit that she recognizes from decades ago. Shockingly, it still has stickiness to it, and she peels off the paper and wraps it around his finger. There's a moment, while she's making sure the cut is fully covered, that he stares at her for a beat too long. She can feel him looking, and she peers up at him. Before she can say anything, he looks away and turns back to the stove, and in another minute, the air is thick with the smell of bacon.

"Dad," she says, but he can't hear her over the sound of the fan, which is sucking up the pan's smoke. Or he acts like he doesn't hear her. "Dad!" she shouts, and this time he has no choice. He puts up his bandaged finger to tell her, *"One sec."* He places a splatter screen on top of the bacon and turns the fan to low. Then, with an air of resignation, he sits across from her.

"What's up, Sophie-beans?" He doesn't look her in the eye.

With what feels like a great effort, she pulls the journal from her chair and plonks it on the table, taking care to peel the sticky note off and shove it in her pocket.

He scratches his head. Then looks up in confusion.

"I found it in my room." She speaks slowly, testing him, hoping he'll…hoping he'll…what? Is she hoping he knows why it was there? Hoping he's the one who put it there? That he's the one who has been writing in it at night? She hasn't let herself think yet about what that would mean, though she can't lie to herself and say the possibility hasn't occurred to her. She can't decide if it's better than the alternative, which is the idea that someone came into the house while they slept. Her foot bounces under the table.

"Huh," he says.

Sophie leans forward, opens the front cover, and points. "It belongs to Quinn Winter."

He narrows his eyes at the book but does not speak.

"Why, why, *why* is this in your house?"

He swallows, picks at his teeth.

Sophie lowers her voice, anxiety crawling its tiny spider feet up her spine. "Why are you acting weird? What is going on?"

There's a significant pause. He still doesn't look at her. Why isn't he looking at her?

Eventually, he closes his eyes and lets out a helicopter breath through tight lips. "The clothes," he says. "I wanted to tell you. I knew I should have told you. You're a smart girl. I knew you'd figure it out eventually, that I knew, but I was sure you'd think it was strange, and so I got scared and didn't say anything. Which, by the way, was much easier when you never came around. I didn't have to hide anything from you. But then…"

Sophie doesn't move. She just watches him, waiting for him to finish.

"Oh, it doesn't matter, does it? I know the clothes in your closet aren't yours. They're… They belong to someone else."

"Oh," she says, not sure what she thought he was going to say but not expecting this. "Whose are they?"

He closes his eyes again. "Barbara's."

She screws up her face. "What? Why do you have Barbara's clothes?"

He buries his face in his hands. "I understand if you're mad at me."

She doesn't know what she's supposed to be mad about. She did not imagine the conversation going this way, and she's honestly relieved. She'd thought they were about to cross into dark territory, and thankfully, they did not. But then it dawns on her. "Wait, are you dating Barbara?"

He winces but, hearing the lightness in her tone, uncovers his face. His sheepish expression is all she needs to know. Calm floods her now. It's such an innocent explanation that she inwardly berates herself for letting her mind spiral.

"Why did you think I'd be mad about that?"

"I don't know. You're always saying how proud you are that I'm a rock star single dad who played two roles for you. I got the impression I was some superhero to you, like you liked me better alone. I didn't want to dive headfirst off that pedestal. And also..." He cracks his knuckles. "I wasn't sure if you'd be upset on a different level, because it's Barbara."

"Why would that bother me?"

"Well." He leans back and scratches at his hair as if he's not sure how to put it. "I know how hard it was when Quinn died. I didn't want to stir up any undue pain for you by telling you I was seeing her mother."

Sophie reaches out to take one of his hands. "That's crazy. I would never, ever begrudge you for choosing to be happy. I'm thrilled for you, got it?"

His eyes are wet. It's strange having a conversation that includes both her dad and Quinn, but she's grateful they're not discussing something else, something she feared but couldn't quite name. "Did you put off asking Barbara out all these years because you thought I'd disapprove?"

He shakes his head. "No, no. Barbara and I connected a few years ago, after she sold the coffee shop and we got a little pickleball group together."

"A few years ago?"

He grimaces. "You were busy with your own stuff. Talia, your wedding. I didn't want to piss on your fireworks. Besides, it took me a while to come around. I didn't recognize her intentions until..." He coughs. "Well, anyway, she told me she liked me, and I, well I think she's a great woman. Not sure what exactly she sees in me..." He makes the kind of ridiculous, screwed-up face that would make Leah giggle, and Sophie knows it's his way to diffuse the awkwardness.

"Me neither," she says, making him laugh brightly.

Just like that, his anxiety has evaporated, and he turns his attention to the journal on the table between them. "Still no clue about this, though," he says. "Maybe Barbara brought it over once and forgot to take it home with her. I know she misses Quinn something fierce, and it wouldn't be unlike her to keep a little token of Quinn's with her. Why don't you ask her? You can tell her you know about us. I'm sure she'll be ecstatic I finally fessed up."

Sophie helps him with the chili and manages to keep down a few bites. Part of her is, of course, relieved that he doesn't know where the journal came from. And part of her still wonders about it. It makes sense that Barbara could have left it in the closet. But then, is Barbara the one writing in it overnight? That would be so strange, but maybe there's a good reason. Or is it actually infused with some kind of magic?

Finding out either way feels crucial. She'll bring it to the spell circle tomorrow, just in case, and then she needs to ask Barbara.

31

JOEY

Joey yanks her hair into a tight ponytail. The night sky is swollen with clouds, exaggerating the darkness. She clicks on her headlamp and runs beneath the streetlights to start, then dips onto a darkened trail where she can see nothing outside a five-foot radius. Her legs burn with the effort as the terrain begins to slope upward, and she pushes harder, over rocks and branches and winding through trees and along the arterial path.

The run is working. Only a few brave thoughts dare enter her mind. Her body is practically ablaze. Endless stamina comes from somewhere down deep. Her lungs press against her ribs, taking up all the space inside her that exists. The darkness around her is a thrill.

Thirty minutes later she is at a lookout point. She stretches her hands above her head and drinks in the sky. It's so close, she feels like she could reach out and grab clouds. They pillow and overlap above her, deeper in the night's shadow the higher up they get. She tugs an electrolyte shot out of her waistband and chugs it. It's sticky sweet. There's an energy bar in there too, and she unwraps it and sits on a rock. Its jagged points stab her in the pelvic bones.

This is when the thoughts come. She has to let them. She has no choice now. And they go right for the soft spots, as she knew they would. First up is River and the heart-hammering idea that he could have been lying to her for their entire adult lives. He's careful and warm and sometimes obstinate, but she didn't think—she had *no idea*—he could be a liar. Until she found the antler in his closet, labeled with her name on it and that word again, *bloodspell*, just like underneath the deck, just like Quinn's journal. How could River not have known such a haunting thing existed in his house? She feels a roll of nausea deep within her. She's just realized that the antler she found would have been an effective way to stab someone, say, in the abdomen several times. It was sharp enough and was covered in what looked like old dried blood. She takes a sip of water and spits it into the dirt.

But it couldn't be River. Joey spoke with lots of people in the year after Quinn died, and of them all, River's was the only alibi that she knew for certain to be rock-solid. She hadn't had to ask him where he was the night Quinn was killed because she knew exactly where he was.

From four in the afternoon until eleven that night, he was with her.

He was with Joey.

She no longer wants to sit, so she heaves herself up and makes her way to the edge. The mountains are powerful shadows pressed against the dark sky. She has a view of the town from here too. It's illuminated by yellow streetlights. She traces the streets she knows by closing one eye and trailing a finger through the air. Immediately, she finds Aspect Coffee and the inn. The Hollywood dirt they poured along Front Street looks odd from up here. It makes the town look plasticky, Disney-ish, and surreal. She keeps tracing. There's the house where she grew up, and the house she lives in now. There's Quinn's and Sophie's and Elena's. On the other side is River's. It's all there, her whole life, her entire thirty-two years in miniature. With her finger, she traces Elk Horn Road out of town to the approximate location of Tom Winter's. She can't see the house, but she wonders if Tom is there, passed out on the lumpy floor mattress or praying before his Quinn shrine. She thinks again of the sweatshirt. Should they have taken it to the police? Maybe they could have found out whose blood it was. But then Elena's voice is in her head, dismissing this idea. It was the cops who decided not to mention the seven stab wounds in the police report. Another wave of nausea. Another sip of water. Are they digging into some kind of police cover-up?

A cold wind bites at her bare ankles. Quinn was always her dad's biggest advocate. *"He doesn't want to go,"* she told Joey once about rehab, while they sat hip-to-hip in the cafeteria, sharing a bag of vending machine pretzels. Joey had the acute awareness back then that Quinn didn't talk about her dad to everyone. She was compassionate, empathetic to a fault, but she was also a teenager. The day Tom rolled his truck into a streetlight and puked onto the sidewalk was one that Joey would never forget. She wonders if that day, the public humiliation of it, was the turning point. It was right around then, Joey realizes, that Quinn started acting strangely. The lies began. The sneaking out. The avoidance. They were all close—Joey and Elena and Sophie—but Quinn was like a mother duck. She kept them all together, and after she dipped out of their friendship, they never unified. If they had, they would have had enough awareness to convince her to come back to them or force her to tell them what was going on. But they didn't. And then Joey made a choice on Quinn's last day that would haunt her forever. To make a stupid, insignificant point, as if their friendship meant nothing to her at all, she chose a boy. She chose River over Quinn.

Joey is starting to feel cold. Spent. She wishes she didn't have to run back down. Waiting for her down there is a decision she doesn't want to make, a conversation she doesn't want to have.

Quinn died that day, and Joey never got the telling off she deserved. There has been no punishment for her but the slow decay of guilt. And guilt is a pillar holding up her grief. It's why she will never be able to let go of Quinn's death.

A sudden sound from behind her shakes her out of her reverie. The rev of an engine. A dirt bike, maybe, from somewhere down the mountain, but still close. It's after eight. Usually, she has the whole mountain to herself at this time of night. She sits perfectly still, listening as it seems to approach slowly. All her muscles tense. She prepares to stand, to run. And then, just as she's about to launch to her feet, the sound fades and eventually dissolves into the natural sounds of night.

She waits a minute, listening to the wind whistle through the trees. Then, she wets her lips and rubs at her face and runs back down the mountain.

32
ELENA

Elena shows up twenty minutes early, just to be as professional as possible. As early as it is, Gael insisted on walking her to set before going to explore. He waves his phone at her when she yells at him to keep it handy, and she feels a flicker of deep unease thinking of him on his own, especially after the creepy photos he seemed to be collecting. But theirs is the kind of relationship where her son doesn't so much ask for permission as just lets her know what he's doing.

Before he disappears down the road and Elena's dark thoughts can consume her, a production assistant finds her and sits her in a chair, where she is told to wait. Her back is beginning to ache when, exactly three hours later, she is abruptly called, handed a costume, then yanked and jostled into place. Then, she waits again until the actors get set. She idles in her position on the dirt road with a handful of other over-enthusiastic extras, including Ken the bartender and an older woman who Elena thinks she recognizes as Kathy, the owner of the Whisper Ridge Inn. There have been moments when she's felt like the whole thing is a little beneath her—like when Ken couldn't do a surprised face without making a loud gasping noise, and she had to stand in position while they decided whether to boot him out of the scene, do a nineteenth take, or just edit out the sound. For her part, she's made sure to be as easy to work with as anyone they've ever seen. The rub is that there hasn't been a single moment of downtime to get Phillip Granger's attention, to bend his ear in this professional setting like she had planned to.

Finally, though, they break for lunch. She pulls her phone out of her bag, which she stashed behind the catering table. She's still wearing the old-timey costume—a floor-length dress with a dirt-smudged apron. Her hair is knotted in a tight bun. Walking as confidently as she can toward video village, she narrowly misses horse manure that has yet to be cleaned up. The guilty horse is tethered to a parking meter, looking like he'd rather be anywhere else but here.

"You and me both, buddy," she says.

When she spots Phil, she calls his name and gives him a small wave, even though he's only a few yards away. He turns, and so does one of the production assistants, who is showing him something on an iPad. He wears a black hat, like he's Ron Howard, and even at this distance, she can see a crumble of food caught in the corner where beard meets mouth. Her wave is friendly, but inside, she's mustering as much brass as she can manage. She is going to get what she wants if it kills her. Then, he looks away from her, and her stomach drops. That absolute ass. He's pretending he doesn't see her.

She turns away, ready to lose her cool, but she catches a glimpse of someone leaving the corner store in the distance. She almost trips over a cord as she moves to get a better look. The man's graying hair and glasses are unfamiliar, but his ski-slope nose and broad shoulders are unmistakable, even this far away. She stands there for what feels like hours but can only be seconds, just watching him walk across the street. He doesn't see her, doesn't seem to care about the film at all. He just walks and walks.

"Elena."

She turns abruptly at her name. Cal Pierce is striding toward her. Not sure if what she's just seen is real or imagined, she glances back at the street. Mark Collingswood is gone. Before she left, before Quinn died, before any of it, Mark Collingswood changed her life. He's the reason her kid exists. He's the reason she has never come back to this town. All this time she's been terrified—but of what? Looking at the stretch of street where he just was, she honestly has no idea what she was so afraid of. Because, strangely, in this moment, she finds she does not give a single fuck about him.

"Everything okay?" Cal is beside her now. She turns to look at him, snapping to attention and pushing Collingswood out of her mind, possibly for the last time. Cal's hair is slicked back in a way that should be corny but somehow isn't. He is in costume, wearing scruffy boots and suspenders.

"All good. You?"

"Actually, I wanted to ask you something." He looks wary, like he's not sure he wants to reveal what it is, but then he says, "There is a walk-on part available. I don't know if you'd be interested, but one of our bit actors got some kind of insect bite yesterday, and they're having trouble getting the swelling down. I think they're taking her to the hospital. Anyway, Phil and I are assuming she's not going to make it back, and we're scheduled to shoot her scene tomorrow. It's hardly anything at all, just three lines. And you'll only have one day to prepare, which I realize is highly unprofessional, but we do need someone. You said you have acting experience, which is why I thought of you. It's a long shot that you would even want to, but if you do..." He's watching her face, which she is working hard to keep as neutral as possible. "Are you at all interested? If not, we can work with production to—"

"Interested," she says quickly. Inside, her heart has started to beat hard against her ribs, but she does not want to betray any emotion.

Two men with headsets walk behind Cal talking about continuity errors, and he lets them pass before he speaks again. "Full disclosure." He leans in, fidgeting. "There is no bug bite. She quit. Harassment."

"Oh, wow," Elena says, genuinely surprised. Her eyes flick to Phil in his smug director's hat.

"Just want you to know what you're getting into," Cal says with meaning. "Anyway, I assume you have a reel?"

"I do." She fumbles with her phone. "I can send it to you."

"Good. I want to go through the proper channels."

To the right, Elena spots Nicola Bianco approaching. She wears a faded dress, similar in shape to Elena's, but Nicola looks striking. Her hair, like Elena's, is pulled into a severe bun, but wisps of it have been teased out, a sign that her character is in some distress. For some reason, this small detail makes Elena flush with anger. Nicola's character may be a victim, but Nicola is certainly not.

"Hey," says Cal. She offers a cheek, and he gives her a peck. Toward Elena, she flashes a lightning-quick smile.

The way she is hanging on Cal's arm—feigning feminine ineptitude while, in fact, she has been scheming behind the scenes—it's infuriating. Elena can't help the rise in temperature that suddenly overtakes her. "Why the fuck did you go to Tom Winter's house?"

Nicola blinks her doe eyes at Elena, then steals a look at Cal. He's looking at the ground, pushing around dirt with a toe.

"Why does it matter?" Nicola says defiantly.

"Because a man's child died. It was a long time ago, but grief is long. What kind of person does that?"

Nicola rolls her eyes, which comes across as almost comedic because of their size and beauty. Elena has the impression of a cartoon princess.

"I was just curious."

"Curious about what? What it's like to die? To lose someone you love?"

As Nicola's eyes move, Elena catches a seemingly involuntary bite of her lip. A nervous tic. But she doesn't look at Cal like Elena thinks she's going to. Instead, she goes quiet. Her gaze finds its way back to Elena, and there's a new, surprising intensity there, almost as if it holds a message, but it's impossible to interpret. Someone calls Nicola's name from the other side of the tent.

She unlocks her gaze from Elena's. "Come on," she says to Cal. "Save me from *him.*" She tugs at his arm the way a daughter might pull at her father.

Without wriggling free of Nicola, Cal turns to give Elena his attention one more time. "Send me your reel," he says. "I'll have the casting director reach out to your agent just so I'm not going completely rogue. I'll email you the pages and maybe some notes."

"Sounds good," says Elena, feeling buoyant, despite Nicola's presence. What she really wants to say is, *"Sounds fucking amazing."* And what she really wants to do is give Cal Pierce a big, wet kiss. But she won't. She definitely, definitely won't.

33

SOPHIE

Brunch.

The only thing close to brunch Sophie has had for eighteen months is cold pancakes peeled from her toddler's plate. They enter beneath a freshly printed sign that says *The Scrambled Egg*. She tries to think of what used to be in this building. The brick overlay above the door is familiar, but she can't remember.

She ran into Marissa at the coffee shop this morning, and because she was alone and she has no willpower, Sophie was strong-armed into an imminent brunch date. Sophie tried to wrangle Joey and Elena into it too, via the group chat, claiming it would be a chance to get information from Marissa, maybe the cop perspective, but Elena had to work. Joey, however, agreed to tag along and said she wanted to get a read on what Marissa's police chief dad knew about Quinn's case. Sophie was relieved.

She feels a little silly that she's brought her giant bag, which is actually a diaper bag, but it's passable as a purse, and she's really only brought it because she was planning to take it to the spell circle. She is still trying not to think too hard about the possibility that someone could be sneaking into her room while she sleeps. The idea makes her cold with dread. Last night she clutched the journal to her chest and woke at every sound. Even the absence of noise had her eyes peeling open, her half-asleep body involuntarily preparing for something terrible. At about four in the morning, she started to confuse panic about the journal with panic about Leah and ended up calling Talia, who—sanely—did not answer.

She spots Marissa in a booth, dressed in a maternity shirt buttoned all the way up to the neck. Sophie wishes she'd had a chance to remind Joey not to give any clues that they've seen the case file.

"So glad we did this," Marissa says after they've hugged. Sophie and Joey sit across from her. "It's been so long, Soph. What's new with you?"

Sophie pushes out a smile. "Not much. I have a daughter. Eighteen months."

"Oh my gosh," gushes Marissa. "I can't wait. But we're hoping for a boy." She runs her hands over her belly.

Sophie decides on a morning bun with a side of bacon and a tea. Marissa gets an egg white omelet. Joey just orders coffee.

"So, Marissa," Joey says as their drinks arrive. "I never asked you why you ended up a police officer."

Sophie's senses go on alert, and she hasn't even gotten her food yet. Joey is so blunt. It's hard to help her navigate conversations so they go smoothly.

But if Marissa senses there is an agenda behind Joey's question, she doesn't let on. "Well, my dad was police," she says, adding a little laugh that says, *"You should have known that, silly."*

"It's...in the blood, I guess. He worked Quinn's case, actually. You might remember."

"I do," says Joey. "Did he ever talk about it at home? Quinn's case?"

Sophie presses her knee into Joey's under the table. *Easy.*

"No." Marissa shakes her head. "He was a professional through and through. But the case was closed within a couple of days I think. It was pretty clear to everyone what happened. But you... That's right, you continued to *investigate* for, what, another several years?" She puts air quotes around the word *investigate*.

Sophie notices Joey scowl into her coffee mug.

"So, when are you due?" Sophie asks quickly. She wants to show Joey that Marissa is the sort of person you can't ask direct questions to. She needs to be buttered up. "Hopefully you'll get good maternity leave?" Sophie adds.

"Oh gosh, mid-October. My dad's birthday, actually. I'm so blessed that both of my parents are still around."

Sophie blanches. It could be just an offhand comment, but it's not, she knows. It's a dig because everyone in this town knows Sophie's mom left her at an early age, and she is sure everyone knows Joey's mom took her own life. Her attempt at buttering Marissa up was a waste of breath. This entire conversation is a waste of breath, and she wishes she had just said no.

Their breakfast plates arrive, and a gluey silence spreads. Marissa was always a rule follower, rigid and self-righteous. She once told the principal that Sophie's skirt was too tight, and the principal evidently agreed because Sophie was forced to change into a spare pair of slacks borrowed from a teacher. But most of Sophie's clothes were tight. It was the shape of her body that made them that way, not that she was buying them tight on purpose.

"That's what Tanner thinks, anyway," Marissa is saying to Joey when Sophie checks back into the conversation.

Distantly, she registers the name. "Tanner McGrath?"

"Mm-hm." Marissa stabs at her egg whites. Sophie watches the omelet jiggle unnaturally. She once heard that eggs are a complete protein, containing all ten essential amino acids. But not if you eliminate the yolk.

"You two still talk?" she asks, looking down at her bacon.

Marissa looks at Joey and then back to Sophie with an unreadable expression. Then she smiles. "Didn't you used to text with him?"

"That's not exactly how I would describe it," Sophie says. Tanner was a bully and a coward, an irredeemable person who made her hate herself for a very long time. That's how she would describe it. He even stole her grief—grief for her dead friend that she should have been allowed to work through purely and wholly but couldn't because he chose two weeks before her death to assault her. Sophie has spent too much time and money unpacking this with her therapist to go into it with Marissa Berg, so instead, she just says, "He used to pick on me a bit."

"And yet, you still fucked him," Marissa says bluntly and without pause, adding a small out-of-place smile.

Sophie almost chokes on her morning bun. "Excuse me?"

"I know you two slept together. He told me. He said you begged him to take your virginity, that you loved him, and he felt bad for you so he did it."

Sophie has an uncharacteristic urge to throw her hot tea in Marissa's face. She wants, suddenly, to stab her fork into her plump pregnant hand. And she honestly thinks she might do it until Joey stands abruptly. "Okay," she says. "I think we're done here."

"Quinn came to see him, you know."

Sophie looks up. Joey pauses with her fingers wrapped around the back of her chair.

"I think it was…two days before she died. I was at his house that night. In his room. Quinn came to his doorstep. When he got back upstairs, he was crying. Like, red-in-the-face sobs. He told me about how he slept with you out of pity and how Quinn made him feel guilty and wanted him to dump me to be with you. She was trying to play matchmaker apparently, but he just wanted to be with me."

Sophie feels goose bumps prickle beneath her clothes as she shares a look with Joey. She doesn't believe for one second that Quinn would have wanted her to be with Tanner. But the fact that she visited him at his house just days before her death means something. She's just not sure what.

"Anyway, that's all in the past," Marissa says coolly. "Back to present day." Slowly, she looks up at Joey, who is still standing, then she glares at Sophie again. "You do know the whole town knows what Elena said to her celebrity friends. That Quinn was murdered. Then, Tom Winter tells me you broke into his house. At first, I didn't believe him because, well...but then it dawned on me that I saw you that day, all of you, in the car heading down Elk Horn Road, toward his house." She lowers her voice to a whisper. "I don't know what you three are up to, but this town has its eye on you. And now, *I* have my eye on you."

Then, she pats her mouth with a napkin and smiles broadly. "Should we get the check?"

34

JOEY

Jesus, what happened to you two?" Elena slides a beer toward Joey and a margarita with a half-salted rim toward Sophie.

"Brunch with Marissa Berg," says Sophie, who is visibly flustered. Her hair is sticking out on one side of her head where she keeps running her fingers through it.

"Oh god, I forgot. How was it?"

The Strike is busy again, although the atmosphere is different than the last time they were here. The rowdy, excited film crew is now subdued, perhaps worn down by the monotony of getting a job done. It's dim and dull and perfect for the way Joey feels right now.

Sophie leans in, casting a confirming look at Joey. "She thinks we're up to something. I think she threatened us." Then she takes a long pull of her drink.

"I'm guessing you didn't find the book," Joey says to Elena.

Elena shakes her head and twists up her mouth. "It's not at Barbara's."

Joey hesitates. Then she steels herself. "Me neither. But I did find... something else."

They blink at her, rapt. "You didn't tell me that," complains Sophie.

Joey shrugs. She wanted them all to be together. She needed Elena's natural-born skepticism so she wouldn't write this off as nothing. Elena, she knows, will see the bald truth, no matter what it is.

"Just warning you," she says, "it's a little weird." Joey feels a gallop of anticipation inside her chest. "I found a deer antler in River's closet… covered in old blood."

"Oh," says Sophie.

Elena presses her palms against the table as if to push herself away, disgusted.

"And I found this stuck to it." Joey unfolds the small pink note and smooths it out on the table.

Sophie squirms in her chair while Elena reads aloud. "Ask Joey about bloodspell."

They all go silent. Joey wonders if her heartbeat is audible to them because it is a concert inside her own head.

"Okay, you're right. That is weird as hell," says Elena.

Joey folds and unfolds the corner of the sticky note, relieved to have the words out but not sure what will happen next.

"Matching notes," Sophie says carefully. She reaches into her bag and sets the journal on the table between them. She runs her fingers over the pink sticky note on the top. *Read me.* There's a small silence, then she sits up suddenly, grabbing onto the table and almost tipping their drinks over. "Remember, under the deck, next to *bloodspell*, the heart with the letters inside?" She glances at Joey, who knows what is coming. She feels it like a pressure drop before a storm. She claws around the bottle in front of her like it's a rip cord.

Sophie says, "Quinn plus River."

Joey tries with everything she has to remain stoic.

"Are we thinking River could have…?" Elena makes a stabbing motion with her hand. "With the antler thing?"

Sophie runs a finger over the rim of her glass. "He cared about her though. Why would he hurt her?"

"Hmm," says Elena.

"And who would keep a murder weapon in their house for fifteen years with the blood still on it? Pretty risky." An ice cube slides between Sophie's teeth. She crunches down.

Joey does not feel capable of participating in this conversation. It's all she can do not to stand up and run out of here.

Oblivious, Elena takes a pensive sip. "Maybe it wasn't risky. Maybe it was confident. All River had to do was ask his cop daddy to cover up a murder for him."

Joey hides her face in her hands to mask her immediate reaction. She doesn't want to think about this. She can't think about this. Then she fills her lungs and straightens her back. "We are going to ask him," she says. "I told him to meet us here."

"Wait, what?" says Elena. "Tonight?"

Joey checks the time on her phone. "Now," she says. Her mind is scrambled. She doesn't know what to believe. It strikes her as strange that, instead of Tom, who she was so sure about twenty-four hours ago, everything is now pointing toward River. She knows he wasn't out that night. He was with *her*. But maybe after she left his house, he could have gone out... But what about the trees? They whispered about Tom Winter, and Joey was *sure* it was him. Could she have misheard? Confused *Dad* with some other word? It is possible. It's all possible, she realizes.

She understands with clarity now, as the bar hums around her and two of her oldest friends sit across the table from her, that justice for Quinn is all that matters. Not her happiness, not her allegiances, not even her own beating heart. She cannot choose River over Quinn. Not again.

Elena sits up suddenly. She looks past their heads toward the front of the bar. "He's here," she says through clenched teeth. And Joey feels the floor drop out beneath her.

He approaches the table, and Joey avoids his eyes, trying to focus on her breath.

"You started without me, I see," he says. She can't bear to hear his deep, unassuming voice. There's an awkward silence during which, under normal circumstances, Elena and Sophie would say a few polite how-are-yous and you-look-wells. But it quickly becomes obvious that these are not normal circumstances.

"How about I get the next round?" he says. She still can't meet his eye, and she feels his touch on her back, but she wiggles away. There's a moment of confusion, hurt, even, but then he slides his wallet out of his pocket and makes his way to the bar.

When he comes back with more drinks, Joey's throat is dry, and she takes a swig of beer. Then another, and then a third. Then she sputters a cough because it's gone down the wrong pipe. She knows the moment she opens her mouth, her whole life will change.

"What's going on?" River asks with a self-conscious smile.

"Why was that antler at your house?" she asks quickly, letting the words spill out before she can stop them.

He laughs, as though she just told a joke that he doesn't quite get. He looks from Joey to Elena and Sophie, who are both watching him carefully.

His smile disappears, and it begins to dawn on him that this is not, in fact, a friendly gathering. This is an ambush. "Joey, come on. I told you, I never saw it before yesterday."

She is quick with her response. "Whose blood was on it?"

He's silent, and Joey notices that Sophie and Elena are also quiet. Everything hinges on what he says next. Only, he says nothing, just stares back at her, the disbelief and hurt written there as if on paper.

Her hand shakes as she fumbles with her phone. "This was Quinn's," she says, and she pushes it toward him. The image of the sweatshirt is already pulled up on the screen. She trails her finger along it, stopping when she gets to the bloodstain that covers the front of it. She pinches and expands it until it fills the screen. River glances from the image to Joey and back again. Against her better judgment, she lets her eyes connect with his, and there's something there. A plea, maybe. Or fear. Or maybe just plain confusion. She looks away and jabs at the screen. Her esophagus is pulsing. She is forced to swallow before she speaks. "Was it you?"

It takes him a second to register her question, but once he does, his reaction is instant. His hands fly to his hairline and peel through his hair. Still, he says nothing.

Joey can feel Sophie and Elena like a forest of support around her, propelling her, encouraging her to keep going and find the truth, no matter what. "Did you do this to her?" Joey keeps her voice devoid of emotion. Robotic. It's all she can manage.

River, on the other hand—he is full of emotion. So much so that tears are starting to fill his eyes. This takes Joey by surprise, and suddenly she is speechless. An inner voice is screaming at her to stop. His hurt looks real. But she steels herself. She cannot crack, not even for him. She has to know the truth.

His voice is thick when he finally speaks. He looks directly at Joey when he asks, "You think I hurt Quinn?"

Joey is hot, so hot. And her mouth is a desert. She wants to reach out and down the rest of her beer, but she can't get her arms to move. She forces herself to stare back at his face. She has come to know it so well. There looks to be some vulnerability there, but she can't tell if it implicates him for lying or if it implicates her for accusing him. If there's a lie, she knows he will betray himself. And when he does, it's going to hurt like hell, but that's what happens. People lie. They leave, and you move on.

"Wait," he says, leaning backward in his chair, which looks like a toy beneath his six-foot-six frame. "You don't just think I hurt her. You think I *killed* her." He turns to Sophie, then Elena. "Do you think this too, or is it just Joey?" He laughs sharply when they don't reply. "I'm such an idiot. I thought this was a reunion. It's been fifteen years. I didn't realize this was...whatever this is. I honestly can't believe you think I'd do something like that. Joey, come on. You of all people. I know it's been a long time, but Quinn and I were... I cared about her too."

Elena, who is inclined toward confrontation, looks about to respond, but Joey stands abruptly, hearing nothing but her pulse thumping in her eardrums. "Just tell me you didn't," she says.

They stare each other down like this for a second or a minute—it's hard to tell how long. And then, exactly what she feared would happen happens. River says nothing. He throws her a look of such profound disappointment, she feels it beneath her skin, beneath her bones, in her very soul.

Then, he is gone.

35

ELENA

Elena watches Joey, who is still half-turned toward the door. Her face hangs slack in a way it didn't before River arrived. She seemed to lose something in that exchange.

"It was him," Elena says.

Joey seems to blink her into focus, and Elena presses on, committing now because she has information that might be valuable. "First, he was carrying a lie like a bad smell. It was all over him."

Joey casts her eyes down at the table.

"Second—and this one is going to be a bit of a blow, so buckle up—he said he cared about Quinn as much as we did, but I know for a fact that's not true." She can feel the latent energy at the table increase. The bar around them is noisy again. Someone has put a song on the jukebox.

"Why do you say that?" Joey's voice is gravelly.

"I just remembered this," says Elena, tapping on the table with her fingernails. "Quinn and River may have dated those last few months of junior year, but it wasn't what we thought. Quinn didn't feel that way about him. At least, not toward the end." She draws a breath. This is harder than she thought it would be, discussing Quinn's love life when she isn't here to give her side of the story.

"Why?" says Joey, tearing at the napkins again.

"Oh god, I started this, so I might as well finish it," says Elena. And then she does. "Quinn had a little action on the side that she didn't want River to know about. She was in love with someone else."

Sophie asks, "With who?"

Elena blinks at her. "With you."

36

QUINN

MAY 2011
TWO WEEKS BEFORE THE FALL

"What the hell is this?"

Elena is in my room when I get out of the shower. My skin is clammy, and the towel over my hair feels too tight. I knew she was here. I just didn't know she would be looking through my things. She's perched on the side of the bed. My mind instantly goes to the book, but as I step into the room, I notice it's not the book she has but my phone. She's scrolling furiously. It takes me a minute to process what she could possibly see there that would make her so upset.

Elena holds the screen out in my direction. I take in the curves of a human form in a picture I recognize. I start to speak, to defend myself, but then I realize I'd rather do it while wearing clothes. I slip on some underwear and tug a T-shirt over my head. My hair is slimy against my neck.

I turn back to Elena, who is scrolling back and forth. She can't take her eyes off the images, and her mouth is open in shock. I'm about to tell her what happened, from the beginning. I'm about to tell her that while Collingswood was feeling her up in the woods, Tanner McGrath was assaulting Sophie. Suddenly, I'm so angry I can't speak, but I'm angry because—why, exactly? I'm angry at Tanner for being a despicable human, angry at Collingswood, angry at Sophie's mom for running out on her when she was a baby, angry at Joey's mom for not getting the help she needs, angry at Elena's mom for trying to snuff her fire out, and angry at my own dad for hiding behind his disease. It's irrational and unfair, but I'm just angry in general—at the multiple, ridiculous ways people are awful on purpose and by mistake, the way their minds betray them and make them into bad people when we need them to be good. It can't be that hard to be good, can it? And the magic…so far, it's done nothing to keep my friends from getting hurt.

Mostly, I'm angry at myself. I tried to unlock the hidden spells in the book—the ones we've never been able to access before. It didn't work. But I'm not giving up because I know, I *know* there is a mind-healing spell somewhere in those pages. I take the phone from her.

"Are you two hooking up?" Elena asks.

I jerk my head up. That's her takeaway? Then, I look at the picture again. Sophie sits on a bed with her arms folded over her naked chest. Her eyes are watery and unfocused from alcohol. Behind the camera, I know, is Tanner, who is not just a run-of-the-mill asshole. He's a predator. My heart sinks. Sophie must still be feeling awful.

Elena doesn't wait for me to respond. Instead, she asks, "Is this why you've been acting so weird lately?"

"I haven't been weird." I turn away to run a brush through my hair. It snags on a knot, making my eyes water.

"You've been avoiding us, sneaking out. You haven't wanted to do magic, not really." She hops off the bed and swipes the phone from my hand. "What the hell is going on with you? And don't say it's your dad because I went over the other day, and you weren't there. I knocked, and no one was home, even though that's where you told me you were going. Before the party, it had been weeks since we hung out. Even before that, you were sneaking out. Backpack by the door at all times, furtive glances at the window, leaving us in your room when you thought we were all asleep?"

I think about *him* and how he has encouraged me to keep things secret. But what if... What if I just told Elena about him right now? There is a little voice inside me. It asks if I've been spending too much time with him. Asks if I am drifting from my friends because of him. But it's only a small voice, and it's easily quieted. Because he is right. If we involve them, I'll have to explain that he knows about the magic. That I've been trying to do magic by myself. I'll have to explain that I didn't trust them the way I've trusted him. He supports me, believes in me. In fact, he thinks that, together, we can do far more than just help my friends. Together, he says, the two of us can show the world what healing really looks like.

"Fine, yes," I say. "Sophie and I are together."

Elena looks even more shocked than when she saw the pictures.

"It's not public knowledge, so please don't say anything to anyone. Including Joey. And don't tell Sophie I told you. We're supposed to keep it a secret."

Elena's hand drops to her side. "Wow. Is it just hooking up or are you together, together?"

I close my eyes for a second and decide which response would hurt Sophie less. "We're together."

"Damn, okay." She nods. "It's cool, obviously. I'm glad you're both happy, but I had no idea. Why didn't you tell me?"

Elena's words make my stomach pinch. What I've just done saves my skin. But this lie will crush Sophie. I formulate my plan then and there, as if doing so will exonerate me. Maybe it will. Tonight, I'm going to pay Tanner McGrath a visit.

37

SOPHIE

Sophie tucks her hands into the pocket of her sweatshirt and wants more than anything to cinch the hood tight around her face.

Elena just said that Quinn was in love with her.

It makes no sense. They were friends. They were always just friends.

"How do you know?" she asks. She can hear the desperation in her voice, and she hates it.

"She told me." Elena's face says, *"Don't even try to deny it,"* but Sophie doesn't know what, exactly, to deny. The bar around them is growing noisier every minute. This already feels like the longest day ever. She thinks about River, about the journal, about her dad and Barbara, about Leah's fever. Her thoughts flutter around like a bird trapped in the rafters.

Elena interrupts. "You don't have to lie, Soph. I saw the pictures."

This makes the frantic bird stop dead. "What pictures?"

Elena juts her head forward in a show of disbelief. "The naked pictures. Of you."

Joey inhales sharply. "Wait, Quinn had naked pictures of you?" She looks hurt, as if this is something that was done to her.

Sophie feels the world blur around the edges of her vision. She tries to respond, but Elena cuts her off. "Just admit that you were in love with her too and save us all some time." She picks at tiny balls of wet napkin that have accumulated on the table.

Joey brings a hand to her chin, like she needs the extra support.

"I wasn't in love with her." Intensifying heat inside Sophie's clouds any rational thought. She pushes her cocktail away.

"Well, I found pictures of you with your tits out on her phone."

"Those weren't—"

"What the hell, Soph?" It's Joey now, coming at her with an aggrieved tone. "You didn't think this was pertinent information to share with us? This whole time we've been thinking Quinn and River… But it was you all along."

"It's not—"

"Honestly, there's no use lying," interrupts Elena. "Quinn told me everything."

Sophie tries to speak, but Elena cuts her off again. "It's not a big deal. It was a lifetime ago."

Not a big deal? Sophie knows what pictures Elena is talking about, and the thought of them being witnessed by someone else makes her feel violently sick. *Quinn showed Elena?* Why would she do that? Sophie has shut out that night with Tanner for so long. It feels impossible that it's being thrown in her face again after a decade and a half. By people she thought she could trust. Starting with Quinn, who told her she got Tanner's phone and deleted the photos that day. But instead, what? She kept them on her own phone and showed them to Elena, making up some story about the two of them hooking up? Betrayal tears through her. Not only did Quinn lie to Sophie, but she also used Sophie's sexuality as a cover story. Or maybe the whole thing was just a sick, twisted joke, and Quinn just never got around to telling Sophie the punchline. She tries to bring Quinn's face to mind so she can ask her, *"What the fuck?"* but she can't. For once, she can't.

"Listen—" she starts, but she's interrupted again.

"I have a theory," Elena says to Joey, completely ignoring Sophie. "What if River saw those pictures? What if he realized what was going on between Quinn and Sophie and he didn't like it? What if he and Quinn had a fight..."

"What, so he pushed her because he was jealous of Sophie?" asks Joey. Sophie can't believe this. They are speaking about her like she's not here, totally oblivious to her rising fury.

Elena shrugs. "The pictures could have triggered him—"

Sophie jumps to her feet, and her chair falls backward from the sudden movement. "Oh my god, stop. Both of you."

They blink at her, silently.

She's seething now, and it makes her feel like she's outside her own body. A fleeting thought about nervous system regulation floats through her mind. She can feel her cortisol spiking, adrenaline bouncing through every fingertip. But she doesn't back down. "Did you even think to ask *me* what I think? No. Of course you didn't. And because you didn't ask, you'll never know how fucking terrible it was to have my picture taken like that. You think I wanted to have naked pictures of me on anyone's phone? You think I wanted it? Well, that's a big fuck-you-very-much." She doesn't pick up her chair. She just yanks her bag free and steps over it. The thought of those pictures being seen by anyone when she thought they were destroyed is making her feel unhinged.

"Soph, please calm down," says Joey, like she's placating a horse. "Let's talk."

But she rounds on Joey. "You know, back then, I sometimes used to wonder if any of you really cared about me or if I was always just the butt of the joke. Ultimately I decided that, no, those thoughts were just my own insecurities. But now, you guys dredge this up, and it fucking *hurts* that you haven't even asked me anything about it. You just informed me what your theories about my life are. So no, I don't want to calm down. And I don't want to talk about it." She's breathing heavily, too heavily. She needs to stop, but she can't. It's all coming up now, and, honestly, it's a relief to say some of this out loud. "Maybe the three of us have been apart for too long," she says. "Other than the memory of our dead friend, what else do we have? Nothing. We're strangers."

"That's not true," says Joey.

"Oh please, Joey. You haven't done a single thing since Quinn died. You refuse to even try to be happy. Why do you think that is?"

Joey looks hurt, and Sophie wants to cry, but maybe just this once, she is done trying to pretend they're still friends when their friendship shattered a decade and a half ago. She is tired of trying to piece together this irreparable thing.

"Whoa," says Elena with a laugh that turns Sophie's blood up to a boil.

Sophie turns to her, spite moving through her. "Oh Elena, I know not giving a shit is your thing, but you take it too far. Do you even know where your kid is right now? Do you even care?" Sophie reels back slightly, surprised by herself.

Elena's eyes widen with something—disbelief. It was an awful thing to say, but for once, Sophie doesn't apologize. Instead, she inhales a single, shuddering breath before pushing her way toward the exit.

Outside, there's still a sliver of daylight, but everything is blurred by tears. She clatters into someone who steadies themself with a grip on her arm. Startled, Sophie wrenches away.

"Everything alright?" It's Marissa Berg. Sophie has the primal urge to get in her face. *Don't fucking touch me.* But she drops to her knees to scoop up her phone and old tissues and baby binkies that have spilled all over the ground. The journal has escaped too, and she slips it back inside.

She pushes herself to her feet, ignoring whatever Marissa is saying to her, and wipes at her face. She feels the journal practically throbbing from inside her bag. She was just beginning to wonder if there was a reason she found it. Like she was meant to find it, like it was a clue. But now Sophie thinks of Quinn in her room that day, assuring her she was going to take care of the photos. Did Sophie misread their closeness all those years ago? Did any of them, even Quinn, ever have her best interest at heart?

She honestly has no idea.

"Our magic is benign. Benevolent when necessary. Never malevolent."

–Rule #4, *The Book of Aspens*

38

QUINN

MAY 2011
TEN DAYS BEFORE THE FALL

My lie to Sophie was for her own good.

Immediately after leaving her house, I went to the spell circle alone and summoned the photos from Tanner's phone. I didn't want her to know I was doing magic alone—I've been doing it, or trying to do it, for weeks. Now, the pictures live on my phone, which Elena saw and hopefully will keep to herself. I should have deleted them, but I decided, that day, that I needed to keep them. Maybe as collateral or something because Tanner needs to be stopped. At first, I thought I could unlock the book to find a spell to change Tanner for the better, but no luck yet. I did, however, think of another way I could use magic to stop him in the meantime.

It's night and there's a drizzle. I pull my sleeves down over my hands because I don't like how it feels on my skin. The streetlight blinks off and on again as I pass under it. I make the right onto Sixth. Then a left on Pine.

He comes to the door within a few seconds of my knock and looks me up and down. "What do you want?"

"Can I come in?"

He looks behind him. There's some chatter from the kitchen, the sound of the dishwasher being loaded, maybe. He has a younger brother, and I wonder if he maybe shouldn't witness what I'm about to do, but then I think, *Whatever*. I don't care if his brother knows what kind of person he is. Maybe hearing this will prevent him from becoming like Tanner.

He crosses his arms at his chest in response to my question.

"Fine," I say. I pull my phone out and find the first image. I hold it up to his face. He glares at me, then tries to swipe it. I dodge his hands. "Look with your eyes," I say. My voice is hard.

He looks then, and I see it in the way his face changes. He's confused and then outraged and then confused again. "What the fuck?"

I shrug and pull the phone toward me. It's a photo of Tanner leaning over Sophie, but it could be any drunk girl, really. He's grinning. And holding a knife to her throat.

I scroll to the next image and show him.

This time he grabs my hands and phone together and pulls them toward his face. "That is not me," he says.

"Looks like you," I say. Here's what I don't say: I don't say that it's not him. Not really. I created this photo using a simple illusion spell. These photos are not real, but I needed evidence that showed how disgusting he is because people don't always believe drunk girls who claim they were assaulted. The real pictures of Sophie had no trace of Tanner—he was smart to keep himself out of them—but these versions do. These versions, that a simple illusion spell helped me create, definitely do.

He stares harder at the phone, and I know he's wondering what the little green pills are that sit like candy in his palm in the picture. "It's fucking photoshopped."

I yank my hand free of his and glance at the image. The spell work is impeccable. "That's pretty good Photoshop," I say, going back to the first picture. "The scar on your chin is exactly the same."

"But I never… How did you get those?"

I give him a look that I hope conveys I would never reveal my source. Then I shrug again, waiting for him to understand.

"Wait, why are you showing me these? What do you want?"

Satisfaction thumps inside me, like a heartbeat. "Leave Sophie alone," I say darkly.

"Sophie Stringer?" He looks baleful, like he's hardly ever thought of Sophie, like he barely knows who she is. It enrages me.

"Don't speak to her. Don't message her. Don't even look at her ever again or I swear to god, I'll show these pictures to the police."

He hesitates. "That's not even me."

I suppress a twitch of the lip because I can hear desperation in his voice, even doubt. He doesn't think he's ever held a knife to a girl's throat before or slipped Rohypnol into a girl's drink, but he's not entirely sure, maybe because he was too drunk to remember clearly. It seems like something he would do, doesn't it?

He protests again, but this time there isn't any real feeling behind it, and I know I have him. I zip the phone into my bag and take a step back. "I have worse too, you know. I can make your life a living hell. So stay away from Sophie. Stay away from any girl that doesn't give you her consent, you fucking creep."

His eyes betray him before he makes his move. He lunges toward me, hand outstretched, and he tries to grab the bag from my back. I am far enough away that I avoid him, but then his other hand finds my hair. He tugs, hard, and my head whips painfully to the side. I reach behind me, into the pouch of my backpack, fumbling with a canister. One of his hands is still ensnared in my hair and the other is roving, searching blindly for the zipper. Then, he has it. He starts to pull the zipper open, and panic flutters in my chest, but then I have hold of the canister. I clutch it in my palm and point it toward his face. I can tell he doesn't see the pepper spray until it's too late. I press down with one finger.

He lets out a cry like an animal.

I stumble backward. Then, I run.

39
SOPHIE

Sixth and Pine.

That's where Marissa told Sophie she lives now. She walks by several houses before she sees a cardboard box next to a trash bin with a picture of a crib. She approaches the front door, painted a garish red, and knocks. She cried all the way to her dad's and made herself a sandwich to try to calm her breathing. She hates herself for what she said to Elena and Joey. She didn't really mean any of it, did she? Eventually she pulled out her phone just to see Talia's name, just to see something that would ground her. But all she saw there on the screen was the black-and-white picture of an ultrasound scan. Marissa's ultrasound scan.

Nothing happens for a minute, and Sophie wonders if Marissa is still out, but then, just as she's about to turn away, the door clicks open.

"Sophie." Marissa wears wool socks and her hair is pulled back severely.

"We must have mixed up phones," Sophie says. She can't summon her usual friendliness.

Marissa smiles. "All good. Come on in."

It is, honestly, the last thing Sophie wants to do. She just wants to go back to her dad's, pack up, and maybe even head home. But she needs her phone, so she just says, "Sure."

The inside of Marissa's house is sterile. White walls and bright lights jar against the mountain view out the windows. A pair of black police-issued boots sits by the door next to a pair of men's running shoes.

"I discovered nonalcoholic gin a few months ago, and I'm obsessed." Marissa gestures to a barstool on the other side of a white Formica kitchen island. She goes to the other side and pulls two glasses out of a bottom cabinet. There are sharp edges all over this kitchen. She's going to have a terrible time baby-proofing. Sophie wonders if she's thought about that yet. She accepts the mocktail. Marissa slides a phone toward her, and Sophie gives her one in return.

"So, you're getting ready for the baby already?" Sophie pockets the correct phone, already wishing she hadn't come inside. It's about as inviting as an ICU in here.

"Mmm. You saw the evidence by the recycling bin, then." She smiles. "You know what it's like."

Sophie has the urge to ask if Marissa's single, but she spots a modest ring on her left hand and recalls the men's shoes by the front door. "The first year is hard," she says, offering an ounce of polite conversation. "But it gets easier once they're sleeping through the night."

Marissa nods and smiles as if sleep deprivation won't happen to her. "Is your daughter at home with your husband?" she asks.

"Wife, actually."

Marissa makes an O shape with her mouth, and Sophie feels a sudden flush increasing her internal temperature.

Sophie always felt guilty that Marissa hadn't been part of their initiation into the magic, but it wasn't her choice. That decision was made by Barbara and Carly, Quinn's and Joey's moms. They never explained why they chose the four of them beyond saying they chose only the most trustworthy, but Sophie is starting to piece together how such a decision is made. Marissa would never have been chosen. Some people are innately repulsive.

"All those years. I am surprised you never came back to see Joey." Marissa puts her glass down and wipes the condensation from her fingers on her pants. "I always thought you two were close."

Sophie realizes there's no question in this statement, and she feels herself bristle inwardly. She has been through her relationship with Joey and Elena with her therapist but still feels an ache when she thinks about how they missed so many years of friendship. And now...she doesn't know if it can be repaired. "We used to be," she says honestly.

"Well, I don't blame you," Marissa says. "Joey is absolutely obsessed with Quinn's death. She thinks someone killed her. Did you know she basically questioned everyone here? Sometimes I think—" She waves a hand as if to say, *"Never mind."*

"What?"

Marissa scoots her stool closer to Sophie's, and Sophie leans away instinctively. "I probably shouldn't say anything, but Quinn's case file is missing. And we have files stored as far back as the sixties, so we should still have it. But I've checked, and it's not there."

Sophie is immediately on alert. She looks down at the floor, just in case her eyes betray her.

"You know what, I should ask River Hunstad," says Marissa. "His dad used to be the police chief. He might know. But it just has made me think. River and Joey..." She lets the sentence trail off.

Sophie beats a thumb against her glass. She takes a sip.

"They're sleeping together."

Sophie coughs as the floral drink slips toward her windpipe. "What?"

Marissa's satisfied expression is tantamount to gloating. "Oh yeah, they've been hiding it"—she puts air quotes around the words *hiding it*— "for months now, maybe even years. Did you really not know?"

This last question is unnecessary, but Sophie bites her tongue. Joey never said anything about being with River, and the way she peppered him with questions just an hour ago—the internal turmoil when she found that antler must have been excruciating.

Marissa seems to interpret Sophie's silence as shock, and it is, in part. "It's weird, right? Dating her dead friend's ex. That's probably why they're keeping it a secret."

"Huh," says Sophie. She cannot picture Joey and River together, but she hasn't been here for fifteen years, so she supposes anything could have happened in that time. Though it would be out of character for Joey to betray Quinn like that, even Quinn's memory, unless she really cared about him.

"So tell me, what is going on with you three? I can tell there is something brewing." Marissa picks an ice cube from her glass and watches Sophie's reaction.

Sophie struggles to keep her face blank. "Nothing's going on. We're just visiting."

Marissa laughs without smiling. "You haven't been back in years, and suddenly you're here, breaking into people's homes, arguing in public. I'm not an idiot, Sophie."

Sophie winces inwardly but forces her face to remain passive. "Allegedly," she says.

"What?"

"Allegedly breaking into people's homes."

"Is there anything you want to tell me before I find out myself?" Marissa leans in even closer, and Sophie realizes that she's suddenly become Officer Berg.

Sophie holds her nerve. "Is this an interrogation?"

Marissa pauses for a beat, searching Sophie's face intensely. Then she leans back on her stool and rubs the crest of her belly. "Nope."

A door clicks open in the front hall and thunks closed. There's the sound of keys being hung on a hook, and then a man tosses out a distracted, "Hey." The sound of it snaps Sophie's taut nerves about Marissa's questions in half. She knows that voice.

When he walks into the room, Sophie feels herself drifting out of her body. The man is stocky with blond hair and a square jaw slashed through with a scar, with some pockmarks on his cheeks—shadows of his youth. She recognizes him instantly.

His eyes find hers, and he shows surprise, at first, that someone who is not his wife is sitting in his kitchen. Then, his surprise turns to something else. He knows who she is. He leans in and gives Marissa a kiss, but he doesn't take his eyes off Sophie.

She shoves her stool back and mutters something about having to go to the bathroom. Marissa, apparently oblivious, points her down the hall to the right.

Tanner McGrath. Marissa is married to Tanner McGrath. Her thoughts spin and whirl as she flushes, washes her hands, looks at herself in the mirror. She's thrown back to that night. His demands were clouded by alcohol. *"Take off your bra now. Just one more. You like it, don't you?"*

She tries to steady her breathing, but it's coming too fast. She is lightheaded, swelling with the acute need to leave this house. She shouldn't have come inside. She should have known.

The hall is dark when she turns off the bathroom light. She takes one step in the direction of the kitchen and bumps into someone. He's as thick as a brick wall and smells of sweat. Her senses fire with alarm.

"Sophie Stringer," he says. "I heard you were in town." She can't look at him, even though she feels his gaze on her. She wants to push past him, but she finds she's rooted to the spot, just trying to catch her breath. "It's nice to see you again." His voice is like claws scratching at the insides of her ears. It sends bile bubbling up her esophagus.

"Get out of my way," she says. She's suddenly shaking.

"What's wrong?"

Sophie can't believe it. Beneath her panic about what happened a million years ago in that room, what he did to her, how he made her feel as small as an insect—beneath all that, Sophie can feel it. He's still a predator. He might have a baby on the way, but she knows who he is at the core. He leans in toward her, and she wants to scream. She wants to vomit. She wants to leave. Above all, she wants to fucking leave.

Tanner reaches above her right shoulder, toward her hair, and she holds her breath. The light above them blinks on.

Then, a voice. "What are you doing?" Marissa stands at the end of the hall, staring at them. Sophie feels like a teenager caught doing something she isn't supposed to. And Marissa is all shock and reprimand now, glaring at her like the devil incarnate has cursed her home.

"Babe." Tanner slides away from Sophie. "I was just turning on the light."

Marissa looks at him, hard, and then she nods, like she believes him. She looks like she always believes him. Her next movement is a jerk of the head. Her eyes find Sophie's, and they bore into her.

"You should go."

"I'm sorry." It's not what Sophie means, not even close, but here she is, apologizing for existing like she always does because it doesn't matter what she says. Her body is insisting: *Leave. Leave. Go now.*

"Marissa, don't be rude to our guest." Tanner looks down at Sophie's lips and reaches for her arm. Her stomach lurches. "Stay," he whispers.

She clocks the distance between her bag on the stool in the kitchen and the front door, and then she wrenches free of him. She thinks she hears her name on the way out, but she does not stop.

40

JOEY

Joey is at River's door at six thirty the next morning.

"It's Saturday, Joey." He's puffy with sleep and looks worn-out, even hungover.

Inside, it's early-morning quiet. Her red bra, the one she said she thought was missing, sits neatly folded on the small table to her left. "I came to tell you it's over." She says it just like this, right where they are, before the front door is even closed behind her.

"Good morning to you too," he says, running a hand through his hair. There's a silence. "Do you want to talk? There's coffee."

She shakes her head.

He seems unsure, wary, like she's a bomb that might go off at any moment. "Is this about last night? Listen, I was just shocked that you'd think—"

"I can't do this anymore."

He looks away, as if searching for some way to convince her she's making a mistake. She knows what is going through his mind. He's relentlessly rational, and her ending a two-year-long relationship with no explanation is likely killing him.

"I didn't hurt Quinn. You know that," he says.

Inwardly, Joey flinches. She can't look at him. "I'm sorry." She turns abruptly.

"Wait," he says. She hears him place his fingers on the doorframe above her head. "Look, I don't want you to go, for whatever that's worth. I was hurt last night. I couldn't believe what you thought of me. But now, standing here with you, I understand. You're looking for answers. I told you how I feel, and that hasn't changed. It will never change. I love you. I still want us to move in together."

A neat row of trees stands guard at the front of River's house. She remembers when they were planted. They were in fourth grade. Now, those trees stand over six feet tall, all of them.

"Everything's changed," she says.

"Listen to me, Joey. You can't carry this guilt forever. If Quinn were here today, she'd tell you to stop beating yourself up. You know she would." He waits to see if she is going to respond, then clears his throat. "Besides, Walter needs you. If you leave, whose sweaty legs is he going to lick after a run?"

When he doesn't get the laugh he was hoping for, he goes silent. The mention of the dog brings the days after Quinn's death back to her, when between bouts of crying, the guilt for spending Quinn's last living hours in River's bedroom surfaced like a sewer rat. And then one cloud-white afternoon, River was there, at her front door. At his feet, a damp ball of fluff paced back and forth, not understanding the leash. River explained that he found the puppy wandering at the edge of the woods, looking hungry, and had eventually lured him into his arms with a few strips of beef jerky, then took him home and gave him a bath. The puppy, she believed then and still believes now, was River's umbrella, intended to repel some of the shock waves of Quinn's death. River invited Joey under it that day. At the sight of him with that squirming fluffball, she became lightheaded with pleasure. If she had to pinpoint it, that was the exact moment she knew she couldn't be with him. She closed the door that day and kept it closed for years. Even after her mother died, when she longed to sink into him, to smell him, to hear him tell her she'd be okay, she just couldn't.

Until one snowy afternoon two years ago. It started with showing up to shovel the same elderly neighbor's driveway and turned into microwave popcorn and half a bottle of tequila. A mistake that was a long time coming. In the end, it was his heartbeat that ultimately did it. It was so steady, so rhythmic. He asked her on a date, and with one ear pressed to his chest, she said yes, but she made him swear to keep it secret, as if doing so would absolve them both.

"I feel guilty all the time." She says it so quietly, she wonders if he has heard her.

Behind her, he lets out a loud, long, frustrated breath. "Do you think...?" he says before lowering his voice. "Would you still feel this way if Quinn hadn't died?"

"If she didn't die, we wouldn't be together." She isn't sure where this thought came from. But as she says it aloud, she wonders if it's true. Has she been drawn to him all these years because he somehow makes her feel closer to Quinn?

"Ouch," he says. "Not sure I agree with that."

She knows she has wounded him, but defenses are hardening around her, brick by brick. "There's something you're not telling me," she says.

"Like what?"

"You can't explain the antler, for one."

"You're right," he says, pulling his fingertips off the doorframe and scratching his arm. "The antler is fucked up. I talked to my parents and my sister, and none of them know anything about it. I am literally clueless. In fact, I'm kind of freaked out because I've been in that closet a few times over the years, and I'd never seen it before yesterday."

He pulls at a drawstring on his sweatshirt and studies it, like he's not sure what her reaction is going to be.

She doesn't turn away, but she can feel herself pulled in two very distinct directions. "So you expect me to believe it's just a magic antler that appeared at random?" she says eventually.

He lifts one shoulder and then drops it. She watches him, playing back her own question in her head. Something about it gives her pause, but she's not sure why.

That's when the rain starts.

"Tell no one."

–Rule #5, *The Book of Aspens*

41

QUINN

JUNE 2011
ONE WEEK BEFORE THE FALL

I've done it.

I've discovered a whole world of hidden spells.

I'm running now, frantically putting one foot in front of the other, careful to avoid roots and rocks. My breath consumes me. Aspens whir past. Ideas try to wriggle free from my muddy mind because it's not just late spring outside. It's like there's a kind of late spring inside me too. I know now. There is so much more that this magic can do.

Finally, my feet bring me to his doorstep, and he is there, watching me catch my breath. My hands drop to my knees, and my chest expands with the air I'm desperate for. He is patient, as he always is, and eventually, we go inside, where he brings me a glass of water.

"I did it," I say. I tell him everything, how the book filled right up with spells that have been hidden for generations, spells my mom doesn't even know about. The blood-inked words flooded every corner of every page with what I can only assume is the scrawl of past witches. Because I believe now that we really are witches. And this isn't just a book. It's a grimoire. It contains hundreds of witches' spells.

He listens, nodding along, letting me spill my discoveries. It feels like I'm offloading a heavy stone with every breathless revelation. I tell him about the curses and the hexes and spells to change the weather and spells to shapeshift into a bird and spells I don't even know what they are for because I couldn't read fast enough before they disappeared again. Some were written in clear, plain English, and others in languages I don't know, in script that was barely legible. With every word I tell him, I feel more electric, like lightning itself.

"And your crown jewel?" he asks once I've exhausted my list. I'm not sure what he means, and it must show on my face because he says, "The mind manipulation spell. The one you thought would be in there?"

I'm still not sure what he's talking about, but then I realize he must be referring to the mind-healing spell. *Manipulation* makes it sound ugly, but it has the potential to be so beautiful. It has the potential to change people and, most essential of all, it has the potential to help my friends.

"Yes," I tell him. I dream of what I can do with that spell. I will start with Tanner, probably, because, after the other night, I'm afraid of what he might do. Then Joey's mom. Then Collingswood. Then my dad. Then, who knows? There are millions of people who need healing. This magic could change the world.

"I can't wait to tell my friends," I say. And it's true. This changes everything. I finally realize that even though it would mean telling them I've broken the rules and facing their confusion and disappointment, it's still a whole world of magic they didn't know existed. They deserve to know.

He smiles, and I see a hunger in his eyes that I've never seen before. "I'm not sure they'll understand," he says. "You went behind their backs. You lied to them. I think it has to be just you and me now. We need to stay together. I want to be by your side when you change the world." He brushes a stray hair away from my cheek and looks down at me, cupping my neck in his hands. "I want to change it with you."

Then he runs his fingertips up through my hair, over my shoulders, and down to my chest. His palms flatten against my rib cage, right above my heart, which is still skittering. His eyes meet mine as he leans down to meet my eyes at the same level and says quietly, "Now, I want you to tell me about bloodspell."

I can't hide my surprise. I know what bloodspell is. I saw it in the spell book. But I don't know how he knows about it. Somewhere from the depths of my brain, I can hear Joey saying, *"We have a responsibility to keep the magic safe."*

But Joey isn't here. And maybe he's right. Maybe it has to be just the two of us now.

So I tell him.

42
ELENA

Elena sees Gael rounding the corner onto Front Street, loping the way fourteen-year-olds do. His camera is tucked under his shirt and out of the drizzle like it's an appendage. She is not one to self-reflect, especially when she's insulted, but she can't help wondering if she's been a good mom. She can't help but think that she's done it all wrong, that she should have maybe come back here all those years ago and tried to make it work or at least find someone else who could have been a father figure. She's tried so hard, done the best she could to make sure he was always fed and always clothed. But is he happy? Does he love her?

Gael sees her then and offers her a nod like he's on his way, but he doesn't hurry. It's not cool to hurry; she gets it. She wipes the rain off her face.

She's distracted by an incoming text. She lifts her phone, protecting it with one hand, and sees that the message is from Cal Pierce.

Rehearsal at the house (out of the rain) at 5?

"Hey," says Gael, who is standing in front of her now. They begin to walk toward Barbara's. He clears his throat with obvious intention. She thinks he's about to regale her with tales of shutter speed and overexposure—and other photography details she is completely clueless about. But instead, he says, "I know you think I came here so I could find out who my dad is."

Elena almost stops dead, but she forces herself to keep her momentum going.

"Mom," he says. "I'm fourteen and a half. And you're thirty-two."

Elena swallows. She doesn't speak, just lets him get it out.

"I know you were a teenager when you had me. And I know you lived here when you were a teenager. And I know I'm supposed to care. I guess maybe a part of me is curious, but mostly, I don't really care. I don't feel like I'm missing anything by not having a dad, honestly. I just always assumed you thought he wasn't a great guy. Otherwise, he'd be in our lives. And I was totally okay with that. I am okay with that."

Elena has to take several deep breaths. She feels like she should speak, that she should apologize, but he doesn't sound like he needs it.

"Want to know why I really came this week?" He asks her this in full stride, without looking at her.

"Yes," she manages.

"I wanted to see your hometown. I've been dying to come ever since you told me about it. And then you said you were going back for the first time in however long I've been alive, and you weren't going to bring me with you? Hell no. I was not going to let you come without me. And now that I'm here, I'm just—it's awesome. Your friends are cool, the locals are cool. The mountains are insane. It's been fun to hear stories about what you were like as a kid, to see the school where you used to go, to look at old pictures."

She looks at him sharply, and he laughs. "Barbara showed me." He lowers his voice. "She also told me lots of stuff about your friend Quinn. She seemed like a cool person."

Elena is struck by the sheer maturity of this boy walking next to her. Where did he come from? She bites her lip to keep the tears at bay because, goddammit, she will not cry. She will not.

"Okay, last thing," he says, pulling at her arm to stop her. They're at the end of Barbara's street now, standing beneath the streetlight where she saw the figure on their first night here, where they saw the photo of the man watching them. It sends a chill through her. It's daytime now, but she thinks of that first night, how she thought she had to protect Gael, and here he is, showing her that he didn't need her to. But Sophie is wrong. Elena has had almost no bearing on who he is at his core. Because Elena is certain that, however emotionally intelligent he is, that's just who he is. No matter what she did, he would always be that person. She looks into his eyes, as deeply as she can, hoping to send him a message this way. *"I'm so proud,"* she wants to say. *"And I'm so sorry for the way our lives have been."*

Before she can say anything, he clears his throat. "Promise me you'll keep up with the acting," he says. "That you won't find some excuse to give up. Because I know you can do it. I know that one day, you will be rich and famous, and we will move out of our apartment and into a mansion with a butler, and we will buy a house here too, and maybe one in Maui. And Joey and Sophie and Barbara can come stay with us whenever they want."

She laughs, but in truth, Gael's words have filled her. Elena thinks of Cal's message. She thinks of her role as Teacher Number Two. Beneath the cold of the rain, she thinks she can feel the tingle of it beneath her skin. It's so cheesy, so horribly cliché, but Gael saying these things to her makes it feel true: This is her big break. In more ways than one.

She is not going to fuck this up.

43

SOPHIE

Sophie kneels on the edge of the crag, noticing the rain sliding down her nose. She takes in the panorama before her: lakes of wildflowers and forests spotted with tennis-ball-green aspens.

The snippets she remembers from that night fifteen years ago with Tanner are blurry—ironically, like they were taken with a bad-quality camera. But they also linger in the way that a bad dream lingers. The smell of the duvet. Musty, like it had sat in the washer for days. The flash of the camera in the dark room. As soon as he got near her last night, his breath sulfuric on her face, she wanted to gouge his eyes out, but that didn't happen. It couldn't, not with fingernails as chewed-down as hers.

She tries to pull her thoughts out of that hallway. Tries not to think about the abject revulsion on Marissa's face, tries not to think about his jeans and the way they pressed against the back of her hand. Suddenly, a violent longing makes her miss Talia. No call from her yesterday at all. Sophie tried again this morning, but it went straight to voicemail. And for some reason she hasn't responded to her texts. Worry has coiled around Sophie's logical thinking, squeezing the air out of it. After the fourth unread message, she started to spiral, and the worst-case scenarios emerged. An out-of-control fever from an unknown virus. Emergency room. A nose cannula pumping oxygen just to keep her baby alive. It took twenty minutes and a solid talking down from her dad to snap Sophie out of it.

If Talia needs me, she will call. This is what she has to keep reminding herself, though she can still feel the electrode prod of anxiety all over her body. It's satisfying to know in a small sardonic way that even after Elena's baseless accusations and her own explosive cruelty, after her conversation with Marissa, and even after her run-in with Tanner McGrath, that her anxiety is still centered around her family. Right now, all she wants is to see her little girl's face and to wrap herself in her wife's arms.

The journal is butterflied open before her knees. There are even more pages with handwriting now, as if more appeared overnight. She knows now that no one has been sneaking in, thank god. She kept the journal cradled to her chest all night as she cried herself to sleep.

Most of what's here is a hurried and nonsensical stream of consciousness that Sophie will have to decipher later. She is scanning it frantically, looking for Tanner's name, because since she woke up this morning, she has been wondering something. Quinn knew how upset Sophie was, how traumatized. What if she didn't make light of the pictures? What if she did do something about them? Quinn could have done a summoning spell on her own to get the pictures from Tanner's phone. She shouldn't have done magic alone, but maybe she did. If the pictures were really that bad, maybe they drove Quinn to do something stupid. She could have gone to Tanner's, like Marissa said, but not to play matchmaker. Maybe she went there to warn him to stay away from Sophie.

Sophie can't seem to marry the two versions of Quinn. There's the Quinn who kept the incriminating photos of her and lied to Elena about being in a secret relationship with her. Then there's this version of Quinn, the one who Sophie realizes now might have threatened Tanner on her behalf. She wants to believe in that version, the loyal friend. She really wants to. Ordinarily, it wouldn't be difficult. But now, she doesn't know. Sophie naturally turns toward the positive like a plant leaning toward the sun. But believing that Quinn stood up for her means believing something else too—something unthinkable. Tanner, fresh from being threatened by Quinn, would have been angry, so angry that he retaliated. Years of being the target of his obsessive bullying meant Sophie knew him. And he hated to be told what to do. He liked to be in control. He wouldn't have taken Quinn's threat lightly, and he had already proved his capacity to do real harm.

Did he push her? The theory reverberates through her as if she's a Tibetan singing bowl, growing louder and suddenly becoming the only possible explanation.

Sophie gets to her feet, still clutching the journal. She leans forward, just slightly. Enough that she can see what's below her. The creek is there—a milky yellow, thanks to the ore sediment leached from the ground—and the rocks. Years have washed away any trace of a death here, and yet it feels as raw as if it happened yesterday.

Cradling the journal in one hand, she forces herself to resume skimming for Tanner's name. She doesn't get far before a new page catches her eye, and she trails a finger over the words.

I asked my mom if The Book of Aspens *is hiding something. She said yes, lots of things. She told me a story about the women who were initiated with her. She said this very question fractured their friendship. It drove the four of them apart. She told me to let it go, that it can only lead to greed. But I know she's wrong... because I unlocked them. I unlocked the rest of the spells.*

Behind Sophie, footsteps. She holds her breath and listens. The steps grow louder, closer. Someone is coming, and the idea sends all her thoughts fluttering away completely. Fear grows roots beneath her. Is it Tanner? Is he following her?

Slowly, she crouches down, too afraid to look behind her. She carefully tucks the journal away and slides her bag onto her shoulders and starts to think of an escape. She could break into a run through the brush. But, oh god, what is she thinking? She can't outrun Tanner. She hasn't exercised properly in years. She could stay low, but how long will that last for her? It's only a matter of seconds before he sees her here.

Or, she realizes, she could jump. The option blows through her like a cold wind. It's not really an option, though. Is it?

"Sophie?"

Sophie yelps, and her foot slips an inch. Her shoe catches on a flat part of the crag. It's drizzling, she realizes with a panic. Slippery. She steadies herself with fingertips against rock and then realizes she recognizes the voice. It's not Tanner's, or at least she doesn't think it is. She stands with a surge of courage and turns to see.

44

JOEY

Joey's house feels empty.

She has come to think of River as an extension of this space, she realizes. And the dog. God, she's going to miss that dog. What Sophie said broke something inside her. Because she was right. Joey *hasn't* lived.

She sorts through day-old mail. Most of it is trash, but there's one bill for the coffee shop. A second notice with a fee attached. That is not what she wants to think about right now, and apparently it's something she didn't want to think about before, either. She leaves it on the counter, promising to finally sort it. She needs to make plans to get that place back in shape. The extra business from the movie shoot will be a huge help, but it needs more than that to become what it used to be. The problem is that Joey just doesn't care about it like Barbara did. She has tried and tried to muster the enthusiasm for community events, maybe an open-mic night, a teen night, a guest speaker, or live band. She knows what it will take, but she just doesn't have it in her. She's not the kind of woman who gathers friends and community members together. She's the kind of woman who runs alone on mountain trails at night, who hides from herself.

Sophie and Elena coming back has brought her a speck of hope, she realizes. It's only been a few days, but she somehow feels more herself than she has since Quinn died. They've had their disagreements, and they are far from perfect, sure, but she understands now that these are core friends, the kind that form the foundation of a life. They are the kind of people you are lucky to have when they're with you and who you miss like a limb when they're gone. What she wouldn't give to just go back in time and do it all differently. Stay in touch. Stay close.

She sits, staring at her phone. The rush of emptiness in her bones weighs her down into the stiff contours of the couch. Her lock screen is a photo of her own feet that she took during a run a few years ago. There are no texts from Sophie or Elena. Nothing from River. Not even a message from Zach, and she knows he's this close to quitting. She is truly alone. Joey's obsession with the truth has poisoned everything. It's kept her from living, from having friends, from reconnecting. Fifteen years is a lot of time to miss. This thought makes her so fundamentally sad that she finds it hard to breathe properly. Elena and Sophie will leave in a few days, and Joey will be alone all over again. She stands, then, and makes an impulsive decision.

It takes her ten minutes to take down all her pictures and notes and strings from the wall. She doesn't let herself keep anything except one. She finds an old frame and slips a photo that has all four of them inside it. This, she sets on the dresser. The case file, she tucks back under the sweater in the closet. Then, she opens her laptop. With several click-and-drags, she brings everything involving Quinn to the trash icon in the corner of her home screen. Her mouse hovers over the Empty button. She and Quinn once promised that if they both hadn't left Whisper Ridge by the time they were thirty, they would leave together. Quinn had laughed. *"I'm going to be an inspirational speaker, so I'll have to leave for all the international speaking engagements."* Joey said she couldn't wait to go with her, but even as she'd said it, she had a strange fermenting feeling in her gut. She knew, even then, that she would never leave Whisper Ridge, no matter what they promised each other. She couldn't imagine a life anywhere else. She ignored that little premonition until...well, until she manifested it. She's thirty-two and alone and still here.

"I'm sorry," she says aloud to Quinn's picture. "I'm sorry for that day. I'm sorry for what I did."

She knows it's not nearly enough, that she'll never forgive herself. But she cannot do this. Not anymore.

She clicks Empty.

45

ELENA

Elena sweeps her arm across her middle as she walks toward the spell circle. "She was right over there," she says to herself, "waving goodbye to the children." She pictures the scene. Teacher Number Two. The sheriff watching her, listening to her account. Curious children hovering nearby. Horses braying in the distance. She thinks about her inflection and wonders about her character. At this moment, is she more afraid of the wolves or the sheriff? This woman knew the victim. She was probably friends with her. Her friend was brutally attacked by wolves, and then the sheriff comes asking questions of the townspeople? It would have anyone rattled.

Rattled. That's the word she needs. That's what she will try to portray.

She looks up and pulls in a sudden breath. Someone is there, squatting on top of the crag.

"Sophie?"

Sophie lets out a terrified shriek when she hears her name. Elena inches toward her. "What are you doing?"

"Oh my god," Sophie says, closing her eyes to recover.

"Get down from there." Elena reaches out a hand. A smattering of raindrops has darkened the rock, making it slick.

"You just scared the shit out of me." Sophie sounds defensive. "What are you doing out here?"

"I was trying to find a quiet place to rehearse. What about you?"

Sophie tilts her head back to look at the sky, which is slowly bleeding into darkness. "Where do I start?"

"Why don't you just come off the rock and we'll—"

"You know how there are people who get shot, but the bullet never comes out the other side and they have to live with the bullet inside them for their entire lives?" Sophie is staring over the jagged side of the crag. Elena stiffens, suddenly aware that if Sophie slips, she will be required to access something instinctual she's not sure she possesses.

"Sure," she says carefully.

"It's like ever since we found Quinn, I've wondered what she went through that day, how she must have felt. But we'll never know. We'll never get the answer."

"Soph, please come down from there."

Elena watches Sophie try to turn fully. But she's unstable. Her toes step on something wobbly, a loose pebble or something, and her momentum shifts. Panic screams inside Elena's head. Sophie is falling. *Shit, shit, shit.* She's falling. Her arms circle helplessly, and Elena moves toward her, but there's nothing to grab. Elena is too far away. One foot dangles over the edge, and she can't seem to get purchase with the other.

Elena feels herself leap with everything she has, and in one desperate motion, she somehow gets her hands around the backpack. Careful not to slip, Elena hauls her back and into her arms. Sophie's legs drag on the ground, and together they fall onto the dirt.

They stare at each other. Elena can see the fear and relief in Sophie's eyes. Her heart feels like it's going to lift off; it's pounding so fast. She stands and reaches down a hand.

Sophie sits. She rests her elbows on her knees and bows her head to catch her breath.

Elena shifts her weight. "Why the hell were you so close to the edge?"

"We really let Quinn down. We really let each other down." Sophie grasps Elena's hand and pulls herself up. The aspens shudder around them as droplets of rain bounce off their leaves. "I'm sorry about what I said. I didn't mean it. You're not a bad mother at all. Gael is really great."

Elena sighs and scrubs at her face. "Let's get out of here," she says.

They only take a few steps before Sophie says, "It did bother me that you didn't think to ask me what the pictures meant. You just assumed."

"I didn't assume," Elena says, but she's not defensive, more cowed. "Quinn told me."

"What Quinn told you wasn't the truth." Sophie sounds indignant.

"What's the truth then?"

"Tanner McGrath took those pictures." The smattering of rain has matted Sophie's hair to her head.

Tanner McGrath. A human stain. Elena remembers letting him finger her once, in the woods behind the school, near where she used to go with Mark. She only did it because she couldn't stand the way his girlfriend Marissa shoved dippable tortilla chips into salsa at her house at their Wednesday Bible study, cozying up to Elena's mother like she was the next prophet. She lets out a long breath. "I'm assuming you didn't want him to take them?"

Sophie breathes out through her nose. It could be a laugh, but it is hollow.

"When was this?"

"Two weeks before Quinn died."

"Why were they on her phone?" she asks.

"She told me she was going to make him take them off his phone. Said she was going to convince him."

Elena tries to remember. Sophie must have lent Elena her phone a hundred times over the year between when she got it and Quinn's death, since Elena's mom forbade her from having her own. At some point that number became stored in other people's phones as "Sophie and Elena." Sophie never once complained.

Suddenly, a memory sharpens into focus. "I texted him," Elena says, breathless. "The day of that party, Tanner sent you something really pervy, and I wrote him back, pretending to be you."

"What?" Sophie has stopped walking.

Elena doesn't do naked emotions, even though they're brimming now. She tamps the feelings down and keeps explaining. "I knew he was bullying you, and I was planning to show everyone what a creep he was. That night, I thought I'd lure him somewhere and leave him stranded with his dick out." She thinks back. She had a half-baked plan. She doesn't even remember what it was now, but she did intend to humiliate him in front of everyone.

"I just didn't get a chance to see it through. I got distracted. That night, I got distracted, and..." She looks down at herself, and even now, even after so much time has passed, she has no idea if she's a good person or a bad person.

Moments pass. They walk. "You're not the only one who made mistakes," Sophie says quietly.

Elena looks at her, thinking Sophie is about to offer her forgiveness, and she feels a vehement, almost physical rejection of it. Elena hates that Sophie relentlessly sees the good in people. And yet she also feels a deep sorrow that she has missed out on her optimism for fifteen years.

"I think I'm the reason Quinn died," Sophie says.

"Of course you're not."

But Sophie explains what Marissa Berg told her, that Quinn went to Tanner's house a couple of days before she died. Then Sophie adds her own analysis. She thinks Quinn threatened Tanner, told him to stay away from Sophie. Maybe she said she would go to the police or something. Tanner, with his infamously short fuse, was probably enraged by Quinn's threat and followed her out here.

Sophie thinks Tanner pushed Quinn. She hides her face in her hands and mumbles that it's all her fault. *No*, Elena thinks. If this is true, then it's Elena's fault. She's the one who encouraged Tanner that night. She's the reason Quinn had an injustice to avenge in the first place. So she's the reason Tanner retaliated. Elena marvels at her three best friends and their ability to take on guilt like they're pack mules.

"There were more words in the journal today," Sophie says eventually. "I feel like there will be answers in there."

"Fair enough," Elena replies. "But it's starting to rain. Why don't you go home and read? I'm going to find Joey and run this by her. We need to find out if our Tanner theory has legs. And we need Joey's knowledge of that day to do it."

Sophie agrees. They walk urgently, and Elena shoots a text off to Joey, asking if she's free. Soon, she sees the buildings of town rising in front of them.

"Oh my god, I forgot," says Sophie, breathless, at the intersection. "Did you know about Joey and River?"

"What about them?"

"They're..." She doesn't finish the thought, just raises her eyebrows.

"No shit." Elena wonders about the demons Joey must be battling to keep such a thing under wraps. Then, like a forceful wind, she feels an onrushing sense of disquietude. This whole week it's just been one secret after another. Each secret has pushed the three of them closer to some unseeable cliff.

What happens when they reach the cliff's edge? Soon, something is going to push them over. She can feel it. And then they will fall.

46

QUINN

JUNE 2011
ONE DAY BEFORE THE FALL

My dad asked me to come over again.

It's been so long since I've been to his house. I felt bad. He sounded sincere this time. He promised he'd be around all night, and we could play Jenga and watch *Die Hard*, and that he'd bought a frozen pizza already and mint chocolate chip ice cream.

It was so hard to say no. It was even worse when I lied to my mom. I told her I was going to my dad's, told her he seemed to be doing better, even detailed what he had planned. She looked so pleased, and guilt tore at me from both sides.

He is walking next to me now. The woods are quiet all around us. A few evening birds find their way back home but mostly there is just the sound of our boots on earth. He carries a rifle down by his side. Seeing it surprised me at first. I physically recoiled, but then I collected myself.

He grabs my hand as if to tell me this is where we should stop, and I suddenly realize this is really going to happen. A part of me is still squirming internally. I think about asking if we can just stop, but he entwines the fingers of his other hand with mine and pulls me closer. He leans in until our foreheads press together. I feel his breath on my face. He closes his eyes, but I keep mine trained on his face. He's acting as if we're soldiers preparing for battle, or lovers about to face an enemy that wants to tear us apart. Us against everyone else. Until a few days ago, I thought we were deeply, inextricably bonded. But now I understand. It's bloodspell he's been after all this time.

We wait a whole hour. He asks me in whispers about my friends, my parents. It's as if he can't get enough of me because I've told him all there is to know already. I ask him to tell me more about his mother because it's the only thing I really know about him and I want to stall, to keep this from happening. But he doesn't respond, just changes the subject. He tells me he called his cousin at an alternative medicine clinic in Wyoming to see if a "new kind" of mind healing would be of interest. Only, he called the clinic Blue Valley Recovery Center. The thing is, when he first told me about it a few weeks ago he said it was called Blue Lake. I remember those exact words because I thought of lupine wildflowers and how they look like beautiful blue lakes in the springtime. It's a small thing, and I don't know what it means, but I realize I think he's lying about something.

He toys with my hair, and I try not to tense.

That's when we see a movement in the distance. Dozens of yards away, I can barely make out a buck bending down to tear at a leaf. Immediately, putrid regret roils through me. I told him that this is how bloodspell works. This was the necessary first step before the spell work.

He said he's never killed before, but there's something practiced in the way he raises the gun to his shoulder and aims with one eye closed. A knife of doubt cuts through the shell around my heart. He knows I'm lying. Any second, he's going to turn that gun on me.

But the shot rings out before I'm prepared, and in another second, the animal is down. There's an echo in my ears because he was too close to me when he fired. I follow him, stamping through the brush.

The bullet, I see as we approach, has gone straight through to the heart. There's so much blood, and the buck's eyes bulge with terror. I turn away and throw up into the dirt. At the sound of the splash, the animal jerks and writhes to life. His legs flail as if he's trying to stand. His antlers carve at the air, inches from my thigh. Fear seizes my limbs.

Another shot. I cry out. The animal thunders down again. We wait in silence for at least ten seconds. Eleven. Twelve. Bitter bile sticks to the sides of my tongue.

He decides to take an antler and a jar full of blood with us. He uses a knife sheathed at his side, and I turn away, feeling the nausea bubbling up again. We leave the rest of the corpse behind. All evening, my mind is a torrent of thoughts and plans. My belly feels hard to the touch, like my internal organs are rejecting this new me.

We wait for hours just to give it enough time. I try, several times, to leave, making excuse after excuse—that I need to be with my dad, that I need to do homework. Because I need to leave before he realizes this isn't actually how bloodspell works. But he tells me he needs me here, and the way he says it, with his eyes spearing me, prodding me, searching for the lie, it feels like I have no choice but to stay.

He rubs my back, and I try not to flinch. He tells me how excited he is to finally do something great with the magic, together, and I offer the appropriate sounds, but inside I am screaming.

He falls asleep easily, with one arm wrapped around me, as if he knows I will try to escape. All night I stare at the ceiling, trying to understand how I got here. I feel like I'm waking from a dream, only just blinking into the bizarreness of these last few months. I think of my friends. I think of the magic. I think of what I've done.

In the morning, he wakes abruptly. I tuck the book under my arm and lead him to the spell circle, feeling like a prisoner walking to her own execution. He sees no path as we walk, not really, because of the illusion spell. All he sees are aspen trees and thick underbrush. But it doesn't matter what he sees. At the spell circle, I speak an incantation, and we wait. And wait.

But nothing happens. And even though the sun hits me through the trees, I am suddenly freezing, all the way down to my bones.

"It didn't work," he says. Of course it didn't work. I tell him to give it the day, and he agrees. He has to go to work, but before he leaves, he places his hands on my chest, just above my heart, as he's done before. Only this time the pressure of his weight on my chest intensifies for a moment, and I'm afraid he's pressing too hard. I'm backed up against an aspen tree. My lungs begin to struggle for air, and my vision starts to blur. I can feel my ribs begin to give slightly. Could they be about to crack? Fear grips me, and I try to breathe deeper, shake him off me, but I can do neither. Suddenly, he is pressing against me with what feels like all his weight. I can see the effort in his face, which is reddening. It feels as if my body will collapse under the pressure, and I start to panic. It's like he's taking his frustration out on my body, but I can't do anything to stop it.

Then he lets go suddenly, and I double over, gasping for air.

He smiles then, kisses me on the forehead, and tells me, pointedly, that he will see me later and we will talk about what to do next.

I run all the way to school. For the whole day, I have an upset stomach. It's only when I see Elena and Joey and Sophie in the lunchroom, sitting together without me, that everything I've done over these past few months cascades over me.

I need help, I realize, almost collapsing into tears. I am deeply ashamed, but still, I need help. It's the only way out. And I feel so stupid because, actually, help is what I've needed all along. If only I had understood that from the beginning.

How did I not see it before? He wants this magic so badly, I know he'll do whatever it takes. And once he realizes I lied, once he realizes what bloodspell really is, he will come for me.

47

SOPHIE

Sophie bursts through the door and runs to her room. She plugs her phone into the wall and slides to the floor with her back against the bed. As she waits for the phone to power up, she pries open the journal. She finds the page where she left off and reads.

Immediately, she finds something that sends goose bumps shooting up and down her arms. But it's not a mention of Tanner. It's something else. A different name. She reads and reads until the surprise turns into realization and then back to confusion. Soon, tears are streaking down her face and dotting her T-shirt. Quinn *was* in a relationship with someone that spring, and at some point, things tipped sideways. Quinn placed her trust in him, and in the end, he turned on her. Eventually, the entries become less sensical and more manic. Most are just a few sentences, some just a single incomplete thought.

She may not fully understand it, but as she closes the last page, Sophie has pieced together one devastating fact. Quinn was being hunted.

Her phone blinks to life, finally, and she shoots off a quick message. I need to talk to you, she types. Are you home?

"Soph?" In another minute, she hears her dad calling her from somewhere deep in the house, just as her phone vibrates with a response. She leaves it plugged in and runs out the door.

48

QUINN

JUNE 2011
THE DAY OF THE FALL

I find Joey by her locker.

We're the only ones in the hall, and I'm breathless, growing more and more aware of the time.

"Can you talk?" I ask. I bring the tip of my thumb between my front teeth and bite down hard. This is neither the time nor place to say what I have to say, to ask of her what I have to ask of her, but I have no choice.

She is digging in her locker, her face hidden by the two-foot metal door. She takes down some magnets that hold up photographs, stuffs two old notebooks into her backpack. Then she pulls out a stack of unopened sticky notes and holds them out toward me. "Want these?" I take them, noticing that she's avoiding my eyes. She's not being cold exactly, just guarded.

Help me. The thought tsunamis to the front of my mind. Because I need her help. I need her steady, loyal logic. But Joey speaks before I can. "You broke up with River," she says. She scuffs her shoe against the floor. The singular squeak fills the hallway.

I close my mouth, momentarily damming up my own words. Slowly, I nod.

"Why didn't you tell me?" She looks at me now, mournfully. It's as if she's lost something irredeemable. *"I'm sorry,"* I want to shout. *"None of it was me. I chose a stupid dream over you and a stranger who made me feel like he saw the real me. Just help me untangle myself from this mess, and I promise I'll make things right. I promise I'll fix us."* But I stay quiet. Her face is slack, disappointed. It's paralyzing.

The bell rings, and Joey closes her locker. Desperate panic floods my chest, overriding my guilt. I'm aching to talk to her, to talk to someone, and I know Joey is the only one who has a level head enough to help me through this. I just need to know what to do now so I don't ruin things forever.

"After school?" I ask.

The cafeteria door opens and a deluge of shrill voices and laughter escapes. Then, there are bodies. Dozens of them. They scatter in all directions like fruit flies from a rotting apple. It is the last day of school, and so they are oblivious to us, busy flooding the hall with their violent shrieks that mark the impending freedom of summer. Joey glances over her shoulder, and I can see that I'm losing her, that she's about to be pulled in one direction and I'm about to be pulled in another.

"Last English class of the year," she says and indicates down the hall with her head. "You coming?"

It's an invitation. A lifeline. Her way of saying that she won't abandon me, despite it all. But I can't stay. I can't go to class. I can't be so easy a target for him. I have to get out of here.

"No," I say, and at first she looks surprised. It makes sense that she would be. I should go to English class with the rest of them and then clean out my locker and start making summer plans. I should be doing normal things. But if I do normal things, I know what will happen to me. After a few beats, she opens her mouth like she's going to say something, but she doesn't. Instead, she shuts her lips tight and nods in resignation, almost in defeat. And then, she goes.

I walk the other way, toward the gym. I duck out the back doors and start to plan. Home first. Then I'll go to Joey's. I pray that she will head home right after school. She will help me come up with some way to stop him. Maybe she'll tell me to go to the police. Or maybe she will hide me. Maybe I can do an illusion spell to hide myself. I'll have to tell her about the book and all the spells, but I don't have the time or capacity to worry about what she'll think. She's the best one to have around when you need to solve a puzzle. The only one.

He gets off work around five, so we'll only have an hour, give or take, but I know she'll help me. I know she will. Because she's Joey.

49

ELENA

Rain taps at the windows, like it would prefer to be let in.

As if in defiance, the lights have been turned up to industrial-level brightness. A glance over her left shoulder reveals Cal clinking away in the kitchen. Elena is drained. They've been working for two hours already. She read through her lines, changed her inflection, read through them again. They went through it several times, using the entire length of the room as their set. The real scene will involve a horse—standing next to one, not riding one, thank god. It's not a major part, and she had it down pat an hour ago, but Cal suggested they run through again and again so he could rehearse his own lines. She was glad they did. It will be different on set tomorrow morning, of course, but for now she thinks she's got it. She hid a smile when he told her she elevated the scene. Her delivery is apparently much more convincing, more emotional, than the "bee-stung" actress who quit. This is the start of something; she knows it in her bones.

Rain taps persistently at the windows as Cal stirs with a long spoon and ice clinks against glass. The flurry of texts from her agent this morning told her she's not wrong to be prepared for more opportunities after this. *Finally*, she thinks. *Finally*.

Since being here, though, she still hasn't felt her phone vibrate with a message back from Joey, even though she's kept it in her pocket the whole time. Sophie's theory about Tanner is still pinging around in her head, and she wonders why Joey hasn't responded. She feels, deep down, that Tanner could be their guy. He was dating and eventually married the daughter of the police chief. A police chief who somehow failed to report seven stab wounds on Quinn's deceased body. Clearly, this whole thing has been a cover-up for Tanner.

She pulls out her phone to tap out a follow-up message. We need to talk, she types quickly. Meet at the bar later?

She hits Send and watches the text fail to send just as Cal comes up behind her.

"Tequila mule," he says, holding a glass out to her. She pockets her phone and takes a sip.

"So good," she says, and she means it. She can tell that he, too, is riding the high of a successful day of rehearsal. They've run through their lines and exhausted their opinions on technique and style and delivery, and now it's time to relax.

He touches the rim of his glass to hers. "Thank you for doing this. I'm going to annoy my casting director until she hires you again. I know she has a cool sci-fi adaptation on the horizon, and I have a good feeling about you."

The fizzy drink crackles inside her mouth. "Thank *you*," she says. "Looking forward to tomorrow."

In a few minutes, she pulls out her phone again while Cal goes to the bathroom. Nothing from Joey or Sophie. She can feel a little tingle at the tips of her fingers. Something doesn't feel right. Sophie is constantly on her phone texting her wife for updates of the little one, and Joey is a woman with a secret boyfriend, so she's tied to her phone as much as either of them. Sure she's overreacting, Elena decides to let it go. Ten minutes is not a long time to wait for a response, and she almost laughs aloud at her lack of patience. Ironic when you consider that, before Monday, she hadn't really spoken to either of them in fifteen years.

Antsy, she walks over to the bookshelf. She remembers seeing it the last time she was here. The books are still neatly aligned, most of them old, a few untitled. One book is tipped over and looks about to fall off the shelf, which is something Elena would normally never notice, except everything in this house is intentional and pristine. She's surprised at the flaw. She rights the tipped book and realizes there's something missing. She looks around because she remembers what else was on this shelf the last time she was here. That gorgeous sculpture of the mountain peaks.

Elena spins around at a sound. Cal is back from the bathroom, leaning against the window wall, watching her with an amused expression.

"Whose place is this anyway?" she asks, uneasy but trying to make conversation. "I never asked."

He looks around as if seeing it for the first time. "That depends. Do you hate it?"

"I love it," she lies. She takes a sip of her drink.

"Well then, I'll tell you the truth. It's mine."

"Oh," she says with genuine surprise. She thought this was a rental property. Why on earth would Cal Pierce want to own a home in Whisper Ridge? It feels strange, and even stranger that he didn't say something sooner. "How often do you come here?" she asks.

"It was my mother's. I only come every few years."

She nods, noticing that he's moved closer to her. She doesn't know why, but she glances behind her to see how near she is to the wall. "So you knew about Whisper Ridge before the film then?" she asks.

He smiles and crunches ice between his teeth. "It was my idea to shoot here."

She doesn't know what to say to this. She'd thought this was a Phillip Granger film, but Cal seems to have much more of a hand in things than she thought.

"So what's with the…?" She gestures to all the massive window walls.

He laughs. "For the view."

Elena nods. His voice has grown quieter, and she realizes that he's only a couple of feet from her. Her cocktail is perched on the slate table next to his, so she doesn't have anything to do with her hands. She needs to pick something up, to fidget. She thinks about plugging her hand into her pocket to feel for her phone, but she stands stock-still. The energy in the room has shifted. She sees, now, that he is holding her in a dark, intense stare.

She knows that look.

He wants her.

50

JOEY

Violent flashes of distant lightning foretell a bitch of a storm.

The boxes by Joey's front door are half-empty their contents gutted and strewn all over her floor. She told Sophie that they were things she kept meaning to get rid of, and it's true. Some of it was her mother's. Old shoes and purses and makeup and books that she treasured, a hideous brooch passed down from Joey's grandmother, and other trinkets. She shoved these all into this box ten years ago on that hotter-than-average September day when her mother didn't wake up, and she hasn't opened it since. She's never been through them. But now that she's free of the obsession with Quinn's death that's occupied her for the last fifteen years, she might as well keep going, cut her life wide-open, expose the underbelly of all her problems, and discard what isn't necessary.

She looks at her phone, at Elena's text from hours ago. Quinn update. Joey didn't reply, ignoring her own curiosity. She is done talking about Quinn.

She pockets her phone and sifts through a stack of old *Cosmopolitan* magazines and sees a small note. It just says *Love you, Mom*! written in the laborious hand of a young child. The love she had for her mother was more than normal, she always thought. Because it went beyond love. It was admiration, adoration, obsession. Her mother would get dressed to go on dates with men she met through a friend of a friend, men from distant towns, and Joey would watch her from the bedroom door. Carly Close had deep blue half-moons under her eyes, even then. "*The exhaustion of living*," she told Joey when she'd asked what they were from. And that was the thing, in the end, that killed her. Exhaustion. Joey tried cracking jokes, making meals, letting her lie in bed for as long as she needed to, and trying to lift her mother's spirits even as she was weighed down with grief for Quinn. But the summer just after Joey turned twenty-two, her mom's latest boyfriend left her for a younger woman in Santa Fe, and that was it. Carly couldn't fight it any longer. She let go and was pulled under. It was the second time Joey had discovered the dead body of someone she loved. The second time she both recognized and didn't recognize a face that she had seen thousands of times. It was a Friday evening when they folded up the wheels of the gurney and slid her mother's body into an emergency vehicle. The sunset was one of the most beautiful Joey could remember, and all she kept thinking was that her mom could have seen it. If she had just hung on for three more hours, she could have seen it.

Joey swallows and sets the note inside the garbage bag. Rain is scratching at the windows, at the roof. She's swimming in a sea of memories, and she needs to come up for air. She slides the pile off her lap and peels open the other box. This one isn't full of her mother's things. This one is filled with Joey's keepsakes from high school, and, she remembers with surprise as she rifles through, some of Elena's things.

They found Quinn's body on a Thursday morning, and the very next day, Elena came and dumped a shoebox of trinkets into Joey's arms before leaving without an explanation. Elena wasn't allowed to have posters or pictures on her walls at home, so there wasn't much. Joey had never looked through it. She'd just put it in her closet, expecting Elena to eventually come back for it. But she never did. When Joey moved, she brought Elena's shoebox too.

She digs through it now, distracted immediately by a group photo, capturing a moment of pure glee, the four of them with their smiles wide and open, their eyes closed, heads tipping toward each other.

At the bottom of the box, she lifts a small Bible that seems out of place among Elena's things. Beneath that, the first thing she sees is a pink sticky note. The room sways around her. On the note is the same scribbled handwriting she found on the one in River's closet. The same handwriting as the one on the journal that Sophie found. Joey starts to peel it off. Then she looks at what it's stuck to. She blinks and looks again because she doesn't quite understand what she's seeing.

It's a DVD case. On it are two names. One she doesn't recognize. And the other is Nicola Bianco.

51

QUINN

JUNE 2011
THE DAY OF THE FALL

Yesterday, Elena cornered me in the bathroom at school and asked if we could do magic for something important. It seemed secretive, like it had something to do with Collingswood. But I was preoccupied, so I lied to her and said I couldn't find the book. It was shitty of me, I know, and, in hindsight, deeply ironic too.

Because now I can't find the book.

I try not to panic, but it's kind of hard when you've torn apart your entire room and it's still nowhere. Nothing in my nightstand but my journal, some pens, a lighter, and a few small candles. Nothing in my closet but clothes and bags and shoes. I did a brief search of the house, but then I spotted my mom in the garden, and I didn't want her to see how worried I was.

Because I am worried. Actually, I'm freaking the fuck out. And my heart won't stop clattering against my rib cage. A ringing in my ear has started, and I can't make it stop. I don't have to think too hard about this. I know he took the book. Maybe this morning on his way to work? I know what it means. It means he has figured out what bloodspell is. And in my stupid ignorance, I told him exactly how to access it when I told him how I revealed all those spells in the book. The fear that tears through me is like physical pain.

My heart is thrumming and thrumming, and my head spins because it's only a matter of time now. I don't have time to worry about the book. I have to go. I spin my grandmother's ring around my finger, as if this fierce, witchy piece of jewelry might give me strength. Then, I race to the front door, but my sweaty hand stays plastered to the handle. I can't bring myself to turn it. Not yet. I need to say goodbye.

I swallow back tears and force myself to keep my head.

I walk through the kitchen and peel open the screen door. I can't seem to slow my heartbeat. "Hey, Mom," I say.

She looks up, startled, from her crouch over the seedlings. "What are you doing home?"

"I forgot a textbook," I say. "I'm just going to grab it and head back."

She stands and glances at a watch on her wrist. "It's the last day." Her hands are covered in dirt.

I offer as much of a smile as I can. "I think I'm going to dad's after school," I lie.

"Okay." The surprise is still not gone from her expression. "I'll see you tomorrow then?"

"I think I'll stay with him tomorrow too." I hold on to the porch railing. Then I look at my mom. The backs of her wrists are perched on her hips, like she doesn't want to get her outfit dirty. I'm sure she has somewhere to be right after this, but she came home anyway to make sure she got the planting done on the right day. She looks down at her garden, counting to herself.

"Love you," I say.

"Wait, wait, wait." She hurries over and brushes my hair away from my eyes with a forearm. She dips her face down so she can look into my eyes. "Everything okay?"

"Yep," I say. I can't really say more, or I might cry. And I can't cry, because then it will all come out of me. After the spell didn't work this morning, I realized why he wanted it in the first place. And now I know I'm in danger. How could I have thought I could use the magic to heal anyone? How did I let him convince me he wanted that too?

I swallow back my fear and humiliation. Among the unspoken thoughts swimming in my brain, one needles through. "Mom, did you ever do a summoning spell without the book?"

She knots her forehead in confusion. "No, I didn't do any spells without the book. It's not possible."

I nod without betraying my deep disappointment. I knew this, but I thought maybe I was wrong and could somehow summon the book to me, that I could make all this go away. But I can't do a damn thing. Not anymore.

"Have fun with Dad," she says.

I pull her in for a hug, crushing our bodies together. She is warm and smells of lemon cookies. "Love you, honey," she says, hugging me back. Love oozes from her the way it always does, like it might be the last hug we ever have.

I can't say anything, so I just nod. I don't want her to read my face or notice that I've changed into my hiking boots, so I turn away quickly and give her a backward wave.

At Joey's, Carly lets me in. She's wearing a simple white T-shirt that exposes her long slender arms and bone-thin wrists, and I think about how she might have deep scars right there on those wrists—or worse—if it weren't for her daughter.

I wait in Joey's room and watch the clock on her dresser as rain begins to spatter the window. Four o'clock arrives. Four fifteen. Four thirty. Dust motes float past me as my panic grows. She's not coming.

I glance at the door, praying that I'm wrong, that she's just late, held up by a teacher, or waylaid by a muddy street she has to traverse around. But she doesn't come.

I fold over. My hands drop to my knees, and I squeeze my eyes tight, letting out a soundless scream. I pushed her away. There is no reason she should be here. But I can't wait anymore. Four forty-five. Terror revs my muscles back to life, my brain barking instructions. Grab that paper over there. Write her a note. Find her hiking backpack, her tent, her stove, her rain gear.

I rummage through drawers until I find socks and underwear, extra pants, and a sports bra. I find a spare toothbrush that's still in the packaging and a bar of soap under the sink. I race out to the kitchen, deciding on canned beans and dry rice, and two Snickers I find in the pantry. I fill up the biggest water bottle I can find. The pack is heavy, stuffed all the way up to the top. I cinch it tight and drag it to the front door. There, I swing it onto my shoulders.

Carly is sitting at her computer. She's leaning forward and mindlessly stamping out a cigarette in an ashtray next to her.

"I left Joey a note," I say.

"She's not here?" she asks, looking up.

I shake my head and move a hand to the door handle. I step one foot outside, then stop. I lean my head back in and say, "Tell her I said bye," but I'm not sure if she hears me because she doesn't respond.

52

SOPHIE

Sophie's fingers feel thick and useless as she opens the journal.

Barbara sits next to her and leans in so she can see. The rain, which sounds like it is only getting worse, makes the kitchen feel closed in. A little lamp casts a dim light from the corner near a plate of cookies. Barbara wears a pendant with a jewel-studded butterfly. It catches flecks of light and spills them onto the journal. Gael is busy with something on a laptop in the other room, headphones over his ears, but Elena is not here.

The last thing Sophie wants is to reopen healed wounds, but she also knows that this is critical. Barbara drums her fingers on the table.

The inside cover of the journal is where Sophie decides to turn first, since this will do the most damage. She wants to rip the Band-Aid off.

Barbara's fingers stop drumming. She inhales a small abrupt breath that gets stuck somewhere in her throat. Without saying anything, she traces a finger over Quinn's name. She circles the balloon of the large *Q*, then the rest of the letters, until she reaches the end of them.

"Where did you find it?" she asks. She wipes at her face.

"In my closet," Sophie says quietly. "At my dad's."

Barbara's eyelashes are wet and clumped together. She keeps her hand on the page, as if preventing Sophie from taking the journal away from her now that she has it. "You've read through it?"

Sophie nods. "It's..." She doesn't know exactly how to explain it. "It gets a little dark."

Barbara presses her lips together and nods. She pulls her reading glasses down off her head and starts to flip the pages with a tremulous hand. Quinn's handwriting assaults Sophie's eyes again. Eventually, she turns to the page Sophie hates to look at. Its words are etched into the paper with a ferocity she didn't realize Quinn possessed.

Bloodspell. Bloodspell. Bloodspell... The single word is written out ten, twenty times in a row, with nothing else on the page. It's the underlining that does it for Sophie. The words are static, and yet it feels as if they're going to crawl up and under her skin. She brings her arms to cross in front of her chest. "Do you know what it means?"

Barbara shoves her reading glasses back up into her hair, while Sophie shifts in her seat. She longs for a glass of cold water but doesn't get up. Then Barbara leans back. She puts her fingers to her temples and massages slowly, rhythmically, as her eyes close. There's a long silence that allows them to listen to the oncoming storm. Sophie feels the rumble of distant thunder in her bones.

"Bloodspell is folklore," says Barbara at last. "Years ago, well before my time, the book was different. It was full of spells written by generations of powerful witches." She inhales long and deep and looks toward the window where raindrops streak down the glass. "Remember I told you about Tammy Kallinski, who was initiated with me? How she came to me with a request? Well, of the four of us, Tammy was the one with the true heart of a witch. She was fierce about the magic, always going on about our power. She wanted to expose all the spells in the book that we knew had been hidden long ago. She gave me a whole list of reasons, and honestly, she was pretty compelling. Part of me agreed with her.

Why shouldn't we have access to all that magic? Why shouldn't we be trusted with it?"

Barbara closes her eyes again for a long moment, and Sophie isn't sure if she's done or not. Then, she fixes a renewed expression on her face and keeps going. "In the end, I said no. I was the keeper of the book, and I didn't see how anything good could come from unlocking spells other witches deemed too dangerous. And thank god I did because I watched the greed grow inside Tammy like a tumor. She was not going to let it go. But eventually, she realized I wasn't going to give in. She was just power hungry. It was becoming obvious to all of us. She turned on me, tried to pit Carly and Winona against me—Joey's and Elena's moms. I guess she succeeded at that in a small way. Soon Winona turned her back on magic altogether. Carly folded into herself. She was never quite the same again. And Tammy left. Moved away. Took her kid to follow her ex and his money. Maybe being wealthy made her feel powerful. I don't know."

Sophie stands up slowly, processing. She tips two cups out of the cabinet and runs the tap, drinks deeply from one, and fills it again. The other, she places in front of Barbara, who gives her a distracted nod but doesn't touch the water.

"Anyway," says Barbara, "one of the hidden spells was called blood-spell. It was a way to steal the magic from a witch and transfer it to someone else."

Before Sophie can process this, there's a sudden sound from the hall, and Gael rushes in carrying his laptop. "Have you heard from my mom?" His hair is rumpled, and he looks wide-eyed around the kitchen, as if Elena might be hiding somewhere.

"No honey, but I'll text her," says Barbara. "Dinner in about an hour."

"I just messaged her," he says quickly. "But she hasn't responded. I need to talk to her."

"Could be that she's on her way."

"Can you let me know if you hear from her? It's kind of important."

"Of course," says Barbara, standing to give him her full attention. "Everything okay?"

"Yeah, just want to show her something." He glances at the laptop screen. "It's fine, I'll wait till she's back." He carries his computer out of the room, and Sophie hears his socked feet take the steps two at a time.

"Where is she?" Sophie asks quietly.

"She didn't want me to say—I think she wanted to surprise Gael—but apparently she got a last-minute part in the film. She's up at the glass house doing a bit of rehearsing."

"That's exciting. But why up at the glass house? Kind of random."

"That's where the director and Cal Pierce are staying, I think."

Sophie thinks about asking more about this rehearsal, but the rain picks up with a sudden intensity that reminds her what they were talking about. "You said that bloodspell was a way to steal magic and transfer it to someone else. What exactly does that mean?"

Barbara puffs out her cheeks and exhales. "Well, those of us who are initiated are the only ones who can do magic. That's the way it's always been. However, bloodspell, if I am correct, is essentially a loophole. It allows someone who is uninitiated to do magic."

"Huh," says Sophie. "But how does that work?"

"I'm not entirely sure. I think there are two steps. The second step is the actual spell, the transfer. But it's the first step that I think gives them the ability to use the book, to see through illusion spells, to start feeling the magic..."

"Okay," says Sophie, afraid to ask her next question. "So, then what about the first step? What is that?"

Barbara looks at her for a long moment before she speaks. "The first step is a blood sacrifice."

53

JOEY

Joey sloshes through the rain, umbrella clutched in one hand and paper coffee cup in the other. The rain is really coming down now, though she doesn't even try to avoid the puddles.

She steps into the lobby of the inn and shakes out her umbrella. Her socks are soaked through, and she is freezing. The wood paneling is supposed to be charming, she knows, but it looks kitschy and cartoonish.

"Hey, Kathy."

The woman behind the front desk looks up from her phone. "Joey," she says warmly. "What are you doing here?"

Joey lifts the coffee. "You have room service now."

Kathy gives her a quizzical smile, and Joey asks, "Which room is Nicola staying in? Nicola Bianco. She called the coffee shop. Didn't want to come out in the rain. And I don't blame her. It's torrential."

Kathy's smile drops slightly.

"I want to get this to her before it gets cold, but I forgot to ask her which room," says Joey quickly.

Kathy hesitates. Joey wonders if she's had instructions to give the cast members top privacy. "It will just take a second. It's just, I promised I'd hand-deliver it. She likes the local touch, I think."

Kathy seems satisfied by this explanation. "Gotcha," she says, then leans forward conspiratorially. "She's in room three."

"Thanks, Kathy, that's amazing." Relieved, Joey moves toward the hallway behind the front desk.

"Wait, wait, wait."

Joey stops and closes her eyes. She's sure Kathy knows she's lying. She has no idea what to do, so she turns back and tries to smile. "Nicola's not there," says Kathy. "She left an hour ago. I think she was going to dinner. Not sure why she would have called you for that coffee. Maybe she wants you to bring it to her at the tavern?"

Shit, thinks Joey. She just needed an excuse to talk to Nicola, one that would be believable. Bringing her a coffee in a restaurant is not going to work. "Great, I'll go see her there," she says, trying to think. "But actually, I'll get her a fresh one so it's hot. You want this one?"

Kathy looks at her like the offer is straight from heaven. "Really? Thank you. I can hardly keep my eyes open." She takes the cup, pops off the lid, and takes a sip. "You don't have sugar, do you?"

"I don't. Sorry."

"Hmm."

"Is it just Nicola staying here, or do any of the other actors have rooms?" Joey asks.

Kathy stands up, and her chair swivels with the release. "Tons of them. The whole place is booked up." She raises her eyebrows in a show of pride.

Joey's heartbeat quickens. "Did they all go to dinner together?"

"Could be. Not sure. I just remember Nicola. She's so beautiful. It's hard to miss her." Kathy snaps her fingers. "You know what? I have sugar in the kitchen."

Joey is still processing what to do with this information. Should she go to the restaurant to find Nicola? But she won't be able to ask what she needs to, not in public. She watches Kathy leave the room. This is the kind of inn that serves sausages and pancakes in the morning, freshly cooked in-house. It's a Whisper Ridge landmark, and just about anyone who has spent their twenties in this town has worked the front desk of the inn, including Joey.

Which is how she knows there is a master key locked in a safe in the cabinet behind the desk.

As soon as Kathy is out of sight, she slips around and kneels down in front of the safe. Surely it can't be the same passcode it was six years ago. Surely Kathy's changed it since then. But she tries it anyway because she can hear Kathy open the kitchen door, and she knows she only has a minute before she's back. 1-6-9-6, Kathy's son David's birthday. The buttons beep louder than she'd like them to, but she pauses to listen and doesn't hear Kathy. She presses the Unlock button—it works. The safe opens with a hard tug. The master key, just as she remembers it, clings to a ring with keys to the maintenance room, the back door, the cleaning closet, and the mailbox.

A sound from the hall brings her back to her senses. She closes her fist around the key ring and swings herself back around the desk.

"You do make good coffee over there, Joey." Kathy is back, head bent over her drink. Meanwhile, Joey's heart races. She's afraid she might give herself away if she speaks, so she just turns to go.

"Come back anytime," she hears Kathy shout after her, and she wonders if the offer will still stand once she realizes what Joey's about to do.

54
ELENA

Elena feels her phone vibrate.

Relief moves through her, and she reaches into her pocket, happy to deflect what seems now to be an overt sexual advancement. Are all men the same? It's the kind of thing she hates to think because she has a son, and it's not fair to judge half the people in the world based on a handful of shitty interactions. But here she is, judging. The look in Cal's eye is darkening, pupils dilating. His hunger for her is obvious, though his smile is placid, which, to be completely honest, is throwing her. She thinks it's desire she sees in his face, but maybe she's misreading it. Maybe it's just the harsh lighting.

"Sorry," she says, pulling out the phone and fumbling to unlock the screen. "One sec."

There's a moment's hesitation, during which she's not sure he's going to back away. But then he ducks his head politely and reaches for his drink. "Take your time," he says, reverting back to the relaxed professional she spent all afternoon with.

The first text she sees is from Barbara. Will you be here for dinner? I'm making chicken.

Elena is temporarily grateful for the connection to someone else who's not in this room. Cal is good-looking, obviously. He's probably one of the most famous, well-regarded men on the planet. He's kind and *real.* Honestly, it would take a will of steel to say no. But she really doesn't want to sleep with him.

The second text she reads is from Gael. I know who the guy is that's been following you, it says. A square pops up on her screen with a little circle to show that a picture should be loading. She stares for a few seconds, but it's taking forever.

She pockets her phone, deciding that it's time for her to leave anyway. She's about to say so when Cal places his glass back on the table and picks something up. It's the little glass sculpture of the mountains. The one that was missing from the shelf.

"I really like that piece," she says, stealing a glance past him toward the door. Where did she put her stuff?

"I had it commissioned," he says. "It's the Three Elks." He touches each of the points in succession and then looks at her. Elena senses that he's going to make a move any minute now.

"I think I should go," she says quickly, placing her cup on the bookshelf. There's no coaster under it, and she sees him frown. "I'm meeting someone for dinner."

She expects him to say something awkward, to look bummed, or to ask her if she'd like to stay for one last drink.

She does not expect him to take a step toward her. Far too close to be considered polite.

An alarm bell inside Elena's head begins to trill.

55

QUINN

FEBRUARY 2011
FOUR MONTHS BEFORE THE FALL

I'm freezing outside on my dad's doorstep. It's still firmly winter. Scabs of snow dot the ground all around me. New Year's passed with a trip to the spell circle and a sleepover at my house after. Elena brought a bottle of André, of course, and we did an illusion spell to change my hair color to lavender. Then we summoned some sparklers and danced around, ringing in the new year. We're only two months in, and it already feels like this year is going to be…different.

I knock three more times and call out. "Dad?" No response, so I try the door. It's unlocked. Inside, he's right there, ten feet from me, asleep on the couch. Passed out, actually. I shake him, try to wake him up, but he doesn't rouse, just lets out a snore. We were supposed to host his friends for poker tonight, but maybe they're avoiding him after what happened. Two days ago, he drove his car into a telephone pole in town. It was awful. I pull a blanket over him and let him sleep.

I drop my overnight bag in the kitchen. A box of stale Triscuits sits in the pantry next to a few cans of beans. In the fridge, there is just a crusted jar of mustard and a cloudy pickle container. And a pizza box. With a flicker of hope, I open the lid, but it's empty, stained with grease.

I steal another look at him on the couch, his leg dangling off the side like he wanted to get up but couldn't quite manage it. It's so early. It's not even four. I wring my hands and look up at the ceiling, hoping for an answer to this mess to be printed there. I wish I knew how to save him, but alcoholism is in the mind as much as it's in the bottle. Even I know that. And it's powerful. River's grandfather was an alcoholic, the asshole kind. He told me horror stories about his grandfather's physical decline and drunk driving incidents that never landed him in jail—probably because River's dad is a cop—and how he punched a tourist right outside the Strike for no apparent reason—again, no charges—at sixty years old. Booze makes people lose themselves. I'm losing my dad, and I wish there was a way to help him.

I sling my bag onto my back and head out the front door. Around the back of the house where the yard meets the woods, I look down the hill and see the spell circle. I wonder if I could do a spell to help him. I turn a fraction, thinking about the merit of this idea. Would I even consider doing a spell on my own?

That's when I see it, all the way at the top of the hill. The glass house. It's lit up, which makes me pause. I've never seen lights on in there before. I thought the place was abandoned. But bright white lights shine out from the windows. I have no idea what compels me toward it, maybe it's boredom, or maybe it's because it looks like a beacon.

Either way, I start to walk up the hill.

56

SOPHIE

"A what now?" Sophie can feel the disbelief rising inside her and nearly lets herself smile because surely this is a joke. But then she sees how serious Barbara is.

"A blood sacrifice." Barbara's voice is funereal. "My chatty great-aunt used to tell a story about one of the girls who was initiated with her... and her fiancé. The fiancé was a miner. He had next to nothing. One day, he must have found the book. At the time, all the spells were right there, on the page. Anyone could see them. One of the spells he saw was bloodspell. He figured he could use it, take her magic for himself, and get rich." She cuts off with a look of resignation. "Anyway, he tried to murder her."

Sophie feels a violent roll inside her. "Oh my god."

"That tough woman refused to back down without a fight. There was an axe involved, and the fiancé was killed. Blanche actually went to prison, something women didn't often do in those days. But I guess the crime was so brutal, self-defense didn't cut it. Anyway, from that point forward, the spells in the book were hidden. All of them. And most of them, save for illusion, summoning, and healing spells, are hidden away for good, or at least I don't know how to reveal them."

Sophie watches Barbara tear the tape from the butcher paper around a whole chicken. Through the window, lightning thrusts the backyard into momentary brilliance.

"I understand hiding bloodspell, but why hide the entire book?" Sophie has so many questions.

The chicken is in a deep pot now, and Barbara pushes pads of butter beneath its elastic skin. "It's a great question. Protection is the only explanation I can think of. There are probably more spells in there that, if they fell into the wrong hands, would be catastrophic."

Sophie picks up the peeler and slides it down a carrot.

"The secrets were passed down to me, not created by me," says Barbara. "I only know that there is a way to reveal the rest of the book's contents. I just don't know what that is."

"Quinn knew." The carrot peels pile on top of each other like a nest of snakeskins. "In the journal, she says she unlocked the entire book."

"Ah, well. They say once in a few generations a highly intuitive witch comes along..." Barbara dusts salt over the pale flesh of the chicken; then she lets her head sag. Sophie thinks she's going to keep explaining, but she doesn't. Instead, she pushes the heel of her palm into one eye, then the other. She takes her time putting the chicken in the oven, then opens a bottle of wine.

Sophie traces a finger along the edge of the journal. "Do you think this could be like the book?"

Barbara frowns in response and then takes a long sip with her eyes closed.

"When I first found it," says Sophie, "it was empty. There were no words on the pages. But now there are, obviously. Maybe it's a similar kind of magic?" This explanation doesn't feel quite right, but she truly isn't sure.

The kitchen fills with the smell of cooking. Barbara taps her finger on the stem of her wineglass. "Did the writing appear slowly over time? Or was it all at once?"

"Over time."

Barbara takes a sip, thinking. "It doesn't sound like the kind of magic in the book. It would have been revealed more immediately. At least that's my understanding of the old magic anyway. To me, this journal sounds like an illusion spell."

Inside the oven, the chicken crackles as it begins to cook. "I thought about that, but an illusion spell only lasts for five years," says Sophie. "It's been fifteen since Quinn would have written in it, so wouldn't the spell have faded years ago?"

Barbara toys with the stem of her glass. "Which could mean someone is updating the illusion spell every five years."

There's a low growl of thunder, and the lights above them flicker.

"Let me ask you this," says Barbara. "Is there any way someone else might have gotten their hands on *The Book of Aspens*?"

"We haven't seen it since Quinn died," she says, shame making her spit the words out as quickly as she can.

Barbara inhales sharply. "Oh, honey, is that true? Why on earth didn't you tell me?"

"We couldn't find it after Quinn died. She was the keeper, and then we just grew distant, and the book stayed lost. We should have looked for it. We've been looking for it since we've been back, but we can't find it. This is bad, isn't it? This is so, so bad." She is breathless. She knows the answer to her question before Barbara gives it.

"Yes, I think so." She taps her finger on her wineglass. "If this journal has been hidden by an illusion spell for fifteen years, that means someone's been updating it every five years. So, someone knows where the book is."

Thunder reverberates off the mountains and through Sophie's mind as she absorbs this. "Are you saying the illusion spell was never meant to reveal the words in this journal? It was meant to *hide* them?"

Barbara gives her a solemn nod. "I believe what we are seeing here is the fading of an illusion...because someone has yet to update it."

Sophie's next words are almost silent. "Which means I was never meant to see this journal. I was never meant to know what I know. No one was meant to."

They both stare at the journal sitting alone in the middle of the table as if it will come to life and confirm that they are right.

The world tips, and Sophie feels an unmistakable plunge of fear.

57

JOEY

The back door of the inn clicks open, and Joey slips inside. Quietly, she makes her way up the stairs. She can see Kathy's hair-sprayed coif from here, but she's busy with a noisy game of *Candy Crush*. Room three is just at the top of the stairs on the right. Joey silently unlocks the door.

Inside, it smells faintly floral. The bed is made, and there are clothes draped over it. The closet is open, and there are more clothes, mostly neutral in color but all delicate and pretty. A slender woman with dark green eye makeup and nude lips pouts at her from an issue of *Vogue* on the nightstand. Joey wonders, momentarily, what it would be like to be a glamorous public figure.

She sees nothing masculine in the room. Not a watch or a shirt or a pair of shoes. She steps into the tiny bathroom, which to Kathy's credit, has great light and is appointed in soft white porcelain with matte black fixtures. Makeup is scattered on the counter. A case of brushes catches Joey's eye, and she digs through it. A hair straightener and an electric toothbrush sit next to a cosmetic shop's worth of face creams. She's not sure what she's hoping to find. Some clue that will point her in the right direction, perhaps.

Back in the bedroom, she opens the drawer beside the bed. Empty except for a remote control and a laminated paper with the Wi-Fi details. She closes it with her hip and looks around the room. This was not worth stealing the master key and breaking Kathy Renner's trust forever for. There is nothing in here that can help her. She is about to leave, about to make her way silently down the stairs and try her luck at the restaurant, when she spots Nicola's suitcase peeking out from the closet. It's gorgeous white leather and looks as if it's never touched a luggage carousel in its life. She wheels it out of the closet and finds the zipper. Splaying it open on the floor like she's doing a dissection, she examines the interior. Empty. But when she reaches a hand inside one of the pockets, she feels something square and flat, about the size of a book.

She pulls it into her lap and instantly recognizes it. It's the painting of the old general store, with a carved wood frame around it—the one that, until recently, hung on the wall of Aspect Coffee since Barbara had it commissioned in the nineties.

Processing the bizarreness of this discovery, Joey digs around again in the pocket and feels something else. A kitschy wooden bear holding a sign that says Whisper Ridge Inn. Excitement and curiosity make her dig her hand into the same pocket a third time.

This time her fingers find something small, cold, and solid. She already knows what it is before she pulls it out, and she feels a sudden burst of anger. The ring. The gold one with the black onyx stone and single gold droplet. She knows now, holding it in her hand, that this is not from a vintage shop in LA. It was a birthday gift to Quinn from her grandmother. She holds it under the lamp to examine it closely. The light catches on an inscription on the inside of the band. *Quinn Winter, 12/13/1993.*

A sound makes Joey look up. Someone is at the door. She searches around for somewhere to hide. In the closet? Under the bed? But there's no time. In another half-second, Nicola's block heels appear, and the door thunks closed behind her.

"*Oddio!*" Nicola throws a hand to her chest when she sees Joey, who is crouched on the floor with a suitcase wide-open in front of her. Nicola is dry and unruffled, despite the weather outside. They stare at each other for a long moment, and Joey wonders if she is going to run away, call for help, or attack her. She stands up slowly with her hands out.

"What the hell are you doing?" Nicola clutches her purse to her chest.

"Nothing, just..." Joey says, taking a careful step over the bag. Nicola backs up, as if Joey is about to lunge at her. "I was looking for you. The door was open. I thought—"

"The door was not open."

"It was. I just wanted to come and bring you a coffee."

Nicola looks around her, waving her hands in exaggeration. "Where is it?"

"I left it downstairs. But I was just about to go get you another one."

Nicola eyes her. "I am calling the police," she says finally, digging through her purse.

"No." Joey grabs her wrist, and the look of shock and fear that Nicola gives her makes her let go quickly. "Please. I was just leaving."

Joey looks back down at the suitcase on the floor. She remembers what she saw and decides to change tack. She reaches down and snatches up what she found in the suitcase. "What are you doing with this?" Nicola looks wrong-footed, and Joey uses it to her advantage. "This painting was hanging in my coffee shop."

Nicola frowns, but she lowers her hand from her purse. "Give me your phone," she says.

"Excuse me?"

"Your phone. I do not want pictures or video recordings of this. Give it to me."

Joey puts up two surrender hands and then reaches slowly into her back pocket. "Here." She offers up the phone. "Look, I don't care what you stole." Joey chucks the painting and the carved bear onto the bed. "I want to know where you got this." Joey takes a chance by holding out the ring. "Just tell me honestly. I won't tell anyone about your *little habit*. I don't care. I just need to know where the ring came from."

There's a silence during which the rain barrages the window. Nicola could still call someone. She could simply shout, and Kathy would be up here in less than a minute. Joey accusing her of being a thief would be so inconsequential; it's not as if Nicola couldn't just apologize and return everything and take Joey down for breaking and entering.

"I will put them back," says Nicola. Joey's not sure she believes her, but she honestly doesn't care. The way she's looking at Joey tells her that this is far from the first time she's stolen. The objects—everything besides Quinn's ring—may not have any monetary value, but drawing attention to them could do real damage to a glamorous public figure like Nicola Bianco. Joey waits.

"Almost as soon as I took it, I realized it was strange," she says, clearly on the verge of distress. She's trying to hide it but she's gripping the shoulder strap of her purse so hard her knuckles are turning white. "The inscription," she says at last. "It's that girl's name. Quinn." The way she says it sounds like *queen*. "I recognized the name when Elena mentioned her the other day. I was so curious because I thought, *There's no way the girl in Elena's story is the same girl whose name is on this ring*. It makes no sense. So I came to see you. I thought, you are a café owner in a small town. You will know. And you recognized the ring right away. I did not even have to ask. I knew then that it belonged to her. I just did not understand how he—"

"*He?* Who's *he*?"

"I wanted to find out what happened to her, so I pretended I needed to learn about her for research for a role, but that man, her father, he was so angry. He tried to push me. I had to run."

"Who did you take it from in the first place?" Joey asks, but she thinks she knows already.

Nicola's eyes are focused on hers. "He and I have been friends for almost twenty years. He has never said anything about this place or anyone he knew here. Not once. I don't know how he got it." Her voice is growing cold with every word, a lake freezing over. "Then I thought, *Maybe he knew her some other way*. Maybe he somehow knew the girl, and I tried to ask him without asking him, you know? And it suddenly became clear."

"What became clear?"

Nicola smiles mirthlessly. "That he was lying."

Joey suppresses a chill. "Where is he now?"

Nicola waves an insistent hand. "I don't know. And I don't care."

"Listen to me, do you think...?" Joey speaks slowly. "Is he the kind of person who could...kill someone?"

For a second, the question hangs in the air between them. How could either of them know this?

Nicola is clearly horror-struck. "You have to go," she says quickly.

"Wait, please. Where can I—"

"He will know it was me who told you." She makes a show of striding toward the door.

"Nicola, wait."

But she doesn't wait. She gives Joey an unapologetic look and then opens the door violently. "Kathy?" she calls down the stairs.

Joey grits her teeth and glares at Nicola for a beat. It feels like a betrayal of trust. They were on the same side. She doesn't waste a second, though she is bombarded with memories. Suddenly things she wondered about for so long—like who Quinn spent all her time with that spring—appear in vivid color.

Joey lets the door close behind her and drops the master key right outside it. She sprints down the stairs, past Kathy, where she pushes open the back door and runs into pelting rain.

58

QUINN

FEBRUARY 2011
FOUR MONTHS BEFORE THE FALL

Up the hill I go. It's a mountain, really. It takes a half hour because my terrible hiking boots have me sliding all over the place, but once I make decent progress on the incline, I know there's no turning back. I shed my dad's winter coat, which I piled on top of my own for warmth. The lights are still on in the house, and now I can see there's definitely someone there. There's a dirt bike parked out back, its wheels caked in fresh mud. I stand surveying the yard, which has been cleared of trees to offer the best views, I'm sure. I let my eyes scan the house. There are so many windows. The place isn't as modern as I remember it from when we played truth or dare as kids. The siding is a fading gray-white, and there are cracks along some of the windows. There's one tall section made of what looks like glass bricks. The style is very eighties, outdated. I see a figure pass between rooms upstairs.

I tuck my dad's coat into a ball in my arms. I've just walked up a mountain to investigate a house that I've never seen with lights on until now, which means there's someone inside. It could be anyone. It could be a serial killer. I know all this, and yet my fear instinct isn't firing like it should. I'm nervous, yes, but for some reason, I'm not scared. I should be hauling it out of here. But something makes me stay.

When I look back at the upstairs window, a man stands there, staring straight at me.

My heart leaps into my throat. There it is. There's the flicker of fear.

The man looks to be in his mid-twenties, maybe. He's wearing jeans and work boots, which I can see because the window stretches all the way to the floor. He has wild hair that looks like it could use a trim.

But the thing that catches my attention the most, the thing that keeps me from running away, is the puppy. He's holding a small fluffy dog in his arms and is scratching behind its ears. I watch him come down the stairs because I can see everything he's doing. The house is completely lit up. I don't think there's a single lightbulb that's not switched on.

In another minute, the man pokes his head out the door. The puppy wriggles in his arms. "Can I help you?"

"Oh, sorry. I was just…" I'm not sure how to finish the thought. *Curious* doesn't seem like quite the right reason to trespass on someone's property. I'm saved from having to come up with something because the puppy squirms free of the man's arms and tumbles to the ground. I gasp, thinking he's hurt, but he rights himself in one bumbling motion and dashes toward me. I squat down to greet him. His fur is so soft. He licks and nips playfully at my hands and falls over.

"Pip, no biting," calls the man. I look up to see him smiling and walking toward us. The dog bounds back to him and then around his legs and then back to me. We're both breathless with laughter by the time he has made several trips between us and, exhausted, lies in the dirt watching us with his tongue lolling out of his mouth.

The man invites me to stay. He's making nachos. I wonder, for a second, if my dad will worry about where I am, but I know he won't. He's too drunk to remember I was supposed to spend the night at his house. Then I wonder if this is smart. I have no idea who this man is. But I am feeling reckless, so I say yes.

We pour salsa on top of tortilla chips and then sprinkle on cheese before sticking it into the oven. We eat with the back door open so Pip can come and go. The man tells me his name is Robbie, and he used to live here, but he hasn't been back since he was two years old. He was born at Sacred Heart down the road, and I tell him that's where I was born, and that's when he admits he's a little older than me, but I already guessed that. He and his mother moved to follow her ex, Robbie's dad, the man who had this house built. They ended up in LA. It was a lonely childhood, or at least that's what I gather when he tells me his mom spent more time getting dressed up and waiting for men in bars than helping him with homework. "She did always seem to have money though," he says. "I think that's why she kept doing it. To make sure I had enough. It was all for me. That's what she told me before she died, anyway. It was always all for me." He tells me that, eventually, he met a really nice girl from Italy who convinced him to take an acting class, and he loved it. When I press him, he bashfully shuffles over to the living room where a duffel bag sits on the floor.

"We only have a DVD because my friend made it. It's not official or anything." It's a movie case.

"So you wanted to be an actor, and you just...did it?" I ask, a little starstruck despite myself.

He laughs and says he has a long way to go yet. He has dreams to hit it big in LA, but all the directors and hiring managers in Hollywood are stuck up and don't see his potential. He ran out of money, which is why he's here. He's been living in the glass house for a few months, doing construction work over in Vail. He thinks he'll stay until summer. He looks at me when he says this in a way that makes me feel like he's just decided, and I go warm with pleasure. As we talk, I can tell he's a genuine person. His demeanor is relaxed and welcoming. I'm surprised I feel like myself around him. I'm also surprised that I don't really think about my dad or about River or anything else. It feels like he could be a new adventure, something I didn't realize I needed until right now.

"Nice ring," he says, as I press my palm against the table.

"It's my favorite," I say.

And then we watch Pip trail in snow and mud and zoomie around the kitchen, and Robbie doesn't seem bothered by it, which makes me smile. He pulls out a joint, putting his lips to it and lighting it in one fluid motion. As he exhales, he passes it across the table to me. I take it without hesitation. He's a little older than I am but clearly sees me as his equal, which gives me a kind of thrill.

As we smoke together, he tells me something else.

He explains how his mother told him there was something strange about Whisper Ridge. Something like magic. I shift in my chair when he says it, trying to hide my discomfort. He says she told him the trees here have magical powers or something and that she used to practice magic before he was born. He laughs with self-deprecation, as if this is a ridiculous thing to say, and I can feel him staring at me, as if I might confirm or deny it. I deflect slightly and ask him if that's why he's back.

"She died," he says. "But before she did, she wanted me to come here. She wanted me to learn about the magic. Stupid, right? But I had to honor her last wishes."

I eye the joint, which rests on the side of a plate, a finger of smoke rising from it. "Not stupid," I say and offer him a smile.

He leans in. "Hear me out." He's buoyed by something, maybe the fact that I didn't laugh at his reference to magic. "I think there is magic here, and it's been locked away so no one but a handful of people knows about it. And if that's the case, I think that's terrible. It's power hungry and wasteful. If there's magic, it should be used for the greater good, don't you think? If I had magic like that, that's exactly what I would do. Help people."

I pinch the joint between my fingers and take another deep, satisfying inhale. The high flows through me. I have found a kindred spirit.

59

SOPHIE

The wipers are frantic, but they're doing no good. Sophie can barely see out the windshield.

She has to find Joey. She has to at least warn her that someone else has access to the magic and they could be dangerous.

Sophie didn't say what she was thinking—even though Barbara was most likely thinking the same horrible thought—that whoever this person is must have hurt Quinn to get the magic in the first place. Quinn was the blood sacrifice.

She leans forward, the seat belt cutting into her neck. Is she at Second or Third Street? She can't tell with all this rain, and she doesn't recognize this town like she used to. She rolls down the passenger window, but that doesn't help either. She puts the car in park, unbuckles, and jumps out of the car, running toward the street sign. Third. She has two more blocks to go then. The rain is relentless, and a jolt of lightning followed closely by a crack of thunder forces her back into the car.

She creeps along until she passes Second. There are no other cars out in this weather, and she's glad she doesn't have to navigate other vehicles.

Without warning, someone appears in the glow of her headlights. She smashes her foot onto the brake, and the car skids to a stop. The figure looks up, as startled as she is. Sophie's heart is thundering, but she unbuckles and swings open her door.

"Are you alright? I couldn't see—Joey?"

"Soph." She looks like a deer, wild-eyed and terrified.

"Are you hurt?"

"No. I just…"

A chill moves through Sophie. "Come on, I'm getting soaked." She points to the car. It takes Joey a minute to understand, but then they both climb in.

The car is instantly warm and dry. The windshield wipers still frantically flip from side to side, keeping Sophie on edge, but it doesn't occur to her to turn them off. "What are you doing out here?"

Joey is wet to the bone. Her hair is plastered to her face, and that look of terror hasn't gone away. She dries her hands on the dashboard vent as Sophie cranks up the heat.

"I know who did it," Joey says. She is looking out the front window, searching through the dark and the rain. It's like she thinks whoever it is will just appear in front of the car. She's manic, Sophie realizes. She's in shock. Something has happened. Sophie turns in her seat. She's about to say something, but Joey sticks out her fist. When she uncurls her fingers, there's a ring there, gold and black and familiar. And then suddenly, Sophie knows what she's looking at. She hasn't seen this ring for fifteen years.

"You know who killed Quinn."

Joey doesn't respond, but her face says it all.

Inside Sophie's mind, gritty, rusted screws turn into place. "Listen," she says, carefully. "I think whoever killed her is going to kill again."

Joey blinks at her.

"I know what bloodspell is. It's a hidden spell, buried in the book.

It's a blood sacrifice. It's a way to steal the magic. Whoever killed her did it to steal the magic that was in her blood."

This takes a second to sink in, Sophie can see. Joey leans slowly back into her seat, thinking. She spins the ring around in her hand. "You said they're going to kill again. Why?"

"The journal I showed you. Quinn's journal. It was hidden with an illusion spell."

She pulls out the journal and puts it in Joey's lap so Joey can see for herself all the pages that are full now that were blank before. "The illusion spell has faded. I think whoever killed Quinn has done the spell every five years since then to keep the magic in their blood and to keep the sacrifices hidden. In fifteen years, that's three murders." She pauses and tightens her hands on the steering wheel. There have been others. Of course, why did this not occur to her before? It wasn't just Quinn. Three. It seems impossible.

"Who were they?"

"I don't know," says Sophie. "I guess they'd have to be witches from here, probably from other generations. But listen, I think we need to focus on right now. Because whoever it is, they're going to kill again. Very soon."

Joey rifles through the pages again, and Sophie can see realization blossoming. "The sweatshirt," she says. "He used an illusion spell to hide that too. That's why we don't remember seeing those stab wounds. It wasn't the raincoat covering them. They weren't there. It's why the police never said anything about stabbing as the cause of death. He used an illusion spell to hide the real cause of death and make it look like an accident instead."

"It's Robbie, isn't it?" Sophie turns back to the right page in Quinn's diary and points at the words there. *Quinn + Robbie*. "She wrote about him. She was infatuated with him. But then, I think he turned on her."

Joey nods, and Sophie feels the theories stringing together. "I found a note today," Joey says. She takes the note out of her pocket and hands it to Sophie. It's soaking wet, but the permanent marker is clearly visible in its all-caps handwriting.

"*I told him*," Sophie reads. "Who does she mean? Robbie?"

"Yes and no." Joey pulls a DVD case out of her coat pocket and hands it over. It's slick with rain, and Sophie wipes it on her jeans. "The note was attached to this."

Joey waits a beat as Sophie looks, skimming the all-black cover for words. The inside of the windows are sweating from their body heat. She reads the title. *The Last Truth*. Beneath that, it says *Starring...* "Hang on," she says. "*Starring Nicola Bianco and Robbie Kallinski*?" She's about to ask for clarification when she looks at the faces on the cover.

There he is. At least fifteen years younger, and it's a bit grainy, but Sophie has watched his movies. She follows celebrity gossip. It's him.

Sudden nails of fear rake down her spine. "Oh my god," she says. "Elena."

"Elena?"

"She's with him now."

Joey doesn't bother to hide her alarm. "Where? Where are they?"

Sophie points ahead, though she can't see a thing beyond the streaks of rain. The sweat on her spine becomes a deluge of terror.

60

ELENA

He's standing right next to her now. She wants to push him away, to give him a good shove because who does he think he is, trying to intimidate her? Why is she again in that gray area between what she wants and what she has to do to get it?

Cal looks like he's studying an insect under a magnifying glass. He doesn't say anything, just looks at her. They lock eyes, and she pushes at his chest. He grabs her arm. The violence of it rattles her. He is not going to let her go. She jerks toward him shoulder-first, but he doesn't even budge. His face is neutral.

"Get the fuck away from me," she says with venom she doesn't have to dig deep for. She half turns away from him, but there's not much room. She's pinned between him and a corner of glass windows. She has a ridiculous thought that if she can find something sharp, something heavy, maybe she can smash the glass, get out, then run away.

She sees his reflection in the window. Soberly, as if he wishes things didn't have to be this way, he shakes his head. "It's nothing personal," he says.

And then, before she can react, before she can even wonder what exactly isn't personal, something cracks against her skull. She feels an orchestra of pain reverberating through her head. It consumes her. She feels herself wobble. And then she looks back at him. He's holding something up, raising it over his head. The familiar object is arresting, the way it catches the light. That's the last thought she has before the pain comes again, this time following a thud that she hardly registers. She thinks of nothing else as the room goes dark.

61

QUINN

JUNE 2011
THE DAY OF THE FALL

The back door of Sophie's house is unlocked. Like a thief, I slip inside.

Clues, I told myself after leaving Joey's. I'll hide clues for them. I've brought Joey's sticky notes with me. I don't want them to find the clues right away. I just need some time to get enough distance. Hopefully, in a week or two they'll find them and understand.

A voice inside my head asks the question I've been suppressing all day. *Why run? Why not stay and fight?* I could go to the police. River's dad. I could tell him—but what would I tell him? I think someone is trying to kill me so they can use my blood to do magic? This was part of the reason we aren't supposed to tell anyone about the magic. Because it sounds insane. If I stay, I'll have zero protection, even with the police. Because now Robbie has the book. The only way I survive is to run.

I drop my journal in Sophie's closet. I press it up against the back corner, next to a pair of sandals I know she'll go digging for on the first hot day of the year. I want her to know, I want them all to know, but they need to find out later, after he's long gone. My hope is that he'll come looking for me. I hope I can lead him far away from this town. I don't know what I'm going to do then, but I'll figure something out.

I'll fight. He may have the book, but he doesn't have the magic yet. He needs to do the bloodspell to get the magic. If he does find me, at least I'll be far from here, beyond this place. Even if he kills me, he won't be able to finish the bloodspell without the aspens.

Next is River. I see no car in the driveway, which tells me his parents are still at work. Nerves swim through my body, bouncing off the inside of my skin. I try the handle, and it's locked, but I know where the spare key is. Inside, the sound of muffled music accosts me. He's a collector of music, practically a hoarder of it, refusing to use an iPod like a normal person and instead insisting on vinyl records. The music comes from his room upstairs. I put a hand on the banister and hover a foot over the first step. He's up there. I start my ascent as quietly as possible. When I reach the top of the stairs, a thump reverberates off the walls, and I hear the baritone of River's laugh. I run on my toes to the game room where his Xbox sits on the floor next to a low TV stand with glass-doored cabinets. The choice to leave the antler here with him came to me at the last minute. As I slip it into the tiny closet and press the note onto it, I hope that it will serve two purposes. To leave him a clue and to push him toward Joey.

Once I leave River's, I stick to the side streets to keep from being seen. They're gravelly, which makes them less slick from the rain. Under half an hour now until Robbie's shift is over. I run to Elena's, trying to think of an excuse I can give to her mother, who will surely answer the door, but I glance inside first and see Marissa Berg of all people standing in the living room. There are a handful of others looking expectant, nibbling on Ritz crackers. Wednesday afternoon Bible study. I hesitate but decide to go around the back. Elena's first-floor window is perpetually unlocked—her parents don't know she disabled the lock months ago so she could sneak in and out easier. I crawl inside and open the box under her bed where she stores her weed and see a picture of the group of us, our awkward fourteen-year-old selves, arms draped over each other, unfettered joy in our eyes. My insides clench as I force down tears. Inside the box, I place the DVD with a pink sticky note on top of his face. I tuck it all back under the pocket-sized Bible, the thing Elena swears makes this box an infallible hiding place.

Finally, I run to my dad's, Joey's pack bouncing on my shoulders. I'm out of time, but I'll leave directly from there. I'll hike deep into the mountains, where no one will find me, and camp and channel some of Joey's outdoorsmanship. But first, I have to say goodbye to my dad. I can't leave without saying goodbye to him. What if something happens to me? I'll never forgive myself, and, more importantly, he'll never forgive himself.

His truck isn't in the driveway.

He's semiretired and never works afternoons. Poker games don't start until dinnertime. Unless he's run out to get more liquor, I can't think of what he's doing at four thirty on a Wednesday. But then I realize I've answered my own question. I go inside anyway, just in case. The door is unlocked, which gives me hope. I push it open, expecting to see him sitting there on the couch, beer in hand, some game or other on the TV, telling me that he had to take the car in for service. But the room is empty. The couch is sunken in from years of lonely evenings spent drinking his worries away. Eight empty beer cans on the coffee table indicate that he hasn't cleaned up in a while, or just since last night. My heart wrenches with pain. Over the past week, I've used magic to heal exactly no one. And now I have to leave without helping my dad, which was all I wanted to do in the first place. I miss him fiercely, and I won't get a chance to see him because I have to go now. I walk out through the back door and pull the backpack straps tight, clipping them in the front.

As I step outside, a shadow paints the dirt in front of me. I look up, hope in my heart. "Dad?"

But it's not him. It's Robbie. I look at him, and I know he's seen me.

I know it's over. "No!" I scream so loud my head feels like it's going to split.

Those two words seem to reverberate through the trees around us. *"Dad? No!"*

I was so close to getting away. So close. He's holding a knife, I realize now, and the violence of his stillness sharpens my fear into dread.

62

JOEY

They wind up the steep driveway with their hearts in their throats, silence screaming in their ears.

Sophie's headlights pale compared to the massive glass house and its clinical halogen glow. Joey catches a movement inside a ground-floor window. It's him. It's Cal. He's doing something with his back toward them, but he turns when he notices the car. And when he does, the screaming silence turns into a real scream. It's coming from Sophie, and one second later, Joey realizes why. Because now she sees it too.

Someone lies on the couch, at the level of Cal's knees, unmoving.

Joey's not even sure Sophie puts the car in park as they both leap out and race toward the house. Cal is clearly visible through the floor-to-ceiling windows, and it's as bright as the middle of the day inside the house. He looks concerned at first, calculating something. And then he turns back around, kneeling.

Elena. Her beautiful hair is two-dimensional beneath her, flattened on the slick black couch. There are no wounds that Joey can make out, but she isn't moving. Her eyes are closed, like she's passed out or—

Joey watches Elena's chest, waiting for it to rise. Any second now, she's going to see her ribs move up and down. She waits. She searches her body for signs of movement, for a twitch or a blink. Cal has finally started to check her vitals, or at least that's what it looks like. But then he moves down toward her feet and tugs up one of her pant legs. He runs a finger along her bare skin, in a motion that makes Joey's own skin tingle. He shifts Elena's leg and lowers it so it hangs limply off the side of the couch. Joey runs to the front door and slams her fists into it. She calls for him to let them in, but he only gives her a half glance and then continues doing what he's doing. She tries the handle, but it's locked. She runs back to the window, and when she gets there, she thinks she sees the smallest movement: Elena's chest rising an inch, then falling. Did she imagine it?

"Joey." Sophie's voice has the thin timbre of sheer panic. Joey can't see Cal clearly with his back to them, but she can see needles and vials and strange medical devices and a very sharp knife.

She runs away from the window, leaving Sophie to bang on the glass and scream. Joey slips in mud as she scours the ground around the driveway.

"Soph!" she calls as loud as she can, hoping she is heard over the torrent of rain. A colorless flash of lightning momentarily brightens everything around her.

She sees Sophie splashing toward her. Soon, she's there, at Joey's elbow. She doesn't stop to ask questions. She doesn't need to. She sees what Joey needs and bends down to help. Their motions are completely in sync as they lift the enormous rock. Their hands are slick, and they almost drop it several times on the way over to the house. It has to weigh a hundred and fifty pounds, but somehow they manage to lift it up to chest height. They nod a countdown in unison and then hurl it at the glass with a duo of guttural roars. It chips the window and drops with a violent crack. When it hits the pavement, a piece slices off the side, like glacial ice cascading into the sea. Cal jerks straight up at the sound. He does not seem to meet their panic with equal emotion. Instead, he looks annoyed, no more than a father about to demand they keep the noise down so he can concentrate.

Joey thinks about calling the police, but her phone is with Nicola. "Hurry, call nine-one-one," Joey says.

Sophie looks stricken. "I don't have my phone."

They turn back to the window. "Please!" shouts Sophie at the same time Joey yells, "Let us in, you piece of shit!"

Joey looks down at Elena and sees that she is still lying awkwardly on the couch. Joey thinks, in a moment of elemental relief, that, yes, she does see Elena's chest lift and then fall. Lift and fall. And again. She is alive.

Cal chooses to ignore them and grabs a glass bowl, then kneels next to Elena's leg. His body obscures Joey's view. She can't see what he's doing, but only a few seconds pass before he stands decisively. What Joey sees there alerts every cell in her body, and they respond with rigid shock. He's sliced her skin. No, deeper than that. He's sliced an artery by the looks of it. Blood gushes from the wound like oil from an impaled gas can. It begins to collect in the bowl beneath her. Joey cannot breathe. Her muscles are incapable of movement, except for a slight involuntary tremor, but her brain—her brain revs like an engine in a stalled car. She has to figure out how to get in. There must be a way in.

She scans the side of the house for any cracks or open windows. You'd think a glass house would be fragile, that there would be vulnerabilities somewhere, but it seems in this horrible moment to be a fortress.

Sophie, meanwhile, has collected fist-sized rocks and is hurling them at the glass, to no effect except to further irritate Cal.

"Stop!" he shouts. It's the first time he's spoken, and Joey's shocked that she can hear him so clearly despite the barrier between them. He holds his head between his hands as if the noise is too much for him. "I just need a minute."

Sophie, unbelievably, seems to find words. "Cal," she says. "It's not too late. You need to apply pressure. Stop the bleeding." Her voice is steady, and Joey has no idea how since her own body is quaking so hard, she thinks she might start convulsing.

He doesn't move except to curl his fingers around a vial in his palm. "Elena came to *me*," he says. "Just like Quinn."

Joey feels like she's going to burst open. "Don't say her name," she manages. She doesn't clarify which name she means. She's not even sure she knows.

Joey joins Sophie and launches a rock at the glass, and then when it makes no more than a tiny scratch, she picks it up and does it again. And again. Cal half turns to them again. "Stop it!" he shouts. "I need this. It's as much mine as it is hers," he says.

Joey keeps looking around, keeps assessing. How is there no way in? Sophie joins her in the barrage of rocks being chucked at the glass. Cal's eyes drop to the nicks the small stones make, which are just next to the deep chip the bigger rock made. For one flash of a moment, he looks worried. But, just as quickly, the moment is over, and he turns back to work.

The sole of Elena's foot is submerged in her own blood. The bowl is filling up fast with crimson liquid. It's obvious now that her face has lost its normal color. Her hands, too, look pale. She is being emptied. Cal takes a vial in his fingertips and dips it into the bowl of blood. Joey watches in horror as he pulls at the fat syringe. Thick red blood fills it to the top. He inverts the syringe, then replaces the tip with a thin intravenous needle with practiced deftness. Looking directly at Joey with red eyes and a manic smile, he pulls his shirt up, revealing the muscular shadows of someone who exercises compulsively. He jabs himself and presses the blood—Elena's blood—through the syringe, from the needle into his body.

A surge of bile finds its way to the back of Joey's throat. She forces it down with her rage at this glass house—impenetrable, and yet somehow the only thing keeping her from saving Elena. Elena is dying, and Cal Pierce is a fucking lunatic. Beside her, Sophie is alternating between desperately calling, "Cal, please," and kicking at the glass with the heel of her boot.

Suddenly, Joey is all adrenaline. She races away from the house and ducks into the car. "Sophie!" she calls out. Sophie turns toward the headlights. She must understand what Joey wants because she runs toward her and leaps into the passenger side. They each take a steadying breath and nod a synchronized mental countdown. And then Joey's foot is on the gas, and the car is squealing forward. In a few seconds, they're at the window. Joey closes her eyes as the car smashes into the house. The sound of shattering glass is everywhere.

They're inside. The window wall is gone. Cal stands, wolfish, just on the other side of the couch. Joey tumbles out of the car, shards biting her knees as she scrapes her way to her feet. She has no plan. She has no thoughts other than one: He will try to stop her from getting to Elena, but she also feels, primally, that it doesn't matter. She will get to Elena anyway. Shards crunch beneath her shoes. Sophie climbs out of the car and stands behind her. Joey and Cal are squaring up now, two boxers in a ring.

He watches her for a moment and then bends down slowly. When he stands again, it's with something in his hand. The knife he used to cut Elena. Joey's heart is a ticking bomb in her chest, but she does not falter. As if in preparation, Cal closes his eyes. This is it. He's going to come after her, and Joey takes a second to work out a plan. She can dive behind the couch and try to trip him up. She can dodge him to the side and attempt to run around. She thinks of the car and wonders if there's a way she can use it again to her advantage. Cal opens his eyes, and he wears an expression of having won. Joey has no time to understand what it means because without warning he turns and runs. Within seconds, he disappears down the hallway, pulls open a heavy door, and slips through it.

Joey's instincts pull her toward him. She has a distant thought that he's going to the spell circle to finish the bloodspell. She wants to tear him apart, to scratch out his eyes, to smash a rock into his skull. But her body, and the rising sobs from Sophie, force her to resist.

Instead, she hurries over and drops to her knees, where Sophie has already lifted Elena's dripping foot up onto the couch. She is leaning on the wound with all her weight, trying to stanch the blood. Joey can see, though, that she doesn't need to. Elena's not bleeding anymore. Joey's hand goes to Elena's neck, where she wants more than anything to feel a pulse, but she doesn't. She keeps her fingers there for as long as she can bear it. Still, she feels nothing. She buries her face in her own hands and tugs at her hair, screaming until her throat is raw. It's a release, a powerful fuck-you, and it doesn't feel good because how can it? It is not nearly enough.

Eventually, she wets her wounded throat with a swallow and looks around. The blood that splashed onto the floor, the bowl of blood, and Cal's footprints leading out of the room—all of it reflects the bright lights overhead. *There are traces of him everywhere*, she thinks as she feels the tremor returning. There is no way he's going to get away with this. Distantly, she hears the revving of a dirt bike, but there's a shrill ringing in her ears, and she recognizes it. It's the cry of burgeoning grief, and it drowns everything out, even Sophie next to her, who sobs into the neck of their dead friend.

63

QUINN

JUNE 2011
THE DAY OF THE FALL

Robbie moves toward me, slowly, and I lean away, my backpack pressed against the closed door.

"You got off work early," I say, trying to buy time, calculating how I can maneuver myself to block his view while I twist the door handle behind my back. I'm not looking at the knife in his hand. I'm looking right in his eyes.

He flashes a small smile, and then it's gone. His eyes cast down to my feet. He almost looks repentant. "Did you know?"

I swallow, nod.

"After the deer sacrifice didn't work, I realized it," he says. "Bloodspell requires a human sacrifice. Someone with the magic in their veins." Then he says, "I'm sorry," and presses his lips together. He might be apologizing for showing up late for a date; that's how casual he is. Behind me, I find the door handle and grip it. I attempt to turn it, but it's stuck, and the backpack keeps me from getting a good purchase.

He sees. Pauses. Watches my hand with curiosity. My breathing is erratic, and I sense that I have no choice. I have to commit. I spin around and use both hands to try to unstick the handle. And then, I have it. It turns, and for a second—no, less than a second—I think I've done it. I imagine myself running through the house, throwing chairs and tables behind me, sprinting out the front door, my dad pulling up at that exact moment…

Instead, I feel Robbie's arm hook around my neck and jerk me backward. And then, I feel the blinding sensation of something sharp piercing through skin. Then it sinks into me even deeper, through muscle, and the pain is like nothing I've ever known. I only have enough time to look down, to see a dark blot of blood forming on my favorite pink hoodie, and to hear him say, "There's no other way."

The pain comes again and again, and I want it to stop. I just want it to stop.

Until, finally, it does. Until, at last, there's nothing.

64

SOPHIE

Sophie dreamed of Quinn's lifeless open eyes for years. Therapy eventually helped her detach herself from the dream, and slowly, over time, she learned how to change it or wake herself up before it could start.

Now, she's struck with the hopeful thought that Elena will wake up, that she will stand and dab the blood out of her hair with a towel and tell them it was all for a movie. But Sophie also knows, of course, this isn't going to happen. Elena is gone. Her complexion is pale. Her mouth is open, unnatural, and still. Her eyes are closed, but the lids aren't fluttering or twitching like someone who's asleep. They're devoid of color. All of her is devoid of color.

Sophie swallows, trying to erase images of the vial he filled with Elena's blood. The needle he shoved into his skin, like it was insulin. And then his face fills her imagination, and she doesn't want it there, but she can't help it.

Unwittingly, she's transported to a cold evening curled up on her couch at home, her legs over Talia's lap, and Talia's mother, visiting their new baby, sitting on the chair. One of Cal Pierce's recent films—for which he had just won an Oscar—was playing on the screen. Sophie's mother-in-law had gone on and on about how *cute* he was, that Cal Pierce. Sophie was called to Leah's bedroom by a shrieking monitor, so she didn't hear the rest of the conversation. But she remembers his face filling the screen when she eventually came back into the room. Even Talia knows him and likes his movies. He's *that* famous. He's one of the most known faces in all of Hollywood, in the world, maybe.

Sophie vomits violently.

Rain spews in through the once floor-to-ceiling window that now lies in pieces on the floor. She wipes her mouth, eyeing the car that plowed through glass. If they had only done it sooner, they could have saved her. Guilt claws at her. She should have figured it out. They could have been here before he knocked her unconscious. Minutes would have been enough. She knows this now, but hindsight has never been her friend, only an antagonist reminding her of all the ways she's fallen short.

"Sophie." Joey is standing, and Sophie is reminded of when they found Quinn at the bottom of the crag. Sophie was all hands. She grabbed at Quinn and hugged her. She didn't shy away from the nearness of death, and she's doing the same thing now. She can't help herself. She smooths down Elena's hair, presses out a wrinkle on her shirt with her fingers, as if it matters. All the while, she is choking back the sob and the taste of her own vomit that nest together inside her throat. Dead friends. That's what she collects. She has failed to save two people she loves from terrible ends.

"Sophie." There's an urgency in Joey's voice that makes Sophie glance up. Joey doesn't say anything else, but she's staring at the smashed window. The car has disappeared. And the window is somehow being repaired. Before their eyes, it's whole again, not a single scratch on it, and the car is parked outside. Inside, where just seconds ago, there was debris and rain splatter and jagged shards, there is now a spotless floor and a wall of glass, perfectly intact.

"What the fuck," says Joey. Sophie tears her gaze away from the window. Elena's body no longer lies across the couch. She's splayed out on the floor as if she has fallen.

Sophie examines the scene, trying to understand. Is the horror of it all making her lose her mind? Streaks of red on the floor where Cal inadvertently smeared Elena's blood—they dissolve. On his way out, he left a footprint, shiny from blood, but now it's like it's being mopped up by an invisible towel. Gone.

Shock and confusion drive Sophie to her feet. She stands next to Joey. The bowl of Elena's blood vanishes. The scene before her is somehow cleaning itself up.

It's a kind of optical illusion. That's all she has time to think before the next strange thing happens. This time, it's counterintuitive. A puddle of blood now halos Elena's head and sticks her hair to the floor. Even the wound itself has shifted from the ankle to the left temple, and it's gruesome. That's where it appears the blood has come from. Sophie and Elena stand in silence, watching the world change shape before their eyes. *No,* she thinks. *This is all wrong.*

Sophie feels something heavy filling her right hand. She grips it instinctively, not wanting to drop whatever has appeared there. When she looks down, she sees a jagged glass sculpture. It looks like it's supposed to be mountain peaks. It's slimy with blood, and strands of long black hair stick to it.

"This is him," Joey says quietly. "He has the book. He must have reached the spell circle."

Sophie instantly knows what Joey is saying. It's an illusion spell. He's masked her murder with magic, like he has done before. Made it look like he's had nothing to do with it. And in this particular case, he's decided the best way to cover his tracks is to make it look like someone else's fault.

"It's fine," says Joey in a voice that suggests it's anything but. And honestly, Sophie feels like she can solve this. She feels like there is a way out. There has to be. She doesn't feel fear, not the going-to-jail kind, until she sees the blue light outside the window. Someone flings the car door open and hobbles through the rain, peering in through the glass window with a face like a ghost. It's Marissa, in her police uniform, and she looks at Sophie, then down at Elena, then back at Sophie. Her face says only one thing: *"I knew it."*

65

JOEY

Fuck. Fuck. Fuck.

Joey is not prepared for this. Elena dead, watching her murdered and not being able to stop it. The sick asshole running away with the book, with the magic. His illusion spell that has suddenly changed the entire crime scene. And now the police, Marissa Berg, outside the glass house looking in, thinking she's seeing evidence of a horrific crime. But she does not see the truth.

"Joey, what do we do?" Sophie's words wrench Joey out of her thoughts. Marissa is right outside, waving at the vehicle behind her, which spits blinding blue and red lights everywhere, and someone else gets out of the car. Another police officer. Marissa says something to him and then takes her gun out of its holster and points it directly at Sophie through the window. The other officer is running, and Joey knows he's heading for the door.

There is no talking their way out of this. Sophie has a murder weapon in her hand, covered in what looks like Elena's blood. Joey has only one thought. "Run," she whispers.

Sophie doesn't hesitate. She drops the sculpture, still dripping with blood, and races down the hallway where they saw Cal run just minutes ago. Joey follows her. They move fast, checking doors, looking for a way out. A solid door at the end of the hall looks like it might lead somewhere outside, and when they get to it, it's heavy, but it creaks open with a shove. They hear the front door of the house crash open and a man's voice yelling. Joey can't hear what he's saying, but she knows they have to be quick.

They're in a garage now. There are three dirt bikes lined up against the wall, and Joey can't believe their luck. Sophie sees them at the same time, and they both make a run for it. Joey grabs the helmet from one of the seats and pushes it onto her head. She climbs on, feeling the bike rock beneath her. She turns the throttle slightly and kicks down the starter. It whirs to life beneath her. Behind her, she spots a garage door opener on the wall. Kicking the kickstand down, she leaps off the bike, smashes her palm against the button on the wall, and then darts back to the bike. The garage door hums and cracks. Darkness and rain swell inside. Lightning and thunder warn them.

"How do I start this thing?" Sophie is twisting her hand forward and backward, looking all around her bike for an answer.

"I'll do it," says Joey. She finds the starter with her foot and steps down hard. Nothing happens. She does it again, this time only stepping until she feels resistance and then starting again. One more kick, and nothing. "Come on," she says. "Come on." Then, with one last kick, it starts with a whir.

Joey sprints to her own bike and peels out of the garage, feeling unsteady. She stops a few feet away, expecting Sophie to be right here with her, at her side, but she isn't. Joey looks back to see Sophie kicking at the starter again. The engine has turned off. The bike is dead.

There's a moment when the world slows down. Joey can hear voices shouting inside the house, and she knows it's only seconds before they're in the garage. She finds Sophie's eyes and tries to communicate something to her, but they only have a moment. There seems to be understanding there, maybe even a slight nod, but honestly, Joey can't tell. The rain is splattering her visor. It could be shock or helplessness that she sees on Sophie's face for all Joey knows. But she doesn't have a choice.

The door that leads from the house to the garage swings open, and Sophie's head snaps around. Joey watches as she raises her hands, gesturing for surrender. She wishes she could stop this right now but she is out of time.

Joey Close has no use for religion, but she prays to the trees as she turns her head and curls her fingers around the bike handles. She prays as the bike lurches forward. In seconds, she's peeling away, tires digging into mud and pebbles. Behind her, she leaves Sophie and the cops and Elena and everything that happened tonight. She's muttering an idea to herself, to the aspens. One more glance back and the mountain terrain has swallowed the view of the glass house.

This better fucking work.

66

JOEY

Joey careens downhill without any semblance of control.

She hasn't driven a dirt bike since high school, and she's reminded why she hates them. They're too fast. Too loud. Too disruptive. The bike is moving fast, away from the glass house, and the only thing she knows is that she needs to go down. Once she's close to the bottom, she'll figure out where to go from there. The rain, of course, is making sight impossible. She bumps over something, a rock or a root, and nearly slides off the seat. When she looks up again, there's a tree trunk directly in her path. She swerves inches from it, a maneuver that sends her skidding out. The tires stop on the uphill side of a boulder, which is the impossible luck that saves her from tumbling to her death. She catches her breath for a second, feeling the rain relentless against her helmet.

She hears something through the din of the storm. A voice. Or voices. They seem to be coming from every direction. Up, down, all around her. From the trees themselves. *"Not much further,"* the voices say. *"Just beyond the next ridge. Keep going."* Joey doesn't need to search for the source of the voices. She's heard this before. Not these exact voices. These are more generic, more ethereal. Not like the voice she heard in the woods days ago, before all this started, before Sophie and Elena showed up. That time, it was Quinn's voice, clear, spoken through the trees. These voices, though. They don't sound like a resurrected human voice but like the trees themselves, and Joey doesn't have time to question her sanity. She doesn't have time for doubt or disbelief, not only because she knows, she *knows*, these trees can talk, but also because she knows the rules. And the rules clearly state that when the trees talk, you must listen.

A faint growl echoes in the distance. Another bike.

The trees whisper once more. *"He's coming."*

67

JOEY

Joey jumps off the bike and lets it clatter to the ground.

The spell circle welcomes her with a tingling inside her blood, a buzzing of hornets in her veins. She's grateful for the feeling and desperate for the magic to fill her as quickly as possible. She thumps onto the ground in her usual spot. Doubt seizes her. This won't work. No one has done magic without the book for centuries. It's not possible. She has a flash of inspiration. She might have a way out. But then she realizes why she's wrong and curses—she needs the book to do any kind of magic, including a summoning spell that would bring the book to her. She wants to scream, to cry out in frustration, but instead, she decides she has to try something. What choice does she have? The police have Sophie now. There is no doubt about that in Joey's mind. They'll take her in, and there's ample evidence to put her away. Joey thinks of Elena. Her snark and style and her magnificent fuck-you attitude that Joey always secretly envied. She thinks of Gael. Elena's son. Joey's chest tightens, and her resolve hardens.

She closes her eyes and starts to feel the magic fill her up. The feeling is pure power, like she is being alchemized. She focuses, but then she shifts as an idea comes to her. It's a ridiculous idea that absolutely should not work—it's not how she's ever known the magic to work—but for some reason she is compelled to try. So, she turns her thoughts to the trees. Out loud, alone in the woods, she speaks. She asks the trees for exactly what she needs. A moment passes when nothing happens, and Joey repeats herself. She can feel the magic thickening her blood, and she knows not to give up yet.

To her astonishment, the whispers begin. The trees speak an incantation. Joey could cry. It's working. She doesn't hesitate. She listens and repeats the incantation as loud as she can. She stumbles over the words the first time, but the trees speak it again and again, and she thinks she can hear Quinn's voice and other women's voices mingled in the whispers, and so she listens and tries again, hoping that something will happen. She can feel the magic within her coursing with power, but nothing is happening. Desperate, she recites the incantation she hears from the trees one last time.

Then the trees go quiet.

Joey goes quiet.

Out of that silence grows the hum of an engine.

Joey hardly has time to gasp before the bike appears from behind the shroud of rain. He's less than seven yards from her with a direct path. Six yards. Five. He's going to mow her over. Moving out of the way is impossible. There's no time. Four yards. Three. She makes eye contact with him for a fraction of a second, and that's when she knows it's over. Two yards. One. She closes her eyes and prepares for the end.

68

SOPHIE

Sophie and Barbara sit in silence.

Barbara's just revealed that Quinn's journal is likely under an illusion spell. A fading illusion spell, which means whoever Robbie is, he probably doesn't want a journal out there with his name in it, accusing him of trying to kill Quinn.

The rain has picked up again, and it seems like it's going to get bad. Sophie gets up to make tea.

"None for me, hun," says Barbara. "There's some lavender in the cupboard over the coffeepot."

When the water is done, Sophie fills a mug with shaking hands. "Who do you think Robbie is?" she asks.

"Robbie Kallinski is Cal Pierce," someone says from the doorway.

Sophie whirls around. Joey is standing in the kitchen, dripping rainwater onto the floor. She's panting like she's just sprinted, and it takes a minute before Sophie realizes what she just said.

"The actor?"

"Mom?" A voice shouts from upstairs. Then the sound of feet on hardwood. Gael slides into the kitchen, still clutching his computer.

"Someone's been following my mom," he says, panting, when he sees Joey. "I think she's in trouble."

"Wait a minute, Robbie Kallinski?" asks Barbara.

Joey nods. "Soph, I need you. We have to go."

"Go? Where?"

"As in Tammy Kallinski?" It's Barbara again. She sounds shaken.

Joey shrugs impatiently.

"Hang on now, Tammy Kallinski. She used to be one of us. I told you all about her. She was initiated with me." She tents her hands over her nose and mouth. "She had a baby," she says, muffled. "I remember now. His name was Robbie."

"He changed his name, I guess," Joey says, with rising urgency. "Soph, please. Elena needs us. We have to go now."

Barbara nods, distracted by her own bewilderment. Sophie's hand wobbles, and hot water splashes over her finger. She flinches and steals a look at Gael, who turns his screen toward them. They all lean in. Cal Pierce stares back at them. It's a grainy zoomed-in photo, but it's absolutely him. "This guy's been following her ever since she's been back," Gael says. "I finally got a picture that shows his face."

Sophie puts a hand on Gael's arm and turns to Joey. "Is she really in trouble?"

"She is."

Sophie can feel her pulse quickening. It all somehow feels connected. "Joey, I need to tell you about—"

"Bloodspell, yeah, I know all about it."

"How?"

"You told me."

Sophie's eyes narrow. She thinks back. She's sure she didn't. She only just learned about it from Barbara a few minutes ago. Unless Joey somehow found out before?

"I'll explain on the way. Right now, we need to go. We're running out of time."

"I'm coming too," says Gael bravely.

"Not in a million years," says Barbara, grabbing hold of his shoulders.

He wriggles free of her and bounds upstairs. "I just need to get my shoes," he calls down.

"You better go before he chases you down the street," says Barbara.

Joey turns abruptly. "Barbara, I'm so sorry. I just want you to know that if I had known, I would have done it. I would have tried to save her. We lost the book, but this whole time, I could have done magic, and I didn't need the book. And if we had known, you know we would have done everything we could to—"

"None of that will do any good," Barbara says as she stands and takes the steaming mug from Sophie. Then she says, low and sure, "Go. Save Elena."

Sophie is lost. "What is going on?"

Barbara's face cracks into a tiny smile. "It's obvious, hun. Joey here has just turned back time."

69

JOEY

To her credit, it doesn't take long for Sophie to absorb the whole story.

"You just *left* me there?" she says in mock fury, but then her face breaks out into a torment of worry. "Let's go over the plan one more time so I know what I'm doing."

She looks nervous, so Joey repeats what she thinks would be the best approach. Slow and quiet, so they can get Elena's attention without alerting Cal. This seems to be enough for Sophie, and they don't waste any more time talking.

The spell circle is wet, and a little pool has formed in the center, somehow giving what they're about to do more reverence. They take their seats anyway, both of them too frantic with what's at stake to worry about the rain. Joey waited for Sophie's doubt, to hear hesitation in her voice when she told her she'd done magic without the book. But Sophie had given her a supportive nod and just said, sagely, "Intuition."

Now, Joey is nervous that it's somehow going to fail her. It might not work a second time. It may have just been a fluke. But when she looks over at Sophie, she sees resolve. She tries to imitate that feeling and finds herself being filled up with the magic. She closes her eyes and speaks out loud.

Within seconds, before Joey has any time to think about whether it worked or to worry that it didn't, the trees whisper. The sound is almost like a melody, and it soothes Joey's ears. It's beautiful, she realizes, when the trees whisper. There is nothing that could sound any more like magic. She thinks she hears the faint sound of Sophie laughing, and honestly, Joey feels like doing it too. But she doesn't. She concentrates, listens, and then repeats the incantation the trees are whispering.

It takes time, but Joey doesn't doubt that it works. Not this time. She knows with all the cells in her body that she has command over this magic. The trees have been here this whole time, and they haven't been agnostic like she'd always thought. They have only been silent because no one asked for their help.

And then, just before she opens her eyes, she feels it. There's a book in her hands. A weathered cover she hasn't felt in a long time. Tears prick at her eyes and her face feels hot.

"You did it," says Sophie. A summoning spell. Without the book.

"He's going to notice," says Joey, standing and wrapping the book in a wet bag and stuffing it into her trail running backpack. She reaches down for Sophie's hands. "Time to go."

70

ELENA

The rain is really coming down. Elena is looking out the window, her senses heightened by a spark of something she hasn't felt in a while. Excitement. She finally, *finally* feels like she's on track. She tries to imagine what Gael will say about this role that's fallen in her lap, and she doesn't know, but it will be perfect, whatever it is. She wants to thank Cal too. Thank him for what he's done for her because he really does have no idea. But she won't gush. That's not her style.

Cal is mixing drinks in the kitchen, and he's put music on to signify that the work is done, and now it's time to reward themselves. She looks up to see his reflection in the glass. He buries himself in the refrigerator.

Past the reflection, she sees something moving outside. A person. No, two people. They're coming closer. Elena's heart leaps into her throat. She cups her hands around her eyes and presses up against the window. What the hell?

Joey is sprinting, hunched over, toward the front door. Sophie is right behind her. They both throw a finger to their lips. *Shhh.* Elena has no idea what is going on, but she gets the sense that they do, so she spins slowly to look at Cal out of the corner of her eye. He's still doing something with his back to her. She creeps along the wall and behind the staircase to reach the front door and pulls it open. Rain splashes on her shoes, and she pulls her friends inside.

Sophie reaches out and touches Elena's sleeve. "Thank god," she whispers, and she looks desperate, relieved.

"Listen to me," says Joey as quietly as possible. Her eyes are wide and flecked with fear, and seeing this is what finally makes Elena realize something serious is going on. Joey is looking around. "Where is he?"

"In the kitchen," whispers Elena. She feels Joey's hand on her wrist. She pulls, but Elena yanks her hand away. "What's going on?"

"He's dangerous, okay?" Joey reaches for her again, but she doesn't tug this time. "He murdered Quinn as a blood sacrifice so he could steal the magic, and he's going to try to kill you tonight for that same reason."

Elena frowns, confusion jumbling her thoughts.

"Please, Elena. We'll explain everything. Right now, we have to go." Sophie's now tugging on Elena's arm.

Elena only has a minute or so before Cal comes back with the drinks. She doesn't know if it's the lack of Sophie's typical positivity that does it or Joey's uncharacteristic frenzy, but she suddenly knows what they say is true. She can feel the truth moving through her, slipping along with the blood in her veins. There's an echo of something, a memory or a dream, that calcifies her thoughts. He's dangerous. Elena knows this. She didn't realize it before, but suddenly, unequivocally, she does.

And then she just feels rage. "I'm not going anywhere," she says.

Their faces drop.

"You say he stole our best friend, that he drove the rest of us apart, and you think he desecrated our magic." Elena doesn't ask this. She is just laying out the facts as she sees them. They both nod. Joey cranes her neck to try to see beyond the staircase. Elena continues, "But you want to let him get away with it?"

"No," says Joey in a whisper-yell. "We'll go now and deal with him later. Let's just get somewhere safe."

"I said *I'm not going anywhere*," she says, wrenching her arm free of Joey's grip. "Quinn deserves fucking justice." Joey and Sophie are apparently speechless. The seconds are ticking away, and there are no more sounds coming from the kitchen.

Her friends are anxious. That much is obvious. But then—and the sight makes her want to let out a war cry—both of their expressions shift. It's slight, but she knows she has buy-in. One small nod from each of them, and that's it. They're in agreement. Joey cracks her neck, like she's preparing to fight. Even Sophie looks feral all of a sudden.

Cal Pierce will pay for what he's done.

In a flash, Joey's gaze drifts past Elena's shoulder.

Elena turns.

71

JOEY

Cal tips his head to the side. He grips one glass in each hand. "Hello," he says.

Joey searches his face for signs of malice, of ill intent, but there is nothing. He's blinking at them, seeming to try to work out who they are and what they're doing here.

"These are my friends," says Elena casually. Her words aren't careful or measured at all. It's solid acting.

There's a moment of quiet during which Joey thinks Cal might not know he's about to kill Elena. Maybe he hasn't thought that far in advance.

"Welcome, friends of Elena. Come in," he says. "I'll make more drinks."

They don't discuss any kind of plan out loud, even when Cal disappears and pours two more cocktails with the calm of a man about to host a dinner party. The only sign that he is at all wary is his small glance up at them while he twists open a fizzing ginger beer.

In minutes he's near them again, and Joey feels her body react involuntarily. She has already changed the course of history tonight, simply by coming here, and it strikes her that she's the only one who knows what happened in the previous version of events. Not even Cal knows. The horror of watching her friend bleed to death—she's glad neither Elena nor Sophie has any memory of it. She watches his eyes glide between the three of them, and she can tell he's thinking on his feet. She knows then that he still plans to go through with it.

Elena cradles her drink up by her face, pushing the lime around the rim. Sophie puts hers on the bookshelf and starts to browse the books there. She holds one hand with the other, plainly steadying her nerves. Joey is relieved to see that neither of her friends have taken a sip because it's just occurred to her that his plan will almost certainly have changed. Anything could be in those drinks.

"How long have you lived here?" Joey asks. She's risking glances around the room, searching for potential danger. He's only one man, but the way he's standing between all of them and the door makes Joey nervous. She's not sure how she let him block their best escape.

"I don't actually live here," he says. "But I fixed it up a few years ago. I do love it, don't you? It's peaceful." His voice is thick with charm, and Joey grinds her teeth back and forth. Elena's face is locked on his. She's watching his every move. They are all taut, tolerating the small talk while they wait for the right moment.

"Huh," says Elena. "Was that before or after you killed Quinn?"

Joey makes eye contact with Sophie, whose face opens in dismay. Neither of them risk a look at Cal, but Joey tries to imagine what he's thinking now. Her heart is suddenly a hammer, and she opts to paper over Elena's outburst. "Listen, we shouldn't keep you. We'll just go."

His eyes are quick, moving back and forth between them again, and Joey expects him to step closer, to corner them. He won't let them just leave. Joey knows this, and there's a part of her that has just realized how insane this is.

Cal doesn't move an inch, but he leans to examine the bookshelf. For a minute, Joey thinks he might relent and try again another time. But sensing something, she follows his gaze. There's a row with books leaning in on each other. It looks like there's one missing. He has noticed.

For a breath, they're all frozen. Then, several things happen in quick succession. Joey throws her drink into Cal's face, and he, undeterred, pulls something out of his back pocket with one hand, grabbing Elena with the other. His arm links around her while the barrel of a slick black gun digs into her neck. It dimples the skin, and Elena bucks once, knocking the books and knickknacks off the shelf. But she must see the fear on Joey's and Sophie's faces or feel the pressure of the gun constricting her airway because she checks her anger instantly.

"Where's the book?" He literally spits the words. His face is soaked with tequila and ginger beer. His look is wild, and Joey has no doubt he'll use that weapon at Elena's throat.

Joey puts her hands out, low, as if backing away from a startled bear. "I don't know what you're talking about," she says.

"Give me the book." He's calmer than Joey expected him to be. He is a thinker, a planner. He has had to be. But Joey and Sophie's presence has thrown him off balance just slightly, and he's rotating on an axis he didn't plan for. Which means he's improvising.

"What book?" she asks.

He flashes a nervous smile. "Don't insult me." Then, he smiles more confidently. "I'm one of you."

Cal notices her flicker of doubt and bites his lower lip. "My mother had the magic in her. She told me to come back and claim it for myself. I promised her I would. That's how I met Quinn."

"Don't you dare say her name," Elena growls, and Joey is aware of an echo of the previous version of events. He tightens his arm around her. Muscles strain at his shirtsleeves. *"Elena,"* Joey tries to tell her with a look, *"for once, shut up."*

He doesn't look away from Joey, and his glare is so intense, it makes something inside her give way, turning her insides soft. "I know you most of all, Joellen Close. I know exactly who you are. I thought it would be you who I'd kill to get the magic this time around, before this one walked right into my life, like a puppy who needed a home." Elena jerks, and he suddenly looks furious. He shoves the barrel of the gun into her mouth.

Sophie makes a small shocked sound, but Joey doesn't flinch. She doesn't move her gaze from Cal's.

"I knew your mom, Joey," he continues. "Carly or Carla, was it? She tried to fight me too, and if I'm remembering correctly—it was ten years ago—I made that one look like a suicide. She didn't understand that these sacrifices are necessary. I'm supposed to have this magic. It's as much mine as yours. And thanks to her, really, I have all of this." He widens his arms to the side, as if to envelop the room, the house, around them. "Her blood bought me my most lucrative years."

It's as if the floor has just opened up. Joey's legs feel weak, and her thoughts congeal. "My mom took her own life," she says weakly.

He smiles. "I'll take it as a high compliment that you believe that."

Thunder rattles the house.

"What about the other one? Your other sacrifice?" It's Sophie now. There's a confident, compassionate lilt to her voice. Like a therapist, or a hostage negotiator.

He looks at her as if for the first time all night. "The other one, as you so compassionately put it, was an old woman, ninety-two. Eliza Hunstad. She was the easiest of them all. I made her death look like natural causes. No one batted an eye, not even her family."

Joey swallows. She wants to scream, to punch a hole right through the middle of him.

But Sophie speaks before Joey can make a sound. The hostage negotiator voice is back. "You're right," she says with perfect calm, almost curiosity. "I believe that the magic is as much yours as it is ours. We would have done exactly the same as you have. All of us. And you promised your mother. I get how important that is." The irony of this statement coming from Sophie, whose own mother walked out on her, is lost on Cal, but she's so captivating, so believable, even Joey is lulled by her words.

He nods, maybe thinking, maybe perplexed that someone claims to actually understand him. "I'm not a bad person," he repeats.

"Of course you're not," says Sophie, and her words are their own kind of magic. Joey's head is pulsing with adrenaline. Elena looks pissed off, but there's a sliver of fear keeping her from trying to free herself again. Sophie continues. "You're just like us. If you hadn't left, you'd probably *be* one of us. You probably would have been initiated too. Rightfully so."

Joey only dares to look at Sophie for a millisecond, but she sees that, since she's started talking, she's inched closer to him.

"You had no choice," Sophie is saying. "I know that. I can see how painful this is for you."

He nods. She is disarming him. It's incredible. She's peeling away his aggression word by musical word.

But she makes a mistake then. During one of her micro-steps, her foot collides with something that slides noisily across the floor. He realizes, then, how close she is, and he whips Elena away in one frenzied motion. Sophie has lost him, and Joey can see the fear growing as she backs away. She looks at Joey. What now? There's nothing more to say because Cal takes the gun away from Elena's face and points it straight at Joey. "Open your bag," he says.

"Okay, okay, okay." Slowly, she slides the backpack off one shoulder, then the other. She chances a look up. His rage is obvious. He is not rattled. If anything, he's more focused on the book than ever. And he's guessed correctly. The book is in the backpack.

But Joey notices Elena's hard eyes staring at Sophie. Something is passing between them. Joey doesn't know what they're silently communicating, but she can feel her rib cage thrumming. She moves slowly to try to buy them time.

"Okay fine, you're right. I have the book," she says. "I'll give it to you. Just..." She works at the zipper, pretending it's stuck.

"You know what, never mind," he says. His patience has snapped. "I think I'll just shoot all three of you and take it myself." He aims.

"No!" It's Sophie who has shouted. And then, she's charging at him. He looks at her, startled. Elena uses this fraction of a second to join Sophie. They both lower their shoulders and barrel into Cal like two tight ends making the tackle of their lives. Joey crashes in too, and all four of them clatter onto the slate table.

There's a ringing in Joey's ears. Cal manages to shove them off with a show of massive human strength. He takes a step backward. Joey and Elena and Sophie wrap each other up. He raises the gun at their huddle once more, and they curl into each other. Joey sneaks a look under someone's arm.

He is crimson with rage. "You—"

Then, suddenly, his foot slips on something—a book, it looks like—and he goes down hard. He lands on his back, choking on his words. The gun flies out of his hand and skids away. His head snaps back. And with it, there's a crack like a wet branch. The sound hits one glass wall and then another, until its echo fills the whole house.

It's a lifetime before they come up from their nest of arms and hair. He's lying face up, eyes bloodshot and slick and wide-open. Blood is filling the grout between the tiles beneath his head, gushing out like a dam has been let go.

Joey drops to her knees and puts two fingers to his neck. She looks up at her friends. "Oh shit," says Elena. Sophie cups a hand over her mouth.

Joey grimaces as she reaches behind his head. Grunting, she manages to lift him enough to see the wound.

Beneath his head, doused in his blood, is the glass mountain sculpture. Its peaks point upright and undamaged, but they're caked with flesh and hair and bone.

72

ELENA

Joey and Sophie hike down to the spell circle while Elena waits with the body, just to make sure it all goes to plan. And it does, for the most part. It's a strong illusion spell. She watches the mountain sculpture reappear, sparkling and pristine, on the shelf by the books. She watches the pool of blood collapse in on itself like it's being sucked up with a straw. She checks to make sure Cal's wound has closed up. Elena looks at his smug face. It's still handsome, ghastly but undeniably good-looking. Brain aneurysm. That's what they're making it look like, and it is—to Elena's inexperienced eye—pretty fucking realistic.

He is lifeless, but there's no blood, no trace of what really happened. No trace whatsoever. Elena stands over him for too long. She didn't realize she'd enjoy seeing him lying there. Never mind that he tried to kill her. That he *did* kill her, according to Joey. But he took Quinn from them, and that was what Elena keeps thinking as she watches his corpse. Surprisingly, she thinks of her mother at this moment, and wonders, for once, if some of what she said was actually true. Elena hopes to god that hell is real. And that Cal Pierce is in it.

She walks down the mountain, this time boots not at all a hindrance.

She observes her own footprints scrubbed away behind her, though she can't tell if it's the rain or the spell that's doing it. *That inexplicability*, she thinks, *is the magic of magic.*

Eventually, she meets Sophie and Joey at the spell circle, where they're pacing, the spell work long finished. Sophie's face is twisted with nerves, and Joey is stoic. Elena nods—"*job done*"—and they return the nod. A collective breath moves between them, between the trees, between the mountains.

They walk, single file, and head—of all places—to Tom Winter's.

Gael is waiting with Barbara and Tom. He looks shell-shocked when she walks into the kitchen, and she pulls him close to her. She smells him. She feels his skinny body in her arms. And she lets herself cry, something that shocks them both because he has never seen her do it. Barbara must have told him some things, but not all, because he has no questions. She is sure there will be, but not tonight. Tom's house isn't perfectly clean, but it's clear Barbara's been at work because it's not at all like the last time they were here. Four steaming mugs sit on the tidied table—one for each of them and one for Gael. It's like she knew exactly when they were coming. Hot chocolate, because of course it's hot chocolate. She's a hot chocolate kind of mom and always will be.

Barbara agrees to be their alibi right then and there, so if anyone is curious about their whereabouts, they'll be cleared. Gael nods along, as if to say he'll vouch for her too. Elena should be worried that he is caught up in a lie now that he knows nothing about. But she is not worried. In fact, she is certain the spell is so good it will fool everyone. This town has been duped by an illusion spell before, and no one, except Joey, ever gave it a second thought. It is perfect magic.

Tom is here too. He sits in a corner with a splotchy face. He hiccups a thank-you through his tears because Barbara has told him what happened to Quinn—glossing over some of the more inexplicable elements. It hits Elena that they still don't really know exactly how Quinn died. They'll probably never know.

At some point, Barbara drives them to her house, where Gael dives into his sofa and passes out. Elena, Joey, and Sophie trudge into Quinn's room. They chat for hours. Around two, Elena sneaks chocolate chip cookies and a bottle of whiskey from the kitchen. Then, much later than they should, they squeeze into Quinn's bed and under her covers. Their bodies curl into each other. Their breaths in sync and steady, and eventually, eventually, they fall asleep.

73

SOPHIE

"Mama."

Sophie nearly bursts into tears when she sees Leah on the screen. She's lying facedown on her childhood bed with her feet kicked up behind her, like she's a teenager. Leah's little face lights up when she sees Sophie, and she starts babbling nonsense, but very seriously, like she has something critical to share with her mother who's been gone. Talia is there too. She's holding the phone and turns it around for a second.

"Hey, love. All good here," she says. Her hair is a mess, and she's wearing Sophie's sweater with an indistinguishable green stain. She looks about as unkempt as Sophie has ever seen her, and she swells with gratitude that her daughter has two moms to make her feel safe. "No more fever," Talia says. "Back to our old selves." Sophie feels something tight inside her body relax, something she's been holding on to for too long.

"I'm coming back tonight," Sophie says, but she's cut off by a whine.

"Okay, here's Mama," says Talia, and Leah appears on the screen again.

"Hi, baby."

Leah's face beams at the word she recognizes. "Baby," she echoes.

"Tell Mimi I'll be home tonight. Oh, and Tal, I invited my dad to come if that's okay…with his new girlfriend."

Somewhere in the background, Talia gives a surprised "Ooo." There's so much to explain, Sophie knows. And she isn't sure how much she's going to share, but she does know that she loves her family more than anything in the world. No matter what happens, that will never change. She suddenly longs to lie in bed with Talia's warm legs entangled with hers, to watch trashy TV and eat bed snacks, with Leah asleep in the next room. She wants it so bad, it takes everything in her not to run and jump in the car this instant. But she can't. Not yet.

"Are you planning to go back soon?" Talia asks.

This is the question that Sophie has been batting around the whole time she's been here. She has stayed away for fifteen years, and for what? To avoid retraumatizing herself with reminders of her friend's death? But Barbara stayed. Tom stayed. Joey stayed. Sophie could have stayed. She understands now, with the kind of clarity you only get after an emergency virtual therapy session, that her avoidance of Whisper Ridge has been tied to Tanner and her fear of him. She told her dad this morning about what Tanner did to her, and he vowed that he would *"make that boy's life hell"* for her. She told him not to, but secretly, she was overwhelmed with the lightness of having let just a piece of it go.

She smiles at the screen. "Actually, I thought we could come up here in September, all of us, when the aspen leaves change. It's the most beautiful thing. Leah will love it."

"Sounds perfect."

"Oh, and we're doing a girls' trip," Sophie says. "Over the summer. I promise I'll give you advanced notice this time."

"That sounds really great, Soph. I'm happy for you."

"Mama!"

Sophie looks at the time and climbs off the bed. "Mama will be home soon, baby. I love you."

"Lo' you!"

Sophie's eyes dampen.

"Love you, Soph. See you soon," says Talia, and they click off. Sophie wipes her face. She grabs her shoes and heads for the door.

74

ELENA

"Acapulco," Elena says, pouring two cups of coffee. Gael is in the other room, packing.

Barbara accepts her cup with a contented sigh. "Lovely."

She's talking about the upcoming girls' trip. "I'd kill for a margarita on the beach," says Elena now, just like she said to Joey and Sophie. She pulls up a picture of the coastline on her phone.

When she turns it around, Barbara reaches out and smiles devilishly. "I think I'd have to agree with you there. And the acting?" asks Barbara.

Elena savors her bite of pancake, then speaks. "My agent has something in the works for the stage, believe it or not. And I'm just going to keep taking my chances with any films that come my way. In the meantime, commercial work can be financially rewarding."

"You seem calmer about it all."

Barbara's right. She is calmer about it. That desperate, would-do-anything-for-a-big-break attitude evaporated the minute Cal's skull split open on his living room floor.

Elena hears Gael in the next room, zipping up a bag.

"Do you still own this town?" Elena asks quietly.

Barbara laughs, looking at her with curiosity.

"Thought so," says Elena. "In that case, I need you to do something for me."

Barbara has grown older, even in the last twenty-four hours. The evidence is under her eyes, in the wrinkles around her mouth. Elena doesn't see it as age because she knows it's more than that. Barbara exudes immense strength. What fortitude this woman has, she realizes, to have endured all these years without her daughter, to bear the impossible weight of a lost child.

Elena doesn't tell Barbara about why she left Whisper Ridge. She doesn't tell her how Marissa Berg *let slip* to her mother at Bible study, of all places, that she saw Elena with a pregnancy test in the girls' bathroom, or how only days after that, her mother wrenched her from this town and locked her in a foreign bedroom all the way in SoCal for long enough that, when she finally escaped, it was too late to have an abortion. Elena didn't tell her how she'd run away after her twenty-four-week doctor's appointment, to nothing, just a cheap apartment she found on Craigslist and a waitressing job.

She doesn't explain any of it. She only says, "Get them to search Mark Collingswood's computer."

Barbara says nothing but raises her eyebrows.

"I have a feeling they might find illicit images of underage girls on there. Just a hunch."

After breakfast, Elena heads out to meet Sophie and Joey. She couldn't have written a better ending if she tried. *Woman thanks her childhood friends for saving her from a psychopath murderer, then makes plans to drink heavily on a beach in a few months' time.* If it wasn't for the fact that she grew up in a town where there was magic in the woods, this would all seem surreal. But very few things are beyond the realm of possibility, it turns out.

She's wearing black—not because she's mourning, but because, in the mountains, which always seem to carry a chill, it's the best way to feel the true warmth of the sun.

75

JOEY

Joey shoots off a text.

While she waits for a reply, she gathers up Elena's old shoebox, planning to take it to her this morning. She's almost done sorting through her mother's things too, the mess she'd strewn all over her living room floor yesterday. There is some junk, to be sure, but she finds her mother's favorite brown mug—a hideous thing that Joey cleaned and filled with hot coffee for her every morning—and a marble jewelry box that she dusts off and sets next to her bed. There is also a framed photograph of her and her mom hiking together, taken when Joey was ten years old. Joey smiles and tears up at the same time, which is very unlike her. It's been a long week.

There's a light knock on the front door.

She stands and brushes invisible debris from her pants. She licks her lips and swallows.

River stands there, looking sheepish, with his hopelessly adorable dog and a question in his eyes. She invites them in and splashes water into Walter's favorite mixing bowl. "We'll have to decide whose house we're going to live in," she says over her shoulder. "I'm not going to just automatically move in with you."

He waits a long painful moment before doing anything at all, and Joey is sure she's made a mistake. She's misread where they are now. She broke something that she can't mend, not with this meager gesture, this playful acceptance of an offer made days ago.

But then, he nods and holds in his eyes a mock seriousness, and she finds herself melting into a smile. Not just on her lips, but deep within her. Then it all comes to the surface. Relief and the hot sting of tears. She wants him, and for once, Joey is going to let herself have what she wants.

"We could let Walter decide," he says. They look at the dog and the puddle forming underneath his dripping mouth. It's the warmest Joey has ever felt.

After River leaves, with a promise to come back later, Joey puts what she loves of her mother's things on a shelf for display and boxes everything else up to donate. She has plans to meet Sophie and Elena. They're going to the spell circle to lay a ring of wildflowers for Quinn. Her favorite.

As she collects the stray scraps of paper, mail, and old receipts that have fallen to the floor, a folded-up note catches her eye. On the front, written in a familiar hand, is her name. She sits up straight, brushing aside an envelope and picking up the note. It's rigid between her fingers, and the edges don't line up, as if it was folded in a rush.

And then she is thrust into a memory. She had such an amazing time with River that night, fifteen years ago, laughing and goofing around. They kissed, and it was like something hummed to life inside her. But the walk home was long, and Joey decided to shower immediately, as if she needed to wash it all off, to erase River's smell and her shame.

And then her mom came into her room and told her that Quinn had come by after school, that she was looking for her, that she left a note. Joey spent an hour tearing apart her room, whipping blankets around and throwing the contents out of dresser drawers. She desperately wanted to find it because she thought, she hoped, that reading a note Quinn left would somehow absolve her. She concluded, in the end, that her mother was wrong. There was no note. And no absolution.

But now, sitting on her faux wood floors, she knows this is it. Cal's illusion spell, in all its omniscience, must have included this note, hiding it from Joey fifteen years ago. And now, the illusion spell has worn off. With steady hands, she unfolds it.

Joey,

I'm writing this from the desk in your room. Your mom let me in. You didn't come talk to me this afternoon, even though I asked you to, but I want you to know that it's okay. I'm not sure I would have come either. I've been really terrible to you—to all of you. I've been lying and sneaking around behind your back and, I guess, getting myself into some really deep shit. I came today because I needed your help, because I thought I couldn't manage this on my own. But I can. I got myself into it, I can get myself out.

Here's what you should know:

The trees. They do speak. I spoke to them, asked them to show me the spells in the book, and they did. They showed me everything we never knew was inside. It's not just a book, Joey. It's a grimoire, filled with really old spells from other witches, generations of them. And one of those spells is called bloodspell. It's why I'm in this mess. It's a spell to take the magic out of a person, to steal it, by sacrificing them. Murder. I don't want to scare you, but that's what I'm facing right now, because I told someone I shouldn't have about the magic. He knows about bloodspell. That's why I have to disappear. I'm borrowing your backpack and tent and camping gear. Sorry! I know you're probably going to freak out when you see this, but you can't come after me. You can't. And you can't tell anyone. Not yet. Because he's dangerous. I'm hoping me leaving will lure him away from this town and buy me some time.

I really fucked up. I'm so so so so sorry.

Oh! Also, on a lighter note before I forget. Please be with River. You guys like each other. I'm sorry I used him as a cover so I could keep lying and no one would question me. I used him so you *wouldn't question me. But you saw straight through me, didn't you? You knew something was going on, and you tried to help, plenty of times. I just didn't want help. Not then. And now that I do, I don't deserve it. So, yeah, do us all a favor and just marry River and have his babies, okay?*

You and Sophie and Elena are my best friends. I love you three so much. I'm really sorry to leave you with my mess, but I really really hope I'll be back soon and everything will be just like it was before. Miss you already.

Love,
Quinn

SIX MONTHS LATER

Joey stands behind the counter surveying the crowd.

Aspect Coffee is as busy as it ever was, including during Barbara's years. River moves behind the counter, refilling cups and chatting with Ken from the bar. Most of the town has shut down to be here this afternoon, and though she's sure Barbara may have had something to do with it, she's proud of what they've come to witness.

Blue velvet upholstered armchairs surround antique coffee tables and rest on top of bright Persian rugs. The exposed brick walls have been washed clean of paint. Wildflowers adorn every surface. The vibe, as Ingrid and Jasper Hardy called it in *Around Town*, is "somehow bohemian and authentic at the same time."

The espresso machine whirs as sunlight tilts into the room. "Chin chin," says a voice to her right. It's Sophie. She must have gotten a break from wrangling Leah, who has been running around, energized by all the attention while simultaneously trying to knock every coffee cup onto the floor. Sure enough, Joey spots Talia in the corner laughing with Otto, and hears over the din, "Uh-oh, Grandpa." Then little Leah is at Joey's feet, asking for a towel so she can clean the spill. She reaches for a rag, but Sophie slips it from her hands, trading her for a glass of champagne. "Go give this to Grandpa," she says to Leah and sends her on her way with the towel. Then, unexpectedly, she turns to Joey for a fierce, tight hug. "I'm so proud to be your friend."

"Oh my god, let the woman breathe," says Elena, sliding up beside them. She's surveying the room too, and just for a second, Joey watches her friends next to her and slings an arm over each of them. A little champagne drips onto Elena's shoulder—apparently she's a little tipsy—but no one says anything. They all just laugh, like they belong right here together.

They watch Gael talking to Barbara and Tom Winter as he adjusts one of the frames. A few weeks ago, Gael called Joey out of the blue and asked her if she'd be interested in featuring his photographs in the shop for her grand reopening. She almost didn't have the words to reply when she opened the envelopes. Seeing them here now, lining the walls all around them, gives her chills. Joey made him agree that these were not a donation, that she would price them out and let patrons buy them when they came into the shop. She'd Venmo him with every sale. And so far, already today, twelve photographs have sold. The kid is absolutely glowing. There are forty-six photos in total, and each of them is so raw, so beautiful, she can't decide which is her favorite. When he and Elena were here last year, he spent the whole time exploring the town and snapping pictures. He captured several breathtaking photos of his mom, some of Sophie, including one blurred-motion one that is absolutely stunning, and a few of Joey too. He even took a handful of candids of the three of them together, sitting on Barbara's back porch, smiling and talking like the old friends they were. There are images of historical buildings and of neighbors talking and of Walter's different-colored eyes and of the school doors and a sign that says, "CONGRATS, SENIORS!" Not one, she notices now, is of the cast or crew or equipment from the movie that was shot here. A movie that was abandoned during filming, or so Elena has reported. Apparently, they did not get to finish the last few scenes due to Cal Pierce's unexpected and tragic death, and most likely won't be continuing with production because of it.

She feels a kiss at the top of her head and looks up to see River there, leaning over her.

"A good day?" he asks.

She nods and pulls Sophie and Elena close to her as the people of this town fill her coffee shop. *Quinn would have loved this*, she thinks. But also, and maybe more importantly, *she* loves this.

"A good day," she says.

READ ON FOR A LOOK AT
CHELSEA IVERSEN'S
*THE PECULIAR GARDEN
OF HARRIET HUNT*!

UPPER HOLLOWAY NEWS

SUNDAY, FEBRUARY 18, 1866

A ROMANTIC DISAPPEARANCE: HUSBAND AND WIFE BOTH MISSING

Mr. Christian Comstock, the son of Mr. George Comstock, has been missing for over two months. The young clerk has not appeared at his role in the London National Bank, nor has he been seen at or anywhere near his premises during this time. The Comstocks are a family of great repute in Upper Holloway, our northern suburb of London, thanks to the senior Mr. Comstock's successful career at the bank. For the son of such a champion of capitalistic progress and well-touted member of London's financial hierarchy, the junior Mr. Comstock's absence is highly uncharacteristic, so say family and colleagues. The suggestion of foul play is, of course, being investigated, though nothing conclusive has come to light.

It appears that Mrs. Christian Comstock has also been missing since late last year. The wife is known throughout Worthing Road to be "strange" and "a recluse." One particular acquaintance of the married couple expressed his "suspicion" upon hearing about her disappearance. Neighbors have no idea as to either of their whereabouts.

Police are investigating, but with so little information, we may be left only to wonder: What has happened to the Comstocks?

ONE

Though the letter lay on the small table, Harriet did not open it.

Instead, she watched a fox begin its work on a plum just outside. The fruit that fell from the plum tree in her garden was a deep violet in some light, golden in others. They grew in plump clusters along generous branches. A fallen plum, an abundance of which was often shaken free by the train rumbling by, smelled sickly sweet when it began its slow rot. The aroma each plum gave off was both familiar and intoxicating.

Harriet knew it well.

The fox sniffed the plum first. It was easy prey, already lying on the ground, waiting for someone to claim it. Harriet could almost see the little creature drooling from here, so indulgently it licked its mouth in anticipation. And then, it began to nibble. The plum rolled a short way away at the first breaking of the skin, yellow flesh exposed, and the fox chased it hungrily. Now that he had a taste, it was going to be hard to resist.

The fox played this game of nibble and chase until half the fruit was consumed, and then he took the last of it in his mouth and chewed with fervor.

Just then, the train roared past. The little fox gave the machine a brief, wary look, and Harriet did too, watching blurs of black cross her vision like splatters of ink.

The greens and pinks and whites of her garden glowed in the hazy morning light while the train burst through, a violent shadowy interruption. She had become quite used to the train over the years, so much so that it was a part of the garden's natural rhythm. It used to drown out her father's thundering commands, and for that, Harriet had been grateful.

But now that it was just her, she found she did not appreciate the train quite as much as she once had.

A shower of overripe fruit thunked to the ground near the fox. The animal was too distracted by the juicy finale of his dessert to care. Now, he stumbled over the fallen plums. There was a distinct imbalance to his gait, and then he lay down right where he was, part of him shadowed by the thicket of blackberry brambles that stood guard along the garden wall and part of him glinting in the brightness of the day. He curled his head around so he lay snugly on top of his tail, a little white tuft sticking out like the corner of a pillow.

A tendril of leafed ivy, as alive as a hand, slunk up to the tiny fox, then another, and another. Soon, the animal was shrouded by vines and covered in veiny green leaves.

The garden explored the visitor, and the visitor slept.

Harriet turned away. The room around her was still and quiet, such a contrast to her garden. The flowers that adorned the walls in here were stuck in a flat, lifeless existence. The paper peeled away at the corners, exposing spots of bare adhesive and plaster. She had lived in this space since she'd been too small to see out of the window. Now, the neatly made bed lay half illuminated, stripped of its bed curtains, posts prodding the air like spears. A faded blanket that had once matched the wallpaper covered the bed, and a droopy pillow peaked limply, though she'd tried, and failed, to help it sit upright. The room smelled faintly stale, like dust trapped too long under layers of damp.

Though she had lived at Sunnyside house her whole life, it wasn't exactly homey. Her father no longer paced the halls, shouting her name, making sure she was not out running through the streets barefoot and wild. He was no longer here to force her to stay indoors, closed off from the garden she loved and the world beyond it. That much was true. With her father gone now, she should have been happier in this house. She no longer had to cower in corners or lie on the floor peering beneath locked doors for hours at a time. But even now that she was alone, this place still did not feel like home. Perhaps even less so now that it was mostly bare. Her footfalls echoed in the emptiness as the floors moaned beneath her, and the walls appeared even more askew, leaning in as if taunting her.

And the off-key chimes of the Dutch clock that stood guard outside the basement door never trilled at the correct hour. It was enough to drive anyone mad.

Harriet knew she could leave these dark corridors for good. He was no longer here to keep her locked up, hidden away. The daughter he wished he'd never had. And yet, despite all this, she decided to stay. To her, the reason was obvious. It wasn't the constricted rooms within Sunnyside's tired, sagging walls that kept her here. It was the small patch of land just outside its doors.

She felt the urge to go down there, as she always did first thing in the morning. But her eyes fell again on the letter, and she sighed. She knew what was inside and could not bear to read it. They continued to arrive, these letters, getting more frequent and menacing. She always burned the letters as they came. What else could she do? Harriet could not pay down her father's debts. The truth was, he left nothing behind for her. He had simply vanished. In the meantime, she had taken to pawning nearly everything of value in the house just so she could live. For most of her life, animal hides and ivory tusks had adorned the rooms of this house. Growing up, she'd been terrified by the sad, hulking remnants of dead animals that he paraded proudly to guests when they arrived for parties, which he spoke of as if he'd hunted them down himself, even though Harriet knew he'd never left England. But, in recent months, she'd earned enough to live off of when she pawned them. Now she kept her life minimal, specifically to avoid such extravagance—an order from the butcher once every fortnight, small amounts of butter, oil for the lamps, paper and ink, tea, milk.

Yesterday, she was going to destroy the letter, just as she had done with the others, but there was something odd about this one. It was not addressed to her father as all the others were. It was addressed to her.

She stuffed the letter into the pocket of her dress—the same dress she wore every day. Perhaps she would have the willpower to open it later.

Glancing in the mirror as she pinned her tawny red hair up without bothering to comb it through first, she nodded at her staid and sturdy reflection. She was no beauty—her plain features blossomed only in the best lighting. And then there was the darkened imprint of the scar that trailed gruesomely from lip to cheekbone on her right side.

Harriet grabbed her boots, though she did not put them on, and hurried down the worn stairs, which drooped and moaned. She passed the clock in the hall and shouldered her way out through the back door to her garden. Relief flooded her as she did, and she drew in a deep breath. She squinted happily into the late-summer glow.

The garden itself was enjoying the painted-on brightness of the day. The flowers were in full bloom—the dramatic pink of the Duchess of Sutherland roses and the flesh-colored Madame Audots met Harriet's eye as she stepped out of the house. Flanking those stood the La Reines with their silvery undertones and the cabbage roses to the right. The cabbage roses, though they did not have a grand name, were Harriet's favorite. More layers inside one flower than she could even count. She inhaled the sweet smell of the Duchesses and watched as every last bloom turned to face her as she padded barefoot from the door onto the stone walkway, bordered by lush green moss. Satisfied that Harriet was content, the flowers resumed their nourishing tilt toward the sky. The stones were cool beneath her feet.

And then there was the plum tree. The tree was the central presence in her back garden, spreading out freely between the house and garden wall. Its branches hung low with thick clusters of fruit that, indeed, looked sumptuous, but they were not exactly the kind of plums she could bake into a tart. Harriet felt guilty about letting most of them rot as they fell to the ground, but such was the fate of wild things that did not want to be tamed. The moss and earth beneath the tree were churned up, as if the roots were continuously growing and stretching. As she watched, small patches of green sprouted up before her eyes, blooming and covering the fresh dirt with expediency.

"You never sit still, do you?" she said aloud to the tree.

As she turned, she saw the familiar vines that snaked up the walls of the house on all sides, covering the brick up to her bedroom window. More roses perched high up on the walls too, woven within the evergreen ivy—spots of white that added to the garden's feral dreaminess.

From the outside, the house showed signs of dilapidation. Though its structure was not falling down, not really, the roof did sag in places. The side door had become warped from incessant fog and rain, and the color of the brick was fading. None of this was from age. The house was no more than a few decades old. It was simply from a lack of care. Harriet's father had decorated the rooms with his treasures, but never once did he repair the peeling paint of the parlor or the chipped wood of the banister. Though, over the last seven months, she couldn't say she'd paid Sunnyside much attention either. It was far too damp and closed-in, like shackles around her. To get some relief—a sensation only truly available now that her father had gone—she let her garden grow up around it, let it snake in through windows on summer days, allowed it to grow wild and thick. If Harriet's home would not be supported by love—and by now she knew better than that—it would have to be supported by plants.

And yet.

The garden could not be allowed complete freedom. Not after what happened. Because she was the sole keeper of this garden, she must remain as diligent as ever. She felt a small shudder at her feet in response to her thoughts. *Yes*, the garden seemed to say. *There would be no limit to my wildness without you.*

"And that is why I must always be here."

It's no wonder they all thought she was mad, speaking aloud to her plants.

The garden was, of course, more unruly than the neighbors appreciated. She heard as much from passersby almost daily. *Unkempt. Too much. A waste.* They did not even try to keep their voices low. But Harriet didn't mind. They had always said the same about her too. She never interacted with neighbors except for the odd furtive look when she dared to venture out or the unabashed stares from children who had surely heard of the mad young woman of Sunnyside. It struck her as ironic that, despite her father's best efforts, many people seemed to know about her, and they kept their distance. It was just as well. Harriet was fidgety and nervous around strangers. It had always been so. Years of being hidden, of being told she was unnatural, of being made so small it was almost as if she did not exist. She supposed that ought to take a toll on a person.

Her only visitor was Eunice. Dear Eunice, who never judged her and always overlooked her quirks. What a breath of fresh air it was to finally throw open the gate when she did come, and laugh freely, loudly, together in the garden without Harriet's father barreling through the door or casting his dark shadow.

She strode over to the brambles, which resembled a thick, thorned tangle of hair. She knelt where the fox had curled up only minutes ago, looking for traces of the animal, but she could see nothing—no orange or white tufts, no beady black eyes. He was gone. Once again, she had been abandoned, and once again, she was surprised that she cared.

Aloneness was freedom, she supposed, but it was also empty.

The man in the round hat arrived an hour or so later, while Harriet sat beneath the plum tree, rereading the same passage from last month's issue of *Gardener's Chronicle*, wondering about garden ferns and, for the hundredth time, whether she would ever invest in a greenhouse. If she did not have to tend to this garden, if she could live where she wanted and create a home of her own, what would her garden look like? She often imagined trees. Dozens of them. Of course, she would need more space for that. A place out in the country with sparrows and forget-me-nots and evening primrose. She thought she would like a greenhouse. The purpose of such a structure would be to have summer blooms in winter, and vegetables if the conditions were right, and it would be wonderful to have fresh summer roses all year long.

But, of course, all these thoughts were pointless. She must remain here. This garden was hers, and without her—

"Mr. Hunt?"

An unfamiliar voice roused her from her thoughts.

It was the nasally twang of a busy man, and she heard a faint rap at the door around the front of the house. Harriet remained unmoving, hoping that her silence would encourage him to leave promptly. She was acutely aware that the silver-lavender roses at the corner of the front garden, just next to the hawthorn, perked up at the sound, swiveling to face the front gate.

The man rounded the corner and spotted her all the way at the back, sitting beneath the plum tree. His small legs carried him over to her so quickly, she barely had the chance to cover her exposed toes, which rested naked over the moss, as they often did when she sat outside. She could feel the garden's attention buzz to life all around her, the roses standing pert and cautious. This small signal was enough to put Harriet on edge.

"I am looking for Mr. Hunt."

The man wore a thin mustache, which curled up at the ends quite intentionally. He had a short but sturdy stance to him, like he wouldn't necessarily instigate a scuffle but was ready for one at any moment.

"It is quite urgent that I speak with him," he said when she did not respond.

Harriet fidgeted, aware of ivy snaking subtly along the edges of the house, which she could see behind him. She willed the garden to be at ease as she laced up her boots beneath the cover of her skirts.

Her fingers grazed a pointed corner of something in her pocket. The letter.

She wondered if the man in front of her could be a debtor who was fed up with her silence and had finally come to collect what he was owed.

Out of the corner of her eye, she caught a nest of thorns separating itself from the garden wall and billowing forward, ever so slightly, growing inch by inch, sharpening in the glinting sunlight that muscled through the clouds.

She let a small nervous laugh escape her. The plants had become more and more unruly the more time she spent here by herself. She feared it would take some strain to keep them in check.

The man frowned deeply. "Is he within?"

Finally, boots secured, Harriet stood, wobbling slightly. She had a small height advantage that made the man take an involuntary step back, and the wrinkles on his forehead creased dramatically as he cleared his throat and stood up straighter. She dipped her shoulders so she would appear smaller and smiled weakly, still without speaking. More than half a year had passed since her father had disappeared, and the debt seemed to be mounting higher every day. Harriet had been naive enough think that if she ignored all their inquests, they would eventually stop harassing her and simply accept that he was gone—that they would give up. Naive indeed.

"He is not within, Mr.—" she said with a shake in her voice. A thick, momentary silence followed.

"Inspector Stokes," he said firmly.

Harriet was thrown for a moment. Inspector. So, he was not here to collect on debts after all. Her vision caught on his blue uniform and white striped cuffs. Of course. She should have put it together before. He was reading her carefully, she noticed now.

"He has not been within for more than seven months," she managed. "My father has left the country."

"I see." He raised his eyebrows. "Have you any idea where he is, exactly?"

She did have some idea. He had run off to Denmark to live with his wealthy cousin, no doubt, as he had threatened to do many times before. It seems he was keen to avoid debtors' prison, though he did not think of what would happen to her in his absence. Or perhaps, more accurately, he did not care. It hadn't been a surprise to Harriet that he had left, in the end. Not really. The only surprise was that he did not send her away to the asylum before he left, as he had also threatened to do many times before. She tried not to fidget. "Denmark, I think, Mr. Stokes—Inspector Stokes—" Was it just her imagination or was he narrowing his eyes at her?

"Denmark." He rubbed at his dimpled chin with stubby fingers. "Curious."

From what she could glean, the man did not, in fact, think it curious at all. He appeared to have made up his mind on the matter. And those eyes. They told Harriet that he wanted to pry something from her.

"Tell me—Miss Hunt, I presume?"

Harriet nodded.

"How did you and your father leave things the last time you saw him? Did he seem agitated?"

Heat rushed to her face. The last time she saw her father, the night had been frigid. He'd stood in the threshold, barring her from escaping to the garden, which Harriet watched rise behind him like a thundercloud before he kicked the door closed and dragged her by the arm up the stairs, his fingernails slicing into her flesh. His shouts were manic. Unhinged. She had flinched when he raised a hand, but he'd only tugged at his hair so that it stuck straight up like horns. His eyes bulged red and unseeing. This time, when he threatened her, she'd gone cold, sensing some finality in his words. Locked inside her room, she'd tried to pry open the window, but, of course, he had jammed that shut too. She'd heard him thunder down the stairs and throw open the door. The silence that followed echoed throughout the empty house. Harriet had still been shaking, back pressed against the wall, fingers digging into her scalp, an hour later, maybe two. She'd clutched a candlestick in her hand, waiting for him to come back, to try to take her away. But he hadn't come back at all.

"I—we had an argument."

Stokes raised an eyebrow.

"It was brief, and then he was gone."

Stokes tapped his fingers against his trouser leg. "Can I ask, what is in Denmark?"

She shook her head. "He has a cousin there, I think."

"His name?" He pulled out a small piece of paper to capture her words in ink.

Harriet shook her head again. "I don't know…"

"Hmm." He dropped his hands to his sides and tipped his head slightly, never taking his eyes off her. "Not close with your father's family then?"

"No." Other than an unnamed cousin referenced when her father was particularly incensed, she didn't think he had any family. The only kin she had ever known was her cousin Eunice—a second cousin, really—and she was related on her mother's side. Harriet could sense Stokes's gaze on her. She didn't like the way it made her feel. Like a liar, somehow. She wished she knew what exactly he wanted.

She suddenly noticed the thorns peeling away from the garden wall, creeping up behind Stokes at shoulder level. Her eyes widened, and she tried to breathe slowly—hoping that the plants would sense her calm—but she could only manage quick, shallow breaths. She stared down the brambles, and the spindly arms paused, appearing to decide something. Stokes swiveled around to see what she was looking at, but thankfully, the thicket had eased back against the garden wall, just in time. Seeing nothing amiss, he turned slowly to face Harriet. She tried to force a confident, polite smile though she could feel the sweat—simultaneously hot and cold—collecting at the back of her neck.

Harriet chanced a reluctant glance behind his other shoulder, worried that she would see watchful vines wriggling and curious rose blooms craning their necks to see what was to come. Inspector Stokes turned again. All was still. The house stood weakly behind the vines, like a drunkard leaning into the arms of a steady companion. The ivy pressed up innocently against the house and the roses looked perfectly demure.

Though when the man turned his back on the house again, they peeled themselves out of their stillness and began to hover.

Stop it, she mouthed at the vines. They did not retreat. Instead, she saw the ivy twisting and curling overhead, gathering momentum. *Don't you dare.*

Stokes was looking at her. "Your neighbors say you have a history of...strange behavior, Miss Hunt." He punctuated the word *strange*. She pulled her eyes from the garden, her attention snagging on his tone. He had spoken to the neighbors, then. About her. She could feel him searching her, as if she were an interesting object, a curiosity, or something even more rare.

Stokes looked her up and down with squinting eyes, as if bringing her stained dress and mussed-up hair into focus. "Where did you get that scar?"

She blinked to bring him into focus now too. There was a flash in his eyes that made her pause. Was it contempt? No, she knew quite clearly what that looked like. It was more like cunning. She could not pinpoint it, exactly, but it made her skin prickle. It also made the thorns on the cabbage roses thicken and sharpen. The garden had sensed it too, then.

"It's from when I was a girl."

Hearing a rustling behind her, Harriet took a panicked sidestep toward the front garden, hoping he would turn away from the roses. The pale blossoms of the Madame Audots bobbed, leaned in, listened.

Thankfully, Stokes swiveled to follow her. She closed her eyes tightly, willing the garden to relax. *Stop it. Stop it. Stop it*, she mouthed silently again.

"Have you been living here alone, Miss Hunt?" Stokes asked.

Harriet barely heard him. *Leave it*, she muttered through clenched teeth, her eyes still on the roses. The advancing stems hesitated, and she dipped her face to try to hide her hard glare. After a beat, which felt surreally like disappointment, the garden subsided, and she watched the flowers settle back into place.

"Miss Hunt." His impatience was unveiled now, as if he were addressing an unmanageable child.

"Sorry?" A single bead of sweat dripped down Harriet's back, but she let her shoulders release.

"Who supports you? How are you able to live here on your own, a young woman, with no husband or father?" He had his pen and paper out again.

Now that the garden was still, she could finally think. Who supported her? She supported herself. What choice did she have? A monthly trip to the pawnbrokers was how she had gotten by so far, but she would soon run out of carpets, dishes, trinkets, ornaments, candlesticks, and her mother's jewelry—all of it. Thankfully, she had convinced her landlord to allow monthly, rather than annual payments. Her father had been quite fond of expensive things, for better or worse, and it had been helpful for the past several months, but by now, the interior of the house was all but bare. Just a few necessities remained in Harriet's possession: one chair in the parlor, a breakfast table, a few dishes given to her by Eunice, a worn-down, old-fashioned kitchen table. There was the Dutch clock in the front passage, which was lacquered oak and brass, and which she would be happy to be rid of—but the glass face was cracked. She was sure it would sell for very little. And of course, there was the lovely Henry Pickering landscape hanging in the parlor, which she hoped would be worth a fair amount should she need it, but it was the one thing in the house she didn't mind looking at.

As she stared back at the man's small eyes and curled-up whiskers, heat crept up Harriet's neck. She wondered if she should tell him about the debtors. Perhaps that would explain her father's absence better. It might at least stop him from looking at her that way.

"Did he explicitly tell you he was going to Denmark when he left?"

The shift back to the subject of her father shook her. Perhaps Stokes had already made up his mind about how Harriet supported herself. "Well, no. But—"

"And did he tell anyone else about his travel plans?"

"I don't know. I—"

"And did you ever wonder where he was? Why he didn't come back?"

Harriet's muscles went rigid.

"You see, it's strange. His colleagues say that he has never mentioned any relations at all. No cousin in Denmark. No sister in Spain. No wife in Wapping. And no daughter in Upper Holloway. Now, why would that be?"

The moss at Harriet's feet suddenly radiated heat, friction mounting between her boots and the ground. She knew exactly why that would be. She shifted from one foot to the other and back again, swallowing her retort. She wished he would just leave. All around her, she could feel the rapt attention of each plant—each bud, each leaf. Fingers of ivy lifted off the wall above them, quivering with tension. Thorns resumed sharpening their points, and roses widened their blossoms. These were the small signs of battle preparation that Harriet feared. The garden was waiting, ready to act in her defense, but she could not afford to let it go wild. Not now. She watched anxiously, pinching the skin of her forearm to try to regain some control.

She forced herself to look back at his face, knowing that if she kept staring at her garden beyond his shoulder, he would turn and see what she saw. But he did not seem to care about the garden. Instead, he was watching her, a dark expression written on his face. Realization prodded at her. She needn't fear looking mad in front of this man. To him, she was already suspicious.

"We were not often in accord," she said breathlessly, feeling suddenly cornered. "But there have been letters—"

"Letters, yes, of course," he said, his words snipped. "Well, I will look further into this journey to—where did you say?"

He was trying to trip her up, to catch her in a lie.

"Denmark," she said with a small degree of defiance. She was not lying, and she did not want to look like she was.

"Denmark," he said, snapping his fingers. "That's right."

He tipped his hat and cast out his next words slowly, dangerously, like a fisherman with a hook, hoping to catch on something. "It's unusual for a daughter not to miss her father, Miss Hunt. Begging your pardon."

She did not like the way the man said her name. It sounded like she was his to wonder about, that he would now put more thought into *her*. She thought she ought to respond, to say *something*, but before she could, he was backing away. "Not to worry," he called to her. "I will find out what happened."

She did not move until his rounded hat disappeared behind the wrought iron gate and the Ayrshire roses that spilled over it.

The train roared in its approach, and Harriet exhaled. The ground shook, and as the railcars passed, one by one, she clenched and unclenched her fists. She could curse herself. In her anxiety over keeping the garden in check—though an essential job, indeed—she had completely failed to appear composed. She'd probably looked mad, in fact. And Stokes likely believed she had been telling him falsehoods about her father too.

But she had no reason to lie. She knew that in a few weeks' time, Stokes would find her father holed up in a houseboat along the Copenhagen waterfront and she would be forgotten. Her father, who had never had the decency to pretend to care for her, had taken every ounce of her freedom. Then he had gone with no word, no explanation, and Harriet was left exposed and vulnerable in his wake. Now, she was under the scrutiny of a police inspector and her freedom was in question again, suddenly, all because Clement Hunt hadn't bothered to leave a note.

She could not shake the impact of Stokes's parting words. *I will find out what happened.* It was a threat more than a promise.

Still unsteady, Harriet leaned her weight against the side of the house. Soon, the vines entwined themselves with her hair and around her back, embracing her, strengthening her. But she did not open her eyes to look. She only felt the now-tender garden rise up to provide her with whatever comfort it could offer.

She let her legs give way, and as she did, something jabbed at her waist. It was the letter in her dress pocket. Unconsciously, she slid her finger into the corner and prized it open, welcoming the distraction.

Dear Miss Hunt,

There is something important you should know about your family, and I hope you will find that it is a great deal of help. Let us meet at the time and place of your choosing. I will explain everything then. Please excuse the mysteriousness of this letter. I cannot offer any details until I see you in person. I await your response.

Humbly yours,
Nigel Davies
10 Kensington Square
London

Harriet read over the letter two more times. It was not what she had been expecting. She'd thought it would be another question about the payments her father owed, but it clearly was not. Her father's debtors never couched their intentions in secrecy. They wanted their money, and they were as explicit as they could be, down to each heavily dotted *i*. For a fleeting moment, she was curious what kind of help this Mr. Davies could offer her, but she quickly recovered. She would not meet with this man. She could not. If his *something important* had anything to do with her father's financial dealings, she did not want to get involved. She must stay as far away as possible from his business.

Instead, she thought as she leaned back and released her frustration against the soft ivy, perhaps she should try to locate her father, to keep Stokes from coming around again. If she had proof, a letter maybe, to show that her father was safely in Denmark, the inspector would leave

Harriet in peace. She did not like the way he had looked at her, with that dark accusation glinting in his eyes. She didn't know what the accusation was of exactly, but she went cold when she thought of the possibilities.

He had said she was *strange*.

Harriet knew what *strange* really meant. Women who were strange ended up in the asylum, whether they chose to or not. It had been her father's most haunting promise, spat at her with his hands vise-clamped around her arms. Inspector Stokes couldn't commit her to an institution, could he? But if he kept coming back and asking questions, she would have to keep her garden calm, and that required the exact behaviors that would have her in a straitjacket.

Balling up the letter from Mr. Davies, she tossed it and watched it skitter across moss and stone. She did not need more mysterious men probing into her life. What she needed was a warm bath and a plan to clear everything up before Stokes decided to come back.

ACKNOWLEDGMENTS

This story wouldn't exist without a whole team of people who nudged and encouraged it to life every step of the way. Thank you to my wonderful agent, Nicole Cunningham, who is smart and tough and genuine and thoughtful with a great eye for edits—how can one person be so many things? Thanks to my editor, Jenna Jankowski, and Gretchen Stelter, and the team at Landmark for helping whip this book into shape—not forgetting Rebecca Andersen and Jessica Thelander for copyediting and proofreading genius. More thanks to the brilliant marketing and publicity teams at Sourcebooks, especially Aubrey Clemans, Hartley Christensen, and Cristina Arreola, and to Sarah Brody for a gorgeous and haunting cover that I love. Special thanks to Pat Collins for chatting about the film industry with me. And many thanks to my earliest reader, Courtney Iversen, for being as astute and helpful as usual, and to Nichelle Giraldes and Chelsea Conradt for two truly wonderful blurbs. Appreciation has to go to my husband who embraces my book-writing playlists as his own and shares the childcare so I can write stories like these (while sidestepping some mom guilt). Thanks to my kid for keeping me laughing and creative and just shy of well-slept.

To my supportive family, you are amazing. Finally, to readers who love stories about women as much as I do—thank you for taking the time to buy and read this little book. You are appreciated more than you know.

ABOUT THE AUTHOR

Chelsea Iversen has been reading and writing stories since before she knew what verbs were. She loves tea and trees and travel, and reads her runes at every full moon. Chelsea lives with her family in Colorado. This is her third novel.